WILL AN ASSASSIN
IN MUNICH
DECIDE THE OUTCOME
OF AMERICA'S
MOST CRUCIAL ELECTION?

THE TIME
Election Eve

THE PLACE
The Olympiahalle in Munich—where the President of the United States will deliver a crucial speech...and where limitless places of concealment are an assassin's dream.

THE AGENT
Roger Wagner—CIA supersleuth with a gift for wry jokes —and too smart for his own good. When the Company gives him 10 days to uncover an assassination plot against the President, Wagner finds himself on a frantic search which leads from German underworld thugs and neo-Nazis to glossy jet-set salons and the highest levels of government. But is the joke on him? After Wagner gets entangled in a lethal web of murder and double-cross, he realizes it isn't only the President's life that's on the line!

THE TERROR ALLIANCE

Jack D. Hunter

LEISURE BOOKS ∞ NEW YORK CITY

A LEISURE BOOK

Published by

Nordon Publications, Inc.
Two Park Avenue
New York, N.Y. 10016

October 5

"Hello?"

"Herr Wismer?"

"Speaking."

"There's sunshine on the bay."

"Oh. Groot. Where are you?"

"At a pay phone in the Stachus, near the Haupt-bahnhof."

"Did you have a good trip over?"

"So-so. The plane was late, and I had a bit of trouble breaking away from the others at the airport. But I caught the S-bahn, and here I am."

"How's everything going?"

"The plan is hard. I propose to initiate it this evening. Are you ready on your end?"

"Of course."

"It's a slippery business. We mustn't lose control for a single moment."

"Quite so."

"You will personally participate, as agreed?"

"Yes."

"If you have to contact me off-schedule, leave a message at Hendel Kompanie."

"You're sure that's wise?"

"No problem. The lines are secure there and the girl is good. Meanwhile, if I have to get you between-times, I'll use this number."

"All right. If I don't answer personally, leave your code name."

"Very well."

"Anything else?"

"Not for now, I guess."

"Well, then. Good luck."

"Goodbye, Herr Wismer."

"Goodbye, Herr Groot."

1

Quitting time in a Ruhr Valley steel town is about what you'd expect it to be. Whistles hoot here and there; trolley cars squeal and bang; ten thousand Hansels and Gretels scratch their behinds, yawn, and elbow their Teutonic ways to the gates that lead to the twilight city and the warrens in which they endure their midnights. It rarely varies much, so on this particular evening, as Wagner stood at his office window and watched the teeming streets below like some pin-striped Zeus, his eye readily picked out the new picture of Emerson Gurney. Alight on the flank of the street-corner advertising kiosk, grinning in the dusk like a toothy ghost, Gurney sprouted a balloon announcing in giant letters that he, the greatest of the cowboy stars, would be host of the "Saddletramp" series to be televised on the Deutschland channel this fall.

The irony was not lost on Wagner, of course, since he was a compulsive symbol player. Emerson Gurney, star of Hollywood's golden years, had reached the final obsolescence. And so had Roger Wagner, star of CIA's golden years. And here they were, trading stares across the approaching night, each in his own way trying to prevail against the weight of years and change.

He put his tongue between his lips and gave Emerson Gurney a moist and protracted raspberry. Then he turned from the window and went to his desk and withdrew the cassette recorder from the lower drawer. He sat in the swivel chair, punched the garble button, inserted the code card, and began to talk into the microphone.

"Memorandum to the Officer in Charge, from Brandywine, File No. 14. Summary for info and file; copy to Congressional Liaison, Heidelberg Office; copy to AC of S, G-2, American Forces Europe."

He took a deep breath and rubbed his eyes. It was cold in the room, courtesy of the latest OPEC price hike, and he debated putting on his topcoat. He decided it was too much trouble and reactivated the tape.

"Pohl has forwarded an interception which confirms our earlier assessment of Soviet ground and air strength in Eastern Europe. The intercept, a high-level summary sent by Hotrod in Moscow to Reefer in Prague, says the Ivans now have thirty-seven thousand tanks on the East Frontier—fifty-five thousand if you include the western half of European Russia. They've boosted their artillery by seventeen percent in the past year, with almost thirty thousand tubes bigger than 100 millimeters deployed, and about twenty-five percent upgrading in their battlefield missile force. They've got nearly two thousand Frog and Scud surface-to-surface missiles deployed over there, which indicates that Army aviation has a predicted combat-loss quotient of fifty percent—some seven hundred helicopters and support aircraft—in the first twenty-four hours of hostilities. Now that the United States is withdrawing from NATO, the loss quotient on Western aircraft could be considerably higher. Hotrod estimates a Soviet occupation of Western Europe could be accomplished by year's end—even if the President decides to distribute the laser cannon as ballyhooed in the press recently. Full transcript of intercept will accompany my weekly progress report. Out."

He withdrew the cassette and dropped it into a padded

book mailer, which he addressed to Zorn Tool and Die Co., Frankfurt/Main. He affixed the postage so that the third stamp tilted to the right, and then he placed the envelope in his briefcase for mailing from the central post office in the morning. Sighing, he lifted the phone, activated the scrambler, and dialed the place on Wenkelstrasse.

"Pohl here."

"Wagner. I'm going to my hotel now. I may commit suicide."

"Well, have fun."

"Anything from our Russian friends?"

"They're still holed up, waiting for the sketches."

"They aren't exactly the world's most aggressive spies, are they."

"That's all right with me."

"If Ankhanov goes anywhere, I'll want to know about it."

"Sure."

"Nighty-night."

He hung up, stifled a yawn, and turned out the desk lamp. After pulling on his topcoat he took up his briefcase, went to the door, flicked the lock, and let himself into the tide of secretaries and lesser bureaucrats. The elevator purred in a controlled fall that matched the sinking of his spirits, and he tried to be unaware of the humanity that wheezed and murmured all around. In an effort to rally a cheerier mood, he thought of a limerick, the one about there was a young girl in a lift, and he felt a smile rolling over in the ooze. But it seemed somehow blasphemous to smile when surrounded by so many faces set so bravely against Malevolent Forces in the World Today, and so the impulse died aborning.

In the lobby he paused, enduring the swirl and clatter and awaiting a chance to break through to the newsstand and his copy of *Tägliche Anfrage*. And in that tiny suspension of time, immersed in a surf of mankind and his own haze of preoccupation, his basic nature suddenly asserted itself. There was a discord, a Something That

9

Didn't Fit. An infinitesimal juxtaposition of normal and abnormal.

Almost as if they moved under a power of their own, his eyes made a sweep. Still banging the symbol, he pictured an old spider, slow and weary beyond measure, feeling a trembling in a far corner of his decrepit web. Was it truly a fly? Or was he only recalling The Good Times?

A woman, hurrying, brushed against him and, struggling for balance, dropped her handbag. She was a brunette with a Prince Valiant haircut, slim and elegant in her red suit.

He stooped, retrieved the bag, and handed it to her. "Here you are," he said.

"I'm sorry. It was my fault." Her eyes were large and frightened, and she stared at the clattering throng as if it concealed beasts that would leap. Thanking him absently, she placed the bag under her arm and crossed the lobby to stand, waiting, in the shadow of a plastic tree.

All crowds hold their share of frightened people—even frightened, good-looking women. Very few of them, though, contain frightened, good-looking women who carry pistols in their purses. Her purse was one of those knitted things, soft, pliable, and probably no more expensive than an ermine barracks bag. It bulged at one side, and he guessed that it was a .32-caliber bulge. And this was, by the definitions of his grubby trade, a discord.

He made his way to the newsstand, paid for his paper, and sidled into the lee of a fluted column, where he watched her for a time. She was very good-looking indeed.

Time must have been important, because she kept glancing nervously at the big clock that hung from the marble gloom above. Nearly five minutes passed, and just as he had decided she'd been stood up, a man came out of the crowd, took her by the elbow, and half-pushed, half-led her out the lobby door. He was of medium height, chunky in his black topcoat, and he had mean eyes and a mouth pinched by years of unvented angers. Wagner couldn't remember the man's name, but he knew

10

he'd seen him before. In Munich, maybe?

Fascinated, Wagner followed as the man hurried the brunette along Gotha Alee toward the trolley loop, where a dark blue Citroën came out of the honking stream to chirp its tires against the curb. The car's door flew open and the man pushed the girl ahead of him into the back seat. The Citroën had no more than rejoined the traffic flow when Wagner was behind it in a taxi, waving a ten-mark note to convince the cabbie he was serious about seeing where everybody was going.

"Are you a cop?" The driver's German had an Alsatian inflection.

"Why do cabdrivers always ask that question?"

"Cops are always telling cabbies to follow some car."

"I'm not a cop. I'm a jealous lover."

"Your girl is in the Citroën with another man?"

"I don't have a girl."

"Then who are you jealous of?"

"The Citroën. I have an absolute passion for Citroëns."

"You're a smart aleck."

"Just follow the other car, eh?"

"Smart aleck."

The blue car turned left into the Buchner Anlage, then made a quick right and headed northwest on Liedersheimerlandstrasse.

"He's a good driver," the cabbie said.

"You're better. I've got another ten marks that says so."

He was, too. Once, when a bus and a truck combined to block the road, the Alsatian gunned the motor and slid the cab between the truck's tail gate and a warehouse wall with all the flair of a Keystone Komedian.

"Where did you learn to drive like that?"

"In the Gestapo."

"You aren't old enough to have been in the Gestapo."

"And you aren't the only smart aleck in the cab, either."

The Citroën was stopped by a traffic light near the Bahnhof, where the multilane overpass vaulted the marshaling yards on the Riegelsmaier viaduct. The lowering clouds had released a misty rain that formed a diamond glaze on the windows. As they all waited for the light to change, Wagner felt the cold. His gaze wandered, and in the dark of an ancient foundry entrance he saw a drunk curled against the drizzle. The man, indistinct and forlorn in his isolation, had wrapped newspapers around his feet and had placed a bottle within easy reach on the steps beside him.

The night was full of symbolisms, Wagner sighed to himself. First it had been the advertisement and its photo of Gurney, reminding him of all the gone and wasted years; now it was an alcoholic derelict, who suggested Escape from the Intolerable. What the bottle meant to the man in the doorway the Citroën meant to Wagner. Roger Wagner had been a good boy for too long, enduring the confounding and relentless deterioration of the only world he knew. By charging after the frightened woman, he was on a binge, so to speak—trying to obliterate his awareness of the anachronism he now represented. The CIA was now a country day school, an amalgam of computer babies and Brahminism on the half-shell. There was no longer room for the Roger Wagners, those Errol Flynns who'd swing from ship to ship with cutlasses in their teeth. The cloaks were now double-knits; the daggers were now ballpoint pens.

Screw them all.

"Did you say something?" the cabbie asked over his shoulder.

"No I just snorted."

"Snorted?"

"The light's changed. Don't lose them."

The Citroën followed the overpass and made a sharp turn to the right, crossing a spur line and picking up the dogleg that joined Bismarck Strasse. It slackened speed as it entered the dark canyon formed by the abandoned coke mills, and Wagner said, "They're stopping. Keep on going at this speed."

Beyond the block of factory buildings and out of sight for those in the Citroën—which had pulled into a cul de sac and gone dark—he directed the cab driver onto a cinder lane paralleling a line of freight cars.

"Stop up there by the signal block."

"What's going on?" the cabbie wanted to know.

"I have no idea. But I remember that man's face. And any man whose face I remember has simply got to be up to no good."

"I knew it. You're a cop."

"Wait for me," Wagner said. "I want to see where they've taken the woman."

The night had brought a raw wind off the river, and as he left the cab and returned to Bismarck Strasse, a chill shook him, and he turned up his collar against the coming winter. The factory buildings loomed high and black, and somewhere in the darkness was the lonesome dripping of some long-forgotten gutter. His personal theme song. The sound-track dirge of the Life and Times of Roger Wagner, that winsome tad who spies on people's spies and huddles against cold winds in dark and saddened places while the theme goes drip, drip, drip. (Mournful cello music comes under softly, he thought wryly.)

Two shadows, large and fast, detached themselves from the factory shadows and rushed him.

He ducked and spun about and threw his hip into the first one, and the man flew over his shoulders and landed heavily on the cobblestones. He kicked this one in the head, and he collapsed. The second one, though, caught him with a chop that sent him to his knees, ears ringing and eyes stinging with tears. He managed to stay open for business even so, and, reaching, he clasped the second man's ankles and then flipped him into a wall. The man swore and smashed at him with his hands, but Wagner sent two jabs to his face and he was down, blowing saliva bubbles. The first one had come around sufficiently to wobble to his knees, but Wagner kicked him again, and he rolled over, sacklike.

He was crouching, ready for others and puffing and shaking, when the alley lit up and he heard the sound of a pair of hands clapping in lazy applause.

"Bravo," a voice said.

2

The light came from the high beams of a Peugeot sedan parked in an angle of alley. Struggling for breath, Wagner stood uncertainly, blinking at the man who approached him from the shadows beyond the glare.

"Hello, Koenig," the man said.

"Ziggi?"

"Ah. You remember me."

Rattner came up beside him, and Wagner saw that the interval—was it three years, or two?—had brought changes. Ziggi Rattner was trendy now, with a lacquered hairdo, a flared double-knit suit and matching Zirkmann topcoat. There were a lot of rings on his fingers, and he wore those large square spectacles with blue lenses. He was too cute for words.

"Of course I remember you. Who else can manage to make 'hello Koenig' sound like a rooster breaking wind?"

"Are you surprised?"

"Nothing surprises me any more, as the saying goes."

Rattner took Wagner's arm and led him to the car. Wagner sank into the expensive upholstery and took the silver picnic cup that Rattner held out to him.

"Drink it," Rattner said. "It's cognac."

Wagner, still trembling from shock, drained the cup and coughed. "Oh, lord," he said, "I'm older than I thought." He pointed at the woman in the Citroën and the two men, who were now staggering toward the car to join her. "They're yours, of course."

"Not any more. They've just been fired. If they can be taken by an old fatty like you, they're in the wrong business."

"I remember the big guy. What's his name?"

"Brenner."

"The chauffeur for that Albanian I pinched in Munich two years ago?"

"Three years. It was three years ago."

"Why the fun and games, Ziggi?"

Rattner's German was thin and harsh, in the Nordland way. "Two reasons. First, I want to talk a little business."

"You mean you hired two punks and a broad to lure me out here and jazz me around when you could have called me on the phone?"

"You were always partial to melodrama. By staging some, I was mixing pleasure with business, so to speak. I've owed you a good thrashing for a long time. Ever since that night you kicked me downstairs."

"Well, hell. You were waving a gun at me. What did you expect me to do—dance soft-shoe?"

"That was no gun. It was a flashlight. With a burned-out bulb."

Wagner held out his cup for a refill and asked the question that was really bothering him. "How did you find me, anyhow? How did you know I was working this town?"

Rattner gave a supercilious little chuckle and patted his cute hair. "Your CIA is a sieve these days. An absolute sieve. A couple of phone calls here and there, and I had you."

"So what's on your mind?"

Rattner paused to light a cigarette. Speaking through a cloud of smoke, he said, "I thought you and I might do a little dealing. The way we used to."

Wagner sighed and rubbed his eyes. "If you know so much about what's going on in CIA these days, you know there isn't any money for informants any more. Whatever you're trying to sell, Ziggi, I can't afford it. Peddle it to the Russians."

"You'll have to afford this information, believe me. An incredible plot is forming. I know the details. You, too, can know the details."

"Sorry."

"I'm going to tell you just enough to entice you. Then I want you to go to your superiors and convince them that they can have the whole story. Provided their, ah, gratuity is high enough."

Rattner stubbed out the cigarette in the dashboard ashtray and blew a long and concluding stream of smoke at the windshield. "Certain parties are preparing to kill the President of the United States. During the summit meeting in Munich. The week after next."

"So call the Secret Service. They handle voter complaints."

"I'll deal only with you. I know you, and how you work."

"Sorry. I haven't got the money."

"Well, just toddle off to your bosses and tell them what I've told you. I suspect they'll not be nearly so miserly as you."

"You want to bet?"

"I'll be at my home, Richtenstrasse Nine. When you all decide to take my offer, you'll find me there, every evening before 10:00 or after 3:00 A.M. And I'm very expensive. Bring lots of money."

Wagner pulled his coat around him and opened the car door to step into the rain. "Good night, Ziggi."

"You don't seem to be very moved by the prospect of your President's assassination." Rattner's tone was one of mock pouting.

"Vote for one President, you've voted for them all."

"You're the same Koenig. Only different somehow."

16

"Menopause."

Wagner stooped to pick up a paving block that had worked loose from the ancient alley bed. He pounded it three times on the Peugeot's hood, leaving torn metal craters and scarred paint. Then he threw the block against the windshield, which went opaquely white with a web of cracks.

"What the hell's the idea?" Ziggi snarled.

"Have me worked over again, Rattner, and I'll use the brick on you."

3

For the next two days, Wagner was immersed in the helicopter thing. The problem, as usual, was budgetary. He needed a cutaway drawing that would supposedly represent the rotor assembly of the new Boeing, and, since the sketch would be evaluated by Soviet aviation specialists, it would have to be doctored with exceptional skill. The difficulty stemmed from the cross-agency red tape that required Air Force drawings altered by the Technical Service Division under CIA's Directorate of Operations. He had put in his request, through channels and with a copy to Congressional Liaison, but the Air Force rep had balked because no budget charge number had accompanied the requisition. Wagner had not had a charge number to cite, since his expenses were account-able under Counter Intelligence and he was therefore operating on a straight expense account. There had been fourteen phone calls, three of them to Washington, and five cables, but the Air Force was adamant: no charge number, no sketches. And Technical Services had been of no help, electing as it did to remain aloof from the plebian squabble.

He had completed another fruitless call to Heidelberg and was preparing to leave for lunch when there was a tap at the door.

"Come in," he said. "It's open."

It was Groot.

"Well," Wagner said.

"Hello, Wagner. I'm glad I caught you."

Groot was older, of course, and showed it. His body, which had always been chunky, was now thick and somehow ugly, and the hair at his temples was no longer dark. In the reflected light of the corridor, his eyes were raisin-colored and opaque. "May I come in?" he wheezed in his asthmatic voice.

"I was just leaving."

"This is important."

Wagner motioned Groot to a seat. "What is it?" Wagner asked uneasily.

Groot sighed and produced a gold cigarette case. His eyebrow asked Wagner if he wanted one.

"No thanks."

Groot lit one for himself and exhaled twin streams of smoke from his nose, a pocked construction lumped in a face of peculiar shapelessness. They sat silently for a time, their minds reaching back over the years.

"Have you been well, Wagner?"

"So-so."

"I've read your report on Rattner's offer."

"I didn't think my field reports went to Washington big-shots like you."

"I want you to exploit Rattner."

"Up your giggy with a hot-cross bun."

"I knew you'd be pleased."

"I wouldn't work for you again, Groot. I'd quit first."

"And I will become a grandmother next Tuesday at four P.M."

"You are not one of my favorite citizens."

Groot examined the tip of his cigarette. "Your local management tells me you've been working the dark side of counterintelligence operations. Case officer on an information planting."

19

"Purely military. Purely routine."

"Tell me about it."

"So what's to tell? The Army has reorganized its aviation for holding action in case the Ivans attack during our withdrawal from Europe. It's established the divisional aviation battalion with supporting maintenance and logistics units and beefed up the antiarmor chopper squadrons at corps level. And a new aircraft has been introduced to line outfits—a Boeing Vertol thing with low-speed, nap-of-the-earth antitank tactical capabilities. The Ivans are interested enough to have planted some undercover helicopter specialists here in West Germany. They know that the Army plans to hold familiarization exercises at Ansbach. I'm running a counteragent who will feed them phony info based on phony exercises I've set up with our Ansbach people."

Groot nodded. "Nothing that can't be put on hold."

"A venture in futility. Moscow has probably had the aircraft's blueprints for a month."

"Well, it's time for you to have some fun now," Groot said. "I've spoken to your local management. They've agreed to attach you to me for ten days' special duty. They were most reluctant to do so. For some reason, they think you're good."

Wagner sank back in the swivel chair, feeling the half-sickness that accompanies recollections of past delinquencies. "Don't try to jolly me up, Groot. I'm struggling manfully—with steely-eyed determination and unwavering courage—to endure the enormous pain in my ass."

"Be serious."

"I am serious. What's funny about a pain in the ass?"

Groot flicked some ashes from his cigarette and watched them fall to the carpeting. "You seem to blame me for your, ah, discontent. The world has changed, Wagner. It is unkind to those who can't, or refuse to, change with it."

Wagner went to the window and watched the noonday traffic. There had been a time when Groot had been the

20

subordinate. There was no bitterness in remembering this, only the kind of regret that attends a drawerful of old lottery tickets. Somewhere in the years he'd refused his chance at what was deemed to be better things—more power and responsibility and the trinkets of rank— because they required that he trade the breadth of field work for the straits of bureaucracy. And so, while he had remained to wrestle alligators in the Cold War everglade, Groot had paddled beyond him, eventually to find CIA's Holy See, where he'd become a cardinal. Wagner wanted now to resent the I-told-you-so tacit in Groot's comment, but he was too tired to strike poses.

"You're right, Groot. I should have known better."

Groot said, "Your self-pity is tiresome. I need a good day's work from you now."

"Why me? The Company's got other people. Cute guys from Dartmouth with broad shoulders, sparkling teeth, and IBMs where their balls should be."

"Rattner is of the old school. So are you. Our new generation of agents wouldn't know how to handle him."

They considered each other silently, and Groot's eyes reminded Wagner of tarnished coins. Groot was an agent of vast and untraceable experience. Of the man as a professional, Wagner knew only the jobs they'd shared; of the man himself, he knew nothing beyond an awareness of unspoken furies. A German, Groot had arrived in America as a youth in the late forties, and even then, according to those who knew, he had been taciturn and wary and moved by some compulsion to avenge some nameless hurt suffered in the organized greed that had destroyed his Fatherland. After naturalization and college, it was said, he had disappeared into the darkness of strategic intelligence. And while Wagner, personally, thought he knew what Groot was against, he hadn't the least notion as to what Groot was for.

"You think Ziggi's on the level, Groot? You think there'll be a try on the President?"

"It's altogether possible, if one considers obvious, wide-open opportunity."

There was a long pause.

"Odd," Wagner said eventually.

"What do you mean?"

"I think it's odd, the President coming to Europe with the election only a few weeks away. What's he trying to do?"

Groot shrugged. "There's talk of his trying to strike an international statesman's pose. He thinks that, by reassuring our former NATO partners they can count on unilateral U.S. military support, he will offset his political rival's accusations of appeasement and spinelessness. And also, in the process, pick up some votes."

"Not very likely. Not with the national temper being what it is."

"Well, who's to say? I never understood American politics anyway."

Wagner sniffed. Groot's saying he didn't understand politics was like Roger Wagner's saying he didn't understand a hundred-dollar bill. But he let it pass. "There's not a hell of a lot to understand if you look at the situation. A continuing recession. High unemployment. Fuel rationing. Food rationing. Inflation. A third party established and high in the polls and running hard for the presidency. Disarmament in face of repeated Soviet violations of longstanding SALT agreements. Withdrawal. Gloom. Believe me, fancy words in Munich won't land voters in Dubuque."

Groot sighed, a signal he had nothing to say to this.

"Besides, with a Veep in a hospital and not likely to come out for two or three hundred years, the President's one-man campaign is already a one-lunger."

"The media say there's a sympathy vote forming around that one. The President and his sister fighting the battle, back-to-back, in a swirl of circling savages, and other such ad-agency vomit."

"The fact remains: it's too late to drop the Vice President from the ticket, which would be kicking a feller when he's down. And, while that might be de rigueur for you and me and our playmates in the Citroën, it's

22

strengstens verboten on Main Street. The Veep amounts to a real loser for the incumbents, any way you look at it."

Groot hunched a shoulder. "They stand a chance. Robert Goodman and his Third Choice Party are a bit too strenuous for the Babbitts, and they're surely no joy forever for left-wing liberals, either. President Randall might just slide back into office on a coalition, a chunk of vest-and-watch-chain Republicans here, a chunk of coverall Democrats there, a chunk of pot-smoking Independents. That sort of thing."

"I still say El Presidente will never make it."

Groot's raisin-like eyes considered his wristwatch. "Talk of politics wearies me. Let's get back to Ziggi."

"Tell me first: what's the drill on this summit thing?"

"Congresswoman Amy Randall, as Speaker of the House and the President's sister and campaign manager, will come this week. The President, with Senator Logue, chairman of the Senate Armed Services Committee, the Secretary of State, and the pool press will fly to Bonn in a Lufthansa jet one week from today. Two days later, to Frankfurt for the trade show. Then two days in Munich before returning to the States. While in Munich, the President will be housed in special quarters at Schloss Nymphenburg, where he will hold additional meetings with the chairman of the Joint Chiefs of Staff, who's already here to supervise initial preparations for our withdrawal from NATO."

"Why Lufthansa? Why not Air Force One?"

"The President thinks it will be a friendly gesture to fly in a German commercial aircraft. He wants to play up to the Germans now that they're so sore at us."

"That's absurd. Who's idea was that?"

Groot studied the palm of his hand. "The President's sister's."

"She must be out of her gourd. Security will be a nightmare."

"Amy Randall's a powerful member of Congress who, besides wanting to see her brother reelected, is anxious to keep West Germany from abandoning us for Arab oil."

23

"Next thing you know, Congress will have the President standing in line at the Greyhound bus terminal."

"Congress is so splintered into special-interest groups it can't agree on where the terminal is," Groot said blandly.

"Hypocritical clods."

Groot said, "We can't affort to ignore Rattner, no matter what you think of Congress."

"Screw Rattner. Screw Congress. Screw you."

Groot rubbed his eyes and stifled a yawn. When he spoke, his rasping voice was low and without heat. "Your orders will be delivered here to you tomorrow morning. You will proceed to Munich and will interview Rattner at the earliest possible time. You will pay him five thousand dollars to speak his piece. If we find his information valuable to us, we will send him another five."

Wagner stared at Groot. "You've got to be joking," he said, incredulous. "We paid Rattner twenty thousand dollars to break that thing down at Bad Tölz. Peach pits, he called it. Twenty grand was peach pits. Can you imagine what he'll say about ten?"

"Ten thousand is all we can afford."

"Then forget it. Rattner will laugh us out of town. He gets ten grand a week just from the whores he runs."

"Even if I had more to spend, I'd have to detail the expenditure for the Congressional Liaison officer. And to talk to him is to talk to reporters. We can't afford an explosion of publicity over an unchecked remark of a greedy informant. But if there's substance to what Rattner claims, the Secret Service and the entire Presidential Security System will have to be notified as soon as possible."

"Well, that's your problem, not mine."

"No, Wagner. At this stage it's our problem. Yours and mine."

"What about Presidential Security? Haven't you alerted them yet?"

"We have to hear out Rattner first. But if it jells and the

24

alert comes from CIA, it will be quite beneficial to the Company. And I needn't remind you that the Company needs all the applause it can get these days. You'll be finished with this thing in two or three days. Just pump Rattner, pay him, and tell me what he says." Groot handed Wagner a card. "If Rattner jells and you get actionable information, call me at this number. From a pay phone, of course. I will then brief Secret Service."

"This is a waste of time, you know."

"We've got to try."

"Ziggi won't talk for any ten grand."

"Then, Wagner, you'll just have to figure a way to make him talk."

"And get crucified by Congressional Liaison for coercion of a foreign national? Not on your Civil Service life."

Groot went to the door, slowly and with apparent weariness. With his hand on the knob, he turned to regard Wagner with a thoughtful stare. "We cannot—we must not—let our President be shot."

"Why? What's he ever done for me?"

Groot closed the door behind him, and Wagner stood for a time, staring at nothing in particular.

4

A return to Germany always cost Groot dearly, because
the old angers would come despite his will to the contrary.
He was especially out of sorts in Munich, which he saw as
an embodiment of the lunatic contradictions of history. It
was a hundred and twenty square miles of incongruous
architecture lumped in the Bavarian plain, and pervading
its compound of medieval antique and Star Trek modern
was the nearly palpable suggestion of violence and decay.
When it rained, he sometimes suspected he could smell
the ancient blood and rotting bones that mulched the
city's polychromatic flower beds; when he considered the
soaring monuments and noble museums, he would think
of Stadelheim prison and its piano-wire strangulations.
And the white-gloved policeman waving on the traffic
would become, in the cellar of his memories, the
imperious SS man directing Jews to the ovens. To him,
Munich was Germany, and he loved it and despised it
with equal passion.

Passion?

He thought about the word and decided that it no
longer had any practical meaning in his life. In the

beginning he had been driven by it, taut and springy and full of snap, like a freshly wound mechanical doll; now he was winding down, and the kinetic superciliousness of youth had given way to the automatous plodding of one who has endured a lifetime of coping. As a native Bavarian, he had begun life with civility, a good temper, and a sense of humor—conforming to the recipe of an Englishman of his acquaintance who said that if you were to brew a Bavarian you'd "take all the good qualities of the Austrians and Swiss, add a touch of German, and season with a little Irish temperament and the light-heartedness of the French." Perhaps. But the Hitler years had altered all that, and he had left his teens and entered his twenties as a dour and remote old man. There were times of nostalgia, like now, when he'd see the reflected Alps in the shimmering of a black lake, when the cowbells tinkled and the air was sweet with the smell of barnyards and fresh-baked bread. But then he would remember the brass-colored morning in 1945 when they dug him out of the rubble and he could hear his mother's dying moans and smell the stink of the others rotting after three days under the broken beams and plaster. And he would be a thousand years old, and numb with ancient rage.

Seeing Wagner again today had deepened his cheerlessness. He had developed a peculiar resentment for the contemporary native American. No man sees America as clearly as one who has found sanctuary there, and because of this he had little patience with those Americans who, having never been threatened by empty bellies and nights full of fear, found it easy to blur their personal shortcomings with crocodile tears over their homeland's warts. But Wagner was not one of those. Wagner personified the idealistic America Groot had wandered into so long ago, and it was sad to see him again, in the way it was sad to leaf through an old family album. Wagner had been diligent and sensible, more often than not, and he had occasionally demonstrated great courage and dedication. But he was a chronic romantic, and for a man in today's secret-intelligence work, this tendency to hold onto the Kiplingesque could be a gross liability.

Groot had several times considered Wagner for promotion and transfer to the headquarters at Langley, but Wagner's propensity for flippancy and showy derring-do had in each instance intervened. To be sure, no one could be in dirty-tricks espionage for long and remain a Drawing Room Dan; the work is cruel and lonely and, essentially, calls for what once was quaintly known as the man of action. But the world had indeed changed, and it would be inherited not by the idealists, but by the angry. And in the world of espionage, anger could heighten an agent's sense of mission and worth, while quixotism could only confuse him and get him killed. Or worse, cause him to write books.

Groot was angry.

Wagner was incurably romantic. A kid, still playing games.

Groot would survive.

Wagner would eventually die, wondering where all the good guys had gone.

It was as simple as that.

And it was for this reason he regretted having to use Wagner in this little exercise in deception. But with things the way they were, with dwindling budgets and thinning ranks and the consequent rise in visibility, it was Wagner or nobody.

He had flown to Munich and rented a car.

After a late supper at Karli's, he drove the VW west on Nymphenburgerlandstrasse to the crooked creek that wound among the chalky houses of Obermensing. Beyond the church with the gold steeple, he picked his way through the security perimeter, a collection of nondescript sedans parked so as to mark lanes of fire for the men hidden in the dark. When he reached the cottage he climbed out of the car and spoke to Smedley.

"Is she here?"

"Yes, sir. She arrived at twenty-oh-three hours."

"Are the neighbors aware of anything?"

"We took considerable care to avoid a fuss, sir. I'm sure

that the villagers are unaware of our presence."

"I hope so. It's a stupid thing, her wanting this kind of accommodation."

"We can handle it, sir."

"Royalty is always a pain in the ass, Smedley. And she's the closest thing to royalty America has."

Smedley displayed the opacity that enables the Secret Service White House detail to maintain a scrupulously nonjudgmental attitude toward the idiosyncracies of the presidential family. He said, "I wouldn't know, sir."

"Keep my car ready. I'll be only a few minutes."

"Yes, sir."

"By the way. She's expecting a visitor. a Fräulein Berchthold. Daughter of an old friend in Augsburg. The lady will be carrying my business card, marked on the back with an X, a Y, and the number four."

"Very well, sir. I'll inform the rest of the detail."

He went up the walk, his shoes making little swirls among the fallen leaves. He breathed deeply of the autumn night, feeling a nameless yearning. Fall was a sad time, to be sure.

"Identification, please," Bernstein said from the shadows at the door.

"Hello, Bernie," Groot said, holding his ID under the pen light. He blinked when the beam went over his face.

"Good evening, sir. Glad to see you again."

"I'll be here only a short time. Don't admit anyone until I leave." He paused. "Tonight's visitor will be a Fräulein Berchthold, due around eleven o'clock."

"Well, sir, I believe Miss Randall is also expecting Senator Logue any moment now."

"Well, hold him off if he comes while I'm still here. I won't keep the senator waiting long."

"All right, sir. But Senator Logue can be very difficult."

"You've noticed that, eh?"

Bernstein chuckled in the darkness, enjoying the little joke. "Yes, sir. I've noticed."

"The chairman of the Armed Services Committee has

the right to be difficult, Bernie. He's on the wagon again."

Bernstein laughed openly this time.

Groot entered the house and stood in the foyer for a moment, taking in its calculated rusticity and expensive smell and listening to the unassertive music coming from the ceiling beams. The house had been designed, built, and lived in by a Third Reich architect of upper-middle repute, and as a consequence it was overstated. But it was also, for all its Schwarzwald cuteness, built like a fort, and therefore better than most of the hideouts that evolved from Amy Randall's secret proclivities.

She was waiting for him in the library, a thin Scotch swirling idly in the glass in her hand. The lamps were low, the fire glowed and sighed, and she looked softer and more amiable than her patrician construction would ordinarily allow.

"Drink, Groot?"

"No, thank you. Did you have a pleasant flight over, Miss Randall?"

"Hardly. I had the poor judgment to give Albert Lockhart an interview, and he's a pluperfect bore, and he took hours to get to the point. As a matter of fact, I'm not sure he ever had a point."

"Well, he's getting along in years—"

"There's no excuse for anyone to get along in years, Groot. Albert is simply a stuffed shirt. Even his bio reads like the Statistical Abstract, and he's dull, dull, dull. I've never yet stayed awake during one of his newscasts."

"Many people think he has great dignity," Groot said, not caring.

Miss Randall gave an elegant little snort. "Many people are dumb." She held her drink to the light and examined it, as if searching for impurities. "Have you set things in motion, Groot?"

"Yes."

"I don't want my brother endangered in any way."

"Of course."

"Your people are reliable?"

30

"I've done the best I can with the resources that are available."

"How about you, Groot? Can I trust you? Really?" She was using that smile she always used when she teased him.

"I have my flaws, but disloyalty is not among them."

"Ah," she said, "but what is loyalty? All human beings are loyal, Groot. The trick is to discover what they're loyal to, eh? Some people are loyal to Satan, you know."

"I suppose."

She studied him across the rim of her glass. After a thoughtful sip, she placed the drink on a table and said, "I was thinking about you this evening, Groot. About all the years you've been my friend and confidant. How many years has it been, actually?"

"It's been a long time."

"California, wasn't it?"

"Yes, I think so." He could have told her the very moment of the very hour of the very day. But he wouldn't, because she would only gloat and he would be demeaned once again.

"Do you ever get the hots for me, Groot?"

"I'm a rather, ah, dispassionate person, Miss Randall. I rarely react one way or another to people."

She laughed. "The perfect bureaucrat."

"Perhaps."

"It doesn't make the slightest difference to me if you like me or not," she said.

"I'm sure."

"But I trust you. I don't know anybody I trust more."

"Even your brother?"

"Especially my brother."

"I'm glad you trust me, Miss Randall. It makes everything so much easier."

"Anyhow," she said, "it's because of your—dispassion, as you call it—that I've asked for your help on this matter. You don't have the ardor, or zeal, or ambition that can screw things up."

Groot said nothing.

31

"You have an air of seedy dependability."

He knew she was teasing him again, so her insults didn't matter. Besides, she was speaking the truth.

"How many know about this assassination threat?"

"You. I. The original group. But by tomorrow I'll be ready to alert all the security forces on both sides of the Atlantic. Intense countermeasures will be set up along the President's route. You might say our gun is loaded."

"That's a rotten way to put it, under the circumstances."

"Yes, I suppose it is. Excuse me."

"Should I tell Senator Logue about the plot? He's due here any minute."

"Absolutely not. Things are still too tentative, and the senator is, well—"

"An alcoholic bigmouth, is that what you mean?"

"Politicians thrive on what they say, not on what they leave unsaid."

"Certainly somebody in your daisy chain of security will blab to somebody. Nothing is airtight these days."

"That's right, Miss Randall. But we must buy as much time as possible. Also, there's an element of credibility when someone blabs and the press picks it up, and so on, while incredibility results when a politician makes an announcement. Which Senator Logue would most certainly do. With a lot of unpredictable embellishment, I might add."

"I guess you're right, Groot. We have enough problems without the distinguished gentleman from Delaware shooting off his mouth." She picked up her drink and rolled the glass in her hand, her eyes pensive. "I'll be officially arriving at the Vierjahreszeiten at ten tomorrow night. I assume the arrangements have been made."

"Yes. We will have a press conference as soon as you leave the hotel meeting room."

"What if I'm asked about the plot? Somebody might have blabbed by then, and there could be questions."

"Then you should be surprised and indignant."

"All right. So all's in order."

"At this time, yes."

"You seem doubtful, Groot."

"I've been in this business a long time, Miss Randall. I know how often things can go wrong."

"Nothing had better go wrong on this, pal. My brother's safety is involved."

"Yes."

"By the way: who've you provided for my companionship?"

"A Fräulein Irma Berchthold. The Secret Service detail has been told she's the daughter of an old friend of yours."

"Is she cute?"

"A Nordic blonde, I believe you'd call her."

"Does it bother you to be my procurer, Groot?"

"Nothing you do bothers me, Miss Randall. I should think you'd know that after all these years."

"You may go now, Groot."

"Until tomorrow night, then."

He crossed the room to the foyer archway and hesitated when she called after him.

"Yes, Miss Randall?"

"If anything happens to my brother, I'll personally cut off your balls."

"I understand."

He turned and went into the night's softly pattering rain. He was clearing the driveway when Senator Logue's limousine rounded the curve and glided up to the house.

He wondered if Miss Randall's wide-ranging sexual tastes accommodated the distinguished gentleman from Delaware.

Probably not.

Otherwise, he would have had pictures and tapes by now.

5

The orders arrived before noon, as Groot had said they would.

He had packed his suitcase the night before, so as to give himself time to call Pohl before catching the one o'clock train. The phone lifted after the third ring.

"Pohl here."

"Wagner."

"What's up?"

"I'm going to be gone for a few days. I want you to carry on as planned."

"Gone? What do you mean, gone? For God's sake—"

"I'm under priority. You'll just have to carry on."

"What do I do about the technical sketch? Ankhanov is getting spooky."

"Stall him until I get back."

"He wants a cutaway of the entire aircraft."

"I thought he would be satisfied with a sketch of the rotor assembly."

"He says now that his boss wants a cutaway of the whole schmeer."

"Boss? What boss?"

"The KGB has assigned a supervisor to this thing. They are placing considerable importance on the Ansbach tests."

"Did he say who the supervisor is?"

"Somebody named Gregori."

"Oh, lordy."

"You know him?"

"He's one of their best."

"So what should I do?"

"Stall Ankhanov. Tell him you're having trouble getting a cutaway. We'll work out something when I get back."

"What do I do about Gregori?"

"Nothing. Stay out of his way. I'll handle him."

"All right. But you'd better hurry. The whole scene is getting itchy."

"Relax, Pohl. It'll work out."

"You can talk. You'll be safely out of it."

Wagner felt an incandescent anger forming. Pohl was one of the new generation of Company people and therefore a handwringer. Wagner could remember Allen and Scott and Leander and Calucci and Hausmann and all the others who had struggled and endured and sometimes died without a murmur; the catch of complaint in the lockjaw inflections of this limp-wristed law-school idiot was an affront to the memory of big men.

"Don't fret, sweetheart. They wouldn't do any more than kill you."

"Why would they want to *kill* me? All I'm doing is passing them information."

"Doctored information. They always have stiff-legged tantrums when they learn they've been conned. But, hell, you're insured."

He hung up, feeling the heat in his face.

The sense of outrage remained with him all the way to Heidelberg. He detested trains anyhow, and the Company's refusal to authorize private auto transport for reassignment travel compounded a resentment that made the second-class seat virtually unbearable. Lost in his self-pity, he ruled out a cab for himself and instead took a trolley to Safe House No. 2 in Handschuhsheim across the river.

He went directly to the third floor, where Morfey, the Congressional Liaison attaché, maintained a suite plastered with autographed pictures of famous politicians.

"So you're here," Morfey said, looking up from the papers on his desk.

"I'm here," Wagner said, taking a chair.

Morfey moved some sheets from one stack to another, tidily, fussily, and then turned in his chair to stare out the window. "I don't mind saying, Wagner, that there are some peculiar aspects in this thing Groot has on his mind."

"Peculiar?" Wagner was determined to keep his temper.

"The fact that Groot, a deputy director of CIA, flew here from Washington simply to draw you off a case and put you on another is odd in itself."

"Well, Groot has a lot of responsibility. And these days, if you want something done right you've got to do it yourself."

"He says you're going to draw ten thousand dollars from Confidential Funds."

"Five today. Five later, if the case pans out."

"I'm wondering what the money's for."

"Sorry. You'll have to ask Groot. Besides, the CIA doesn't have to explain expenditures to Congress if the amount is ten thousand or less. So you'll have to keep on wondering, Morfey."

"Mr. Morfey."

"You'll have to keep on wondering, Mr. Morfey."

Wagner found it difficult to look at the man behind the desk. Morfey had been the administrative assistant to Senator J. Roland Finucane, senior member from Iowa, and when the senator had been defeated four years earlier,

36

Morfey had wangled an appointment to the Joint Committee on CIA operations. The watchdog committee, burgeoning under a congressional temper that saw evil in all clandestine intelligence matters, had created special civil-service ratings for a small corps of overseers who would be assigned to key CIA branch offices in the U.S. and abroad. Morfey had won early appointment to the Heidelberg station, since he was considered to be a real expert on Germany, having studied German in his senior year at Haverford and having a wife who traded Christmas cards with an old Vassar chum who was now the wife of the Mayor of Pforzheim.

"I don't like your attitude, Wagner," Morfey said.

"I'm not so crazy about yours, either."

There was a moment of impasse. Then Morfey reached into a drawer, selected a paper, and slid it across the desk. "Hold up your right hand," he said.

Wagner showed him his palm.

"Repeat after me: I, Roger M. Wagner, do hereby swear—"

"I, Roger M. Wagner, do hereby swear—"

"—that the operation I am about to embark upon promises in no way to interfere in, or to obstruct the processes and functions of, any other national government. So help me God."

"This is the silliest thing I've ever heard, Morfey."

"Repeat it, then sign the affidavit."

"They're trying to interfere in *our* processes—"

"Repeat it and sign."

Wagner intoned the phrase and scrawled his name at the bottom of the paper. "There. Now do you want me to nail it to the door of the cathedral?"

"Don't be a smart aleck, Wagner. I've got my job, you've got yours."

"Shee."

"If you spend one cent more than ten thousand, I want a complete briefing and justification."

"Groot's in charge. Bug him, not me." Wagner pushed

back his chair and stood up. "Is that all?"

"You may leave."

Wagner descended to the basement and followed the long corridor past the glass walls and teletypes and file cabinets and computers where the blank-faced people genuflected before The System. He recognized only a few of them, the older ones. Most were shockingly young, and he wondered if he had ever looked so lean and guileless. He had always been vulnerable to nostalgia, and the Gurney advertisement, ubiquitously plastered over West Germany, had inspired a particularly intense attack. Making for Central Registry, passing all the youngsters, he decided that Emerson Gurney must be a hundred and seventy years old. Emerson Gurney, who had swashed and buckled across the tiny screen at the Kenmore on Saturday afternoons, where the Crosby Avenue gang would whistle and bellow and throw wads of chewing gum and, occasionally, watch the picture show. Pay your dime and watch Emerson Gurney fist-fight on cliffs and shoot the baddies and give sanitary kisses to broads with batting eyelashes. Saturday afternoon in O'Hara's-ville, USA, and then, as now, Emerson Gurney—but grinning with his original teeth under his original hair from ads whose writers had never heard of TV. Emerson Gurney had seemed old even then, yet here he was in Germany, still grinning, still trying to look clean-cut and earnestly moral, despite the intervening decades of multiple divorce and saloon brawls and nude swims in city fountains and dodging the draft in the Hitler war.

The rot was setting in even then.

Even in those childhood days.

Dusty Rhodes was on duty at Central Registry, and he was glad, because she was his favorite of all librarians, and he sorely needed some cheering up.

"Ah," she said from behind the counter, "Von Peck's bad boy. What brings you out of the woodwork?"

"How you been, Dusty?"

"What kind of question is that to ask a lady who is

between lovers? I've been rotten, that's how I've been."

"You aren't a lady. You're Civil Service."

"I still ain't getting any."

"Well, don't look at me. I'm a retired eunuch."

"Yeah, I'll bet," She gave him a sly wink. "How come you and I never made it?"

"We might have if you'd climbed out from between your lovers now and then."

"How about tonight?"

"It's back to the woodwork, I'm afraid. I only came out for a gulp of air."

"Oh, well," she sighed in mock resignation, "if I can't interest you in my warm and tender body, what else can I do for you?"

"I'd like the dossier for a feller down Munich-way. Rattner. Siegfried Rattner."

She made a note on her checkout pad. "Isn't he the nightclub operator?"

"That's what he tells the police he is."

"What is he really?"

"That's what I've got to find out."

She snickered and shook her head. "Why don't you call him up and ask him?"

"Say, that's an idea. It would revolutionize our business."

She smiled to herself, pushed the button that opened the swing door at the end of the counter, and nodded him toward the viewing booths. He sat in the one by the big window and waited until the computer selected the Rattner material and put it on the screen.

The pictures of Ziggi were old ones, and he hadn't been any better-looking then than he was now. The bio rundown was also colorless: born in Dresden in 1925, illegitimate; trade school, then the Hitler Jugend and eventually the Wehrmacht; undistinguished service in Norway and France, infantry; transferred to the sappers' school at Murnau in February, 1945; captured by the U.S. Army near Rosenheim in April; returned to civilian status

June, 1945. Assorted jobs: dishwasher, chauffeur, stock boy, cabdriver, drygoods salesman, bartender. First arrest in 1952, petty larceny. Second arrest, 1955, suspicion of robbery, released for lack of evidence. Partner in Munich nightclub, the Unicorn, from 1956 to last year. Opened his own nightclub, the Golden Thigh, Munich, in August. Previous service: Informant, Operation Equity (which see).

Wagner sat for a time, alternately planning and dozing.

Rattner was a dreary little man.

Fortunately, all that was known about him had not been entered in Central Registry's data bank.

And this fact was the only trump Wagner could see in his hand.

He went to Supply and Resources, where he was given six one-thousand-dollar bills—five for Ziggi and one for personal expenses to be vouchered. His ID papers were made out in the name of Wilhelm Koenig—the name by which he was known in Munich—and he was issued a set of clothes bearing Rhineland store labels, two cheap suitcases, and, much to his surprise, the keys to an outwardly battered but inwardly fine-tuned BMW sedan.

Groot's priority must be very high indeed, he decided.

Which meant that Groot was truly very worried.

Which worried him.

When people like Groot were worried, people like Wagner seemed always to wind up in some kind of soup.

His uneasiness increased when he picked up the Autobahn and headed south. Traffic was moderate-to-heavy, and there were more high-speed drivers than usual, and so he was compelled to work harder at his driving than he would have liked.

He had the impression that the brown Volvo sedan behind him was a tail. To test the idea, he varied his speed, but it was no real test because the ebb and flow of the vehicles around him made it impossible to isolate the behavior pattern of any specific atuomobile. The brown car was to the rear, and there it remained, sometimes fairly close, sometimes as far as a half-mile behind.

And after dark it all became academic anyhow, since everything turned to headlights and horn-blaring.

6

It was deep night when he reached the city, and the lights were brilliant flecks all around, and the traffic was fast and indifferent to the late hour. He steered the BMW off the Georg Brauchle Ring near Luitpold Park and took some side streets past Karl Theodor Strasse and on into the Schwabing section, where he put the car in an all-night garage and hired a room for himself at the Nikolai, a twenty-bed hotel where the help said nothing and remembered less.

He was very tired and would have liked to spend November and December on the slab-hard bed by the solitary window. But he washed and shaved in the communal bathroom at the end of the hall, then changed from his suit into slacks, turtleneck, and blazer. The repairs made him feel a little better, and he promised himself he'd sleep late in the morning. He dropped his key at the desk, where a fat old man dozed in a chair with a mean-looking cat in his lap. The man was as truly asleep as the cat, and Wagner knew that both of them could have told him how many buttons he had on his clothes.

He tapped his hand on the bell and they both opened an eye. The cat's was friendlier.

"Excuse me," Wagner said.

The man said nothing. The cat yawned.

"Where do I find the Golden Thigh?" He knew, of course, but it was his policy to test the people on his perimeter. Tone and manner reveal a lot.

The cat stood up, stretched into a hump, then curled up again, looking bored. The man stroked its head and said, "You want a woman? I can get you a good one. Clean. Cheap."

"No thanks. I just want to look around the town."

"The Thigh is a whore station. It's a rat's nest. Only fools go there."

"That's me, all right. Where is it?"

"Down the street. Turn left. Next right. Halfway into the block."

"Thanks."

The man closed his eye and coughed, his huge belly rolling.

The night was chilly, yet the streets were dotted with the inevitable window-shoppers. Shopping had always been, next to drinking and fornication, Schwabing's favorite sport. To the native, shopping was a social event to be shared with like-minded souls, an amiable drifting from lighted window to lighted window, pausing occasionally for a snort, or an orgasm, or both, depending on his mood and the opportunity. Schwabing was to Munich what the Village was to New York, only cleaner and prettier, with artsy-craftsy displays and saloons and discothèques and street cafés and basement bistros and screwballs in nutty costumes, and Wagner never tired of it.

The Golden Thigh was all that the hotel fat man had claimed it to be.

Its door opened on an explosion of noise that compounded the fire-gong crashing of hard rock with that high-pitched clamor of drinkers who, pretending fun, think they're having it. There were many more women than men, and they were bosomy and spangled, and their eyes gave Wagner a shopping appraisal as he found a place in the thicket of behinds at the end of the bar. He yawned, showing the universal Schwabing signal that he was not in the market, and the eyes turned away to other considerations. He caught the bartender's attention in the dim light, and he was brought a Scotch.

"Tell Ziggi Rattner I want to see him," he said to the barman over the yammering.

The man's little eyes wavered. "I don't think he's in tonight."

"I think he is."

"Oh? I just said he wasn't."

"You're not a very good liar. Where's his office?"

The bartender lowered his gaze, flicked his towel across the mahogany, then turned to get busy at the cash register. He must have triggered a warning buzzer, because the bouncer materialized at Wagner's elbow and leaned down to say in his ear, "Wouldn't you rather be home, watching television?"

"Don't give me the hard stuff, Bismarck. Just tell Rattner I want to see him."

The bouncer was one of those box-shaped Bavarians, and his face was set in perpetual irritability. "Beat it, pal. Out."

"All right," Wagner said agreeably. "But tell Rattner that The Organization was here. Tell him that The Organization is very unhappy. We are unhappy that he was unavailable to discuss our unhappiness."

If there's anything that gets a German's attention it's an organization. The bouncer examined Wagner with new thoughtfulness. "Organization?"

Wagner stood up and threw a bill on the bar. Then he winked at the man. "It was nice knowing you."

"I don't scare, friend."

"Good. We enjoy the tough, fearless ones."

Wagner made for the door, but the bouncer caught his sleeve. "Wait a second, mister. Have a drink on the house while I check to see if Mr. Rattner is in."

"Just tell him Koenig's here."

The bouncer blinked several times, his mind obviously

44

overtaxed by all the decision-making. Then he turned and shouldered his way through the crowd. Wagner watched him disappear into a small hallway at the rear of the place. He was halfway through the house Scotch when the Bavarian reappeared, caught his eye, and waved the come-ahead.

Wagner made him wait until he finished his drink.

Rattner was behind a glass-and-chrome desk, counting money.

"Hello, Ziggi."

"Well, now. You weren't supposed to come here. You were supposed to meet me at my house," Rattner said, making a little face of reproval. "And you frightened Otto with your talk of organizations and things."

"I always was a great kidder."

"How's everything in the cloak-and-dagger business?" Rattner seemed to be especially nervous this night.

"Tolerable."

"Sit down. Want a drink? A girl?"

"You know better than that."

"Ah, yes." Rattner paused to light a cigarette. Then he said, "It appears you delivered my message."

"My people might want to hear what you have to say."

"Mm. All it takes is money." He glanced at his watch, and again Wagner sensed his tautness.

"How much money?"

"A hundred thousand marks. Fifty thousand U.S. dollars."

"That sound you hear is me, wetting my pants."

"Well, that's what it'll cost you if you expect to get the story." Rattner finished his playing with the money and, after snapping a rubber band around the stack, slid open a drawer in the credenza behind him and dropped it in. Then he unbuttoned his fancy jacket, clasped his hands behind his head, and sank back in the swivel chair. "How about it?" he said. "Are you buying?"

Wagner shrugged. "I guess not."

Rattner came forward to rest his elbows on the desk and to deliver what he probably felt to be an earnest look.

45

"This is really big. Top-drawer stuff."

"So you say."

"Forty thousand?"

"No."

"This information is critical to the United States. You should put a lot of value on it."

"Kooks are always trying to take the United States. We get wary."

"I'm no kook."

"You couldn't prove it by me."

"Still the same old smartass, too."

"Mm-hm."

"Well, how about twenty? Same as last time."

"No. I've decided I won't pay you anything at all."

Rattner blinked. "You're joking, of course."

"No."

"Well, then, get lost. I'll peddle it elsewhere."

"As you wish."

"You aren't the only one who pays, you know."

"Say it isn't so."

Rattner patted his hairdo nervously. "I don't understand you. I'm one of the few people left in Germany—the world—who will even talk to your stupid CIA these days. You should treat me nice."

Wagner crossed his legs and made a steeple of his fingers, which he touched to his lips. He sat in easy contemplation, his eyes fixed on Rattner's. "I know how you financed this pigsty of yours, Ziggi."

"What does that mean?"

"I know you masterminded last April's payroll robbery at the Mueller Gesellschaft factory. And you bought this place with your share of the loot."

Rattner sank back in his chair, his spectacles glittering in the glow from the desk lamp.

"I've got a complete rundown," Wagner said. "You. Ernst Blumentag. Alois Luft. Irma Klagel. That cute trick with the delivery van. Do you want me to tell you where that delivery van is right now?"

There was a silence.

Finally Rattner stirred and said, "Talk like that can get you killed."

"I doubt it. I left a statement with my Agency."

"You're bluffing."

"Try me."

Rattner came forward in his chair. "Let me get this straight. If I tell you what I know, you won't tell the police about the Mueller thing. Right?"

"You've got it."

"That's blackmail."

"Oh, my goodness. Really?"

"Your Agency has been forbidden to use criminal tactics. Blackmail is a crime."

"So write a letter to your congressman."

Rattner's anger reddened his face. "You're crazy, Koenig. Raving. Some people are planning to kill your President and you bicker in petty blackmail."

"I'm weird, all right."

Rattner seemed to be immobilized by outrage mixed with anxiety.

"Well, Ziggi," Wagner said, "how about it? Is it jail or talk?"

"Oh, I'll talk, damn you. But not now."

"When?"

"Later tonight. I've got something to do first." He glanced edgily at his watch. "Be at my place at three o'clock. As I told you in the first place."

"Richtenstrasse Nine, Bogenhausen. Right?"

"That's right."

"You've moved up in the world. No more basement apartments for you, eh?"

Rattner licked his lips and was about to answer when there was a knock on the door. His eyes, barely visible behind the blue lenses, turned quickly toward the sound. "What is it?" he called.

The door opened and Otto, the bouncer, peered in. "You asked me to tell you when Gustav Kahn and Lotte arrived. They're here now, waiting in your suite."

"Well, tell them something's come up," Rattner said.

47

"Tell them I'll have to see them tomorrow. But for God's sake, be diplomatic about it."

When the bouncer was gone, Wagner stood up, his bones aching and his spirit in deep eclipse. The underworld and its seediness depressed him to an unspeakable degree.

"So, then," he said. "Three o'clock."

Rattner sat scowling at the desk top.

Despite his weariness, Wagner did not return to the Nikolai but walked for a time, deep in thought. Eventually he went into an all-night snack bar owned by a retired cop named Kulka. He asked for Kulka but the night man said that the boss came around only in the morning these days. So Wagner begged some wrapping paper and, over a cup of coffee, composed a brief letter to Hans Trille. He folded the note around five of his six one-thousand-dollar bills, wrapped and Scotch-taped the lot, then went outside to hand the package to a cabdriver who'd been dozing in his hack at the waiting zone.

"This twenty marks is for you," he said, snapping a bill. "Deliver this package safely and you get another twenty in the mail."

The cabbie considered the address. "What if he isn't in? It's pretty goddamn late."

"Then leave it for him. He'll get it when he comes in."

"All right. Send the other twenty to my number at the garage."

"Sure."

Wagner went back to his coffee and, sipping and staring out at the gathering predawn fog, reviewed the presidential itinerary Groot had left for him at the Safe House.

Bonn and Frankfurt he dismissed. In both places the itinerary kept the President in closed and protected vehicles or under roof from plane to meeting hall. The exposure to crowds would be within enclosed structures at both places. The President would be protected against

48

crazies, close up, by a platoon of Secret Service bodyguards, and on the perimeter by hand-picked German pistol marksmen. Since the buildings would be fine-toothed for bombs every hour, an assassin would be foolish to try that method: bombs were indiscriminate, unpredictable, difficult to hide, and easy to spot. So, if plotters truly wanted the President dead, they would have to use a rifleman of exceptional cool and skill.

But a rifleman would require a large open space for sighting and placing his shot. He would need routes for quick withdrawal. The buildings in Bonn and Frankfurt offered neither. Too much clutter, too many closed spaces.

Munich was something else again.

The Olympiahalle, where the President's speech was to be delivered, was a major feature of the Olympiapark on Munich's northern rim. It was flanked on one side by the great sports stadium and on the other by the 900-foot tower that dominated the site like a surrealistic finger warning of doom. Surrounding the whole were sweeps of lawn and walkways and artificial lakes and woodland groves planted in the premeditated haphazard that betrays the professional landscaper. According to the dope sheet, the presidential party would arrive by car at 11:45 A.M. The President would go directly to the podium in the meeting hall and complete his address by 12:25. Then he and his party would walk from the meeting hall to the tower and would take the elevators to the revolving restaurant near the tower's top. After a lunch against the slowly turning panorama of Oberbayern, he would make a brief TV and radio address to the German people, thanking them for their hospitality and reassuring them as to America's continuing interest in a partnership with them. Then he and his party would descend to ground level and take cars to München-Riem airport and the Lufthansa flight home.

Wagner guessed that the places of concealment available to a sharpshooter could not possibly number more than four or five million.

It would be an assassin's dream.

A target moving slowly across an open mall overlooked by a square mile of hills and trees.

And adjacent to the hills and trees, a great city of buildings and streets and alleys and subways in which to get instantly lost.

Munich would be the place, all right.

7

Richtenstrasse proved to be a winding side street lined by tall hedges, over which the slates and gables of big, rich houses made forbidding slabs against the night sky. Few lights showed anywhere, and Wagner guessed that Ziggi Rattner would be the only one among the fatcat residents to be out of a warm bed. Which made him dislike Rattner all the more, because bed was where he himself longed to be.

Ziggi's house was even grander than the others. It sat well back from the street at the round of a U established by a tree-lined driveway. Meticulous lawns spread from the house, and discreetly placed lampposts made elegant pools of light in the darkness. Wagner parked the BMW under the vaulted porte-cochere and stood on the steps, listening to the sounds of distant traffic and wondering what lying idiot had first said that crime doesn't pay. Houses like these rarely came to men who worked for salaries and paid their taxes. So what subtle bendings of morality had underwritten their construction and occupation? What market had been cornered to build that one? Who had been fleeced out of what so as to finance that one?

He shook himself free of this dour speculation and turned to the door and pressed the bell. Nothing happened for a time, and he was about to ring again when the door swung open to reveal a shriveled old man in a dressing gown.

"Wilhelm Koenig to see Herr Rattner. He's expecting me."

"But Herr Rattner is at his work, sir. He—"

"I saw him at his office and he asked me to meet him here at three."

"Ah, I see." The door opened wide. "Then come in, please. I'm sorry I'm so disheveled, but it's the doorman's night off, and—"

"Who are you?" Wagner kept the question soft.

"Ludwig. Herr Rattner's butler. Come in, please. There's a fire in the library. Would you like me to freshen it for you?"

"No, thanks. I'm early. I'll just relax in a chair."

"Very good, sir. Follow me."

The house was baronial, with white stucco walls, dark ceiling beams, carved balconies, antler displays, and brooding tapestries. There were even crossed swords and a knight's helmet over the unused fireplace at the end of the entrance hall, and Wagner saw the absurdity in a hood like Ziggi Rattner asserting even so tenuous a link to chivalry. And a greater mockery waited in the library, which was stacked from floor to ceiling with dark-hued tomes that Ziggi was as likely to open as he was to teach the New Testament to the neighborhood kids.

Wagner sat in a tall leather chair, sipped a slow Scotch served up by Ludwig, and waited for something to happen.

At about five before three, the lights of a car flickered through the draperies, and there was the sound of a door slamming. He expected Rattner to come in, but the doorbell rang instead, and soon the creaky butler drifted through the great hall. After some low-key conversation by the door, Ludwig reappeared to usher in a woman.

"Fräulein Pomeraine," Ludwig wheezed, "may I

present Herr Koenig? He, too, has an appointment with Herr Rattner."

She was in her dignified thirties, and her honey-colored hair was tied back with a ribbon. Her eyes were slate blue and set wide under a broad forehead. The effect was crisp, and Wagner decided that she was, all in all, pretty. He wondered what she was doing here.

"How do you do, Herr Koenig."

"Fräulein Pomeraine." He stood up and offered her a chair.

They sat down and examined each other with polite wariness, and he could see she shared his surprise and annoyance at finding a third party attending what had presumably been a two-party arrangement.

"I'll have to admit I'm surprised to find you here," she said. Her German was correct and stilted and flavored by unmistakable Carolina cadences. He considered a switch to English, but it seemed to be an unnecessary expenditure of a small trump. Let her labor a bit. Let her pay for her intrusion.

"That's what my father said when he saw me for the first time."

She smiled faintly, a mere turn of the lips. "A German with a sense of humor? You're a rare bird, Herr Koenig."

"Germans are not nearly so stolid as Hollywood would have you believe." He paused. "You're from the States, of course."

"I'm an American, but I've spent a lot of time in Europe."

"So have I."

She smiled a bit more openly this time. "Who are you, Herr Koenig?"

"I'm in public relations."

"Oh?" She made a little joke of her own. "That's something Ziggi Rattner could use, all right."

It was Wagner's turn to smile. "Anybody who thinks that has to be an excellent judge of character."

"You're not one of his fans, then?"

"Hardly."

"I'm glad. You have too nice a face for it."

"What's your interest in him, Fräulein Pomeraine?"

"I'm a writer. He's promised me a story."

He looked at her carefully, trying not to show his surprise. "A writer. Well now. Whom do you write for?"

"You don't flatter me very much, Herr Koenig. I'd thought my by-line was better known than that. I'm a correspondent of *Chronos*, the weekly news magazine."

"I read mainly Continental newspapers."

"That's rather limiting for a public-relations man, isn't it? I'd think you would read all the opinion-leading publications." Her eyes had narrowed, hinting derision.

"Well," he said, "I'm not a very good public-relations man."

She rested back in her chair and fell silent, studying his face from under lowered lids. He felt vaguely uncomfortable under such scrutiny, and, to disguise this fact, he pretended interest in the Oriental carpet. He was really not much of a ladies' man, either, being aware of woman's capacity for tyranny since his earliest days. His childhood had coincided with the Great Depression of the 1930s, and his family had been very worried about money, and his mother had cried a lot, and he had begun to believe that he was somehow the blame for her unhappiness. His mother had talked a lot about dying, or leaving, or being alone and lonely, and it got to be that he was never certain he would find her there when he came home from school. Now, with the insight of years, he saw that this was how she had controlled her husband and her sons. But the damage had been done early on. He had been so afraid of losing her and having no one in the world who really cared about him he had, in time, willed himself into not caring about anybody too much, since it seemed clear that if he stood to lose his own mother he stood to lose anybody else. His love affairs had therefore been superficial, tangential, and the women would drop him eventually because be remained so obtuse and uninvolved. Yet it would sting like sin when they did, and he'd feel a terrible loss for months afterward.

"What sort of things do you write?" he asked for want of anything else to say.

"Pretty much what interests me."

"Your German is excellent, Fräulein Pomeraine."

"I'm told it has an atrocious American accent."

"But it's precise and unhesitating. Pretty unusual for a Yankee."

"I have an ear for languages. Straight A's in German, French, and Spanish from Carolina U. Which, incidentally, makes me no Yankee at all."

"Ah, yes. The War Between the States, and all that." She dropped the manner of smalltalk and asked pointblank: "Why are you here? What's your interest in Rattner?"

"I'm not sure, but I'm beginning to suspect that he wants his public-relations man present when he tells you his story, whatever his story may be."

"You don't know the story?"

"I'm afraid not."

She reddened. "I'm not sure I appreciate a PR type listening over my shoulder." Her anger seemed for a moment to be put on somehow. It was only a fleeting thing, but he had the impression that she wasn't nearly so angry as she appeared to be.

He was preparing to answer when, somewhere deep in the house, there was a muffled symphony of crashings and bangings. There was something else: a sliding, and what sounded to be a shriek.

Miss Pomeraine flew out of her chair, eyes wide. "What in hell was *that*?" she gasped in English.

"I don't know," he said in his own English, "but we'd better take a look."

They hurried into the entrance hall, pausing for a moment to get their bearings.

"This way," Wagner said. "Down the corridor. I think it leads to the kitchen."

At the far end of the butler's pantry was a swinging door, and they pushed through this to enter the kitchen, which was an enormous square of brilliant enamels and vinyls and chrome. A serving table had been overturned, and shattered glassware made a sparkling clutter on the tiles. Sprawling against the table, pajamaed legs thrust outward from the rumple of his terrycloth robe, Ludwig stared in goggling shock, his mouth working to eject unintelligible squeakings.

Wagner kneeled beside him. "What happened? What's wrong?"

"I—I—"

"Come on: what happened?"

"A—a—snack. I came down for a—oh, my God."

"What *happened*, damn it?"

"I—oh, dear lord. The Terror. The Terror. Oh—"

"What? *What*?"

"The refrigerator—oh, dear lord—The Terror—"

Wagner stood up, spun around, and pulled open the refrigerator door.

Miss Pomeraine said, "Jesus God . . ."

The bottles and containers and sausages and butter blocks had been moved carefully aside.

In the center, directly under the light, sat Ziggi Rattner's head, spectacles neatly in place over the half-open eyes.

8

Hans Trille, being a resident detective inspector of the Bundeskriminalamt, had certain prerogatives, and one of them was to keep an investigation waiting until he had had a proper breakfast. As a material witness to homicide, Wagner had been detained, but the night-side local police management, bemused by the gaudiness of the case and the presence of Miss Ellie Pomeraine (who, it turned out, was truly a well-known journalist), had taken his statement and then permitted him the relative comfort of Trille's office. He was napping in a hard-back oak chair when Trille came in, nibbling a toothpick.

Trille considered Wagner without pleasure and said in English, "You again."

"Mm."

"You are a magnet, Koenig."

"How's that?"

"Whenever you come out from under your rock you attract dead bodies. Like a magnet."

"That's a somewhat mixed and extravagant metaphor, Inspector. Besides, we've met only twice before."

"And there was a body each time."

"Neither of which I had anything to do with."

"Perhaps. But I've never been sure."

"Besides, there's no body this time. Just a head."

Trille gave Wagner a long, sorrowful appraisal. Policemen (Wagner thought in a moment of empathy) have much to be sorrowful about. By the time they have moved beyond the rookie stage they are likely to have seen everything there ever was. A man in clandestine intelligence also witnesses all kinds of depravity and transgression, to be sure, but his mission is to exploit such sins as the raw material of his own ultimate achievement. The policeman, though, is commissioned to halt, or at least to negate, mankind's propensity for evil, and this, of course, is trying to subdue Niagara with a bathtub drain plug. Predestined failure is issued with the policeman's badge, and Trille's narrow face was a bas-relief representation of the human cost.

"That's an interesting present you sent me," Trille said. "I don't often receive five thousand dollars in my morning mail."

"I would like to have kept it," Wagner said, deadpan, "but it belongs to Mueller Gesellschaft."

"Your note says you retrieved it from Siegfried Rattner."

"Better known as Ziggi, the Headless Whoresman."

"Are you really that callous, Koenig? To make jokes about murder?"

"Not really, Herr Trille. I make jokes to keep from screaming."

"I have been a policeman for twenty-nine years. I am still shocked by what people can do to each other."

"I'm glad, Inspector," Wagner said, not believing him. "That means you're a man first, a detective second."

Trille sighed and folded his long and tidy frame into a swivel chair behind the desk. Pulling open a drawer, he rummaged around, finally to produce a meerschaum that had seen better times. He sniffed the bowl gingerly and made a face. "Maybe I should try tobacco in this thing some time."

Wagner waited silently, feeling the gloom of the place.

"May I see your papers, Koenig? I'm sure they're in order, but I have to go through the motions."

Wagner handed him his card case and waited some more.

"Is your name really Koenig?"

"Does it matter?"

"I guess not. You've probably used so many names you can't remember your real one anyhow."

Wagner shrugged a shoulder. "The cops have long known of my affiliation with CIA."

"Correction: I have known. The police, as an organization, do not know."

"You haven't told anyone?"

Trille smiled a faint and frosty smile. "I saw no need. You are an American counterintelligence agent. I stumbled on that fact during an investigation. The fact did not pertain. So I saw no reason to complicate life for you. And my secret knowledge of the fact, I decided, might come in handy some day."

Wagner looked at him with new interest. "I see."

"Which brings me to another ritual: did you kill Rattner?"

"Of course not."

"I had to ask. But tell me again. Only this time without all that public-relations-man stuff in your signed statement."

"I'm working an exploitation. Rattner had some information that could be useful to me. He promised to meet me at his house this morning at three. I arrived shortly before that time. The butler, Ludwig something, let me in. I waited awhile, then the American journalist, something Pomeraine—"

"Ellie. Ellie Pomeraine."

"—showed up. We talked about this and that, the way strangers do, and then we heard a rumpus in the kitchen. We investigated and found Ludwig in shock. He said something about the refrigerator. I opened it and found Rattner. Or his head. I left everything as it was and called the police. While Pomeraine helped Ludwig reassemble himself, I looked around the place. I found nothing significant."

"Did you go outside? Look around the garden?"

"No. My footprints might have confused things."

"When you saw Rattner earlier, did he do or say anything that you would consider to be—unusual?"

Wagner shrugged. "Not really. He seemed a little nervous, I'd say. But a man like that has a lot to be nervous about."

"Indeed."

Wagner sat quietly while Trille made some notes. There had been something peculiar about the inspector's calm admission that his true identity as a CIA agent had been withheld from the official files. This was a discord, a contradiction in the ambient bureaucracy. Wagner decided he didn't like it and that he would therefore have to pick his way carefully in his dealings with the man behind the desk. He cleared his throat and said, "There was one thing. The bouncer, Otto something, stuck his head in the door to tell Rattner he had some visitors. Rattner seemed to be upset about this. He told Otto to tell the visitors to wait."

"Any idea who the visitors were?"

"A man and a woman," he said, ceding part of the truth. "I wasn't listening too closely, because I had been on the verge of acquiring Ziggi's information and I was trying to noodle my next move. You could ask the bouncer."

"Otto Vogel?"

"I don't know his name. But he could tell you."

Trille turned a moody stare out the window. "There's a bit of a complication there, I'm afraid."

"Complication?"

"Otto Vogel's body was fished from the river an hour ago. The butler's body was found in a vacant lot in Harlaching an hour before that. Both had been decapitated."

Wagner thought about this. "It would seem," he said,

"that somebody has been busily shutting doors. It seems that Rattner, the butler, and the bouncer knew something, and their knowledge was an annoyance to somebody."

"Mm."

"How about some of the others? The bartenders. The whores."

"Rattner had a private suite with access off the alley. People working up front rarely, if ever, saw who came and went from those rooms. We've drawn a blank among the employees."

"Pomeraine?"

"She told essentially the same story you did. She said Rattner had called her, hinting that he would give her the story of the century, or some such thing, if she would come to his house and bring money."

"Good old Ziggi: the eternal entrepreneur."

Trille sucked noisily at the stem of the meerschaum, and a smelly cloud rolled to the ceiling. He spoke through these labors: "How about the money you sent me this morning?"

"I have evidence—which I'll supply you, incidentally—that Ziggi masterminded the theft of the Mueller payroll last April. I confronted him with my knowledge of the crime and he paid me five thousand to keep my mouth shut."

Trille leaned forward. "Why send it to me? Why are you being so nice to *me*, Koenig?"

Wagner crossed his legs, trying to establish some degree of comfort in the marble-hard chair. "Two reasons. Ziggi had outlived his usefulness to CIA. Once I had exploited him, I wanted him off the street for a long time. I sent you the five to finger Ziggi. I daresay you and your cops can take the matter from here."

"You said two reasons."

"The second one is self-evident. I'm trying to ingratiate myself with you. I want your goodwill."

"Why?"

"The thing I'm working on is touchy. I might need

some backup from the police. I hope I don't. But I might. And if I scratched your back I thought you might scratch mine."

Trille rested back in his chair again and puffed reflectively at the burbling pipe. His eyes remained full on Wagner, thoughtful and containing a trace of disdain. "You Americans have evidence of a crime and you withhold it from us?"

"Rattner was more useful to us out of jail than in."

"Until now, eh?"

"That's right."

"It's good that you sent me the money before he was killed, wouldn't you say? Otherwise your, ah, ingratiating gesture might not have been so convincing."

"I'm lucky sometimes."

Trille peered into the pipe bowl and coughed gently. He placed the pipe carefully in an ashtray whose ceramic flanks bore witness to the Excelsior Hotel. Then he picked up his pencil and made another tiny note on the pad by his telephone. With his eyes downcast, he looked weary and pained, like the wooden face on a roadside crucifix. "How," he said, crossing a T with a deliberate motion, "do you expect me to scratch your back?"

"You're asking what my mission is?"

Trille's lips showed the beginnings of a smile. "I know better than that. You'd only lie to me anyhow. I simply want some idea of how you would use the police in return for your, ah, favor."

"I won't lie to you. I'll be completely candid. Ziggi claimed knowledge of an assassination plot against the U.S. President."

Trille's doleful eyes placed Wagner under new scrutiny. "Oh?"

"I understand that since the massacre of the Israeli athletes during the Munich Olympics you people have built an extensive file on terrorism."

Trille's expression did not change. "It's adequate."

"Well, maybe you'll let me peek at it now and then."

"Odd that you should mention the subject."

"Why?"

Trille turned in his chair and regarded the city beyond the window. "Just yesterday afternoon we received an alert from one of our undercover agents on the terrorism squad. He said Akim Ri is in Munich."

Wagner felt a sudden chill. "The rifleman?"

"Mm. The nomad who rents his marksmanship to the highest bidder."

"I thought he had been killed in a plane crash a year or so ago. In Crete, or some place like that."

Trille shook his head. "No. We've suspected all along that was a fake. But we'd lost track of him."

"And now he's supposed to be here?"

"Oh, he's here, all right. Our agent is good. If he says he's seen Ri, he's seen Ri."

"Ri's wanted in a half-dozen countries. He's known to have assassinated Cardinal Ritchey in that Mexico City thing. And that CBS commentator in Dublin."

"And the German diplomat in Paris. A spectacular feat of marksmanship."

"You plan to arrest him?"

Trille's smile showed openly now, and it made him seem younger. "Oh, I'd be delighted to arrest him. But knowing he's here in Germany is one thing. Catching him is altogether another thing."

"Would you have a mug-shot of Ri I could borrow?"

"You don't know what he looks like?" Trille was surprised.

"I know what he looks like, all right. But a police ID of him could be useful if I have to ask around."

"You expect an assassination attempt during the summit meeting, Koenig?" The question was quick and silky.

"Ri is a professional assassin. He's not likely to be visiting Germany to view the beautiful scenery."

They sat wordlessly again, the only sounds in the room those of the distant traffic and the wall clock's ticking. Finally Trille leaned to one side, flicked an intercom switch, and told the box: "Karl, Wilhelm Koenig is being released. He will stop at your desk on the way out. Please provide him with a photo of Akim Ri."

Wagner pulled on his coat. "I'm allowed to go now?"

"You may go."

As Wagner reached the door, Trille said, "One other thing."

"Well?"

"You might as well know of my contempt for you and your Agency."

"Oh?"

"I recognize your ingratiating gesture for the impotence it is. You and your CIA are pitiful dilettantes who must beg their way among professionals."

"Well, bless my soul, Inspector. I do believe I detect signs of the bully in you."

Wagner did not slam the door, knowing as he did that Trille expected him to.

9

Leaving the BMW at the Autopark, Wagner took the U-bahn to the Schwabing station and found an outdoor phone booth a block from the Nikolai. He searched his wallet for the Hendel card, and because his eyes were swollen from sleeplessness, he had to refer to the number three times.

There were two buzzes at the other end, and then an officious woman's voice answered, "Hendel Kompanie is closed until nine hundred hours tomorrow. This is a recorded message. At the sound of the tone, state your name and telephone number and your call will be returned." He would not have been surprised if she had added *Sieg Heil*.

"Please ask Herr Nagel to call Wilhelm Koenig." He gave the number and hung up. He waited for three minutes, staring at his reflection in the glass. The phone rang.

"Koenig here."

"What's going on?" Groot asked in his asthmatic way.

"We've got complications."

"Oh?"

"Our supplier is bankrupt. Somebody foreclosed him soon after I made my initial contact. In which he confirmed your worst suspicions, by the way."

There was a moment in which he could hear nothing but Groot's breathing. During the interval his mind tried to picture a shock moving across Groot's oatmeal-colored face, because it would have been good to know that Groot could react to murder; that Groot, too, could be sickened by violence. But the picture wouldn't form, and in that flicker of time Wagner wondered about the Moral Law and how far out its perimeters lay. Ziggi, the grossest kind of hood, would have killed him for his trolley tokens. Why then was he so shaken? And why had he been so drained by pretending for Trille that the matter hadn't affected him at all?

It occurred to him that the silent questions were the aging stonemason realizing he hated granite; the retiring bus driver comprehending the fact that, for all of the hundreds of thousands of miles he had driven, he had seen nothing of the world.

"Are there any strings dangling?" Groot asked, his tone unchanged.

"Akim Ri is in town. The police spotted him, but then lost him."

There was another silence, and Wagner waited expectantly. This news was sure to have jolted Groot, and he felt a strange kind of gratification.

Groot said, "Since Ri is a businessman, he never travels for pleasure alone. It would seem, then, that he's here on business."

"And the business seems pretty obvious."

"You're going to have to stay with this thing," Groot said. "And I'll want memorandum reports from you daily. Send them to me by fast mail at Hendel Kompanie."

"Reports? My God, man, I haven't time to go to the bathroom, let alone compose reports."

"I must have a log. A daily situation report." Groot's voice revealed a peculiar urgency. "It's most important."

"My orders say I'm due back on my job at the end of the week."

"I'll fix that. Meanwhile, you're where Ri is. You must find him and drag him to jail. If he won't drag, you'll have to shoot him. But find him and negate him you will. And until you do, I want daily reports."

The dial tone sounded, and Wagner leaned against the booth, staring, but seeing nothing.

He went to his room, took off his shoes, and fell back on the bed, cold and lonely. The ceiling was cracked, and his eyes followed the trails through the plaster, and he thought about his wasted life and Groot's anger and how they were interwoven.

Oh, Jesus...

Where was the beginning? Where was the end?

Sighing, he reached for the recorder and taped a long report to Groot, summarizing things to date. After mailing it to the Hendel Kompanie, he dropped on the tacky bed and slept.

There was a tapping, and he spiraled to the surface of a deep darkness. Pale dusk was outside the window, and he lay there, trying to absorb the fact that he had dozed in the morning and awakened in the twilight. The tapping sounded again, and he rolled, aching, from the bed. He went to the door and opened it.

"Hello," Ellie Pomeraine said. "The cops gave me your address."

"Hi."

"May I come in?"

He looked back at the room, ashamed of the dreariness there. "Sure. I guess so."

She came in, smelling of soap and fresh linen. Glancing about her, she said, "The public-relations business isn't too good these days, eh?"

"You can see for yourself."

"Where did you learn such U.S. English, Mr. Koenig?"

"Berlitz."

She laughed, and it was a pleasant sound.

"What can I do for you, Miss Pomeraine?" He yawned.

"Ellie. Call me Ellie." She sat in the room's only chair and considered him speculatively. "How about putting on your shoes and taking me out for a cup of coffee? This place gives me the heebies."

"I need a shave."

"In Schwabing, everybody needs a shave. Come on."

She knew an espresso off the Leopoldstrasse where the lighting was easy, the tables were penny-size, and the clientele was soft-spoken and literary. They found a place in a corner among some potted plants. They said nothing at first, and it was his impression that her lighthearted posture was hard for her to come by.

He said, "That thing in the kitchen got to you, didn't it?"

She gave him a thoughtful stare and hunched a shoulder. "I suppose so," she said. "I like to think that I've become weathered by all the grim things I've seen in my life, but every time something like that happens I feel the shock all over again."

"Join the group."

"You do too?"

"Especially me."

"That's odd. I had you down as a very cool onion."

"I try. But it never comes off."

"What kind of work do you really do, Mr. Koenig? You must be an actor if you can manage to look so cool when you aren't."

"Everybody's an actor, Miss Pomeraine. Some are better than others, that's all."

"So what's your thing? What do you do for money?"

He could see no valid reason to keep from her what she had probably guessed. "I'm an American. I'm on special assignment."

"Criminal Investigation Division?"

"No. Counter Intelligence." He was angry with himself for his inability to admit his affiliation with CIA.

"I'm glad you told me."

"Why?"

"Because I already knew."

"How?"

"Ziggi. He said he wanted me to meet with him and someone from American intelligence."

"Ziggi was a bigmouth. I'm surprised he lived as long as he did."

"Don't worry. I'll keep your secret. For the present, anyhow."

"It's not much of a secret anymore. I guess. If Ziggi told you I have to assume he told everybody. The bigmouth."

She brushed the tablecloth with her long fingers and was thoughtful again. She took a deep breath and said, "Do you have any idea of what Ziggi was going to talk to me about?"

"No."

"I think you do."

"So sue me."

"Look, pal. I need a story. I need one bad."

He felt a mild surprise. There had been desperation in her tone, and it surprised him. "The famous Ellie Pomeraine should have stories lined up for months ahead. Why poke at an obscure public servant who knows nothing about nothing?"

"It's none of your business."

They watched the traffic for a time. Somewhere in the lull she made a decision, apparently. She said, "Have you ever been married?"

"No."

She smiled a tight little smile. "Well, I was. And I'm trying to get over it. I'm trying, as the cliché goes, to lose myself in my work."

"Who's the ex?"

"A writer. A novelist. Well, not a novelist, really. He writes spy stories and international intrigue crap. He's a jerk. All writers are jerks."

"You're a writer."

"So I should know, eh?"

"You were crazy about the guy, eh?"

She chuckled wryly. "Hell no. That's the problem. For the two years since the divorce I've been literally writhing over having been such an ass as to play that idiot's doormat. For two years I've had absolutely no self-respect, no sense of worth. I was the world's leading patsy. You know what I mean?"

"I guess so."

"But one day I woke up and decided that things would be rotten just so long as I thought they were. As long as I made no effort to change. So I thought of my ex-husband, rolling around with his airline tootsie on Majorca or wherever, and I decided, Screw you, you bastard, you've done all the damage to me you're going to do."

"So what's the trouble, then?"

"Those two years of self-pity have cost me a bunch, buddy. I wasn't cutting the mustard at *Chronos*. I was riding along mainly on my reputation. Just putting in time and going through the motions. And now that I'm a new me, rebuilding and all that foo, Goddard Dalton, the boss man, is trying to put me on a shelf. Like tomorrow, Dalton wants me to interview a *movie* actor, down in Eigenheim, in the Tyrol. A movie actor, for cripes' sake. Interviews with hams are the lowest form of journalism."

"Why don't you just leave and get another job?"

"I've put in too much time at *Chronos*. Like, *Chronos* is a big tit, and I'm afraid to let it go."

"Oh."

"You see?" she said ruefully. "I'm a well-known writer. But I'm not a successful one."

He took a sip of coffee, using the moment to form a question. Putting the cup down carefully, he asked: "Miss Pomeraine, why did Ziggi single you out for this story he had in mind? Europe is crawling with journalists of all sizes, shapes, and persuasions. Why did he pick you?"

"He said he'd read my article on terrorists. He'd been impressed. He said that with his special information, my savvy on terrorists, and *Chronos*'s money, we could all wind up being happy."

Wagner, who had been watching the traffic outside, gave her a sidelong glance. "You did an article on terrorists?"

"Mm. Last fall."

"What did the article say?"

She hunched a shoulder in that way of hers. "Oh, it was a rehash of the Olympic massacre, when all the Israeli athletes were shot down and so on. I updated the whole thing by giving a rundown on the Greuel, which, as you probably know, is short for das Greuelbundnis, or Terror Alliance. It's a group of German terrorists. A local group, I think. They usually behead individuals who gain their disfavor. Trademark, and like that."

"Why do you think they're local?"

She rested back in her chair and gazed out at the city. Her eyes were very blue now. 'There are many terrorist organizations worldwide," she said, "but most are small and show no overt signs of being coordinated, except, maybe, those that are Maoist-oriented. The Middle East Arab groups—especially the Palestinian guerrillas—are, of course, the most active and high-profile, what with their major cover having been the aim to crush Israel and liberate Palestine. And—"

Wagner broke in. "You're saying the Palestine guerrillas never really wanted to crush Israel and liberate Palestine?"

"Of course they did, silly. But the issue is really much broader. At least I suspect it is. The fundamentalists among them—the intellectuals and philosophers—proclaimed from the beginning the common enemy, the revolutionary's true and classic enemy, to be the world's economy manipulators. Not only the Wall Street tycoons, but the industrialists, financiers, public-opinion molders and owners of the media in all major capitalist nations—U.S., Germany, the UK, Japan, France, and so on. That's why you've seen Middle East radicals bombing U.S. Information Service buildings, shooting up British and French stock exchanges, assassinating West German diplomats, machine-gunning New York and Washington newspaper editors and television commentators."

"How about all the rich Arab guys who own all the oil?"

She shook her head. "No. The revolutionaries see them as kindred souls who are doing no more than protecting a dwindling national resource."

"And you think this Greuel is just another club in the Middle East daisy chain?"

"On the contrary. They are rabid right-wingers. They

threw the Sekigun out of Germany, actually."

"You mean that Japanese student thing?"

"The student group that raises unalloyed hell. They're Marxists—a small but fanatical group that first appeared in Central Japan. Its base for some time was Kyoto. Later it joined forces with another radical group called the Keihm Ampo Kyoto, and the new amalgamation called itself the Rengo Sekigun, or United Red Army. Its members are said to be working for worldwide revolution in Lebanon, Okinawa, Mexico, Cuba, and some South American countries."

"But not in Germany?"

Miss Pomeraine shook her head again. "They were in Germany. But, as I say, the Greuel made short work of them."

"Who belongs to the Greuel?"

She glanced at Wagner and smiled ironically. "I think they're Nazi retreads."

He couldn't help but return the smile. "Ah-hah. The good old tried and true. Nazis: the old-fashioned American's favorite enemy."

She said, "There are about a hundred of them, according to the poop I get."

"All punks?"

"No way. Some of them are said to be upper crust. Even some officials of the government, and like that. Housewives. Businessmen. They think Hitler was right all along."

"Has the Greuel pulled anything yet?"

"They are rumored to have arranged that Bad Reichenhall massacre, where the building caught fire and all the exit doors were jammed shut and eighty left-wing students died." She sighed. "That and assorted beheadings in Oberbayern and adjacent Austria."

"Among them Ziggi's, maybe, eh?"

"Did you hear what the butler said in the kitchen?"

"'The terror.' He kept saying 'the terror.'"

"Right," Miss Pomeraine said. "How many people, even Victorian types like Ludwig, are liable to take a look at a head in an icebox and say, 'the terror of it all'? He wasn't saying how horrible it was. He was saying 'The Terror.' Capital letters."

Wagner considered this for a time.

"You know what I think?" Miss Pomeraine said eventually. "I think that Ziggi Rattner had stumbled onto some facet of the Greuel thing and was about to sell the information to you and me."

"Perhaps."

Miss Pomeraine gave him a level stare. "Look: I need a story, you need—well, whatever it is you need. Let's work together."

"Sorry. It's against Company rules."

"You need all the help you can get, you jerk," she said amiably.

"Amen." He picked up the check and examined it.

"Well, then—"

"Do you really believe," he drawled, "that I'd do that? I'm a professional. The last thing I'd do would be to share my duties with a smooth-talking southern-fried chick who's out to prove her former husband made the all-time world's champion mistake by leaving her for an airline tootsie-roll. I'm not running a rehab center for rejected broads, sweetie. I'm trying, the best way I know how, to earn my laughable salary."

Her blue eyes narrowed to hot slits. "Why, you son of a bitch. Who do you think you're talking to?"

"How many guesses do I get?"

"Nobody kisses off Ellie Pomeraine."

"Well, I'm nobody."

Crimson, she pushed back her chair, stood up, turned on her heel, and strode out the door into the neon night.

Wagner sighed, counted out some money, and went to the cash register.

10

Groot had taken a small room in a prosaic section of the Vierjahreszeiten, and, true to his custom, had made it at once into a combined office, breakfast nook, library, sleeping place, and command post. (Someone—probably Oscar Wadman, who had been a court jester during the Company's Dulles reign—had observed that Groot never took a room, he pulled it on like an old bathrobe. But those were the days when their naiveté enabled Americans to make jokes. No jolly sounds had been heard around the Agency for a long time now.) He was sprawled on the bed, nibbling detachedly at a salami sandwich and making notes, when the house phone rang. .

"Yes?"

'This is Sam Fallon. Senator Logue wants to see you."

"Oh? What can I do for him?"

"Just get your ass up here."

"Well, I—"

But the dial tone sounded, and Groot returned the phone to its cradle. He sniffed and rolled over to place his feet in the shoes beside the bed. Standing erect in defiance of his unwilling muscles, he made his way through the newspapers and books that littered the carpet to stand at the dresser and consider himself in the mirror. He saw an aging face, sagging and pocked and splotched, and he wondered how his life might have been changed if he had been beautiful. His mind went briefly to Emerson Gurney, so handsome all those years ago and now seeking vainly to convey the illusion of beauty retained; Gurney must most certainly be terribly demoralized by his descent into ugliness. So, Groot decided, dismissing the subject, it was better to have been ugly all along: you don't miss something you never had.

He put on his tie, combed his remaining hair with his fingers, and pulled on the coat of a $300 suit that looked, on him, as if it were a $38.95 special from Sears. Then he returned to the bedside table, from whose drawer he took the SCR.

He punched the red button and said into the scrambler: "Groot to Secret Service. Twenty-one-thirteen hours. To Senator Logue's suite, the Vierjahreszeiten. Will return this station for check-in."

He placed the communicator in the drawer and went to the door, where he paused to brush his shoes against the backs of his trousers legs. Sighing again, he entered the corridor and made for the stairs.

Senator Logue was the product of a libertarian guilt carried by a splinter of Delaware's super-rich. Delaware had been virtually owned by wealthy conservatives since the nineteenth century. But in the late 1970s, still drifting in the social remorse of a decade earlier, the "Greenville Groaners" (a sobriquet laid on the hand-wringers by the contemptuous majority of their fellow zillionaires) plunged enormous sums—some of them legal—into the support of Logue, son of a Kent County preacher and the personification of Liberal Morality. Logue had been elected to the Senate, of course, and had promptly become a darling of the national media for his ability to mix down-home wit with parish-house piety. He was quoted widely, and appeared on many talk shows, and thereby became the first bona fide Celebrity ever to spring from Delaware, achieving the ultimate in recognition when his likeness began to appear on the seats of blue jeans sold in discount stores.

Practically speaking, his chairmanship of the Armed Services Committee and his membership on the Finance and CIA oversight committees made him a virtually irresistible force on Capitol Hill and among the agencies. This heroic portrait was tied in ribbon by his friendship with that other personification of national popularity and moral rectitude, Amy Randall, Speaker of the House of Representatives and President Randall's sister.

The Associated Press's patriarchal cynic Al Leone, once seeing them together at the head table with the hockey-star M.C. at an orphans' benefit, drawled, "Father, Nun, and Goalie Host." The gag had been picked up by a gossip columnist and became a great favorite everywhere. The senator, of course, barely spoke to Leone after that, but Amy Randall had laughed and sent Leone a tricked-up photo of herself in which a halo encircled her coiffure, thus enhancing her reputation as a good sport.

When Groot entered, the senator was shaking the hands of two round ladies with blue hair and pointy, sequined eyeglasses. They beamed at the Great Man, showing large and impressively even false teeth. Fallon, the senator's administrative assistant, presided over the historic occasion with a look of contained boredom. Spotting Groot, he nodded toward the inner sitting room.

"Imagine," the senator was saying sincerely, "two lovely ladies from Seaford, Delaware, all the way over here in Munich, Germany. And just imagine them going out of their way to stop by and say hello to me."

Groot eased his way behind the ladies, who chortled and rolled their eyes and presumably creamed their corsets.

"The Good Lord does strange and wonderful things, doesn't he, ladies," the senator crooned. "I was spending a lonely and difficult evening, praying for God's guidance in the matters of state that had brought me to this strange

76

and forbidding land. And I yearned for some sign that I was not truly alone, that I carried the good wishes and hopes of the good people of the great state of Delaware. And here you are: my sign. The Good Lord has directed you here to reassure me, bless your hearts."

Groot sat on a divan and listened to the ladies' burbling, wondering if they really believed the senator's baloney. They probably did, which was What Was Wrong with America, as the tabloids would have it.

"When you get back to Seaford, ladies, ask your friends to pray for me."

"Oh, we will, Senator, we will," said the lady with the larger teeth. "And we certainly hope you will stand fast against the forces of hate."

"You have my solemn promise."

"Remember, Senator: it takes two to fight. All we have to do to assure peace in the world is to hold our arms wide in loving friendship. There would be no wars, no international tensions, if America would only stop making and using guns."

"So true, Mrs. Hershaw. So true."

"Well, goodbye, Senator. And God bless you."

"Goodbye, ladies. Thank you again for making this delightful call."

There was another round of burbling, and the ladies were swept into the corridor by Fallon's solicitous arms. Then, with the door closed, Fallon said, "Groot's in the other room, Senator."

Groot stood up as the senator, a towering and florid man, stalked through the door. "Good evening, sir," he said.

"Groot, what in blue-balled hell are you CIA sonsabitches up to now?"

"I don't understand, Senator."

"Don't give me that evasive who-me crap. I want to know why you flew that lard of yours all the way over here from Washington just to upset Miss Randall."

"I'm on Agency business, Senator. I have no intention of upsetting Miss Randall."

"Well, you have. You've upset her good, and I'm here

77

to tell you that if you so much as involve her in one of your slimy shenanigans I'll nail your rotten hide to an outhouse wall."

"Just what am I supposed to have done, Senator?"

"How the hell do *I* know, you sumbish? All I need do is hear Miss Randall's troubled voice, a voice troubled in the aftermath of your visit to her this evening, and I know you've been doing or saying something that's directly threatening to the President's beloved sister and helpmate. And what threatens her outrages me, and I think you realize how very tough I can make things for you bastards over at Langley when I'm outraged."

"Well, Senator, if you don't know, I don't know."

"What the hell kind of answer is that?"

"I don't know how to answer your questions, Senator."

"You know goddam well what I'm asking: why are you here in Germany? What is your mission here? What trouble are you stirring up? That's the question, dummy. Now answer it."

"I'm not at liberty to discuss Agency business, Senator. You'll have to ask the Director."

"I'm a member of the United States Senate, you know. And I'm chairman of more committees than your ass's got freckles. When I ask you a question I expect you to answer."

"Sorry, sir. Call the Director."

"Sam, throw this weirdo out of here, will you?"

"Very well, Senator."

Logue snarled: "You heard what those two old bags said. They expect me to stand up against the forces of evil and hate. And that's what you and your CIA henchmen are all about—evil and hate. And I'm gonna stand against you. You're not gonna ruin this conference we all have come to. You understand, you putty-face sumbitch?"

"Good evening, Senator."

He returned to his room and stood by the window, staring at the night and thinking carefully.

Senator Logue's scatological tirade had been symptomatic of the frenzy that was mounting, not only in Congress but in what was quaintly called the hustings as well. The United States and the other democracies (as they, too, were quaintly called) were in an economic and political decline so precipitous as to suggest rout. No wonder, then, that the senator, publicly known as a saint, could privately display such unsaintly frustration. The senator, along with most legislators and administrators from Bonn west to Manila, was becoming increasingly visible among those Robert Goodman liked to call the architects of the Fall of the Western World, and the senator didn't like the idea at all. And so he, as they all were, was fighting feathers—blustering, whining, and accusing to little avail.

In what appeared to be an eerie fulfillment of the Marxist prediction, the American people were widely thought to have reached a climactic distrust of their political process and its capitalistic base. The alienation, according to the pollsters, was sufficient to permit an abysmal lack of public confidence in the political professionals who manned the various levels of government. The reaction, ectoplasmic in the years following the liberal inertia of the late 1970s, had by now taken material form via the National Independent Party. The NIP's official membership was numbered somewhere between the minority party's dwindling handful and the disproportionate bloat of the rudderless majority. But the trend was still under way: the polls showed a surging emotionalism, a rising sea of approval for the NIP's titular leader, Robert Goodman, a onetime TV newscaster with the face of an angel and the soul of a Gestapo interrogator. Goodman was merciless in his attacks on the President and the legislators of both parties, denouncing them indiscriminately as "agents of Moscow" and, illogically in the same breath, as "tools of the Zionist conspiracy" and "bootlickers of the black bigots and welfare leeches" who "lost Asia, Africa, and South America, who gave away West Berlin and disbanded NATO and now quaver before the Arab bullies."

Goodman championed a military establishment "without peer" and "nationalization of the key American industries and utilities and the sources of energy both domestic" and, vaguely, "under the sea." The media on all continents had, of course, reacted, dubbing him "the new Hitler" and "a Nazi in Brooks Brothers clothing" and "Buchenwald Bobbie," and he had, early on, been fired by his network.

While President Randall, the classic Wilsonian idealist, maintained a lofty aloofness, Congress was uncertain and erratic in dealing with the Goodman phenomenon, torn as it was by the message of the polls and its own liberal traditions. It alternately dismissed Goodman as a fly-by-night of great noise and little substance or viewed him with alarm as Arkansas's answer to Attila the Hun. Senator Logue was particularly identified with Goodman's opposition, and from his rambling outburst of this evening, it was apparent that his skin, once the consistency of a Tiger tank's, was now abraded and lacy. Men reacting out of frustration and outrage could be unpredictable and therefore dangerous. Men as powerful as Senator Logue, when in such a condition, could be especially dangerous.

Groot thought about all of this, and made a decision or two.

He took a last look at the diminishing night traffic below, then went to the bedside table. He considered the remains of his drying sandwich; he could never bear the wasting of food, no matter how modest or stale. But the acrimony in the senator's suite had gotten to him—a sign of his own rising sensitivity to abrasion—and so he knew he couldn't cope with the arid pumpernickel.

Yawning, he opened the drawer and withdrew the communicator.

"Groot to Secret Service. Twenty-two-ten hours. In quarters. All quiet. Good night."

He did not go to bed, of course, since it was time for a scheduled contact.

There was a pay phone down the hall.

October 12

"Hello?"

"Herr Wismer?"

"Speaking."

"There's sunshine on the bay."

"I've been waiting for your call."

"Sorry. I was summoned to Senator Logue's suite. I've just returned."

"Oh? How is the—what's the name? Elmer Gantry?"

"He's in his usual form, sad to say."

"That bad, eh? Ha-ha. Do you have anything to report?"

"As you know by now, I suppose, the man called Rattner was killed. Also his bodyguard, named Vogel. Also his butler, named Klug. All killed a week earlier than scheduled."

"A bad turn of events, all right. Do you have any idea who did it?"

"None whatsoever. I was hoping you would."

"Perhaps it was a coincidence."

"Do you really believe that, Herr Wismer?"

"No."

"I don't either."

"Who, then?"

"I'll be working on it. Meanwhile, I've got some better news. Wagner says the police have spotted Akim Ri."

"Aha. At least that's going as scheduled."

"Mm."

"What do you propose to do now?"

"We'll keep Wagner alive for awhile. He's a good man, and he should be able to pick up the strings from where Rattner's left off. If he has too much trouble, we'll just feed him more line."

"There's not too much time, you know."

"How well I know. Meanwhile, we must get all agencies looking for Ri. That's absolutely fundamental. All agencies must be preoccupied with Ri."

"Well, don't neglect the original thing."

"Of course not. There's too much riding on it. For all of us."

"Very well. Keep in touch. Good night, Herr Groot."

"Good night, Herr Wismer."

11

The bartender's name, according to one of the girls at the Golden Thigh, was Paul Lincke, and he lived, according to the directory, on Oswald Strasse, a grubby dogleg beyond the west-side railroad marshaling yards. Lincke hadn't reported for work, so Wagner took the S-bahn out of the Stachus and was ringing a man's doorbell fifteen minutes later.

"What do you want?" a large woman asked from the darkened vestibule.

"I want to see Paul Lincke."

"He isn't here."

"Do you know where I can find him?"

"No. Go away. He isn't here."

"Who are you?"

"None of your business."

"Very well. When you see him, tell Lincke the Organization was here."

There was a moment of silence. Then: "What's that supposed to mean?"

"None of your business, Madame."

Wagner turned his back to the shadowed house and

walked off, feeling the silent scrutiny. A mist had settled in, cold and wet, and the streetlights made cheerless circles in the night. He went to the corner, then doubled back quickly to take up station in an alley that afforded a view of the house. He waited for three minutes by his watch, and then the door clicked and a figure descended the steps, a darkness against the dark. It was a man, and he was carrying a suitcase, and he was in a hurry.

Wagner reached out, clutching.

"Good evening, Lincke," he said, his voice just above a whisper. "Going out of town?"

"Christ, you're breaking my arm. Let me go."

"Only if you tell us something we must know."

"Who are you, for God's sake? You're breaking my arm—"

"You saw me last night. In Ziggi's last hours."

"Oh, Jesus. The Greuel—" Lincke was close to sobbing. "What do you want of me? I haven't got anything you want—"

"We know about that girl you've been sleeping with."

"Girl? What girl? Good God, I sleep with a million girls."

"The Communist. The girl who is a Communist. A traitor to the true Germany."

Lincke rolled his head back and forth against the dank brick wall. "I don't know any—Jesus, man, I only screw the girls. I don't talk politics with them."

"Do you know what happens to Germans who keep company with known Communists?"

Lincke groaned. "Ah, God. Please don't cut off my head. I'll do anything you want. What do you want? Please, just tell me what you want—"

"Last night somebody named Gustav Kahn came to the Thigh to see Ziggi. Who is he? And where do I find him?"

"He's just some character Ziggi knows. Knew. He comes around now and then. With some gash named Lotte."

Wagner leaned on the captive arm until Lincke

84

whimpered. "Who is Gustav Kahn?"

"I can't say for sure," Lincke gasped. "I heard Ziggi say once that Kahn is a salesman. Appliances. Works out of Austria. Kitzbühel, or some place like that."

"What does he look like?"

"Tall. Bald. Hard. In his fifties."

"Who is Lotte?"

"Lotte Mahlmann. She's Kahn's secretary or mistress or something. I don't know. Honest to God, mister—"

"What does she look like?"

"Thin. Dark eyes. Quick, sort of."

Wagner eased the pressure on the arm. "You will forget this conversation of ours, Lincke. You will tell no one about it."

"Oh, hell, no. I mean, not a word. Honest. Not a peep. And believe me, mister, you won't have any trouble with me."

"We hope we can count on that," Wagner said.

"You want me to kill the Commie broad? Just tell me her name. I'll kill her tonight. Honest."

"Simply don't say anything. That's all you have to do right now."

"You bet. Not a word. And believe me: I think Hitler was great. A real great man. Yes, sir."

"Now get back in your house and stay there for the rest of tonight. Report to work as usual tomorrow. And if you see me again, I'll expect respectful and helpful answers to my questions."

"Yes, sir. You can count on me. I hate Communists. Jews. You name it. You won't have any trouble out of me."

"Get out of my signt." Wagner threw the man to the pavement.

"Yes, sir. You bet," Lincke said, scrabbling like a crab down the alley.

Wagner kicked the suitcase after him, feeling an overpowering need to cry.

He didn't, of course.

12

It had been strange and good, seeing Ellie again after all these years. For all the women she'd known, for all the little liaisons superintended by Groot, she'd never really had a close girlfriend, and it was her suspicion that, beneath all the hard-boiled, slick-talking journalist crap, Ellie Pomeraine would be someone she could talk to easily, share with—not just in times of need or crisis or in a razzle-dazzle like this one, but on humdrum afternoons when the House was in recess and all the politicking had been done for the day and there was nothing to do but, say, watch the rain outside. Ellie was good-looking and vivacious, to be sure, but not in a competitive way, and she had this ability to be quiet when quiet was needed, to be tender and understanding without becoming sentimental or tiresome. Looking at the dark ceiling now, hearing the breeze in the garden beyond the casements, she decided to do something nice for Ellie. Something Ellie would really delight in and feel restored by, comprehending, perhaps, something of the true dimensions of Amy Randall's capacity for friendship.

He stirred beside her, and she felt his scrutiny in the dimness.

"Are you awake?" he said.

"Yes."

He said nothing for a time, and she sensed that he was considering ways to compliment her. Dirk was a rotten lover, in the sense that he was all physical and had no competence in matters of affection or delicacy. Even in a physical sense, come to think of it, he was inclined toward the wham-bam-thank-you-ma'am philosophy of sex.

"It's good to be with you again," he said, without emphasis.

"I needed this," she said, polite and sparring.

"Too bad we have to go to all this sneaking around. I'd like to be able to walk right into your room in front of everybody, and just slam the door."

There, she thought. That's probably the absolute range of his capacity. The ultimate fervor from the chairman of the Joint Chiefs of Staff, signed and endorsed in triplicate, copy to the Secretary of Defense. Memo to All Commands: The chairman would like to screw in public.

"Well," she said, examining the night patterns on the plaster above, "I was lucky Ellie went for it."

"What'll she do? Just wait until you get back?"

"Oh, I don't know. She has good music, good wine; she seemed taken with Irma, the German girl."

"You mean Ellie's a lesbo?" Dirk chuckled.

"Don't use that word."

"Just joking."

"Speaking of getting back, I'd better get back."

"So soon?" He put on that the idea disappointed him, but she suspected that there was relief in his tone. For a man who all but clicked his heels before mounting a woman, idle chitchat in the night could be taxing.

"We mustn't press our luck," she said, sitting up and reaching for the red dress Ellie had loaned her. "That man Smedley—the Secret Service man in charge of watching my cottage—is bucking for a promotion or something. He's very eager, and he keeps checking things all the time."

"Why don't you have him transferred? That's what I do

with people who give me an itch. I cut orders sending them to Guam, or even Des Moines." He chuckled again, pleased with his own wit.

"I don't want to do anything offbeat or out of the established rhythm of things. I'll just continue to sneak around the Smedleys in my life."

"How about the other agent? The one on duty where you leave the house?"

"He's all right. No problem."

Dirk came up behind her in the dark and put his hand on her shoulder. "Do you really have to go? There's lots more left in the Big Tube." He laughed softly in her ear.

"Too much time's gone by already. Smedley might be giving Ellie a bad scene, or something."

"All right. When will I see you again?"

"I'll call you."

Lord, she thought, driving through the dark, predawn streets, *the things we do to get ahead....*

13

The drizzle had moved on by dawn, leaving a brilliant sky.

The Autobahn to Kufstein was lemon-hued in the crystal morning, and the BMW sang on the flats and whined softly in the curves. The autumn-dappled meadows and high blue mountains were so severe and absolute in their colors they seemed to have been rendered in undiluted poster-card paints. He drove, aware of the tremendous views but indifferent to their pull, unsettled as he was by the understanding that titanic forces were in motion and he was caught up in them.

A horn blared in the northbound lane, and the sound released him, and he was suddenly irritated by his own maundering.

That brown Volvo was behind him again. Or was it the same one? Volvo sure as hell must have made more than one brown sedan. . . .

After he had cleared the border and was well into Austria, he realized he was hungry. He considered waiting until he reached Kitzbühel, where he would treat himself to a mountaineer's breakfast, but as he rounded the curve leading into Eigenheim he remembered a Konditorei ahead that served first-class sweet rolls and coffee as thick as engine oil.

Eigenheim, one of those Disney-cute Tyrolean towns, was a cluster of snowy plaster and ancient wood on the lap of the Wildem Kaiser range west of St. Johann. A restless brook gurgled through its center, and the Bauernhäuser and the church and the gaggle of shops clung to the grassy banks and looked adorable for the rich American tourists and their Japanese cameras.

He parked the car in the shadow of the Gasthof and crossed the square to the Konditorei. He looked around for the Volvo, but there were no signs of it.

Little bells played the opening bars of *Schnitzelbank* when he opened the door, and a rosy woman with braided blonde hair beamed at him from behind the counter, obviously mistaking him for one of the rich Americans.

"Grüss Gott," she burbled. "May I help you?"

"I'll have some of that cinnamon and raisin thing. And coffee."

Her face fell when she heard his German, since it revealed at once that he wasn't a rich Yankee after all. "Very well," she said through her suddenly artificial smile, "take that table by the window, and I'll bring it to you."

He could see that he was her day's first disappointment, and feeling vaguely that he should make it up to her, he sat at the table and said, "Where is everybody? Eigenheim is usually crawling with sightseers."

The woman warmed to his overture. Sliding his kuchen onto a sparkling dish, she said, "You must have come in from the west. Otherwise you would have seen all the activity east of town."

"What kind of activity?"

She brought the cake and coffee and placed it on the table. "They're making a movie out there. Can you imagine? An American cowboy movie being made in Austria? Madness."

"Oh?" He remembered, then, Ellie Pomeraine's bitterness over having to interview an actor in Eigenheim.

"Yes. Most of the villagers don't give a fig for such

goings-on, living in a tourist place. But even most of them are out there today. Emerson Gurney seems to be too much for them to resist."

"It is sort of silly, isn't it—cowboys in the Alps."

She smiled, truly amused. "And red Indians, too. With feathers in their hair. One of the cameramen told me it's supposed to be Wyoming or Colorado or one of those places in the Rocky Mountains. They're making the movie here because it's cheaper than in America. It shows you what money—or the lack of it—can do to things, eh?"

They traded a few additional inanities and then retreated into a mutual silence. The cake was excellent, and Wagner relaxed with the relish of it, chewing slowly and giving courteous consideration to the beauty outside. A flock of geese waddled through the square and went into a flapping frenzy when a dirty red VW clattered through their formation. The car slowed, and Wagner saw that its driver was none other than Miss Pomeraine, who stared straight ahead, angry of eye and set of jaw.

He watched her drive off on the Kitzbühel road, and then he paid his bill and made for his own car.

The highway traced gentle, diminishing arcs on the high meadowlands between opposing Alpine parapets. And roughly in the center of the incredible panorama, where the road pierced a huddle of farmhouses, there was a small traffic jam. And in the center of it all was a motion-picture camera, around which a squad of people fussed with clipboards and waved light meters at each other and smoked cigars importantly.

He parked the BMW behind a generator van and strolled toward the crowd at the camera site, where he could see Miss Pomeraine's pony-tailed head bobbing in animated conversation.

"Look, buster," she was saying to a bearded fatty in sunglasses, "I'm here to do *him* a favor, not the other way around. If he wants to get his name in *Chronos* he's going to have to get off his eighty-year-old duff and come over here and talk to me."

"Mr. Gurney is sixty-two years old, Miss Pomeraine,"

the beard said condescendingly.

"Correction," Wagner said helpfully. "He was twenty-five in 1935. I know this because I lived back in those days."

Miss Pomeraine gave him an angry glance. "You stay out of this."

The beard said, "I'm sorry, Miss Pomeraine, but Mr. Gurney has made it clear that he doesn't want to be disturbed between takes."

"Well, for God's sake," she snapped, "he's sitting right over there in that camp chair. Doing nothing."

"Sorry, Miss. Orders are orders. If you make a move toward Mr. Gurney I'll have the security people remove you from the set."

Miss Pomeraine launched into an oration rich with expletives. Wagner, moved by some bizarre strain of curiosity and dimly remembered hero-worship, dropped back, skirted the crowd, and sauntered over to the large tree under which Gurney sat in splendid isolation.

"Excuse me, Mr. Gurney," Wagner murmured, "but there's something you ought to know."

The famous head turned toward him, and the eyes, old and knowing and wary, traveled over him in irritable examination. "Who the hell are you? I gave orders—"

"I thought you ought to know that the lady there, the one with the pony tail, is a writer for *Chronos*."

The watery blue eyes blinked. *"Chronos?"*

"Mm."

"What's her gig?"

"To interview you. But they won't let her near you."

It was like seeing the past in a funhouse mirror, warped and distorted. The face was still there, even under the pancake makeup, but it was a caricature, terrible and dreary and telling of uncounted gallons of booze and uncountable wallowings in the sties of five continents. Gazing into it, Wagner first felt contempt—the disdain that comes with self-righteous judgment of the weakness in others. But the old blue eyes, reflecting the Alpine sun, revealed an unexpected truth: what Wagner had taken for jungle suspicion was, in fact, loneliness and insecurity. Emerson Gurney was frightened, and in recognizing this, Wagner felt a peculiar sympathy.

"*Chronos?* The big news magazine?" Gurney asked carefully.

"Two million circulation in the USA alone," Wagner said.

"Well, thank God," Gurney erupted, slapping his knee. "It's about time. Where the hell's she been, for chrissake?"

The explosion of sound from the star turned all eyes his way, and a lean, coiffed young man came out of the crowd, fast and intent. "Sorry, Herr Gurney," the man said, reaching for Wagner, "zis one got away. I shall take care of him."

Wagner smiled politely and said, "Put your hands on me, sweetheart, and I'll curl your cuticles."

"Leave him alone, Rollo," Gurney rasped. "He just did me a favor."

Rollo hesitated, torn between orders and an obvious desire to put Wagner down. His eyes were black, close together, and mean, and they showed that he did not appreciate Wagner's having made him look incompetent.

"Leave me alone, Rollo," Wagner said. "I'm one of the good guys."

"Dond't push me, Dadt," Rollo snarled.

"Oo," Wagner said. "Humphrey von Bogart."

"Knock it off, you guys," Gurney said. He studied Wagner for a moment. "What's your name, buddy?"

"Bill Koenig."

Gurney stuck out his big hand. "Glad to meetcha. You a publicity guy, eh?"

"Well—"

"What you doin'—travelin' with the broad?"

"I—"

"You're lucky. She got a nice ass." Gurney lifted his head and shouted. "Ackerman! Hey, Ackerman, you stupid sumbitch!"

"Yes, Mr. Gurney?" the beard cooed.

"Bring that writer bim over here. What the hell's the

matter with you, you stupid sumbitch! She's gettin' it on to do a story on me."

"I'm sorry, Mr. Gurney. You said you didn't want to be disturbed under any circumstances."

"Christ, you really are a dunghead, ain't ya." Gurney waved Miss Pomeraine his way. "Hey, toots, over here. We make pow-wow."

"Mr. Gurney," Miss Pomeraine said, striding up in pink-faced agitation, "my name is Ellie Pomeraine. I'm from *Chronos*. And if that means anything to you, maybe you'll answer a question or two."

"Hell, yes, Ellie-baby. Anything you want. *Chronos* is one magazine that's got balls, I always said. And I been wonderin' where ya been."

"You've been expecting me?"

"Sure." He glanced at Wagner. "You're the publicity guy. Didn't you tell her, for chrissake?"

"I—"

"I don't know what all this is about," Miss Pomeraine broke in. "But I've got ten minutes. No more. If you want to answer a couple of questions, Mr. Gurney, let's get at it. If not, I couldn't care less."

"Hard-nosed broad, ain't ya," Gurney beamed. "Whatcha wanta know?"

"My office tells me you've been invited to attend the Olympic Tower luncheon after the President speaks in Munich next week. Is that right?"

Gurney nodded with satisfaction. "Yep."

"How come?"

Gurney blinked. "What the hell do you mean, how come? Jesus, lady, I'm to America like salt is to pepper. I'm known all over the friggin' world as the typical American. It's only fittin' that I be there when our chief is greetin' Germany and all that crap."

"Who invited you? The President himself?"

"Nah. Amy Randall."

"The President's sister?"

"You bet your sweet ass, Ellie-baby. She's family. The President's favorite congressman. Miss Decency herself.

94

The Speaker of the damn-old House. She wants me to bring some of the movie company to Munich and make a present of an Indian headdress to the President. Then lunch in the tower. A real gas. A politician wearin' a Indian hat in Germany, yet. Christ, what a world."

"She just invited you? Out of the blue?"

"Yeah, sort of."

Ellie Pomeraine began to make some notes, and while she was so occupied Wagner indulged his curiosity. "You don't know Miss Randall? I mean, she's not a personal friend or anything?"

"She knew me, course, me bein' famous and all."

"But you'd never met?"

"Not so's you'd notice it."

"Did she call you on the phone, or what?"

Gurney blinked again, and there was something in his hesitation that struck Wagner as being odd. "Nah," Gurney said, "she came by the hotel I'm stayin' at. Made a real personal thing outa it."

"Where's your hotel?"

"Ain't a hotel, exactly. The Edelweiss Hof. Outside a Kitzbool." Gurney gave Miss Pomeraine a narrow look. "Hey, ain't you goin' to ask me about my flicks? I been inta some good strokes, you know."

"I'm not with a fan magazine, Mr. Gurney. *Chronos* simply wants a sidebar piece for the upcoming cover story on the President's visit to Germany."

"Sidebar? Since when am I sidebar? Lotsa writers wanta do features on me. What's this sidebar crap?"

"Mr. Gurney," Miss Pomeraine said in her snappish way, "you haven't had a stick of publicity in any major U.S. publication for five years. I know, because I did some research before I came out to this godforsaken hole and you are a great big has-been with zero press. That's why you're here, making this Schnitzel Western. You're a big fat zilch, and you ought to be on your knees kissing my hem just for the outside chance you might get a mention in *Chronos*. Now put that in your sombrero, you foul-mouthed phony."

Gurney glowered, ruby-faced, at Wagner. "You're the publicity guy. You goin' to let this tomato get away with this kinda crap?"

Wagner shrugged. "I'm not a publicity man, Mr. Gurney. I'm just a friend of Miss Pomeraine's who happened by."

"You ain't the guy?"

"What guy?"

"Amy Randall said there'd be lotsa publicity comin' up. She was even goin' to put a guy on me, special."

"Well, I don't know anything about that."

"Why would she put a publicity guy on you, special?" Miss Pomeraine wanted to know.

Gurney gave her a flat, malevolent glance and said, "Ellie-baby, I don't think I like you. You got a nice ass and gorgeous knockers, but you're one of them know-it-all broads, so you ruin it all. So I don't think I like you. And I don't think I need you, either."

Wagner, still identifying with Gurney despite the old ham's grotesque insensibilities, felt a small smile forming. He recognized the kind of courage it had taken for Gurney—old, tired, beaten, and frightened—to defy a bully from one of the world's more important publications. Somewhere under all the dissipation and dissolution and despair had been an ember of the fire that had put him on top so long ago; and it had flared a tiny flame, enabling him to refuse to grovel for his publicity supper.

Wagner looked at Miss Pomeraine, selfish and arrogant in her own anxiety, and at Gurney, shifty and defensive and belligerent all at one time, and he realized that he was sick up to here with both of them and everything they represented.

He walked off, climbed into his car, and drove to Kitzbühel.

14

He parked near the center of town and bought a tabloid that made a fuss over Ziggi Rattner's violent end. For all the garishness, the story revealed nothing beyond the fact that Rattner, his bouncer, and his butler had been beheaded and that the police were questioning those who might throw light on the matter. No names, no specifics. Grateful for this, he wandered for a time, staring into shop windows and feeling the distance between him and the tourists who brushed against him. The day's crisp sunniness made blue and gold patterns in the cobbled canyons, and the air was rich with the smells of hotel kitchens and mountain pines. These delights of an Alpine noon infused the crowds with a general holiday *Geist,* but he wandered apart—an alien from a distant galaxy who, having crossed one cosmos, wondered if he should try another.

As a creature sensitive to discord, it was natural that he be bothered by the encounter with Emerson Gurney. Why had the actor been expecting a publicity man, especially one "assigned" to him by Amy Randall? Why would Amy Randall appear "out of the blue" to invite an uncouth

97

has-been she didn't know to attend a Presidential luncheon at which every chair would most certainly be filled by a government luminary? It was a grating discord, and it gave him fits, despite his attempts to concentrate on the job at hand.

The business directory listed three major appliance dealers, all of them located in the center of town. He sauntered past each in turn, and only with the third—the Gipfel Gerät Kompanie—did he catch any vibrations. The place gave no concession to Kitzbühel's resort atmosphere; it was a store behind a plate glass facade, and it could have been on Main Street in Kearney, Nebraska. A sign in the show window announced that Gipfel, while dealing in retail, was primarily a wholesale distributor for the Tyrol. As if to prove the point, there had been no attempts to decorate the window, and a refrigerator and a dishwasher stood in clinical isolation under the fluorescent lights.

He went in and stood by the counter. Heels tapped on linoleum at the rear of the store and then a woman appeared in a doorway flanked by file cabinets. She was youngish, but her blonde wig didn't suit the dark fire of her eyes, and so she looked older, and hard.

"May I help you?" Her tone was indifferent.

"Perhaps," Wagner said. "I am looking for a small apartment-size refrigerator. I've converted a herdsman's hut into a little weekend place and a power line's to be brought in, and so now I can complete the furnishings."

"I see." She gazed about her as if a small, apartment-size refrigerator might have just fallen from her pocket. Despite her blandness, something in her manner suggested uneasiness, a diffidence born of anxiety. "I don't think we have one in stock right now."

"No matter. I'm simply shopping anyhow. The place won't be ready for a while."

She riffled through the papers on the counter. "We have a brochure or two. Perhaps if you were to select something we could order it for you."

"Yes." Wagner waited politely while she continued to

98

search the stack. "By the way, do you deliver, Miss—"

"Mahlmann." She bit her lower lip, as if giving him her name had been a mistake. "It depends on the location."

"My place is above the village of Going."

"Going?" She paused, her eyes opaque. "That seems a bit—" She gave him an indirect glance. "I'll have to check that with Herr Kahn. Excuse me for a moment."

She disappeared through the doorway and Wagner, pretending interest in the washer and dryer beside him, examined the shop for discords. He had already discovered two: the woman's poorly disguised fear and the uncertainty over deliveries. Any dealer in wholesale and retail worth his salt would have hired help that knew precisely where and when the company delivered. The place itself, though, revealed no further departures from the norm, and he had given up his scrutiny by the time Fräulein Mahlmann returned with Herr Kahn.

"This is Herr Kahn, sir," she said, brittle.

The man was big and bald, with a Roman nose flanked by deepset eyes the color of jade. His suit was well-cut, his shirt was clean, and his tie was straight. But his gaze was about as friendly as a sawtooth bayonet.

"You say your place is in Going?" Kahn's voice was a rumbling bass.

"That's right."

"That's outside our zone for retail deliveries."

"Oh, well, too bad. I'll have to look elsewhere."

"We could make an exception if we had a wholesale delivery in the area. When will you be moving in, Herr—"

"Reichling. Oswald Reichling." Wagner consulted a calender on the wall. "Let's see. It should be about December first."

Kahn nodded his big head. "We might be able to handle that. Where can we call you, Herr Reichling?"

"I don't have a phone at present. I'll call you in a week or so. May I take this brochure?"

"Of course."

Wagner returned to his car and, before starting the motor, sat for a time and considered what he had learned.

It wasn't much, to be sure, but instinct told him that Kahn and Mahlmann would prove to be important to him later on. Moreover, he had an edge: he knew who they were, and that they represented a link between the murdered Ziggi and Ziggi's secret knowledge, but they had no way of knowing about him.

It was a comfort to have at least this shred of advantage.

He was about to leave when he saw Gustav Kahn hurry out the store's front door, climb into a dark blue Audi, and drive off. Routinely, Wagner wrote down the license number in his little address book. Then he eased the car out of the lot and turned north to the intersection of the road to St. Johann. The street took him past Gipfel Kompanie, and a glance through the colorless show window revealed nothing. But as he slowed for a stop sign, his rearview mirror showed him an interesting development.

A large black Mercedes nosed out of the alley next to the appliance store and waited in elegant opacity for a delivery truck to pass. Then it crawled into position behind the truck, and the manner of its movements told Wagner that he had picked up a tail.

He decided to test the idea, and, accelerating, he made his way through the thinning traffic and eventually left town at a brisk speed. The Mercedes hung a discreet distance to the rear, peeping now and then from behind the truck. When the truck peeled off on a side road, the black car continued to follow the BMW in majestic indifference, holding back sufficiently to keep Wagner from seeing its driver.

He maintained his speed until he reached the fork where Alpenbergerlandstrasse began its ascent into high country. Rounding the bend and clearing a tractor-trailer rig that belched its diesel smudge in the climbing lane, he launched the BMW into flat-out. The motor keened and the slipstream hissed, and the car settled into the job it did best. A 550 Mercedes was a hot article, but the BMW was smaller and nimbler and, in the hands of a good driver, could carry the day.

It would be a nice trick, though, because the black sedan clung to the rear, glistening and malevolent in the brilliant sunlight and unruffled by the narrowing road and tightening curves.

The only car in sight was far behind, a brown dot on the ribbon of highway.

Wagner, despite his concentration on the physical process of driving at great speed, felt a weird desire to laugh. When he had awakened this morning, he had had only two leads of the most tentative nature—Kahn and Mahlmann. Now, only partly into the noon hour, he had questions to answer about the sister of the President of the United States, an uneasiness about Gurney, the aging ham, suspicions about Pomeraine, the frantic news-magazine writer, and three definite suspects—the Kahn-Mahlmann combo and whoever was behind the wheel of the Mercedes—and seemed now to be fleeing for his life in the bargain.

In checking the car behind, he caught a glimpse of himself in the mirror, and he was surprised. There was an aliveness in his face, a kind of glow, and his eyes seemed young and excited, and instantly in a vagary of the thought process that permits recollection in the midst of frenzy, his mind vaulted the years to the night in the Ardennes when he and Tom Ober had stumbled into the woodsman's shack and had huddled together in the thundering, bullet-snapping darkness. Toward dawn, the firing had fallen off, and there followed an eerie silence, as if the war had been muted by the new fall of snow. Ober, a theology graduate who had inexplicably become a rankless rifleman and was later to be disemboweled by a land mine, had begun a turgid, near-delirious soliloquy. "You're still a child, Wagner." Ober had said, "and can't understand the psychology of war. But let me assure you: men make much of peace, forming all kinds of noble-named organizations with noble-sounding intentions to achieve a world free of war, while all the time they yearn for escape from the dreadful combat that the absence of war implies. Men make war because they can find no peace in their individual hearts and minds. They try to stifle their inner, private, personal wars by waging overt, public, impersonal warfare on others. Because, when a man's fighting another man, he can forget his unhappiness; in peace, he has only himself to blame. And even then he doesn't blame himself. He blames God. And getting no satisfaction from this, he goes back to war. On and on and on. Only when man is fighting does he find a kind of peace."

And other such madness.

Wagner looked at himself in the mirror again, but the moment was gone.

There was a bad curve near the mountain pass known as Wolkenheim. Explosive winds and glaze-ice belabored the place, even in August, and in the autumn they could make passage a pluperfect horror. Only respectful truckers and knowledgeable locals were liable to pass this way after summer's end.

On the flat stretch approaching the curve, Wagner eased off on the gas pedal, and the Mercedes closed fast. Hovering off his left rear quarter, the black sedan pressed its new advantage. Defensively, he swerved the BMW into the left lane, and then he realized that that was exactly what the other driver had wanted him to do. With a warbling of tires, the Mercedes bobbed full to the right and pulled up alongside. He saw no gun, but he heard the dry-stick snapping in the air and the sun visor buckled and stung his face with a spattering of debris.

And he recognized this as his chance.

He slumped, allowing his head to roll, and he played the BMW's wheel, giving the car enough rein to set up a controlled, yet seemingly stricken, side-to-side weaving. Gearing down to brake, he let the careening car skid to the gravel berm and, just short of the Wolkenheim curve and its thousand-foot precipice, he swung it into a stone-spewing skid that halted inches from the edge.

The Mercedes was going too fast to manage a stop behind him, and so it carried through the curve and squealed to a halt a quarter of a mile beyond. Watching from under his half-open lids, his head resting against the side window, he saw the black car execute a neat U-turn. He wished he had a pistol, but congressional overseers of CIA had ruled out sidearms as provocative equipment, and so he was gambling everything on the hunch that the Mercedes driver would come close enough to fire a coup de grace.

The man climbed out of the black car and Wagner felt a moment of fear.

It was Rollo, tall and lean in his dark suit and sparkling oxfords.

And in his right hand he carried a butcher's cleaver—broad, ugly, and glinting in the high mountain light.

Struggling for control, Wagner remained still, waiting for Rollo to open the door. His plan was to sag as if to fall to the ground. Using the momentum as a source of auxiliary power, he would swing his fist into Rollo's crotch, and when Rollo doubled over in helplessness, he would subdue him for a few little friendly questions.

Rollo started across the road, moving the cleaver in little arcs, the way a man does when he tests the heft of a tool.

There was a soft, snicking sound, and Rollo hesitated and turned to glance behind him at the tree line beside the road. Then he looked back at Wagner, smiled a crooked smile, and collapsed in a heap.

The cleaver bounced on the road surface, clattering.

Wagner thought he heard a car start behind the trees, but he wasn't sure because of the pounding in his head.

After an interval of uncertain duration, he found his notepad and pencil and, with a trembling hand, wrote down the license number of the Mercedes. Then he heaved Rollo's body into the front seat, released the brake, set the gear selector in neutral, and, leaning into it with a shoulder, sent the black car rolling over the cliff.

Forty thousand dollars' worth of automobile.

Banging, slamming, squealing, splintering.

And then a distant boom, a finality of sound.

The laboring truck was the only other vehicle he met on his drive down the mountain.

15

The room was rosy in the light of the setting sun, and it smelled of polish and soap and fresh flowers. He sat by the window, appreciating the mountains and breathing the winelike air, still giddy with the sense of survival—that odd exhilaration he always felt when leaving a funeral parlor, when the world would look renewed and full of promise.

There was a polite tapping at the door.

"Yes?"

"Excuse me, sir. It's Frau Lindl, the innkeeper. May I speak with you?"

"Certainly. Come in."

Frau Lindl was a splinter-thin woman with gray hair and a gentle levelness in her eyes. She wore a full skirt and a short jacket in the Tyrolean fashion, and she stood by the door under the low-hanging beams like a sketch from some ancient book of fairy tales.

"What can I do for you, Frau Lindl?"

"It's not my practice to disturb guests of Edelweiss Hof, Herr Koenig. But I couldn't help but notice when you checked in that you seemed to be—"

"Disreputable looking?"

"No, sir, hardly. You appeared—upset. Shaken. Ill. And I'm wondering if there's something I might do for you. A doctor, perhaps."

"I'm quite all right, thank you."

She seemed to feel it necessary to explain further. "My husband and I once failed to do anything when an obviously ill guest checked into our hotel in Munich, in the old days. We thought we had no right to intrude. The man very nearly died during the night. So—"

"It's nice of you to check on me."

"If you need anything, please let me know."

She turned to go, and he said, "I guess I was lucky to find a room here, what with all the celebrities among your guests."

"So you've heard that Herr Gurney stays here, I see." She smiled dimly. "One man doesn't make for a crowded inn."

"How about all the others in his party? Cameramen, directors, and so on."

She shrugged. "They prefer the more lively places in town, I regret to say."

"Gurney is here alone, then?"

"Essentially. He has a suite of adjoining rooms. People come and go. I make it none of my business, since all the space has been paid for in advance."

"Does his secretary, Rollo, stay here?" Wagner asked, off-hand.

"Herr Stoeckler is not Mr. Gurney's secretary," Frau Lindl said with an air of disapproval. "Herr Stoeckler is no more than a dressed-up handyman."

"I take it you don't like him."

The old woman's eyes wavered. "Well," she said carefully, "I've already said too much. I have no right to make judgments on my guests or their friends."

"In Rollo's case you do. To dislike him is an act of true decency."

"You know him well, Herr Koenig?"

"I've seen him only twice in my life. But that was twice too much."

She nodded. "I see. You spoke as if you knew him better than that."

"How long has Gurney been here, by the way?"

"Since August. He's paid through next month."

"Rollo, too?"

"Herr Stoeckler comes and goes." She smoothed her skirt with a freckled hand and cleared her throat delicately. "Which is what I should do. I'm sorry to have bothered you, sir. I hope you have a pleasant stay at Edelweiss Hof." The door closed behind her.

He found a pay phone at a roadside rest area outside town, and he put through a call to the Hendel Kompanie. After the Prussian woman made her nasty-nice speech and he had given the code signal, he hung up and waited for almost five minutes. Then the phone rang.

"Groot?"

"Mr. Groot is not available."

"Who are you?"

"Fitzpatrick. Night duty officer."

"Well, where's Groot? I've got to talk to him. It's important."

"Mr. Groot is not available."

"What the hell is that supposed to mean? Where is he? I'll call him there."

"Mr. Groot is attending a meeting. He can't be disturbed."

"This is national-urgency material I'm calling about. He'll want to hear from me, believe me."

"Leave your number. He'll call back tomorrow."

"Where's the meeting?"

"At the Vierjahreszeiten. Amy Randall, the President's sister, has called a security review. Command performance."

"I'll call there."

"I'm telling you: it won't do any good."

"We'll see."

"What's so hot, anyhow? Maybe I can help you."

"I don't think so. I need some surveillance gear."

"Oh. Well. You know how tough to get that is—"

"I know."

"Mr. Groot will have to handle that with Congressional Liaison."

"That's why I want to talk to him. I've got a crisis going."

"Well, I wish I could help you. But you know the drill."

"Do I ever."

He hung up and rested his forehead against the cool glass of the booth. Then he called the special number in Heidelberg.

"Congressional Liaison Office. Shaeffer speaking."

"I'm with the Agency and I'm calling from Austria. It's necessary that I speak with Mr. Morfey on a national-urgency matter."

"Mr. Morfey is at an important meeting in Munich."

"Is there anybody who can act for him in his absence?"

"Well, I'm on duty."

"I want authorization to bug a building. I have to use some apparatus to keep some spooks under surveillance."

"All I can do is fill out a CL–2 form, noting your request, and leave it on Mr. Morfey's desk for when he gets back from Munich."

"I haven't got all that kind of time. I'm in a situation of national urgency. Considerable wet stuff has already occurred."

"You mean people have been killed?"

"Here and there."

"Well, Mr. Morfey's the one you talk to."

"I haven't got time to wait."

"That's the trouble with you CIA people. If you would only use a little advance planning, a little foresight, you wouldn't always get yourselves into silly crush situations like this."

"What did you say your name is?"

"Shaeffer. Arlen Shaeffer, assistant Congressional Liaison rep. I didn't get your name."

"No matter. I'll be by to see you one of these days. Wear a helmet and teeth protectors."

16

There were no phone listings for Gustav Kahn or Lotte Mahlmann, and the phone rang unanswered when Wagner dialed the Gipfel Gerät Kompanie. Falling in with the dinner-time traffic, he drove past the shop, but it was already in darkness, and the shades were drawn in its show windows. Soft light showed in the windows above the store, and so he parked the BMW around the corner and strolled back to see if he could find an entrance other than the one facing the street. It was in an alley that bisected the block—a small doorway next to the Gipfel loading dock—and two neat white name cards were below the single pushbutton: *Kahn, G.* and *Mahlmann, L.* He felt a compulsion to ring the bell, but he mastered it and instead returned to the car and drove to Munich. With no speed limit on the Autobahn, he made it with time to spare.

On the way, he had the feeling he was being followed, but with all the headlights there was no real way to check it out.

The Vierjahreszeiten was not the largest hotel in Munich, but it was very in, being on Maximilianstrasse and in the so-called cultural center of the city. It was old enough to convince the Beautiful People that they were truly in Germany but new enough to keep this from interfering with their decadence. It was precisely the kind of hotel Amy Randall, the President's jet-set sibling, would choose for the presidential advance party.

Wagner tried to park in the hotel's underground garage, but the entrance was teeming with Secret Service types in their government haircuts and three-button suits, and he was shooed away by an attendant whose officiousness, presumably fed by the glamorous hubdub, seemed akin to bloodlust. So he put the BMW in an all-night garage off the Scharnagl Ring and walked back to the hotel.

He slipped an outside porter a couple of marks and said, "Where's the Amy Randall thing?"

"In the Salon Diana, part two," the man said, pocketing the money in a creamy sweep of his hand. "But you'll never get in there. The security is unbelievable."

"How much to get me to the door of the salon?"

"You haven't got enough, mister. It would be easier to get you to Mars."

He knew a couple of people on the Secret Service White House detail who'd been fellow students in an antisabotage course he'd taken at Fort Holabird a few years back. Frank Kevin was one, and—who? Bill Coad? He could have looked for one of them, but to make a stir like that would simply blow a corner of his anonymity in a needless way. No. He'd just wait for Groot.

"Where are the autograph seekers?"

The porter pointed. "Over there, behind the rope. By the main entrance, where the cops and TV are."

"Thanks."

He managed to push his way to a spot at a small bar off the lobby, and, in a magical coincidence, a bartender saw him, asked him what he'd like, and dished it up. Completing the stroke of luck, a skinny French lady slid off the stool directly beside him, and in a moment he was ensconced as if the place had been built around him.

110

Sipping his Scotch, he watched the reverse-image world in the bar mirror and realized how very little he had missed by not being a wealthy hardware manufacturer from West Frammsville, Indiana. The room was filled with red-faced men, who, if they didn't manufacture hardware, appeared as if they should. They were with round women in dresses that were too tight and perfumes that were too high in octane, and all of them laughed too loudly and waved to people across the room and slapped each other's backs to prove how much fun they were having.

Wagner tried to picture himself as the husband of a large, noisy woman from Des Moines who would ignore him in the clamor of a country-club bar on Saturday nights. The image gave him a moderate chill.

He was nursing his second drink when he caught the signal.

The autograph hunter has an innate radar that puts him on the alert long before the layman has the slightest idea that a celebrity is even in town. And so Wagner knew when Amy Randall's meeting had adjourned by simply watching the group behind the golden rope. When the chatter fell off and there was much jostling and readying of pens, he paid his check and eased through the cigarette haze to a position on the rim of the television jungle.

She erupted from the hotel's labyrinth to cross the lobby in a vortex of earnest-faced sycophants. She was regal and cool and stylishly rumpled in that way of the very rich, and Wagner could see that, despite her repute for wholesomeness and sensible living, her eyes were a thousand years old.

She came to a graceful halt in the focal point of the assembled cameras, and she turned, carefully casual, ostensibly to nod at the applauding admirers to the right and left but really to see that the various news photogs and network lenses had maximum opportunity to catch her good side. She was a beautiful specimen, to be sure, but no more than a glance told Wagner that she was a politician first, a hedonist next, and a woman last of all.

111

The noise in the room seemed suddenly muted, as if some giant volume regulator had been turned somewhere, and in the comparative hush Wagner could hear a newsman's voice:

"—and, as you know," the man was saying in American English, "the polls at home are showing a very high level of disaffection. There is all kinds of evidence that the American people are in an ugly mood over the waverings of politicians, the impotence of our military, the energy shortage and the economic depression and double-digit inflation that have resulted, and so on. And the Third Party is—"

"Mr. Kelly," Amy Randall interrupted smoothly, "are you asking a question or making a speech? If it's a question, I plead with you to get to the point. If it's a speech, please excuse me. I have so terribly many things to do."

The crowd laughed at the good-natured put-down, the sycophants looked more earnest, and the newsmen shouted for her attention.

"Mr. Kelly has the floor," she said, smiling the smile that had adorned a thousand magazine covers.

"Well, as I say, Madame Speaker," the ruffled Kelly said, "with all the tensions mounting, how can the President feel free to come to Europe? I mean at this time."

"Please, Mr. Kelly, ask the President. I don't mean to be evasive, but he must speak for himself. I'm sure you understand. And may I please remind you again, for what surely must be the thousandth time, I dislike being called Madame Speaker. I much prefer—insist on—Miss Randall."

She pointed to another man, and out of the din came his voice: "Is it true that you have presidential aspirations of your own?"

"What do you mean by that, Mr. Potter?"

"There's a rumor that you will seek the nomination once your brother's second term is over. Is there anything to that?"

"Absolutely not. I'm perfectly happy as a member of Congress." She pointed again. "Mr. Ramsdell?"

"In that connection, Miss Randall, would you, as Speaker, have trouble working with—counseling— Robert Goodman? If he's elected, that is?"

She did not hesitate, and it occurred to Wagner that she'd been primed for such a question. "I am an American above all, and America's will is mine, too. If Mr. Goodman is elected and Congress chooses to retain me as Speaker, I'll be as readily available as a congressional consultant to Mr. Goodman as I've been to my brother. Mr. Loggerman?"

"Does your brother resent your remarks in Houston, in which you referred to him as a hand-wringing, do-gooding nincompoop?"

"On the contrary. He laughed and told me I was slipping. That I've called him worse in childhood spats."

"Well, why did you say that, exactly? I mean—"

"Mr. Loggerman, that whole thing has been hashed over so many times I'd think your editor would fire you for asking it again."

"There seems to be a lot of confusion on the subject."

"There's no confusion whatsoever. I've said it a thousand times: when I came out of that meeting in Houston and heard that the President had recommended a thirty per cent cut in military spending across the board, I was greatly irritated, and in a spontaneous reaction I called him a nincompoop."

"Why, Miss Randall? Because you're pro-Pentagon?"

"I'm nothing of the sort. Heavy defense spending is a leading contributor to the deficit which, in turn, has caused severe economic dislocations, and I'm against it for that reason. All you have to do is look at my voting record to see how I stand on that. But our national safety and hundreds of thousands of jobs depend on defense, and arbitrarily and impulsively to cut defense spending without consideration of those factors is unvarnished nincompoopery." She pointed. "Miss Dryden?"

"Miss Randall, do you love your brother?"

113

"I adore him. He's the only family I have. Mr. DeWitt?"

"Miss Randall, how come you're in Germany at this time? I mean, the election is only a few weeks off and it would seem that you'd be back there, running the campaign—"

She smiled again, turning slightly toward CBS. "I must remind you, Mr. DeWitt: my presence here in Germany is in response to a direct and formal invitation from the Chancellor himself. And, as you know, my campaign people and my colleagues in Congress have enthusiastically encouraged me to make the trip. Miss Vereen?"

"Miss Randall, what was your meeting about tonight?"

"Preparations for the President's arrival. The Secret Service and the German authorities thought I should be updated on security measures and so on." Another nod. "Herr Von Richter?"

"Miss Randall, our bureau has been advised that the American cowboy actor, Emerson Gurney, will attend the German-American friendship luncheon in the Olympia-turm, at which the President will address the German people. Is Mr. Gurney an old friend of yours, or of the President?"

She beamed a carefully shaped smile and peered about the crowd in what seemed to Wagner to be a contrived and somewhat elaborate search for a face. "Well, yes. Mr. Gurney will attend. No, he is not an old friend. He is a delightful representative of something specifically and compellingly American, so to speak. I think he's here somewhere. Mr. Gurney, where are you? Mr. Gurney, come up here, will you, please?"

The autograph hounds shuffled and looked bored when the big man detached himself from the crowd beyond the glare. Emerson Gurney was no longer big game in their sport, apparently.

Wagner felt a flare of indignation when, in the shadows behind Gurney, he saw Groot standing with Morfey, the congressional liaison man, and, of all people, Ellie Pomeraine.

114

Making his way around the crowd's perimeter, he tapped Groot on the arm. Groot's shiny little eyes came around to regard him, and if there was surprise in them it didn't show.

"I've got to talk to you," Wagner said over the amplification of Gurney's aw-shucks inanities.

Groot brought his head closer. "Be by the garage exit. I'll pick you up as I come out."

"Make sure you do, damn it. I'm sick of being on the hind tit."

"Give me five minutes."

As he turned to go, Wagner glanced at Miss Pomeraine. If she had seen him, she gave no sign, but stood, curiously apart from the humanity pressing about her and serenely complacent, in the manner of a cat that's been fed.

To hell with her.

A light rain had begun to fall, and the city's lights threw a mirrored dazzle from the glistening streets. The wipers hummed an electric E-flat, and Wagner, chilled despite the warmth seeping up from the heater, huddled deeper into his coat and resisted the sleepiness induced by the metronomic sound.

Groot was a good driver, picking his way through the nighttime clutter with the ease that comes from decades of practice. Once they had broken clear of the snarl and had rounded the monument at the far end of the Maximiliansbrücke, Groot gave Wagner a sidelong glance.

"What is it, Wagner?"

"Let me ask you one first: how come the Pomeraine woman was at your meeting?"

"Amy Randall invited her. She's been a friend of Miss Randall's for years. But beyond that, Pomeraine had gone to Morfey to protest the high-handed way you'd dealt with her. She told Morfey you had threatened her, and as a member of the press, a threat against her was a criminal violation of the First Amendment."

"Oh, Jesus God."

"Morfey brought it to me. When I said I'd look into it, he wasn't satisfied. Nor was Pomeraine. She called Amy Randall. And Miss Randall summoned us all to find out what was going on. What *is* going on, by the way?"

"You mean Pomeraine actually said I threatened her?"

"That's what she said."

Wagner sat for a time, hot and unable to find words. Then he shifted in his seat and said, "So where does that leave us?"

"You're to cooperate with the Pomeraine woman. Help her get a story."

"Why?"

"Miss Randall, counseled by our congressional friend, Morfey, believes it to be, ah, politic. Wise. Pomeraine, they tell me, enjoys wide readership."

"Pomeraine will complicate my search for Ri. And if she shoots off her typewriter at the wrong time, she'll drive him so far underground we won't be able to find him with a seismograph."

Groot coughed dryly and said, "All that aside, where do you stand?"

"You've got my reports?"

"Only the one."

"I've sent you two."

"Well, give it all to me again. From the top."

This was the part Wagner had been edgy about. Here was where he would have to explain the disposition of the five thousand dollars, which, in his memos, he'd simply reported as "used." Now he was faced with making a choice of two alternatives. For one, he could tell the truth, explaining how he had used the money to get Ziggi off the streets and buy Inspector Trille's help at the same time. Or he could, without directly saying so, imply that he had paid Rattner as planned, with the whereabouts of the money unknown, now that Ziggi was dead. Of the two courses he favored the second, because to tell the truth would create some bad side effects. The truth would, if it reached the attention of Congressional Liaison, be

116

evidential of one more CIA attempt to meddle in the domestic affairs of another nation. And the truth, moreover, if it reached the German authorities, would put Hans Trille in an awkward position and alienate the entire German police force to boot.

"I visited Rattner at his nightclub. He indicated that there was a plot to kill the President and for a fee he would tell me about it later, at his house. When I went to his house, Pomeraine was there. She said that Ziggi had promised her a big story, and, adding things up, she guessed that I was from the Company. We sparred a bit, then the butler found Ziggi's head. The police came, and I spent some time answering Hans Trille's questions."

"Does Trille know what you were up to?"

He decided to go all the way and keep Trille out of his story. "I told him nothing. But I think he, too, expects an assassination attempt, now that one of his men has spotted Akim Ri."

"So what happened then?"

"Ziggi had canceled a date with a couple of visitors so as to meet me and Pomeraine. By leaning on Ziggi's bartender, I learned that the visitors were an appliance salesman named Kahn and his girlfriend, a Lotte Mahlmann. I traced them to Kitzbühel. In the process, a hood by name of Rollo Stoeckler tried to cut off my head with a meat cleaver."

Groot remained quiet for a long moment, thinking. Then he said, "Why did Rollo try to kill you?"

"I don't know the answer to that one. On the way to Kitzbühel, I stopped for breakfast in Eigenheim, where Emerson Gurney is making a movie or something, and while rubbernecking; I annoyed the hell out of Rollo, who, it seems, was hired by Gurney as a sort of bodyguard and gofer. Later, after casing Kahn and Mahlmann, I was tailed by Rollo, who attacked me on a mountain road. With a meat cleaver. A la the Greuel."

"The Greuel?" Groot humphed. "A creature of the Sunday supplements. So what did you do?"

"I didn't do anything. While he was coming at me,

somebody picked him off from a nearby woods."

"Any idea who fired the shot?"

"Not one. But either somebody didn't like Rollo a bunch, or somebody loves me a lot. Either way, I owe him or her a kiss on the fevered brow."

"What did you do with Rollo?"

"I pushed him and his car over a cliff."

"That's bad."

"I'm a poor sport. I always lose my temper when somebody tries to cut off my head."

"If there are prints on that car, if you're tied to this death, you could be prosecuted. And a public trial is something I can't afford."

"Well, I'm not so crazy about the idea myself. That's exactly why I parked Rollo in a place he won't be found for awhile."

Groot lit one of his smelly cigarettes and blew a cloud against the windshield. "So what do you plan to do now?"

"I think Ziggi knew where Akim Ri is hiding. And I think Kahn and Mahlmann might know, too."

"Why do you think that?"

"Something in Ziggi's manner told me he was afraid of Kahn and Mahlmann. When a stoolie's afraid of somebody, it's usually the somebody he's snitching on. So I have a hunch that Kahn and Mahlmann pertain."

Groot nodded reasonably. "All right. So how will you exploit them?"

"I want to bug their apartment. Their store."

"No."

"What do you mean, no?" Wagner stared at him.

"To authorize electronics, we have to go to Morfey. If he feels the bugging is a violation of the intent of Congress, we don't get the authorization. But even to apply we have to lay out the whole case for him. And, like all the other congressional satraps, he's a bigmouth. We'd lose Ri, and, perhaps, our President, simply because Morfey might like to see his name in the papers."

"So I can't count on you. Is that what you're saying?"

"We'd be risking too much, talking to Morfey."

"God, Groot, who's the *enemy?* Who's on *our* side? Who cares about *us?* Who wants to help *us?*"

"Not very many, I'm afraid."

"Take me to the Nikolai, will you, Groot? I don't feel so good, and I need some sleep."

As Wagner was leaving the car, Groot said, "Something you might want to know: your successor on the helicopter thing isn't doing so well without you."

"How so?"

"Gregori has stepped up his control of the two Soviet spooks. He holds them on a short leash. And he's making your stand-in look like a real boob. You're going to lose the game, I'm afraid. Gregori is a professional, and he's making your successor look like a boob."

"That's no trick. He is a boob."

"I wish I had three people like Gregori," Groot said. "With three people like him I think I could achieve the best clandestine operation in Europe."

"He's got the wrong politics."

"Gregori is no more a political type than you or I. He works his trade. He works it well. He works it for the Soviets because he's a Soviet citizen."

"Well, I can't generate much enthusiasm for him. He's screwed me too many times."

"You've screwed him, too. And I daresay he doesn't hold it against you. Nothing personal. Like losing a game of golf."

"You're full of crap, Groot."

"I suppose I am." Groot sighed one of his sighs. "Good night."

"I want Ri, Wagner. I want him negated."

"Good night, Groot."

17

After midnight, climbing the Nikolai's musty stairs, Wagner found the door to his room unlocked and Ellie Pomeraine sitting on the bed, reading the new issue of *Chronos*.

"You sure took your time coming home," she said. "Bowling with the boys, *indeed.*"

"I think you spend more time in this room that I do," Wagner said. "How did you get in?"

"I told the fat man at the desk that we are having a clandestine affair."

"Oh? Why?"

"If I told him I was just a friend who wanted to wait for you in your room, he'd have figured I was a whore and thrown me out."

"I know for a fact he doesn't have anything against whores."

"Only those whose fees he skims, buddy. The others he throws out."

"I guess so."

She waved to the inhospitable chair. "Sit down."

He sat uneasily, too tired to be angry at her intrusion

yet not tired enough to lose his wariness. "I thought you were ticked off at me, Miss Pomeraine."

"Hell no. I've come to invite you to a party."

"Sorry. It's late, and I'm bushed."

"Not tonight, dummy. A week from tonight."

"I'm really very busy."

"This is a presidential reception staged by no less a personage than my old buddy, Miss Amy Randall, Illinois's answer to Helen of Troy."

"Why me? A famous woman like you must have all sorts of hotshots to escort her to parties."

She nodded matter-of-factly. "Sure. But I like you. You're a weird bugger, but I like you."

"Oh, come on, Miss Pomeraine. My boss tells me you've charged me with Constitutional rape or something. So spare me all that crap, will you?"

"Don't be so surly. Your boss agrees that there's no reason in the world we can't work together."

"You want to bet?"

— She plumped up the pillow and, rearranging herself on the bed, let her head sink into it. "This is a rotten hole. Do you always stay in places like this?"

"No. I usually take a Hilton penthouse."

"What are you so *mad* at?"

"I want to go to bed. But you're on it."

"Are you married?"

"No."

"Any girlfriends?"

"None of your business."

"You're a very attractive man."

"And you, Miss Pomeraine, are full of more crap than a Christmas turkey."

"Kiss me."

"What?"

"I said come here and kiss me."

"What the hell for?"

"Because I want you to."

"Have you wigged out? Hell, I hardly know you."

"That's all right. I don't have VD or anything."

"Do you really think I'm dumb enough to tell you everything I know in return for a little grooving?"

"I don't want you to tell me anything. I want you to kiss me."

She came off the bed and stood over him, a fragrant silhouette against the glow of the lamp. Taking his face in her hands, she said, "You are a *weird* son of a bitch, aren't you."

"Please. Miss Pomeraine. I'm tired and I want to go to bed."

"What the hell do you think *I* want to do?"

"I—"

"Aw, shut up, you klutz."

"Are you awake?" she said in the darkness beside him.

"Yep."

"They say men either want to smoke or have a sandwich afterward. Which kind of man are you?"

"I don't smoke. And I'm not hungry."

"What do you feel, then?"

"Regret."

"Ah-ha. The old post-coital depression, eh?"

"I always feel this way when I've been raped."

"Are you going to have me arrested?"

"The police would take one look at you and then ask me why I was complaining."

"Well, now. That was a nice compliment. I think." She shifted in the dusk, a warm readjustment of warmth. He thought she was preparing to leave, but she merely pulled the blankets closer around them and settled her head on his chest. "May I stay the night, sir?"

"You're a tough one to figure. First you treat me like some schmuck, then you butter me up; next, you go to my superior and call me a rat, then you knock me down on a bed and eat me alive."

"My unpredictability has always infuriated people."

"I'll bet." He stifled a yawn. "How come you don't exploit your friendship with Amy Randall? She should be good for a lot of stories."

122

"Not really. Not for me, anyhow. She's too political, for one thing, and our regular political staffers cover her on that. And she's too theatrical. She's a ham actor, is what she is, and you know what I think of hams."

"Do you like her?"

"Yeah. She's a phony in a lot of ways, and she ain't nearly so moral as all her churchianity and prayer breakfasts make out. Would you believe she's a switch-hitter? She even made a pass at me one night when she was feeling blue."

"Well, I don't hold that against anybody, if that's what they want."

She lifted her head and gave him a fond look. "I didn't want to get you in trouble with your honcho. Really. But I'd kick my own momma in the bum if it meant getting a story."

"You didn't get me in trouble. You complicated my job, that's all."

"Tough patootie. You were complicating mine, weren't you?"

"What'll you do when there are no more stories?"

"What do you mean?"

"What'll you see when you're old and gray and you look back at all the things you've done? When you say, there, there are the things I did that fulfilled me. What things will you be talking about?"

"Jesus. A philosophical spy, yet."

"Answer the question."

"I told you before: I take one day at a time."

"That's antithetical to your work."

"Oh, shut up and go to sleep."

He did.

When he awoke in the dawn, she was gone, and there was a note on the night table.

> *No kidding I like you a lot. The*
> *party's at 8 in the Klub Monika.*
> *I'll meet you there.*

He lay on the bed for an hour, thinking.

There were some peculiar aspects to this whole thing. Why, for example, had Groot seemed so unimpressed by the fact that a person or persons unknown had fired a shot to extinguish Rollo Stoeckler and thereby save the life of that great and good American, that lover without peer, that clear-eyed two-fisted champion of justice, Roger Michael Wagner?

And who, by the damn-old way, had fired the shot?

Somebody driving a brown Volvo.

But who?

And why?

18

The bad weather had returned, and the morning was the color of lead. The drizzle drifted across the city in a gray wash that made ghostly caricatures of the streets and the life that streamed along them. Even the traffic seemed subdued, as if the mist had lowered a damper on some gigantic keyboard.

The desk sergeant said only that Inspector Trille wasn't due until eight, but breakfast had been implicit in his tone. So Wagner selected the place he might go if he were a hungry detective who lived alone, and he went to the Goldene Bratpfanne, where he found Trille at a table near the door.

"How's the sausage?"

Trille looked up, chewing without zest. "All right."

"Do you talk business at breakfast?"

"I talk business at any time."

Wagner sat across from him and asked a waitress for a coffee. While she was gone, he said, "I need some help."

"Already? You move fast to collect on your debts, don't you, Yankee?"

"I have no choice. Business needs are business needs. And so here I am."

"Business needs can make grovelers of us all."

125

The waitress brought the coffee. She was unsmiling and full of private resentments. Wagner decided that if she had been happy she could be quite pretty. Odd, he thought, how anger paints with so heavy a brush.

"I need some electronics," Wagner said. "I'd like to borrow some from you."

"Bugging gear?"

"Yes."

"What's the matter with your own quartermaster, or whatever you call your supply group?"

"Same old story. To get the gear, I'd have to tell a secret to somebody who can't keep a secret."

"You mean your congressional people, of course."

"Yes."

Trille buttered a piece of toast, a disdainful smile working at the corner of his mouth. "If I live to be a hundred, I'll never understand you Yankees. So preciously pious and moral and puritanical in public; so satanical behind the scenes." The smile broke through and became an open display of Trille's square white teeth. "How in God's name do those Pharisees in your Congress expect to stay in business when the things they need to keep your country in business—armed forces and good intelligence—they snarl up in self-righteous posturing and the Ten Commandments? You Yankees are funny. Actually funny."

"You ought to see if from here, Inspector."

Trille nodded, his amusement subsiding under the demands of the toast. "I suppose so. I suppose there are times when you wake up screaming."

"It's a sad thing to be victimized by your own people. But you Krauts know all about that, don't you. Having been so ill-used by the Nazis, and all."

"I don't like that word Kraut." The smile had disappeared.

"I don't like that word Yankee. At least the way you use it."

Trille raised his eyes to regard Wagner thoughtfully. "For someone who needs a favor, you certainly are a surly wretch."

126

Wagner pushed back his chair and stood up. He put some change on the table and said, "For the coffee."

"How about the gear?"

Wagner shook his head. "Keep your gear."

Trille sniffed. "Is this what you people call cutting off your nose to spite your face?"

"Call it what you will."

He turned to make for the door but Trille held up a hand. "Koenig. Wait."

"Give me one good reason why I should."

"Whom would you use the gear on?"

"None of your frigging business."

"Don't be so huffy. You need me. I need you."

"You need me? Why?"

"I can't afford to have an American President shot in my jurisdiction. You might help to keep that from happening."

"You've got a whole police force to help keep that from happening."

"Correct. But you have something I don't have."

"Like what?"

"Membership in the CIA."

"What's that supposed to mean?"

Trille brushed some crumbs from his lapel. "It would help me to keep current on CIA's thinking on this and related matters."

"You mean you want me to turn informant? To double on my own people?"

"So to speak."

"And for this you will let me use some of your gear?"

"Don't get angry. It doesn't help."

"You see too many movies, Trille. My bosses tell me only what they think I need to know."

"All right. Whatever they tell you, you tell me."

"Sorry, Dad. You aren't offering enough."

"What's your price?"

"Three dollars and ninety-eight cents. Special this week only."

"Come on. Be serious."

"I am serious. You can learn more from *The New York*

Times than you can learn from me, Trille."

"If you change your mind, let me know."

"Up yours."

He walked through the Stachus, huddling against the misty rain, to Rudi Kulka's all-night snack bar. Rudi was pulling on his topcoat and giving some instructions to the day man. He glanced at Wagner and winked.

"*Tag*, Koenig. Something to eat?"

"No thanks, Rudi. I want to see you."

"Hold on a minute. You can walk me to the U-bahn."

"Sure."

He stood by the door and stared out at the street and the pastel facades of the buildings, all darkened by dampness and heavy with that crestfallen look a city takes on in the rain. His mind insisted on returning to the erotic night just past, and he recognized that what he had seen then to be regret had become embarrassment. He had long known of the debilitating effects loneliness and isolation could work on men, but it had not occurred to him until now how very vulnerable he was in this area. He trusted Ellie Pomeraine no farther than he could throw a freight car, but he had hopped in the sack with her at the drop of a brassiere, like some horny traveling salesman.

"Let's go," Rudi said, nudging him.

They went into the rain, and Wagner breathed deeply of the October air, exhaling little clouds in the cold.

"I need some help, Rudi."

"All you have to do is ask. You know that."

"I don't like to ask. But I haven't any choice."

"What do you mean, you don't like to ask? I wouldn't be here, I wouldn't have anything, if you hadn't risked your ass to pull me out of that burning car."

"Well, that's what I mean. I pulled you out because I didn't want you to die, not because I wanted you in my debt."

"So what do you need?"

"A rundown on some characters."

"Police-file stuff?"

"Yes. But these people might not have records."

"I'll call my buddy, Karl Ulrich at Archives. Everybody in Germany has some kind of record, my friend, and Karl knows how to find it."

They walked without comment for a time. Then Rudi said, "How come you people don't have anything on them? I thought you Ami spies knew everything about everybody."

"Sheesh."

Rudi gave Wagner an apologetic glance. "Sorry, Koenig. That was stupid of me. I know how tough it is for you to operate these days."

"No offense."

"It's like that time in the Luftwaffe. We were flying Dorniers out of Holland. The brass orders us to bomb a Limey radio hidden in a boat in a Belgian inlet. But don't hit any of the fishing boats around it, they say; we don't want to irritate the populace. At two hundred kilometers an hour, we're supposed to hit a tiny boat in a sea of tiny boats without hitting anything else. And we're not supposed to irritate a populace whose cities we'd burned, government we'd seized, women we'd screwed. Bureaucracy? Hell, man, I've seen my share."

"I didn't know you were in the Luftwaffe, Rudi."

"Sure. A bunch of us cops flew in that war. Hell, Inspector Trille was a big ace. Ritterkreuz, and all that."

"Trille? A flier?"

"I thought everybody knew that. He had lunch with Hitler even. Hitler and Göring. He shot down a bunch of you Yankee swine, as you were known in those days." He gave Wagner one of his winks and laughed.

"Well, as they say, you learn something every day."

"I suppose so."

"I can't imagine you, or Trille, for that matter, as anything but policemen."

"Lots of us came in as trainees after the war, when any kind of job was welcome. We weren't considered political, being young, uncomplicated fly-boys, and so we were mainly acceptable under the old de-Nazification laws.

129

Trille had some trouble, as I recall, thanks to all his hobnobbing with the Nazi brass in Berlin and so on. But after a while we Germans got sick of wearing a hair shirt and apologizing to the world for breathing, and everybody got on with living. And now it's been four years since I retired from the force, and I still can't think of myself as anything but a cop." Rudi checked his watch. "Train's due soon. Who is it you want lamped?"

"Three people." Wagner handed Rudi a slip of paper. "These three. An appliance salesman named Kahn. Kahn's girlfriend, a Lotte Mahlmann. And a hood named Rollo Stoeckler, who's been working lately as Emerson Gurney's bodyguard, or handyman, or something."

"All right. I'll need a day or two. Being retired, I can't make everybody jump anymore."

"Well, make it as fast as you can, Rudi. I'm being stripped into bacon."

"Where do I get you?"

"The Nikolai here. Or outside Kitzbühel, at a place called the Edelweiss Hof."

"Anything else?"

"One thing. I want to identify a couple of cars. A 1985 Mercedes Benz, model 550, German registration. The number's on that slip. It's a Hertz, from its plates. But I want to confirm that, and I want to know who rented it." He paused, consulting the note. "And this 1982 Audi LS, number attached. O.K.?"

"Glad to do it. You're my favorite Yankee swine." Rudi checked his watch again, winked, and then was gone in the rush for the subway.

When Wagner returned to the Nikolai he found a note that asked him to call Trille.

He dialed police headquarters from a pay phone and got Trille only after enduring a series of clicks and snaps.

"This is Koenig. You wanted me?"

"Oh. Yes. I have some news."

"Well?"

"Akim Ri. He's been seen again."

"Where?"

"In Frankfurt. Near the trade-show complex."

"Any line on where he went?"

"No. A sighting, no more."

"All right. I'll keep it in mind."

"That's another one you owe me, Koenig."

"By the way: I've been wondering about the airport. Ri might make his try there. It's good for shooting."

Trille chuckled softly. "The airport is so good for shooting even we poor policemen are aware of it. That's why, when President Randall boards his plane for home, every conceivable vantage point within a thousand yards will be covered by police officers. Soldiers. Dogs."

"How about the plane? Bombs, and so on."

"Scrupulously checked by Bundespolizei explosives experts. By American Secret Service officials."

"The crew?"

"Handpicked from Lufthansa's best flight personnel."

"By whom?"

"By me. Personally. I've checked and passed them all, from pilot to stewardesses, from chief mechanic to baggage handlers. And each double-checked. No, Koenig, Ri won't be at the airport. He'd be wasting his time, and I think he knows it."

"Well, as you like to say: I had to ask."

He rang off and went back to the hotel.

19

His intention had been to return directly to the Edelweiss Hof, but Trille's report on Ri changed his mind. He drove west through the burgeoning daytime traffic to Landshuter Allee, which he followed north to Olympiapark. He left his car in the tower parking plaza and sauntered past the ice stadium, crossing a branch of the artificial lake on a foot bridge. The pathway wound through the trees to a ridge due south of the tower, and he sought out the highest point. Despite the lowering mist, the rise offered a fine view of the tent-roofed stadium, the Olympiahalle, the tower mall, and the Olympic Village beyond the Brauchle Ring.

He went to a phone and called Hendel Kompanie. Groot was not immediately available, according to the female Prussian general, so he dictated a message for him:

> Unimpeachable source reports
> Akim Ri sighted near Frankfurt
> trade show yesterday. Suggest
> you alert all elements of
> security. I'll continue as
> planned, since I am convinced

Ri will make his try near the
Olympiaturm, no matter where
he's sighted between now and
President's Munich visit.

—Wagner

After hanging up, he consulted the directory and found
the number for the Munich offices of *Chronos* Magazine.
He dialed it and asked the switchboard to connect him
with the bureau chief.

"Mr. Dalton's office," a secretary purred.

"He in?"

"May I ask who's calling, please?"

"Louis Frammsville, U.S. Secret Service. Put him on."

There was a polite snap, then a phone lifted.

"This is Dalton. What can I do for you?"

"White House detail, checking certain aspects of
security. Presidential visit and all that. Got a question."

"Well, I'll help any way I can—"

"You have an employee named Pomeraine? Ellie
Pomeraine?"

"We did. But she was dismissed last month."

"Odd. Understand you assigned her to do a story on
party name of Gurney, Emerson. Motion-picture actor."

"Well, yeah, but I don't see—"

"So why, if she's been fired?"

"Hell, you people ought to know. After all, it was Amy
Randall's idea in the first place. I got a call from Amy, a
longtime friend from my old West Coast days. She said
Gurney was going to be lunching with the President and
her and maybe *Chronos* would do a little story on Gurney
and, as a special favor, assign Pomeraine to write it. I like
Amy, and it was no skin off my ass. So I set it up."

"Would it have been likely that you'd have assigned
Pomeraine to such a story anyhow? Without such a call?"

"No way. By the way: what's your name, pal?"

"Is Pomeraine working on anything else for you?"

"Hey, come on, pal. What the hell's this got to do with
security?"

133

"Answer the question, Dalton."

"I don't see where it's any of your business, but she's doing something special. A one-shot."

"Rattner?"

"Why—how did you—"

"Don't screw around, Dalton. Did Rattner contact her? Or did someone else?"

"Hey, look—"

"Who, Dalton? Who put Pomeraine onto Rattner?"

"I did. What I mean is, I got the initial call."

"From whom? Rattner?"

"Look, pal. I don't have to tell you that or anything else. And the Supreme Court backs me up. So get off my frigging line, see?"

"Do you want to argue this in court? Do you want to put President Randall in danger?"

"Well, hell no. But—"

"Then answer the question."

"What question?"

"Why did you assign Pomeraine to the job?"

"You don't argue with the U.S. Government for long—not when they promise you a hell of a story."

"So somebody in the U.S. Government put you onto Rattner? Then stipulated Pomeraine was to get the story?"

"I don't have to answer that. And if you want to take me to court, go ahead, you son of a bitch."

Dalton hung up.

But Wagner had found out what he'd been after so he hung up, too, and went to his car.

He picked up the Autobahn and headed for the Austrian border at flank speed. He tried to think analytically, but it wouldn't come together.

One thing for sure, though: somebody was putting somebody on.

20

She was thinking of Lola Toomey, for some reason or
other. She hadn't thought of Lola in ages, and that in itself
was peculiar, because it had been at Lola's, during those
long, disconnected Malibu afternoons, that Rae had
taught her The Escape. It had been sort of dumb, really,
because she'd always preferred men—she still did, for that
matter—and Rae Ellen (dear, soft, tragic Rae Ellen) had
been so drunk all the time. But life brings bizarre and
unpredictable instructors and instructions, and she owed
Rae Ellen, and Lola, too, a remembrance now and then
for old lessons learned.

Lola. Where was she now? Rae was dead. But where
was Lola?

The German girl (what was *her* name? Irma?) was a
lovely thing, but, like Dirk, a terrible bore. Which was no
surprise, after all. Groot always picked them for their
bovinity because he understood that amiable stupidity
was expected of her therapeutic companions. Stupidity
and acceptable English. Her life was a boiler room, filled
with clang and clangor and the need to be always with it,
always a shade faster on the draw than anyone in the

clamor around. What a blessed relief it was, simply to sit quietly with some beautiful political zero who thought of nothing but the sensation of now, who aspired to nothing beyond the egocentric comforts of tomorrow. Special men, like Dirk, had to be risked, because they were useful. But mere *Playgirl* centerfolds were too risky, because the glare was always on her, and men—even the beautiful dumb ones—were always ambitious. Moreover, a man was prima facie evidence of hanky-panky as far as the gossip mongers were concerned. A man at midnight was, for the Speaker of the House and the President's sister, cause for possible blackmail and eventual scandal. A woman at midnight—let them all make something of that, eh? How would they, without themselves appearing evil-minded and grotesque, make something of a daughter of an old friend? Or a speech stenographer? Or a hairdresser? Anyhow, thank God for Groot, who understood.

Still, the absence of intellectuality could be endured only so long, and it was now a nuisance to have the girl over there on the sofa, hugging her knees and listening to the hard rock coming from an eight-dollar transistor radio.

"Turn that thing off, will you, Irma?"

The girl's slate-blue eyes were half-closed and preoccupied. She blinked and said in her Hessian inflections, "I regret you don't like me."

"I like you fine. But it's time for me to leave now. I have a very busy morning planned."

Irma silenced the radio, and, after placing it on an end table, sank back against the sofa cushions. "You did the whole night nothing but talk to me of your childhood," she pouted. "And there was so much I didn't understand in what you spoke."

"I wanted companionship, Irma. A listener."

"You didn't want a lover. That was clear." Irma made a little face.

"My mind was too busy with other things."

Irma nodded her exquisite blonde head and sighed.

136

"You are a very rich and famous and important lady, and it's always that way when there is money and fame. A friend I have is the managing director of a great Swiss company, and he asks only that I hold his head in my lap and stroke his hair. As a man he is dead now, he says, because his manship has been lost in the business worries. When he was a boy his mama would stroke his hair when he was tired and afraid, and it gives him pleasure to remember those times."

"I get very lonely. That's my problem. And the world supervises my social life, I'm sorry to say."

"Pooh. Were I you, I would do what I wish."

"It doesn't work that way, Irma, dear." She leaned closer to the mirror to check her makeup. She wore very little, but what was there had to be right.

"Will you be wanting to see me again?"

"Probably. Ellie likes you. But I'll have Mr. Groot keep in touch. All right?"

Irma bent forward to hug her knees again. "What means this—Speaker of the House or whatever? Do you make many speeches?"

"Not really." She began to retouch an eyebrow. "The House is part of the American legislature, and the Speaker has many duties there. I'm a kind of servant of all the members when I preside over their meetings and when they need parliamentary guidance and legislative counsel, and I've got to be impartial in all of this. At the same time, I'm partial, because I lead my party in the House, and, well, frankly, I'm very powerful."

"You earned this job? Or were you given it?"

For favors granted, for men screwed: the thoughts were implicit in the girl's question, and for a moment Amy resented the dumb sow's salacious presumptions. The flash of annoyance triggered a kind of fluttery replay of all those prologue years in the grubby municipal wards and the mayoralty and then the state legislature and the appointment to a dead man's unexpired congressional term and then the reelections, six of them, while all the while guiding the destinies of a motion-picture company and its subsidiary recording and publishing and talent-agency operations. The Eternal Miss Cool, smiling and moral and correct; the Unshakable Miss Churchwoman, pious and sweet-smelling and devout in the Madison Square prayer rallies and on the Bishop Caldwell talk shows and in the Reverend Tom Zansky's Crusade for Christian Love; the Aloof Miss Parliamentarian, efficient and helpful and bookish; the Indefatigable Miss Armtwister, brittle and dedicated and sincere and unwavering; the Empathetic Miss Dealer, with the back-room agreements and the smiles of connivance and forgiveness; the Reliable Miss Everpresent, never missing a vote and always on hand in committees and always ready to assume a duty or to strike a compromise. And always smiling-smiling-smiling through clenched teeth at the powerful men who would deny her power because her womanhood threatened their manhood; the patronizing, the pretense that her femininity didn't matter, when all the time it was the only thing that mattered to them at all. And the men, the uncountable men, she'd pushed away, her secret anger hidden in feigned gratitude for their big-hearted willingness to pat her ass or massage her chest, for their promises of sexual delights beyond all imagining if she could manage a weekend at Rehoboth Beach or Ocean City or even, for Christ's sake, Baltimore. And then, the election to Speaker, not because she was, in truth, the only straw-boss who could possibly govern a House gone indolent and fatuous in years of lopsided majority, but because the Women's Rights lobby had induced the men to Establish a Lasting Symbol. She'd been author and co-author of some of the most significant legislation passed in twelve years—from the Income Tax Reform Act to the Solar Energy Enabling Act—and yet, unless history surprised them all, she was doomed to be A Symbol of Women's Achievement. She'd been chairman and keynote speaker of the national convention; she had served on the most prestigious committees and foundations to be found anywhere, from Big Sur to Big Apple, and yet she was still Amy Randall, the President's kid sister.

Had she earned her way? Oh God oh God oh God. Had she *ever*.

Well, she thought, *the game isn't over yet.*

Their eyes met in the mirror. "I worked very hard for the job, actually. I assure you, Irma, nobody gave it to me."

She checked the contents of her briefcase, making sure she had clipped her schedule to the topmost file folder, and then went to the bedroom door. Looking back, she said, "Do you need anything, Irma?"

The girl hunched a shoulder. "Mr. Groot has taken care of everything."

"All right, then. You can leave when you wish."

"Please call me. I like you. And you need me, I think."

"I need only one thing, Irma, dear."

21

The car radio was crackling with coverage of the President's afternoon arrival in Bonn. There were interviews with the renowned, sidebars on security measures, a lot of brass band music, speculations by pompous political commentators.

He listened to it for a time, then, tiring of the transparent attempts to expand a simple arrival into The Eighth Wonder of the World, he tuned out and set the stereo to playing one of his own Frankie Carle cassettes.

Luncheon was being served when he arrived at the Edelweiss Hof, and the strummings of zithers, plucked by three pink old men in Lederhosen, blended with the dining-room chatter to create an overall Tyrolean benignity. Wagner went onto the sundeck and took a table beside the railing.

He had settled into a brooding contemplation of the valley, now sparkling under the reappearing sun, when there was a general stirring at the doors. Emerson Gurney had materialized there—nobly erect, head lifted, his eyes sweeping the view—like a bleary parody of MacArthur pondering the return to Bataan. His gaze eventually took in Wagner, and there was recognition.

"Well," Gurney said, arriving at the table in a cloud of cologne. "How's everything in the publicity biz today?"

"Tolerable. How's with you?"

"Crappy. I'm still on that gig out at the crossroads. Mind if I crash-land?"

"Not at all. Lunch?"

"Who eats lunch, except press agents and old broads with purple hair?"

"Drink, then?"

"Bingo. You said the magic word." Gurney slumped in the chair opposite and waved imperiously at a waitress. Neither he nor Wagner spoke until she had brought a barrel-size martini.

"What's you name again?" Gurney asked over the rim of his glass.

"Koenig. What's yours?"

Gurney paused in his sipping and sent a quick glance at Wagner. "You're a riot, you are," he said.

"Yeah."

Gurney took a gulp of the drink, rolled it around in his mouth, eyes thoughtful, and then swallowed noisily. "Phoo," he said. "Atomic warfare."

"It smells like the radiator of a Model A I had in high school."

"You had a Model A?"

"Yep."

"I thought you was a Kraut."

"I'm from Buffalo. I used to take girls to see your movies in my Model A."

"You must have been two years old, eh?"

"About."

"You liked my pictures?"

"As a matter of fact, I did."

"Those were the good days. People had fun then. Notice how people don't laugh much anymore? Everybody takes hisself real serious these days. Back then, you could tell a Irish joke and nobody'd laugh louder'n the Irishmen in the crowd. Nowadays you tell a Irish joke and they got you answerin' questions front of a Congressional friggin' committee. The whole world has turned into a great big pain in the ass."

"Yeah."

"It's those friggin' Communists. The Commies have took over all the key partsa our life, see. And Commies are glum sonsabitches. Sour. No sense of fun. So humor's a bad stroke now. Glum's the word."

"Some of the warmest, funniest, most likable people I've ever met are Russians."

"I dint say Russians. I said Commies. The two ain't necessarily the same. But you're right. Even the Russian Commies can have a wild sense of humor. It's the American Commies are the sullen ones."

"Well, I wouldn't know."

"Take my word, buddy. I know."

"Have you been working at the crossroads this morning?"

"Nah. We was supposed to shoot a take or two but the director's got the flu or the creepin' crud or somethin' and so we dint go out." He took another long pull at the martini and sighed. "Phoo."

"All's serene then, eh?"

"I dint say that. All hell's breakin' loose, matter of fact. I can't find that sumbitch Rollo, and he's got the script revisions in his car."

"Oh?"

"Yeah. Ginsberg—he's the director—Ginsberg's all uptight about it, and with the flu and all, he's into rageville."

"Too bad."

"Can't figure it. Rollo's an eager sumbitch. Always around under your feet. Got the door open before you decide to leave. That kinda thing, know what I mean? Now all of a sudden he ain't nowhere and he's got the script revisions in his car. Ought to fire the knocker."

"Where did you find him in the first place?"

"Who? Rollo?"

142

"How did he get on your payroll?"

Gurney placed his glass carefully on the table, and his manner became wary, as if a ghost had passed, leaving a chill. The actor cleared his throat and glanced at his watch. "My God, is it that time already?"

"Yeah. Where'd you meet Rollo?"

"Around. Where do you ever meet the hired help?"

"Rollo's a mean item."

"He ain't my type exactly. Another of them eager, sour bastards. I'm the kinda guy likes his laughs. Back in the old days I wouldn't have anybody around without he made me laugh. Hell, at MGM they used to pick even the gofers and grips I liked when we worked on a reel."

Wagner's impression was that Gurney, for all his bluff reminiscence, was still going carefully. But there seemed, too, to be a trace of worry in the mix, and Wagner wondered why. He decided to keep the old ham talking.

"My favorite of all the pictures you made was *Hell in the Clouds*, that airplane thing with Rae Ellen Ramsey."

Gurney humphed. "Wasn't bad. Change a pace from Westerns."

"What kind of girl was Rae Ellen Ramsey? She came across as being so angelic. Proper. The word was 'sweet' in those days, I think."

Gurney laughed. "Well, you're right about one thing. She sure came across. And she was worth waitin' for. A real article at the scronch."

"What happened to her?"

"Died a booze. Last time I seen her, I think, was at Lola Toomey's place in Malibu. Had a tribe trashin' out there between flicks, like Lola always did. One big long gang-bang, and people would come in for a crash when they felt like it. Rae was a fixture, though. She took to the sauce, and she'd just trash out at Lola's, drinkin' and puttin' out the scronch. Only she turned switch-hitter. AC/DC. That afternoon she put her hand on Amy's box and almost got threw off the sundeck, Amy's bein' so nicey-nice and proper and all." He laughed again, shaking

143

his head with fond recollection.

"Amy? She made a pass at Amy Randall?"

Gurney's alcoholic smile faded, and the look came into his eyes again.

"I thought you hadn't met Amy Randall until just the other day," Wagner persisted. "When she came here to invite you to the presidential luncheon."

"Well," Gurney said uneasily, "I hadn't. Not really. Seen her around a couple times, like at Lola's. But we was never pals or nothin."

"I don't see how you can be at a gang-bang and not get to be pals with the participants."

"Oh, Amy wasn't gangin'. She's really square in a lot a ways, you know? She'd just made a pit-stop at Lola's and Rae was zonked as usual and when we was havin' a polite drink on the sundeck Rae patted Amy on the gatehouse and Amy got sore, it bein' so public and all."

"Still, it seems a scene like that would be pretty much dominated by a famous cowboy actor and the daughter of a zillionaire."

"Hollywood's like that. Hell, I've put the blocks to many a broad I dint even know their names. Once I shacked with a gash for three days before I recognized her as Mary Ann Orion, the famous Broadway hoofer. Everybody looks different off camera. Especially when you're zonked. Beside, Amy wasn't all that well-known in them days. She was just a kid trashin' around the Coast, gettin' it on to bustin' the movies on the business side. She couldn't make a dent, so her old man bought Titan Studios and made her president. She did real good, too. The studio went from zilch to Mach Four in ten seconds. Hell of a organizer. Hell of a salesman. Talk of the Coast, she was."

"How come she pretended she didn't know you at the press conference last night?"

Gurney polished off his drink and waved for another. "Just the old promo crap, I guess. And tell the truth, I don't think she even remembers seein' me at Lola's. Lot a water over the dam since those days."

"Seems weird to me, the idea of you two putting on not to know each other because it might make better publicity."

"Everything in this world is weird, pal. Ain't ya noticed?" He took another huge martini from the waitress and swallowed it. "Phoo. Now that *is* a lunch."

Wagner was about to ask another question when Frau Lindl came onto the deck, squinting her watery blue eyes in the afternoon's golden glare. She came, rustling and birdlike, to their table, managing a faint smile.

"Grüss Gott," she said. "Is everything all right, gentlemen?"

"Hey," Gurney said to Wagner. "The old bim talks English. How about that." To her, he said, "You din't tell me you talk English. Hell, lady, you talk it almost as good as me."

"Thank you," Frau Lindl said. "My husband and I were in the hotel business for years, Mr. Gurney. I've spoken English as a matter of necessity from the first."

"Hat's off to ya. Takes talent." He drained the glass again and licked his lips reflectively. Turning his red gaze full on the woman, he said, "Somethin' on your mind?"

"I apologize for interrupting, Mr. Gurney. But I was wondering if Herr Stoeckler—the gentleman you call Rollo—will be coming back."

"I sure hope so, lady. Why?"

"Well," she said diffidently, "he promised he would pick up a package for me at the central post office and I haven't seen him since."

"Neither have I, Cleo. Neither have I." Gurney belched. "He'll be back. He's probably shackin' someplace. He'll be back as soon as he's had his ashes hauled."

Frau Lindl peered at Wagner. "The idiom is unfamiliar—"

"Mr. Gurney thinks Rollo has a girl somewhere and is spending some time with her and will be back soon."

"I see. Well, I hope so—" Her voice trailed off.

Wagner returned her serious gaze, and he tried to picture her as a younger woman, married, and struggling through the years of bed changes and maids and bellhops and streams of faceless tourists. What kind of woman had she been before the years dimmed her? What had she done with her life? Was she, behind the wrinkles and faded eyes, another soul immobilized by inertia and lost opportunity?

"Hear anything, let ya know," Gurney said.

Frau Lindl nodded, excused herself, and returned to the inn and its shadows. Her shoulders sagged.

God, Wagner thought, *we are all doomed to cope, forever and ever.*

Gurney pushed away from the table, yawned hugely, and weaved erect. "These heavy lunches always make me sleepy. Gotta take a nap. See ya, buddy."

"Sure."

"You liked 'Hell in the Clouds,' eh?"

"Yep."

"Critics panned the hell outa it. Said I should stick to horses and six-guns."

"Shows you how much they know."

"Yeah. Well, see ya around."

"Sure."

He went to his room and sat by the window, watching the shadows of the puff clouds as they marched across the sweep of sunny mountains. The image of Rollo, grimacing and turning slowly as he fell to the road, was clear and oppressive in his mind. How many Rollos had there been in his life? How many had he sent, collapsing, into their separate voids?

He wondered for an irrelevant moment if there was a God.

He broke the spell by going to his briefcase and removing the set of burglar tools from its hiding place behind the lining. He considered taking the dust tubes, too, but decided against it.

The break-in would be fairly unsophisticated and made in broad daylight. Moreover, the apartment, being

146

occupied by Germans, would probably be immaculate, and there would be no need to blow dust over traces of his visit.

He was very tired.

For a reason he couldn't name, he laughed aloud.

22

Outside, beyond the rococco balcony and the courtyard's ornamental yews, the city grieved in the afternoon sunlight over those days in history when art and theology and the salt trade had been its most pressing involvements. Groot, unfortunate enough to have a chair facing the windows and their distractions, found it easy to woolgather. He squinted his eyes and tried to imagine the town as it might have appeared to Henry the Lion or to Albrecht V: the bannered barges at the Isar toll gates; noble horses clattering over the cobbles, their armored riders fierce and erect; the pastel facades and deep-slanting roofs echoing to Medicean pomp. But then someone rattled some papers, and Groot, as was his custom when finding himself sentimentalizing, called up cynicism to break the schoolboy spell. Times change nothing, he told himself. Nine hundred years, and the city still buzzes with military traffic and ambitious bigshots; nine centuries, and the facades splash neon and the cobbles have surrendered to multilaned concrete and cloverleaves, but the pomp and the pride go on and on. We're right and they're wrong, and so we will sit in big rooms and stare at charts and decide how to kill them first.

The meeting had been dominated by a colonel from the Corps of Engineers who droned on about embarkation points and airfield retirements and the phase-out of missile silos and immovable hardware stands. Groot was grateful for having had a light lunch. He had declined Wilson's invitation to share some cutlet Parmesan and chilled Riesling at the French Barn. It was hard enough to keep awake as it was, without a bellyful of cheese, veal, and wine.

There was a question from the chairman.

"And what does the CIA have to say about all this?" The baritone conveyed intimations of expensive prep schools and maple-shaded colonials in saltwater New England.

Groot was practiced enough, thanks to his many exposures to general officers and their ways, to modify his daydreamer's squint so as to make it appear to be the gaze of a staff consultant pondering the verities. Gazing serenely into the eyes of the chairman of the Joint Chiefs, he said, "Well, sir" (here a thoughtful pause), "it sounds as if you military types have put it all together. I have no doubt that you will have shut down our NATO operations in complete good order by February twenty-eighth. My congratulations on a distasteful job well done."

Since General Dirk was used to hearing only favorable comment, he did not react to Groot's, choosing instead to make a neat stack of his papers, which he then tapped on the tabletop in the manner of a card player tidying a deck. "Of course," he said. "But I was wondering if you could give us a glimpse of the view from your foxhole. How does our withdrawal from Europe appear to you and your director?"

This was a loaded question, calculated to embarrass Groot. General Dirk had always been condescending in his dealings with CIA, and because Groot's reticence was easy to misread as diffidence, the chairman enjoyed bullying him with elegantly phrased zingers. Even Groot's invitation to this meeting had been patronizing; U.S. Forces Europe needed CIA beside its deathbed like General Dirk needed a third eyebrow, but the presence of a man of Groot's rank in Cop-out City was too much even for the chairman of the Joint Chiefs to ignore. Especially when the President was now in Bonn and would be briefed by the chairman in less than a week. It wouldn't do for the chairman to admit to the President that he'd ignored a deputy director of CIA. Besides, even if he hadn't been trapped in protocols of his own, Groot would have attended anyhow, since it was an excellent chance for some exploration. Now, because Dirk had irritated him, and because he really didn't owe these uniformed manikins a thing, he decided to shun diplomacy and move into a direct test of the chairman's sympathies. He said, "We are appalled, of course. The United States military establishment is in full rout, and we see abandonment of NATO as the final ignominy."

There was a moment of awkward silence in which the officers on the chairman's flanks turned pink and eyed the carpet or studied their nails. The chairman himself did not so much as blink.

"Oh?"

"The United States has become a second-class power and is now on the run before World Communism. The United States itself will become a socialist society within the decade."

The tension in the room was almost touchable.

"Those are strong words," the chairman said without emphasis.

"To be sure. But the Cold War is over. The United States is no longer fighting World Communism, it's on the road to joining it. Anyone who denies that fact simply hasn't been watching what's going on."

"This is the official view of your Agency?"

General Dirk was not so stupid as the question might imply, Groot knew. It had been, rather, another attempt at teasing him into anger.

"Of course not, General. It's no more than a personal opinion. Moreover, since the CIA is no longer a force to be reckoned with by anyone, it really doesn't matter what official position it takes. Like your Army, my Agency has succumbed to the nation's determination to defend itself by putting up no defense at all. Congress has bought the philosophy expressed by a lady of my acquaintance from Delaware: 'to keep peace, all we need do is throw our arms wide in loving friendship.'"

General Carruthers snorted. "Nobody thinks like that—even in Delaware."

"You want to bet?" Groot said, borrowing a phrase from Wagner.

The chairman put his papers on the table, squaring the stack with meticulously manicured fingers. "It seems to me that you have a defeatist attitude, Groot," he said coolly.

"I'd call my attitude pragmatic, General. Look at the facts. The doom that's befallen your armed forces and my Agency is the natural result of two things: first, disenchantment that followed Viet Nam, and second, an irrational energy policy. Both the Administration and Congress saw the armed forces and the intelligence establishment as Cold War artifacts, and, spurred by the pressures of inflation and drastic fuel shortages, cheered by idealistic organs of public opinion, and indulging its own instinct for self-perpetuation, Congress set up watchdog committees and enacted legislation that brought about de facto disarmament and official disengagement—isolationism. I believe the nation is drifting into a kind of insular socialism, which, in turn, will eventually permit the United States to become a large supplier-satellite of the Soviet Union, like Poland, or East Germany. If China doesn't blow us all out of the water first, that is."

The chairman broke in. "What's to check this—drift—as you call it?"

Groot saw that his extravagant rhetoric had contacted a nerve. He had often rehearsed this scene, but now that it

151

had arrived he felt uneasy and constricted by an awareness of how thin was the ice under him.

"Well," he said, "there's the Third Party thing. The Robert Goodman phenomenon."

There was another silent interval in which the chairman and his colleagues made a business of not looking at each other.

"Mr. Goodman," General Dirk said with elaborate casualness, "is said to be a fascist."

"Of course," Groot said blandly. "He is indeed a Hitler-type event. Because the United States is, in many ways, experiencing today what Germany experienced in the two decades after World War One. That war brought Germany defeat, humiliation, confusion, inflation, unemployment, student agitation, Bolshevik-inspired rioting. Viet Nam and the subsequent loss of the Panama Canal and Puerto Rico and our humiliation in and ejection from the UN, our retreat from Europe, have brought the same results to the United States—in varying degrees, but essentially the same nonetheless. The bottom line in Germany was the Nazi Party in power and Hitler ruling as chancellor. Draw your own U.S. projections."

General Dirk humphed. "You said yourself that the Congress, the Presidency, even the Judiciary is over-whelmingly, ah, liberal. Which means preponderant voter sentiment that's, ah, if not, ah, leftist, then liberal, so to speak. I mean—"

It was Groot's turn to break in. "Correction: the majority of voters reveal a confusion, an unsureness. A yearning for simplistic answers to complicated questions, as the cliché goes. But more important, the rising support for the Goodman movement shows that a heavy reaction could, if harnessed by Goodman or some other demagogue, swing the pendulum all the way to the far right. To American fascism, if you will. Just as in Germany, when unguided liberalism—a mindless lust for reform—went careening into National Socialism, or German Fascism."

General Carruthers, who was seen by his Pentagon peers as a Penn State ROTC man and therefore unequipped for intellectual fencing, made another snorting sound and spoke the unspeakable. "You mean if this Goodman cat gets elected he'll build up the military, like Hitler did?"

Groot felt a kind of relief. This was what all this garbage was about. Now was his chance to categorize General Dirk, whose inscrutability was lengendary. He sighed and shrugged a shoulder. "Hitler's election came only after a careful stacking of the Reichstag deck, a protracted campaign of fixing and bribing and setting up and blackmailing and bullying. A campaign tolerated, if not actively backed, by an angry, disillusioned military officer corps." He gave General Dirk a direct stare. "In view of all that, Robert Goodman has a long way to go before he gets elected, wouldn't you say, General?"

The chairman remained inscrutable. "I leave politics to the politicians, Groot. I am a soldier."

"To be sure. I was simply suggesting that Goodman's fascism is in the eye of the beholder."

General Ferguson, a product of OCS and therefore, like Carruthers, widely pitied for his relative illiteracy, stirred in his chair and sneered, "Communism, fascism, left wing, right wing—I can't keep them all sorted out. Hell, all of them end up screwing the little guy."

Groot had expected a more positive reaction to his elaborate salvo. Militarists are happiest when in charge of wars or rumors of wars, and they can be expected to be pleased when their trade receives an expression of support, however indirect and whatever the source. But these assembled centurions remained impassive, devoid of any display beyond Ferguson's skepticism. Lacking anything else, Groot picked this up and gave it a kick.

"We have difficulty with identifications and definitions, General Ferguson, because they involve people, and, since people are so different and have so many different backgrounds, experiences, educations, biases, phobias, they have their individual conceptions of a single idea like, say, Communism. For some people the name—the idea—connotes something eminently good and constructive, almost a religious, inspirational thing.

153

For others, it represents something detestable, something to fear and hate. But the same occurs when you say a word like 'Christianity'; some people react glowingly, are lifted up by what the word implies to them, while others envision pinch-faced, Puritanical hypocrisy lined up in the pews of a white-steepled church. So, many times, when people are talking about an idea, a philosophy, a political system, they think they're all discussing one thing when, in actuality, they are discussing altogether different things. And so, when somebody hears the claim that Robert Goodman is a fascist, he might think that's good or bad, depending on what his experience with a totalitarian point of view has been. I remember one German to whom Nazism meant midnight arrests and rubber truncheons, while to another it meant Autobahns and parades and good jobs."

"Well," Colonel Draper said from the far end of the table, "I've experienced all of them, from left to right, and I say they all stink. American democracy, for all of its crappy faults, is the only thing I can endure."

Groot nodded. "You say that because your experience of what you call American democracy has been good. However, how does American democracy look to the average black man?"

"I'm a black man," Colonel Draper reminded.

"Yes. But hardly average."

"There's no such thing as an average man," Colonel Stepick said, evincing all the piety of a General Motors recruitment brochure.

"When a black man is the son of a wealthy Chicago dentist and is a graduate of the Air Force Academy," Groot said, "his experience has been different from what most black men experience. He is, therefore, even mathematically, apart from the norm, the average experience. He is therefore likely to have an atypical view of American democracy, so far as his blackness is concerned."

"How did we get off on all this bullshit?" General Carruthers complained.

Groot managed a small smile. "It's my fault, I guess.

I'm sorry. I was wondering what you military types think of Robert Goodman—which is really none of my business anyhow—and I got off the track. I'm a windy fool. Please excuse me, gentlemen."

The chairman's eyes held steady for a long time. Then, with slow purpose, he put the stack of papers in his briefcase, pushed back his chair, and stood up. There was a clattering as the others rushed to rise, too.

"Well," the chairman said, running an elegant finger along his elegant mustache, "we've done enough damage for today. We'll resume tomorrow at 0900."

At the top of the marble stairway, Groot felt a tug at his elbow. He paused in the swirl of uniformed humanity and turned to confront General Dirk.

"Yes, General?" he said, raising his voice above the rush-hour din.

"You gave a little lecture in there, and you asked us what we thought of Robert Goodman."

"As I said, General, I'm a windy fool."

"In all of your gabble, you neglected to mention something. Something I'm curious about."

"What's that, sir?"

"What do *you* think of Robert Goodman?"

"No comment, General. As a member of CIA, I'm forbidden to have ideas. I'm forbidden to think."

"That, as Carruthers would say, is bullshit."

"Perhaps. But I can't answer your question."

Bowing a mocking little Prussian bow, the chairman tilted his head, smiled, and then began to descend the staircase. A few steps down, he paused, peered over his shoulder, and said, "I sleep better these nights knowing Philip Randall is our President. And that Albert A. O'Toole is our Vice President. Eh?"

He laughed openly and went to the lobby and crossed to the revolving doors, where he disappeared into the afternoon.

Groot sighed and went his own way, smiling his own smile.

23

"Rudi?"

"Speaking."

"How's everything in the retired-cop business?"

"Oh, hello, Koenig. I'm expecting your rogues' gallery any minute now."

"That isn't what I called about. I want you to do me a favor. Another favor, that is."

"Name it."

"It's a tail job. Gustav Kahn will be at the Golden Thigh this evening. I want to see where he goes from there. You've got his description."

"Sure. What time this evening?"

"I'm not sure. Let's see. It's four-thirty now. I suggest you be watching the Thigh no later than six-thirty. O.K.?"

"Right. You want me to tail him until when?"

"When he goes home and goes to bed, call me."

"Where? At the Nikolai or the Edelweiss?"

"I'll be at the Edelweiss."

"Anything else?"

"No. Just call me and let me know what Kahn does this evening."

"Child's play."

"Good. But don't take any chances."

"Who, me? Cowardly Rudolf? Not likely."

"I'll pay you for this one, Rudi."

"Like hell you will."

The phone clicked and buzzed.

The booth was next to the antiques shop across the street from Gipfel Gerät Kompanie. It stood in glassy opaqueness in the purple afternoon shadows, and while it gave a good view of the Gipfel location, it would itself be hard to see from the appliance store salesroom and the desk at which Gustav Kahn labored.

Wagner hung up, then, after consulting his little book, called the number of the Golden Thigh in Munich. While waiting for the connection, he watched Lotte Mahlmann show a fat lady the innards of a refrigerator. She looked bored and so did the fat lady.

"Golden Thigh," a man said.

"Let me talk to Paul Lincke," Wagner said.

"I'm not sure he's in yet."

"Well, find out."

There was a click and the sound of another phone being lifted. Glasses clinked in the background, and music murmured.

"Main bar. Lincke."

Wagner said, "What have you done about your Communist girlfriend?"

The music was a Bert Kaempfert number that made doomp-chah, doomp-chah. It commanded the interval until Lincke said, "Who is this?"

"No coyness, please. The Organization makes short shrift of the coy ones."

"Oh, excuse me. I didn't recognize your voice. About the girl. I've got a problem. I'm not sure which one it is."

"So?"

"So I've stopped seeing anybody at all. Would you give me a break and tell me who she is? I mean, I haven't—"

"I did not call to discuss your love life."

"Of course not. It's just that—why did you call?"

"You have something to do for us."

"Anything you say. Just name it."

"Call the Gipfel Gerät Kompanie in Kitzbühel as soon as I hang up. Ask for Gustav Kahn. Identify yourself and tell him that it's important that he sees you. Tell him it's about Ziggi and some plans to kill somebody, and you don't want to talk about it on the phone."

"That's all?"

"When he gets there, tell him that you overheard Ziggi talking on the phone to somebody the night he was killed. You heard him discussing something about a plan to assassinate somebody and Gustav Kahn was mentioned. Tell him you heard that and thought he ought to know."

"That's all?"

"That's all."

"I guess I can handle that."

"You handle it well, we give you the girl's name."

"Right. When will I hear from you?"

"When I decide to call you."

"All right. I want to be as helpful as I can. I'm with you people, you know. I'm sympathetic to you Greuel people."

"Make the call."

Wagner depressed the hook and held the phone to his ear, as if still in conversation, and waited until, across the street and behind the show window, Kahn stopped scribbling and picked up the desk phone at his elbow. The big bald head cocked to one side in an attitude of listening.

After a moment, Kahn placed the phone on its cradle, pushed back his chair, stood up, and called to Lotte Mahlmann. She came over to the desk and, after a brief conversation, nodded, checked her watch, and then returned to the fat lady and the pink refrigerator. Kahn pulled on a sports jacket and disappeared toward the rear of the store. Three minutes later, the dark blue Audi eased out of the alley with Kahn at the wheel.

Wagner watched the car out of sight and then he

rounded the block to the service alley. He went to the door marked with the Kahn-Mahlmann name cards, where, with a flick of his burglar's jimmy, he let himself in. Pausing in the tiny vestibule, he took an umbrella from its stand and placed it against the door. If anyone were to come through the door while he was upstairs, the umbrella would fall and put him on the alert.

The apartment was a monument to hedonism: full carpeting, brocaded draperies, expanses of glass and chrome, plush divans and pillows and subtle lighting and a master bedroom with a round bed and a mirrored ceiling. He began with the desk, an angular construction of wood and leather, and spent at least five minutes on the bills, business letters, car documents, insurance policies, and miscellany he found in its drawers.

The dressers and wardrobes and blanket chests and towel closets were equally unproductive; he found in them exactly what he'd expect to find in them. The bathroom, for all its limited space, was an ingenious arrangement that elevated the mundane to the exotic—literally. The bathtub nestled atop a hill of carpeted, steplike terraces. Mirrored walls, shuttered windows, potted plants, fake gold taps; there was even a small dressing room adjacent to the bath, one wall of which was given over to a vanity and makeup lights. The opposite wall featured a clothes closet concealed by a rank of louvered folding doors.

The appliance business must be very good these days, Wagner told himself, making for the vanity. He was about to have a thought for a change when the umbrella fell.

The distant clatter caused him to freeze for a moment, considering places of concealment. And then he found he had no choice, because Lotte Mahlmann was suddenly in the living room, kicking off her shoes and muttering to herself about sloppy, careless men.

He quickly opened one of the folding doors, stepped in among the perfumed garments, and had just closed the door when she came into the dressing room and sank on the stool with a sigh and regarded herself in the vanity mirror.

He watched through the louvers as she pulled off her wig of red hair and loosened her real blond hair. She looked better as a blonde, he decided. She was in her early thirties, but her face was younger and softer with gold hair, and she was nuts to bother with wigs at all.

She leaned forward to examine herself more closely and to rub at some imperfection she had discovered on her chin. Then she tried her smile, first from the right, then the left, creating several alternative versions between those extremes. She had nice teeth, and she knew how to display them. She should. She practiced enough.

She went into the bathroom and set the tub's taps to gushing. When she returned, she had already taken off her blouse and skirt and was pulling her slip over her head. In her panties and bra, she paused to study the same tiny corner of her chin and to try still another smile. Then, with that combination of calisthenics and dancing peculiar to a woman undressing, she removed the rest and stood nude before the glass.

She was in good shape. Her shoulders were set squarely, her breasts were small but well-formed, her belly was flat, her hips and buttocks were boyish, and her legs were tapered nicely from thighs to delicate feet. She struck several modeling poses and flashed her smile at the mirror over her rosy right shoulder. Then she stood full front, running her hands over her body and pausing to plump up her breasts and to pout at their smallness. He had a crazy impulse to whisper through the slats: *They're O.K. Don't knock those knockers.* And like a goofy high-school boy peeking into the girls' john, he felt an anguishing need to snicker.

She cured him of that impulse at once, though, because she completed a pirouette and came directly to the closet to pull open the door and reach for a robe. He was behind some clothing, but he knew she would see him in the next instant, and so, lacking time for anything fancy, he tapped her chin with a polite uppercut and caught her as she fell.

He lowered her easily to the carpet, since it would be best for her to awaken on the spot. She might, just possibly, think she had fainted.

The vanity drawers were also filled with the expected trivia, along with a truly impressive array of pill bottles containing bennies, seconals, dexedrine and nembutal. There were also two hypodermic needles.

Somebody in this little family was doing a lot of upping and downing and mainlining, and, feeling the pulse in Lotte's neck, he decided it was she.

But there was something else, too. Something very curious.

It was a Polaroid snapshot of a slim, dark-eyed, dark-haired young man. He was leaning against a deep-blue Audi, which had been parked against an Alpine background. He was staring somberly into the lens. Beside him was a fat man wearing a Tyrolean hat, who was talking to somebody to the side, off-camera.

Akim Ri.

Snapped with an unidentified fat friend.

Placing the photo on the vanity under the glare of the makeup lights, he used his Minox to take a picture of the picture.

Then, flicking out the lights and returning the Polaroid shot to its place in the drawer, he prepared to leave. He glanced at Lotte, who, stretched on the nylon pile, slim and oddly boyish, looked like a sleeping youngster.

"Bye-bye, sweets," he said. "Keep smilin'."

24

What should have been the Edelweiss Hof's primary attraction—conviviality in the presence of monumental mountains and intense, unblinking stars—was instead its burden. It was as if the glass walls and planter-lined railings were all that stood between the diners and the elemental forces that had molded the universe itself; it was as if one were asked to sip his *potage à la tête de veau* while God stood outside, nose pressed to the window. So the aging men and their glossy women sat in separated huddles, wide-eyed in the candlelight and whispering hollow reassurances, and Wagner, instantly depressed, considered a fast return to town for a *belegtes Brot* at Wimpl's Imbisshalle.

But time was against it, and so he persevered, taking a table in the corner at the very brink of the eternal. The waitress asked him, in cathedral tones, if he would be having dinner, and he ordered *cotelette Guyere,* subduing an impulse to add an amen. He brooded over his wine and gave himself silent little lectures on how happy he would be when he was done with the Company and its sorry business. Unaccountably, his visions of pleasure to come were broken by thoughts of Ellie Pomeraine, and so he gave a few moments to speculating on her role and person.

It was depressing to know that she was a liar. It was depressing to know that she was treating him as some kind of droll idiot. It was also depressing to know that that's precisely what he was.

It had been a mistake, of course, to become even slightly intimate with her. Women had never been truly important to him; if they had, he would doubtless have been married long ago, enduring West Frammsville and paying the spiritual price of convenient copulation and fresh socks in the drawer. Brittle career women were especially unacceptable as an alternative; although he was privately a champion of Women's Lib—or, at least, the idea of female equality—he was nevertheless repelled by the notion of screwing a hard-hatted steamfitter. And he had the feeling that Miss Pomeraine's ill-fated marriage had not collapsed solely under the weight of her mystery-writer husband's infidelities. She was a formidable woman, and it could be difficult indeed to concentrate on Chaper Three and Sir Gerald's asphyxiation in the greenhouse when your wife is lunching and trading lies with heads of state.

He was spooning up the last of his berries and cream when Frau Lindl ghosted through the room, nodding vaguely to hushed greetings. When she hesitated by his table, he had the feeling that he was why she had come in in the first place.

"Is everything satisfactory, Herr Koenig?"

"The meal was excellent. But my life leaves a lot to be desired."

She smiled dimly. "Life never matches its promises, does it?"

"Maybe we should sue God for false advertising, eh?"

"My husband used to say, 'God keeps many mysteries to himself, but the biggest of all of them is how he can love somebody as unlovable as man.'"

"Your husband said it all."

"He was the kindest and most lovable of all men."

"When did he die?"

"In 1945. In an American air raid. In the last bombing of Munich. A few more weeks and he'd have survived the war."

"You must really hate the Americans, then."

"I tried, certainly. But when you see them face to face, you see that they're people like you and me. Just as worried. Just as anxious and lost. And they did their share of dying in that war, too."

"Your capacity for forgiveness is amazing, Frau Lindl."

"What's to forgive? Americans didn't kill my husband. Politics and politicians killed him."

"Ah, yes. Well—"

She straightened a sagging flower in the vase on his table. "Which brings me to something I must tell you, Herr Koenig."

"Oh?"

"Eva, one of the maids, reports that she observed a man leaving your room this morning while you were out. She says he looked very suspicious."

"Oh?"

"She was taking fresh linens to Number Ten, and as she topped the stairs she saw the man letting himself out of your room."

"Did she describe him?"

"Large. Dark. Black turtleneck sweater. Gray slacks."

"Why did she think he looked suspicious?"

"His manner. She said he looked like a burglar on TV." She smiled a kind of apology. "I ask all my help to watch for things that might annoy the guests. Eva is the most observant, but also the most imaginative."

"Good for Eva. Put ten per cent on my bill for her, will you, please?"

"Certainly. And I'm sorry if you have indeed been burgled. I—"

"I appreciate your telling me. I'll look into it."

As she turned to move on, he said, "By the way, any word on Rollo yet?"

The peculiar, pained look flickered across her seamed face. "We've seen nothing of him."

"He'll turn up." He hated himself for such lies.

"Yes. Well, good evening."

He went directly to his room and began a systematic search.

Since he had brought nothing of value with him, it was reasonable to expect that his visitor had not stolen anything. But it was quite possible that he'd left something, and it was this potential that preoccupied Wagner.

Carefully, from corner to corner, wall to wall, phone to TV set, he examined the room and its furnishings, and finding nothing, he focused on his personal effects. Shirts, ties, socks, underwear, shaving gear—each was moved with slow care from his suitcase, or the bureau drawer, and felt and turned and held up to the light, rubbed, tapped, sniffed, listened to. He even pressed all the toothpaste from its tube and disassembled the stick deodorant, washing the combined goos down the bathroom drain.

He had washed his hands and was drying them when the thought struck him. Returning the towel to its rack, he went to his hands and knees and, with his pen flash, ran light under the hopper lid.

It was there.

A pink capsule.

Set precisely, so that it would trigger with the lifting of the lid and then, after releasing its gas, fall into the water, where it would dissolve in less than two minutes.

With great delicacy, he used the tip of his pencil to reset the safety loop over the gelatin spring. Then, lifting the seat, he flipped the capsule into the bowl and watched as it melted into an impotent pink stain, which ultimately disappeared in the innocent pool. He flushed the john and returned to the sitting room, and he realized his hands were shaking.

He sat in the easy chair and turned off the lamp and stared out at the starlit mountains.

A large, dark man.

Who?

And working for whom?

Who wanted him dead?

Ankhanov? Gregori? Groot? Pohl? Morfey? Pomeraine? Trille? Lincke? Kahn? Mahlmann? Gurney? One of Ziggi's friends? One of Rollo's friends? Irma la Douce? Betty Boop? Mickey Mouse?

Or somebody he hadn't even met yet?

Like God, maybe.

He dozed, waiting for the phone to ring. And the doze deepened and became sleep.

He awoke at eleven o'clock, heavy with the conviction that something had gone wrong and he would not be hearing from Rudi Kulka. He sat in the dark for a time, thinking about this, and worrying.

There was a tapping, and he went to the door.

"Rudi. I was getting worried about you. All this time and no call."

Kulka crossed the room and dropped into the easy chair. He loosened his tie, opened his shirt collar, kicked off his shoes, and said, "Cognac will do."

"I only have some whiskey—"

"That's what I said: whiskey will do."

Wagner snapped the cap on the Black Label he kept in the bureau and poured doses into the pair of sparkling glasses presumably provided by the observant Eva. "Shall I send for some ice?"

"Ice in whiskey? Don't be gauche."

"Cheers."

Kulka drained his glass in a gulp. "Ah," he breathed, "that awoke the one testicle. Now for the other."

Wagner poured him another drink, saying, "What's going on?"

"You first," Kulka said. "You look like yesterday's mashed potatoes. Why?"

"Somebody tried to kill me yesterday. Also today."

"So what's new about that?"

166

"I'm too near retirement to get killed. It would screw up my plans."

"What kind of tries were they?"

"A meat-cleaver attack. Tonight somebody left me a pink panther. Under the hopper lid."

"Aha. So that when you, being a grown-up lad, went to wee-wee, you'd lift the lid and be squirted with an instant heart attack, eh?"

"And the evidence would roll into the water and dissolve."

"The perfect crime. Ta-da."

"It's too perfect. It shows that somebody in the trade is trying to do me in."

"Gustav Kahn, maybe?"

"No. He's not the type. He's a cheap hood. Favors cleavers, is my guess."

Kulka nodded and downed his second Scotch. "Well, pink-panther piss is a bit sophisticated for a hood, to be sure."

"Not only sophisticated. Almost impossible to get. Our people ration those gas capsules as if they were moon rocks. And you have to be a Grade Ten in the Soviet service even to look at its label."

"Mm."

Wagner sat down on the divan and put his elbows on his knees. "All right," he said, "so why are you here? Why no phone call?"

"No time to call, really. I picked up your boy Kahn as billed. He arrived at the Golden Thigh at 1910 hours. Mean-looking bastard."

"Where were you? Inside the place or outside?"

"Outside. I wanted to see where he parked. Then I followed him in. And he went directly to the office at the rear of the place."

"Did he speak to anyone on the way?"

"He traded nods with one of the bartenders, that's all."

"What happened then?"

"The same bartender drifted back to the office and went in and closed the door. Seven minutes later, Kahn came out and went to his car."

"Did you see the bartender after that?"

"No. I was too busy keeping an eye on Kahn. Why?"

"Curious, that's all. Where did Kahn go then? Kitzbühel?"

"No. Here."

"What do you mean?"

"He's here now. He drove straight from Munich to the parking lot outside this haunted house."

"Where here? I mean—"

"I don't know. I lost him. I couldn't exactly clutch his coattail when he came in, you know. When I entered the lobby he had disappeared. He's here, but I don't know where here, if you follow me."

"The registration book—"

"No entry since six. We arrived at ten. That means he's visiting somebody."

"Well, now. That's an interesting development. Where's his car?"

"In the parking area beside the three pines. Blue Audi."

"Will you—"

"Continue the tail? Sure. If he drives away from here, I'll be behind."

"Good. Meanwhile, I'll snoop around the inn."

"I have here another meanwhile," Rudi said, producing an envelope. "The rundown on Messrs. Kahn and Stoeckler and Fräulein Mahlmann. As well as the Audi and the Mercedes. The Audi is registered in Lotte Mahlmann's name. The Mercedes, rented from Hertz by a gentleman named Meyer. Who, in turn, answers to the description of your friend and mine, Akim Ri."

25

Groot was halfway through the *Times* crossword puzzle when she burst through the door in her Loretta Young way: part march, part swirl.

"Miss Randall—"

"Well, aren't you going to invite me to sit down?"

"Of course. I'm simply surprised." He was conscious of his dishevelment, his stockinged feet.

She eased into a chair and smiled. "You make it sound obscene."

"I'm sorry. I mean—I didn't—"

"Oh, come off it, Groot. I'm here on business. Is that all you've got to do with your time? Crosswords?"

He folded the newspaper and placed it on the coffee table. "It helps me think. I do crosswords when I must deal with a problem. And it helps me with my English, too."

"Your English is faultless, you old fraud."

"Only because I work hard at it, Miss Randall. It's not my native tongue, so I must continually practice. As if it were a musical skill. And—"

"Is my brother safe?"

Her habit of breaking in with a new train of thought was as disconcerting today as it had been through the years. He'd never get used to it. "Yes. As safe as anyone ever is in this world."

"We've got to reelect him, you know."

"You mustn't fret over it. He'll be reelected."

"Will you vote for him, Groot?"

"You know I will."

"We simply can't risk having that Goodman creep deny us the election." She was having one of her anxious spells, he saw.

"Well, that's what we're working for. I mean, the whole idea—"

"Robert Goodman's a fascist. A Hitler. If we get him for President, we'll be at war with the Soviets within a month."

He wondered what bizarre twist of her ambition had brought Amy Randall to his room. As a mere deputy director of an agency, he was not privy to much of what transpired in the White House ambience. He knew, and accepted stoically, the truth: Amy Randall had always used him as if he were an appliance, to be turned on or off to suit the needs of her various palace intrigues. Still, for him, she represented the only game in town, and what she needed right now was a little fatherly assurance. Reassurance.

"Well, Miss Randall, it seems to me that your brother has things sufficiently well in hand. The only real political hazard, as I see it, is that the Goodman people learn of the, ah, vulnerability of the Vice President as a running mate—"

She humphed. "Thank God *we* learned of it. My brother has taken O'Toole out of the campaign and put him in a closet."

"Closet?"

"We've taken O'Toole from the hospital and installed him at Camp David. He's ostensibly overseeing the nation's business while my brother is in Europe. In reality, he continues to dry out, beyond the range of unfriendly eyes. The problem is to keep the drunken fool hidden until after the election. Then we'll dump him. For reasons of health. Et cetera, et cetera."

Groot's curiosity couldn't be held in. "I know this is a presumptuous question, but has your brother decided whom to appoint in Mr. O'Toole's place? After the election?"

She gave him a conspiratorial wink. "Me."

"Oh?" Groot concentrated on masking his surprise.

"How do you like them apples? The President appoints his own sister to be Veep. Talk about nepotism, eh?" She laughed, seeming to be genuinely delighted over the arrogance of this idea.

"Such an appointment must be confirmed by a majority of both the House and the Senate. Do you think you can win such confirmation, Miss Randall?"

"You bet your bippy I do. I'm a professional politician whose social and fiscal caution neatly balances my brother's liberalism. I've been identified with the party since the beginning of my career. I've spent more time pushing legislation on Capitol Hill and have collected more IOU's there than anybody else in the Administration. Moreover, the media like me, there are Amy Randall fan clubs in the boonies, and our party is in the overwhelming majority in both houses. To top it all off, there's a hellish screaming for more than lip-service recognition of women in the government."

"Still—"

"Jack Kennedy appointed Bobby as attorney general."

"Well, yes, but—"

"But what? Attorney general is a lot more sensitive than Veep. Everybody knows that the Veep is only a ceremonial dummy."

Groot wondered privately how a whirring gear like Amy Randall could—even for a moment—contemplate a post in which she'd be no more than a ceremonial dummy.

Almost as if she'd heard his thought, she laughed again. "Next stop for Amy, Groot-baby, is the presidency four years hence."

He smiled, despite himself, at her incredible gall. "I see. I'm beginning to fully understand your determination to bring about your brother's reelection. It would be easier to be nominated and elected from a base established in the vice presidency."

"Atta boy, Groot. You're not as dumb as you look. It'll shift the public's impression of me into higher gear. They'll begin to see me as an executive, not as a mere member of Congress."

"Still, Miss Randall, there are powerful forces moving in the United States. I mean, I admire your ambition and audacity—I always have—but for all of the weight of your majority, there's a counterbalancing conservatism that will take a lot of handling. As Mr. Goodman never tires of pointing out, there are many Americans who see your brother and his party as appeasers, as surrendering American interests and initiative to the Soviets. There are some who even suspect his loyalty to the nation. Charges like that, concentrated by the fury of a Robert Goodman, can pose a difficult problem that takes more than luck and sentiment and a congressional majority to subdue for long."

She made a face. "You're being a pedantic bore, Groot. Don't lecture me on politics."

"I didn't intend to lecture. I—"

"What did you think of my advance party meeting?"

"It was crowded. I'll give it that."

"You mean there were too many there?"

"I think there were."

"Explain."

"I think that Frank Kevin, as chief of the Secret Service White House detail, and I, as special security ops, CIA, were the only Americans you really needed there. It was proper to have Interpol, the German police and their antiterrorist detachment represented, to be sure, but General Dirk and delegates from our Army and Air Force and the German military were considerably superfluous. And, of course, a member of the press in attendance was, in my opinion, a serious mistake."

"Ellie? Ellie's almost family. She won't write a scratch unless I permit her to. Besides, her morale needs boosting, and I'm her friend, and I'm thinking of having her do a book on me or something and she has to know how I look and talk in meetings and things. Ellie's all right."

Groot had the feeling she was marking time, groping for a way to get at the real reason for her visit. He considered the suspicion, decided it was probably so, and so waited patiently for her move. It wasn't long in coming.

She recrossed her tidy legs, sank back in the chair, and gave him a level-eyed examination. "If I were President," she murmured, "and if you were the director of the CIA, what foreign developments would you tell me to look out for? In the near future, I mean?"

So, Groot thought, *she's as serious as that. My God, this woman is really too much.*

He sat tentatively on the edge of the bed and returned her stare, vowing he wouldn't be the one to break it.

"Oil," he said. "Energy in total, but oil in specific. Its importance can't possibly be emphasized strongly enough. There's a curious stand-off in international power politics right now. The Soviets have oil, but not enough for major military action. And we have oil, but not enough for major military action. They're maneuvering for additional sources, we're working desperately to bring our oil shale and liquefied coal to levels that will make us self-sufficient. Whoever comes in first in the oil race picks up the marbles."

"Well," she reminded, "all we have to do is keep them docile for three or four years. We'll have our self-sufficiency by then."

Groot shook his head. "You're minimizing the discovery of massive oil deposits in the Adriatic off Lastovo. Ever since Tito, the Soviets have yearned to reclaim Jugoslavia as a portal to the Mediterranean. And now that the Jugoslavs are about to outpump the Arabs, a return to the area to the Kremlin fold is absolutely fundamental, in Moscow's eyes."

"You expect this to happen soon?"

"As soon as we've left NATO. Then, if neo-Stalinist subversion of the Belgrade government won't do it, Soviet military invasion via Hungary is inevitable."

She cleared her throat. "What should we do to forestall such a move by the Soviets?"

"Pray."

"I'm serious, Groot." She broke off the stare, sending a glance out the window at the clammy night.

"So am I, Miss Randall. The world is a house of cards. With our nation virtually defanged—both militarily and in terms of alliances—and with a Federal government absolutely frozen by special-interest dissensions, with Europe neutralized and China preoccupied with enormous internal turbulence, a suddenly oil-rich Soviet would have the world to itself. It'll take a miracle, the kind the religionists pray for, if the Soviets are to be deterred from taking over first Jugoslavia and its new oil fields and, soon after, all the oil fields in the Mideast—from Kirkuk to the Perisan Gulf. In the end, they will take de facto control of the oil in Castroite Mexico as well as the stupendous offshore oil deposits near Saigon, which, as we know, were the real reason, the secret reason, for the war in Viet Nam and Cambodia. And then the U.S. will be all alone and lonely in its relatively puny self-sufficiency."

"What's our current NATO troop status?"

"Units have begun withdrawal preparations. They're still in line and combat-capable, of course, but the logistical activities have been initiated. By March, there will be no more than a few U.S. housekeeping and clean-up detachments in all of Europe."

Her gaze returned from its study of the city beyond the window and locked onto his again. "How does the Kremlin look at all this?"

"From Agency analyses computered just last week—studies based on data gathered in the past two months—it's apparent that the Kremlin attitude is to wait quietly at this time. Why should they make any moves, when the Americans are doing to themselves what the Soviets failed to accomplish in almost four decades of cold war?"

"Has the President been fully briefed on this analysis?"

"The director tells me he has. As have the JCS, the Cabinet, and the NSC. In secret session."

"What are the private reactions of the Cabinet members?"

"Inscrutable, according to the word I get. After all, they're your brother's yes-men, so to speak. And your brothers stands for détente, disarmament, and discretion."

"You're sounding Agnewesque, Groot," she said, dour.

"Whatever I sound like, Miss Randall, the fact remains: our nation has begun its long night of enforced isolation. The Soviets, by controlling most of the world's land and sea masses and all the major oil deposits, will become the greatest power the world has ever seen. The United States will become another Poland—or maybe England—hanging like a market basket on the Kremlin's arm."

She stood up and went to the window and watched the traffic below, and he saw again how very handsome and commanding she could appear to be. What a strange combination of hardness and softness, he mused.

Her question was quiet, almost offhand:

"Did you know that the Navy's Task Force twelve has been ordered to take up station in the Arabian Sea?"

He gave her a quick glance, feeling an electricity in him. "The Indian Ocean unit? It's being moved?"

"Mm. Senator Logue told me at dinner."

"Why?" He leaned forward. "Why was the task force repositioned? Did the senator say?"

She shrugged. "I confess we'd been talking about you. The senator despises you, you know, and I was more or less defending you—as a person, I mean—and one thing led to another. He said you and your slimy Agency probably had instigated the Navy's move as a means to threaten the Arabs for their punitive oil policies."

"I see. Exactly where is the task force to be located?"

"On patrol off Muscat and Oman. Near the mouth of the Persian Gulf."

"Only a thousand air miles from every important oil

field in the Middle East," Groot said thoughtfully. "Did the President initiate the relocation?"

"No. But he approved it. General Dirk, as chairman of the Joint Chiefs, thought the CNO ought to make the change as a tactical training exercise, as I understand it."

"But, my God, a move like that can be misread as a belligerent act in every capital in the world. Moscow, especially. General Dirk is an idiot."

She nodded. "My brother plans to fire him after the election."

"The damage is already done, I'm afraid. General Dirk and his admiral may be just playing sand-table games, but a move like that should have been forbidden summarily by the White House."

"My brother thought it might defuse some of Robert Goodman's campaign rhetoric."

"Your brother should have consulted you first, Miss Randall."

"Did you hear my Houston comment, Groot?" She had changed the subject again, and, as usual, Groot overtly made the change with her while inwardly continuing his effort to digest this little bombshell.

"The one in which you called your brother a nincompoop?"

"Yes."

"I don't think there's a soul on earth who hasn't heard about that by now." *(What in God's name had Dirk been thinking? Or drinking?)*

"What did you think of it?"

"What's to think, Miss Randall? I think your brother's a nincompoop, too, when it comes to U.S.-Soviet relations."

"You agreed with my comment, then?"

"Of course."

"Why?"

"The United States means a great deal to me, Miss Randall. It's grossly imperfect, to be sure. But it's the world's only true haven for those like me—those who've been persecuted by the calculated tyrannies of govern-

176

ments. I hate to see it drifting into the shadow this way. Happily, I'll be dead by the time our light finally winks out, so to speak. Even if I have to arrange it myself, I'll be dead. But it's a sad thing to watch in the meantime. I've been very fond of America. Very fond indeed." He realized that, to her, he must sound dreadfully Victorian.

She did not look at him. "What should we do, then? Take on the Soviets? Attack?"

"Oh, heavens, no. War would only destroy everything."

"You subscribe to 'better Red than dead,' eh?"

"Not really. I subscribe to the idea that talking is better than fighting, that's all. I've seen what fighting does."

"How long would you give us to turn things around? I mean, do you think we could keep the Soviets in a kind of Mexican standoff for the next four years?"

"Well—" *(Jesus God. We may not have four weeks if the Soviets misread the Task Force Twelve repositioning.)*

"Long enough for me to become President?"

"It's anybody's guess. But we have no alternative but to try."

"Would you support me as President?"

"If I support you now, I'd support you then."

She turned and gave him a cool stare. "If this little thing of ours works and my brother is reelected as planned, you're the next CIA director. You know that, don't you?"

"I—"

"And if I succeed my brother as President, I'll need a Secretary of State. So you see, Groot, you have all kinds of incentive."

"I don't know what to say, Miss Randall."

She crossed the room to the door. "Then don't say anything. Just do. Make things work. And the first thing is this Munich thing. And above all, don't let my brother get hurt."

With her hand on the knob, she glanced back at him and added, "With luck, you and I might just save the good ole US of A from itself."

She closed the door behind her, and he stood, listening to the traffic sounds.

October 15

"Hello?"

"Herr Wismer?"

"Speaking."

"There's sunshine on the bay."

"What is it, Groot?"

"The Navy's Task Force Twelve—"

"Don't worry. It's no problem. Yet."

"Oh. Well, then—"

"It was a stupid move, of course. A training exercise in such controversial waters. Stupid."

"I simply wanted to be sure there's no confusion over it."

"I appreciate your calling."

"Something bothers me terribly about all this. I have a strong feeling."

"Feeling?"

"A hunch. Intuition. Something. But I have this feeling that I'm missing something."

"Well, I hope you aren't, my friend. A very great deal is riding on our ability to keep this affair rigidly under control. And with Rattner's early demise, we lost a good bit of control, I fear."

"Yes. That was a bad break. I'm still chasing that one."

"I know. That's among the top priorities, to answer that one."

"I'm counting on Wagner."

"I hope he lives up to your expectations."

"I do, too."

"So, then. Anything else?"

"Not now. I wanted simply to check you out on this thing about the Navy."

"I'm glad you did. Good-bye, Groot."

"Good-bye, Herr Wismer."

26

The Edelweiss, while large and contemporary enough to accommodate the functions of a residential hotel, was built in the general configuration of the classic Tyrolean "Einhaus"—so called because, in its original form, such a structure combined the farmer's living quarters and animal barns under a single roof. The hotel's kitchen and service areas were at the rear of the ground floor, where the cows would have been, and at this time of night the kitchen was a forest of gleaming aluminum and copper whose silence was broken only by the blooping of a coffee percolator. A man with a walrus moustache and a chef's cap was perched on a stool, reading a newspaper. He looked up when Wagner peered through the door.

"*Abend*," Wagner said.

"Kitchen's closed, except for room-service snacks."

"I'm not hungry. I'm just a nosy guest, poking around."

The man rattled his paper and said, "As you can see, there's not much action here right now."

"Have you been with the inn very long?" Wagner, leaning against the door jamb, made the question sound amiable.

"Since the beginning. Close to ten years, all told."

"Must be a good place to work if you've been here that long."

"It's all right."

Wagner could see that the man was in no mood for chitchat, so he decided to move on. "Tell me," he said, "where would I find the maids' quarters?"

The moustache twitched and the man gave Wagner a suspicious examination. "The maids aren't supposed to socialize with the guests."

"I don't want to socialize. I want to find a room maid named Eva to tip her for taking care of something in my absence today."

"Well, you'd better check with the front office. Not with Frau Lindl, though. She's not available. But Sara Kloman, her assistant, will handle things."

"Frau Lindl is out this evening?"

"No. Haven't you heard?" The man looked doleful.

"Heard what?"

"The police came to see her after dinner. Her son was killed in a highway accident. She's taking it pretty hard. Don't ask me why. Rollo was a rotten swine who never did a thing for her."

"Rollo was her son?"

The man shifted on the stool and folded his newspaper. "Swine."

"Why do you call him that?"

"The way he treated the old lady. She was always running around after him, wringing her hands, worrying about his slightest whim. And all he ever did was spit in her eye. He'd been mine. I'd have kicked his ass all the way to Norway."

"I'm sorry for Frau Lindl, though. She seems quite nice."

"Nice? They don't come any better. I could never understand how she could have a son as mean as Rollo."

"How come he had a different last name? Stoeckler, or whatever."

"He just called himself that. To get the old lady's goat.

182

The family name is hyphenated. Stoeckler-Lindl."

"Well, as I say: it's too bad."

The man humphed and adjusted the heat under the percolater. He glanced at Wagner and said, "Coffee?"

"No thanks. I've got to find that girl, Eva."

"Eva Whitney. She's in the employee chalet. Down the lane from the parking lot. Turn left and up the rise. It has blue shutters."

"Whitney, eh? English?"

"No. American. Cute little kid. Works hard, too."

"Well, it's been nice talking with you. My name's Koenig."

"Schultheis. I'm the cook."

Several girls and a young man were giggling by the door of the employee chalet, oblivious of the majesty of the night. They became quiet and respectful while he asked about Eva Whitney, but after one of the girls had gone to fetch her, the group resumed its gossiping, relegating him at once to the other side of the gulf that separates the hotel guest from those who serve him.

She came out of the place, a cardigan over her shoulders.

"May I help you, sir?" Her German was schoolish, but her voice was friendly and soft.

"I'd like to speak to you privately for a moment, Miss Whitney," he said in English. "I'm Koenig, in Room eighteen."

"Well, certainly," she said, and he sensed her surprise at his American inflections. "But—"

"Walk with me on the path. I'll only keep you a moment."

"All right."

The group on the bench nodded pleasantly as they went by, and he knew that, even if his intentions had been misread as a sortie of a middle-aged rake among the help, there would be no judgments passed. It was one of the commendable traits of the New Generation (or whatever it was called these days), this ability to love and let love.

183

They stopped under one of the lanterns that lighted the path and it occurred to him once again how easily misconceptions can form. From Frau Lindl's description of her as one of the "more imaginative" maids who'd seen his intruder as "a burglar on TV," and from the cook's reference to her as "a cute little kid," he'd expected Eva Whitney to be a giddy child—anything but a tallish, serious-faced young woman in her late twenties. She wore her dark hair short, with easy curls at the side, and her eyes were level and cool and of an indeterminate color.

"I want to thank you for reporting my burglar," he said, sparring.

"I hope nothing was taken."

He noted her air of composure, and he guessed that she was waiting for a fuller explanation.

"Everything's fine," he said.

"It's a rotten thing, stealing," she said, and there was real annoyance in her voice, as if she could be as put out by a petty crime against him as she could be by one against herself.

"Well, my caller was the one who was cheated. All that risk, just to find that my other shirt is frayed and my cuff links are plastic."

She smiled, and he was glad she had heard the amusement in his self-deprecation. As a maid, she'd seen firsthand that he had very little to lure a thief, and as a woman she'd appreciated his ability to joke about it. He studied her with new interest.

"He must have been an amateur," she said evenly. "He was so obvious about everything. Furtive, like."

"That's what I wanted to talk to you about. Would you describe him for me?" He added, "I know you told Frau Lindl, but she was sort of vague about it all—"

"Frau Lindl has had a lot on her mind lately. That son of hers has been driving her crackers."

"There don't seem to be too many people who are upset about Rollo's, ah, untimely passing," he said neutrally.

She crossed her arms, hugging the sweater closer in the night chill, and something about her suggested the schoolteacher.

"He wasn't my cup of tea," she said. "But as for your caller, Mr. Koenig: he was tall, heavy in the shoulders. His face was rather long, and he had a full moustache. Black hair, cut medium. Wore a black turtleneck and gray slacks, pull-on shoes with buckles."

Wagner humphed. "You'd make a good cop, Miss Whitney."

"I'm too thin-skinned for that. I'm a schoolteacher. Or was, that is. And I have this habit of watching people closely. Especially kids. You'd be surprised what you learn when you watch people—really watch them."

"You're not teaching now?"

"There aren't any teaching jobs anymore. Stateside, anyway."

"So what are you doing in Austria?"

"I was engaged to the headmaster of a Christian mission school near Kufstein. It didn't work out. So I'm dangling here temporarily, like a diver ascending. I want to surface in Colorado Springs without getting the bends."

"That's your home—Colorado Springs?"

"No. My parents left me a piece of land and a house in the high country west of there. Not much of a place. But beautiful. I'll go there and write little books you'll never hear of."

"Fiction?"

"No. Theological commentaries."

"You're religious?"

"Not really. I'm simply fascinated by the New Testament. It's the story of the only man in the world who could ever be trusted. Completely trusted."

"Well, it's a bit much for me. I could never get with the Jesus thing. Sunday school is not my scene." After a pause, he said, "But back to my caller: was there anything about his face you remember? Features, complexion, so on—"

She shrugged, a small movement of a shoulder. "He had a longish nose, I think. But he was wearing tinted glasses, so I couldn't really see his eyes. His mouth seemed to be wide. Hard to tell, with the mustache and all."

"What did he do? I mean, you saw him leave my room. But how did he leave?"

"He kind of backed out, you know? Pulled the door closed, turned the knob as if trying it out. Then he saw me at the top of the stairs with the linen, and he came quickly to the stairs, brushed past me, and went down to the lobby."

"Anything else?"

"I'm not sure. But—"

"But what, Miss Whitney?"

"It might have been a trick of the light, or maybe it was just my imagination, but I had the impression that his moustache didn't match."

"Match?"

"Mm. His hair was quite dark. Black, even. But I had the impression his mustache was a lighter hue, sort of."

Wagner thought about that for a moment. "Well," he said finally, "that isn't so unusual. Many men have beards that are lighter—redder—than their hair."

"I wouldn't know."

He sensed she was becoming bored by the whole affair, and so he took her elbow and said, "I'll walk you back. It's cold. And I've kept you too long."

"No need for you to come along. I'll be fine."

"By the way, Miss Whitney, there's one other thing." He glanced at her. "Have you ever served a hotel guest by the name of Kahn? Gustav Kahn, of Kitzbühel?"

Her serious eyes pondered the name. "No," she said slowly, "I don't believe so. We don't get many guests from nearby places."

"A visitor of that name, maybe?"

She stared directly at him. "Wait. That name—"

"You've heard it?"

"Yes. I have. But—oh. I have it now."

He felt an excitement.

"There was a phone call," she said. "I was on waitress duty that day. Last week, it was. I was spelling off Gerta Klein. There was a call for Mr. Gurney, and Sara Kloman was on the desk, and I was passing through the lobby, and she said to tell Mr. Gurney, who was in the dining room. Mr. Gurney told me he wasn't taking any calls, and so I relayed the message to Sara, and she told the caller. He must have been very angry, because Sara got quite red, you know, and she said I should tell Mr. Gurney that Gustav Kahn was calling. I told Mr. Gurney, and he got up and went very quickly to the phone."

"I see," Wagner said, the feeling racing in him now. "You've been a big help. A very big help, indeed."

"You're welcome, Mr. Koenig."

She shook his hand, formal and somber in the European manner, as if she were suddenly trying to deny her revelations of American provincialism. To picture one's self as a Bible expositer recovering from a broken romance in the Austrian Alps was romantic, poignant; to admit to being a schoolteacher working as a maid until she could get together enough scratch for a trip back to Colorado was drabsville. It was certain that, for all her careful speech and pensive ways, there was nothing dull or tedious about this young woman, and it pleased him that she seemed annoyed at herself for having possibly given him the impression that she was a klutz.

It meant that she cared what he thought.

And this pleased him.

For a reason he couldn't name.

27

It was a rotten morning, with wind humming in the windows and rain lashing the panes. Groot had breakfasted in his room, using the time to ponder the mystery of who had killed Ziggi Rattner and his employees. Worrisome thing, that. Then, after taking a call from the Director in Washington, who was openly upset about the Task Force 12 thing, he'd taken a cab to the Police Building and the meeting on the assassination threat.

The conference room was already packed, and as he took his chair across the table from Frank Kevin, he could see that the Secret Service man was also very put out. Kevin's public inscrutability as the White House detail chief did not extend to his intramural relationships, and Groot knew it must have been particularly galling to Kevin to learn of a serious plot against the President, not from his own daisy chain but from that old bogey, the CIA. *Well, screw the son of a bitch,* Groot grumped inwardly. *Let him puff and blow for a change.*

Kevin, as the man most responsible, was chairman, and he called the meeting to order with an irritable tapping of his pencil on the glass tabletop. When the room had stilled, he considered Groot directly for the first time.

"Well, Mr. Groot," Kevin said with no nod toward diplomacy, "it's your meeting. Will you fill us in, please?"

Groot let his eyes travel around the table, taking a full thirty seconds to allow a little drama to build. He recognized most of the faces, of course, but it really didn't matter who was on hand. The secret was out now, and irretrievable.

"Good morning, ladies and gentlemen," he said, sounding the properly somber tone. "The matter is serious, and I won't take too much of your time. Actually, there's precious little information to share with you."

He paused to light a cigarette, a business that would be guaranteed to infuriate Kevin.

"As you all know by now," he said through a cloud of smoke, "the CIA has—through diligent exploitation of the most scanty of leads—" (it was great to promote again, even if from a phony base) "uncovered a plot to kill President Randall."

He waited for the stir to subside and then went on: "On October *five*, one of our field agents, working on a routine military counterintelligence project in the Ruhr, came across information that hinted at a presidential assassination. I received his memo to the OIC as a matter of course because I'm charged within the Agency to keep the Director apprised of international terrorist plots having domestic implications."

Kevin broke in morosely. "Why didn't you tip us off?"

"Because," Groot answered smoothly, "we get many reports of this type. There isn't a day that goes by in which we don't pick up whispers of some kind of threat against the President—a fact you are most familiar with, Mr. Kevin. I gave this report more than the usual attention, however, because of two factors: first, the field agent is one of our best, and therefore unlikely to be cluttering his memos with unevaluated crank stuff; second, the informant was demonstrably not a crank or a malcontent—he was a highly affluent and influential member of the German underworld who had already, on an earlier counterintelligence affair, proved his reliability as an information source."

"All the more reason to tip me off," Kevin grated.

"The Secret Service," Groot said, his gaze sweeping the others, too, "as well as all you ladies and gentlemen of other police and security agencies, were tipped as soon as I had a shred of actionable information. I now have that shred, and we are now meeting to decide what to do with it."

"All right," Kevin snapped, "so let's get with it."

Groot pulled a large glass ashtray to him and ground out the cigarette, satisfied that it had served its purpose. He opened his briefcase and withdrew a file folder, which he placed on the table.

"Very well, then," he said. "Our informant was Siegfried Rattner, owner and operator of the Golden Thigh, a Munich nightclub. Rattner's background is quite varied, and I can read it to you in detail, if you'd like." He tapped the folder with his forefinger.

Hans Trille, representing the Bundespolizei, shook his head and glanced at the others with an eyebrow raised in question. "I don't think that will be necessary, do you? Such detail, always available through our Central Information Index, is secondary in importance at this meeting, wouldn't you say?"

All the heads nodded agreement, and Trille regarded Groot with an amiable squint. "Won't you go on, please, Mr. Groot?"

"Rattner told our agent merely that he had knowledge of a plot, which he'd sell to the CIA. I—"

Colonel Dreher, of All-Service MPD, broke in: "Why the CIA, for hell's sake?"

"Rattner was turning to a familiar face. He had knowledge he felt to be worth considerable money. He was not about to trust just any agency. He wanted to work, on a direct basis, with the field agent, whom he knew, as I say, from a previous case."

"So what's the plot, please?" Kevin said with exaggerated politeness.

"To date, here's all we know: Akim Ri, a professional assassin with a number of confirmed offenses on his record, has arrived in Germany. He has been seen by police in widely separated points within a matter of hours: Frankfurt one day, Munich the next, and so on. It was when I learned of this I decided we had actionable info. The very presence of Akim Ri is prima facie evidence of trouble. Ri rarely risks being seen; when he is, he must be assumed to be closing in, because, even for a skilled technician such as Ri, you can't set up for a target without increasing your risks of being spotted. So we must assume an assassination is imminent. We have the tip of a reliable informant and the confirmed presence of an infamous rifleman."

"I thought Ri had been killed," Sir Allen of the Yard said. "Plane crash or some ruddy accident somewhere."

"We believe that to be a false report, floated by Ri and his handlers to lull us." Groot nodded at Trille. "Yes?"

"In that connection," Trille asked around his pipe stem, "why would Ri be sent against the President? What is to be gained by Mr. Randall's death in a foreign land?"

Ah, Groot thought, the Big Casino. The Question. It wasn't at all surprising that it came from the German state police, one of the most efficient and intelligent law enforcement agencies to be found anywhere. They made their mistakes, to be sure, as any organization will; but they made fewer mistakes than most, and they thought big, aggressively, imaginatively, and legally. The others in the room were locked in by their various myopias (with the exception, perhaps, of the Yard people). The others were cops first, thinkers second, ready to ponder the whereabouts of Akim Ri at the expense of the larger, more significant question as to why he'd been sent in the first place. Mere cops would fall happily to the problem of solving a crime from the bottom; true enforcement officers like Trille thought beyond the solution and arrest, and, starting at the top, asked why was the crime contemplated in the first place—recognizing that the larger question of Why, fully answered, would almost always lead to the Who.

He thought momentarily of Wagner, the perfect cop, and he thought of himself, the thinker, and he saw the precise personification of the contrast. He wanted to smile, but he didn't, of course.

"A good question," he said, returning Trille's serious stare. "It's the question which preoccupies us all, I'm sure. Unfortunately, my agent has not come up with any concrete clues as yet."

"How about less concrete ones?" Trille murmured.

"Our agent is, this very day, pursuing a heavy lead. If it develops into something, we'll brief you all at once. At the moment, all I can say is that the motivation appears to be political. By that, I mean above and beyond mere indiscriminate, shotgun terrorism of the kind we're all so familiar with."

O'Shea of the FBI leaned forward, his face pale. "You mean domestic U.S. politics?"

Groot waved a minimizing hand. "I can't say anything of the kind, Mr. O'Shea. All I can say is that our agent currently believes that the spring source of this plot lies in the United States, in American politics, not in Europe."

There was a moment of thought, a brittle silence in which the assembled international bureaucrats weighed the momentous implications. Even the most stolid and unread among them recognized that the President's most implacable political enemy was Robert Goodman. Without even mentioning his name, Groot had just inferentially laid a heinous scheme for murder at the feet of an American zealot who had yet to run for any elective office, anywhere.

"Who is your agent?" O'Shea said tautly. "Can we talk with him?"

"I'm afraid not. He's deep under cover. To call him out could risk our whole house of cards," Groot said calmly.

"Has he filed memorandum reports? Agent's field reports? Is there anything we can read?"

Groot motioned to the girl from Audio-Visual, who had been waiting in the far corner.

"Miss Partridge, are the tapes ready?"

"Yes, sir."

Groot told the assembly, "I have several cassettes, sent to me by our undercover agent. They are simply progess reports, and include none of the speculative material on the plot's political overtones, which have been relayed to me by telephone—direct. These tapes are nuts and bolts, ladies and gentlemen, but I'll be glad to run them if you think they might be helpful."

There was a general murmuring that signified a wish to hear the tapes, so Groot nodded at Miss Partridge and the cassette player hissed, then began to emit Wagner's tired baritone, electronically altered into a deep bass.

The tapes, like Wagner's voice, were carefully edited, of course, and so the group heard only—in tedious detail—about the meetings with Ziggi; the appearances of Akim Ri; the exploitation of Lincke, the bartender; parts of Rollo's attempt to kill Wagner; the frustrations of working without the aid of bugging gear; the descriptions of the Olympiàturm as the logical site for a shooting attempt. The group did not hear Wagner tell of his bafflement over Ellie Pomeraine, his doubts about Gurney, his interrogation by Trille, his concern over the brown Volvo, or, of course, the surveillance of Kahn and Mahlmann.

When the tapes had played through, Kevin said, "Hell, there's a lot of talking on those, but no hard info you haven't already given us. I think we ought to talk to the agent. I think we ought to eyeball him."

Groot said, "I recommend going very carefully, Mr. Kevin. The situation is very awkward for our agent. He could be seriously endangered if he were seen associating with known enforcement people."

"What's all the frigging mystery?" O'Shea said hotly. "You CIA bastards are always so frigging obtuse—"

"Please, Mr. O'Shea, we have ladies present."

O'Shea reddened and nodded an apology to Irmgard Regel, of Interpol, and Mary Thompson, of the U.S. Embassy security detail. Their expressions, deadpan, remained unchanged.

"I don't mean to be obtuse," Groot said in a conciliatory way, "and I assure you that, once Akim Ri has been captured and the case has been resolved, our agent will be readily available for questioning by all of you. Right now, though, he represents the only link we have with the plot, and so we dare not lose him."

"What the hell good will it do to question him after the fact?" O'Shea snorted.

All eyes focused on the outraged FBI man, some in scarcely veiled pity. Everyone but O'Shea could see, apparently, that Akim Ri's capture would be mere preface to the eventual confirmation of the already solidifying notion that Robert Goodman—Buchenwald Bobbie, the Hitler in Brooks Brothers clothing—was probably plotting a coup.

Rage is an emotion to be indulged only sparingly, Groot thought. In the right dosage, it can build roads to the stars; in an overdose, it can kill its host deader than dead. O'Shea had killed himself dead with this group, since he'd revealed a rage that could break harness. Who would want to collaborate with an FBI man whose rage could blind him to the central point of an issue?

He was preparing to answer when Hans Trille bridged the embarrassment with a question. "Can you prove U.S. political involvement? This is most important, you know."

"Not at this point, Herr Trille. In no way. I'm merely reporting that this is the agent's conviction—his sure suspicion, backed by years of experience and as-yet unconfirmed clues. No, there's not the slightest piece of hard evidence. The agent is sure; he's still trying to prove it."

"You'd truly be in a bind if you lost him, eh?"

"Precisely my point, Herr Trille. He must be kept alive at all costs. Even," Groot winked good-naturedly at O'Shea, "at the risk of being obtuse."

Everybody laughed, and O'Shea, trying to retrieve lost face, joined in half-heartedly.

"So then," Groot said, smiling at Kevin, "the ball

194

comes back to you for the thing you do so well: protecting the President. What, Mr. Kevin, can we do to help you?"

Kevin, pleased to find himself in charge of the meeting again, pushed back his chair and went to the blackboard. He began drawing squares and lines and circles, droning on, as he did, of approach routes and intercity linkages and O.P.'s and checkpoints and radio disciplines, helicopter recon and escort, closed-circuit TV surveillance, flank riders, limo escorts, temporary evacuations, building patrols, explosives, sniff-outs by bomb-squad dogs, cordons, alley corks, Kevlar vests, plastic bullet shields, and direction finders. There would be shake-downs of all escort personnel, and nobody would be admitted to the presidential party without passes signed and countersigned by Kevin himself. There would be police atop all buildings along the route of Olympiapark, and all officers, whatever their duties, would be supplied with a photo card of Akim Ri. Units of the West German Army would man weapons carriers and water cannons at all key intersections; U.S. Army armored vehicles would ring the park. The Secret Service would, as usual, ride with and around the presidential party. The President insisted on an open limousine, as everybody knew, but the Chancellor had graciously provided a Mercedes with bullet-proof spoiler windows fore, aft, and on the sides, which made it impossible for a sniper to achieve a clean shot at anyone in the car's rear passenger compartment. Ri may be a hotshot, Kevin purred, but he'd have a cute time shooting curves around those spoilers, by God.

Groot feigned interest in all this, but his mind was busy with the problem of Roger Wagner and what to do with him. And when.

He'd have to keep Wagner going until Wagner could give him clear information as to who had killed Rattner et al.

And then Wagner was done.

When he got back to his hotel room at noon, the phone was ringing. It was Morfey, of Congressional Liaison.

"Where are you, Mr. Morfey?"

"Heidelberg. I drove back last night."

"I see. What can I do for you?"

"I want you to send Wagner up here to see me."

"Well, he's very busy these days. We have a real crisis going, and Wagner's square in the middle of it."

"Tough tit. I want to see him. Have him here by six this evening, hear?"

"I don't know if I can even find him, let alone get him there by that time."

"I'll expect him nonetheless."

"May I ask why you want to see him?"

"No, you may not. Good-bye."

The dial tone sounded and Groot put the phone down. The bastard.

It was precisely the worst possible time for him to indulge his fondness for petty harassment.

28

Rudi's archives contacts had been first-class, Wagner found. The bios on Kahn, Mahlmann, and Rollo were quite thorough, although they contained nothing that would be spectacularly helpful.

Kahn was a War Two type, with the pedigree of a Nazi who loved his work: born in Stuttgart, 1921, son of Alois Kahn, a grocer; Gymnasium in Mannheim; Hitler Jugend section leader, 1935; Adolph Hitler Schule graduate, special class; SS Ordensburgleiter, 1938; military service, 1939–1945, Norway, Denmark, Holland, France; wounded August 1944; instructor, sappers' school, Murnau, November 1944–May 1945; highest rank achieved, Waffen SS Sturmbannführer; seven decorations; released PW Camp no. 4 June 1945; paroled, de-Nazification program; construction worker, Munich, 1946–1953; contractor, Augsburg, 1953–1959; bankrupt, 1959; typewriter repairman, Munich, 1959–1961; cabdriver, Munich, 1961–1963; construction worker, Bad Tölz, 1963–1970; salesman, Munich, 1970–1977; appliance-shop owner, Kitzbühel, 1978 to date. Arrest record: assault and battery, 1961, dismissed; assault, 1962, probation; car theft, 1971, dismissed; larceny, 1972, served four months. Unmarried, no known relatives. Subject's address: Lopezstrasse 83, Kitzbühel.

Mahlmann was also dullsville: born in Tegernsee, 1952; daughter of Lothar Mahlmann, a game warden, forester; parochial schooling; ski instructor, Garmisch, 1970–1972; mountaineering instructor, Kitzbühel, 1972–1974; receptionist, resort hotel, St. Johann, 1974–1980; salesclerk, appliance shop, Kitzbühel, 1980 to date; string correspondent, *Climbing Today, The Piton, Schuss, Ski Time, The Archer, Mountaineering;* member Kitzbühel Sports Club, Women's Ski Club, St. Johann. Arrest record: breach of peace, 1975, dismissed; disorderly conduct, 1976, dismissed; intoxication, 1977, probation. Unmarried; father dec'd; mother, Anna Marie Mahlmann, Klootstrasse 18, Stuttgart. Subject's address: Lopezstrasse 83, Kitzbühel.

Rollo: born Munich, 1945, son of Albrecht Stoeckler-Lindl, hotel manager; parochial schooling, one year Technical School, Munich; auto mechanic, Kitzbühel, 1965–1977; chauffeur, Krystal Film Studios, Munich, 1977 to date. Arrest record: assault, 1968, dismissed; traffic in narcotics, 1972, dismissed; carrying concealed deadly weapon, 1974, probation. Unmarried; father dec'd; mother Lara Stoeckler-Lindl, owner-manager Edelweiss Hof residential hotel, vic. Kitzbühel. Subject's address: Edelweiss, as above.

Wagner read all of this carefully, three times. And then he stared out the window at the rain-washed mountains and thought about it for nearly an hour. He was tired, and he knew he should sleep, but the understanding that time was evaporating brought a great uneasiness.

There was something that kept at him. There was a tremor in the dark corners of his gizzard, or whatever it is that makes a man aware of something seen but unseen. There was something significant lurking in all the insignificance, but it was like an itch maddeningly beyond reach.

He read the data again, weighing each entry under each

name as if it were a stone under a jeweler's glass. And then he related each of the entries to its counterpart entries in the other biographies, searching for a link, a similarity, a relationship that might lead to something vital and conclusive.

The central question kept intruding: terrorism aside, who would benefit from President Randall's death? Why would somebody go to all the trouble of hiring Akim Ri? Why? Give me why, and I'll tell you who....

The phone rang.

"Herr Koenig, Sara Kloman, on the desk. Are you receiving calls?"

"Yes. Put it on."

There was a purring and a click.

"Koenig?" Groot's voice sounded far away.

"Oh, yes. Herr Nagel."

"Sorry to disturb you like this, but I've received a call from our mutual friend Morfey, and he'd like to have you come to see him this evening at six."

"Oh, God. In Munich? I can't come to Munich today. You know how busy I am."

"Not Munich. He wants to see you in his office."

Wagner couldn't contain the explosion. "Heidelberg? He wants me to go all the way to *Heidelberg?* And be there at *six?*"

"Yes, I'm afraid so."

"Well, tell him to kiss my round, rosy ass."

"Command performance. You know how critical Morfey is to our success. In all our affairs. Always."

"Up to my wattles in crisis and trying to keep ten balls in the air, and that bubblehead wants me to drive four hundred kilometers between now and six o'clock just so I can listen to another of his silly congressional lectures? Well, you tell him—"

"I'll tell him nothing," Groot said, suddenly severe. "And I don't want any more argument. Be there at six."

The phone clicked again, and after a moment Sara Kloman's voice came on again. "Are you finished, Herr Koenig?"

"Yes, Fräulein Kloman, I am. I certainly am."

He was about to go out the door when the phone rang again, and he picked it up angrily. The switchboard put Rudi on, and his voice sounded weary.

"I am now going home and go to bed," Rudi announced.

"You called me up to tell me that?"

Rudi humphed. "I called you up to tell you I followed your buddy."

"And?"

"He went home and went to bed."

"Well, even bad guys have to sleep now and then."

"Then there's hope for me."

"Anything else?"

"I went through his car. The blue Audi."

"Find anything?"

"Something weird. He has an amplifier in the trunk. A commercial-type amplifier."

"What for?"

"How the hell do I know? To make a noise, I suppose." Rudi cleared his throat. "Another thing: there was a cassette player attached. And in the glove compartment was a cassette labeled: 'Sound Effects.' It had a Krystal Film Company logo on the label. A notation: 'For Studio Use Only.'"

"That's all?"

"That's all."

"O.K., Rudi. I don't know how to thank you."

"Just send me the rest of that bottle you've got."

"It's on its way, pal."

29

The bad weather had decided Groot against his original plan to lunch at Karli's, and so he ordered *belegtes Brot* and a stein of beer from room service and ate, silent and alone, at the small table by the window. He chewed slowly, taking occasional sips from the enameled mug, and stared moodily at the gray city below and beyond.

The phone warbled, and he crossed the room, dabbing at his lips with a napkin.

"Yes?"

"The senator wants to see you, Groot," Sam Fallon's whiskey tenor said.

"Very well."

"And make it snappy. He doesn't like to be kept waiting."

Groot had been a part of the bureaucracy long enough to have developed a kind of sonar, a delicate sensitivity to nuance and posture, that served as a personal early-warning system. In an enormous and complex structure like the Federal government, it paid dividends to know what was happening in the front office and down the hall; the slamming of a door or an unanswered phone or a secretary's transfer could signify important and impending change, and he who failed to keep alert and to adjust to the currents and eddies was the one who invariably came out somehow worse for the wear. And so, because he'd been accustomed to Fallon's preemptory manner, the husky summons that rang of arrogance and self-satisfaction, he'd been instantly aware that something different had now been added—a special vibration that suggested something new and ominous.

And because he was what he was, Groot opened his suitcase and took out the aspirin box and slipped it into his vest pocket.

He felt a real headache coming up.

The senator was seated at a writing table beside the windows and their panoramic view of the Altstadt and its spires. He was scribbling furiously, his lips moving slightly with the effort. Fallon motioned Groot to a chair by the phony fireplace and then sank onto the sofa, crossing his legs and staring at the carpet in pretense of deep thought.

Senator Logue finished a sentence, pounded a period with the thump of his ballpoint, and, tossing the pen onto the table, turned in his chair to give Groot a triumphant glare.

"I've got you now, you sumbitch," he said.

"I don't understand, Senator."

"I've got you by your scrawny balls. And I'm gonna squeeze 'til you die."

"Would you please explain, sir?" Groot was depressed to hear the senator's affectation of corn-pone language. It meant he was playing the country bumpkin, and it always signaled a coming disaster.

"You bet I will, you knocker." The senator's belly rolled in a spasm of laughter. "I'm gonna explain it real good. Ain't I, Sam?"

Fallon grinned and winked. "You bet, Senator."

Senator Logue picked up a paper from the pile on the table and glanced at it, gloating. Then his small eyes came back to Groot. "I have here," he said, "a little note from a feller named Rattner. Ever hear of him?"

Groot vowed he would not show surprise. "Certainly. He's a Munich nightclub operator, robber, and pimp. Or he was, until he was killed last week."

"Well, that little old pimp seemed to be afraid he might get killed, and as a kind of insurance he wrote me a little old letter, to be delivered if anything violent happened to him. He wrote the famous U.S. senator and overseer of official American morals, about how he was forced by the CIA to cooperate in a plot to kill the President of the US of A. Only his insurance didn't work, it seems, 'cause somebody done killed him dead, and so now the letter is his revenge. That right, Sam?"

Fallon laughed aloud, making it clear that he thought this to be the funniest thing that ever happened.

"The man was obviously mad," Groot said coolly.

"He was mad, all right. Mad at you, Groot."

"At me?"

"Yeah. This note says you contacted him, such-and-such a date, such-and-such a place, and ordered him to set up a scheme that would bring dire harm to our beloved President when he made his visit in this here city." The senator stood up, rubbing his belly and laughing. "He names all the names, too. Not just you, pal. Everybody. We're gonna have the goddamn-dest congressional investigation you ever did see."

Groot used every ounce of will to keep his face expressionless.

"May I use your bathroom, Senator?"

Senator Logue and Fallon began to cackle, pointing at each other in red-faced hilarity and whooping.

"How about that, Sam," the senator gasped, "we just scared the shit out of the slimy bastard."

"I need an aspirin," Groot said.

"Wee-hoo!" the senator cried, "you're gonna need more'n that before I get through with you!"

Groot arose from his chair, numb in the roaring laughter, and crossed the living room and went down the small corridor to the bathroom, where he ran a glass of cold water. He snapped open the aspirin box, placed two of the tablets in his mouth, and washed them down, swallowing hard. He sighed, selected another tablet, kneeled to complete the business, and then returned to the front room, where the senator and Fallon were grinning in red-faced amusement. Fallon was rereading Rattner's letter.

"Let him read it, Sam," the senator chortled.

Falloon handed the letter to Groot, who returned to his chair and read impassively. It was all there, chapter and verse.

The senator, enjoying the taut silence, rubbed his big belly and wandered out of the room and down the hall. So there it was, Groot thought: history was to be made by the famous senator's famous weak kidneys.

Fallon sat in quiet amusement, watching Groot's face. There was a crash.

"What the hell was that?" Fallon barked, jumping up.

Groot, continuing to read, said, "It sounded as if something fell down in the bathroom."

Fallon hurried down the corridor and, in a moment, began making strange, whimpering sounds. Eventually he returned to the living room and, leaning against the arch, stared at Groot with wide, bloodshot eyes. His redness had turned to a gray putty color.

"The senator has had a heart attack. I think he's dead," Fallon said, his voice thin and strained with shock. "He's lying across the toilet."

"How about that," Groot said, still reading.

"He's dead, Groot."

"Well, I suggest you call a doctor or something."

"Groot—"

"Mm?"

There was a long silence, after which Fallon choked, "You win."

"Whatever do you mean?"

Fallon came across the room to stand by Groot's chair. He reached down and took the letter from Groot's fingers and, as they exchanged stares, he tore the paper into small pieces.

"You win," Fallon said. "I can't go up against a guy like you."

Groot stood up and buttoned his jacket with slow deliberateness. Then he went to the door. Before leaving, he said, "I haven't the foggiest notion as to what you're talking about, Mr. Fallon."

"How did you know it'd be the senator who went in there first?"

"I didn't."

"You mean it wouldn't have made any difference if I'd gone first?"

"Lessons are lessons."

"For God's sake, Groot. I won't give you any more trouble. And that's a fact."

"Really, Mr. Fallon—"

"I mean it, Groot. You win. Just don't—don't do whatever you did—I mean—"

"You'd better call for a doctor, Mr. Fallon. And let me know if I'm needed. At the inquest, or whatever."

"Groot. Promise. Please promise me."

But the door was shut, and Groot had gone.

30

There was no sign of the brown Volvo. But a dark green Mercedes, ever present to the rear, was suggesting that his tail had changed cars.

It rained all the way, but he made good time. The BMW was sure-footed and responsive, as ever, and, what with the bad weather and mid-afternoon hours, the traffic was light and undemanding. Under such conditions the Autobahn was a place for thinking and soul searching, and he did a lot of both.

A pattern was forming.

There were holes, to be sure—serious gaps that defied any logical construction, or even audacious imagination. It was clear that Ziggi had somehow stumbled onto something real, in which Gustav Kahn, Lotte Mahlmann, and Rollo Stoeckler-Lindl were, peripherally at least, involved. It was evident that the dissipated and dispirited old ham, Emerson Gurney, was being used or exploited by Kahn in some manner, since a man with a pickled brain isn't equipped to play a direct, active role in something so intricate as premeditated political murder.

It would also appear that Amy Randall, the President's sister and alter ego, was also being used somehow, since

206

she'd been moved—for reasons unknown—to invite Gurney to participate in an event which, in ordinary circumstances, would be closed to him. But what was the connection? What was the reason? Who was behind Kahn? Who was playing the lady congressman and a rheumy old sourball for what kind of patsies?

And what was Kahn really up to? Was he hiding, abetting, Akim Ri? If so, where? And why? That was the important thing: why?

He sighed, thinking that the problem with the CIA bureaucracy—as personified by Groot—was that they all thought like cops. They all tried to solve problems from the bottom. A true investigator, a born field man, would always start from the top, the way that dear ole Sherlock, Roger Wagner, did.

The Groots were always looking for the who and the how.

Wagner knew that if you found the why, you'd automatically discover the rest.

But he was working under a rotten handicap. He was too far removed from the Godhead scene to have even the dimmest idea of why someone might want the President dead. Certainly it wouldn't be the Vice President, who, according to the three o'clock news, was rumored to be very ill with the flu and under doctor's care at Camp David and who, it was known, was soon to inherit a hundred million dollars from his late father's drygoods and hardware empire. Certainly not Robert Goodman, who appeared to have a better-than-even chance of winning the election on his own steam. Certainly not the Soviets, who were so pleased with how President Randall played into their hands they'd vote for him if they could. Certainly not Ellie Pomeraine's international terrorist organizations: President Randall's hands-off-the-Middle East posture had made him almost a dear boy to them.

So, not having the why, he had to go at it the cop's way. He had to work up from the bottom.

Ziggi-to-Kahn-to-Mahlmann-to-Rollo-to-Gurney-to—

Well, who?

Why?

Why, goddamnit?

He flicked off the stereo, which had been offering some muted Chopin, and punched the button for a news update. It came on, surprisingly, in a burst of that special hollowness, the amalgamation of traffic clatter and voices, that characterizes the live, on-site interview. And the interviewer was much involved in asking Amy Randall a question:

"—which is, of course, on everybody's mind at this solemn moment. Who, Miss Randall, do you expect the Senate to name as successor to Senator Logue as chairman of the Armed Services Committee?"

"Well," she said over a microphone squeal, "we're all so shocked at the senator's tragic passing that there's been little speculation on such things among our advance party, naturally. I'd seen the senator only last night at a NATO review meeting with General Dirk, and, as I say, it's all so sudden and overwhelming and, well, distressing, you know. The nation has lost a great statesman, a man of piety and sincere goodwill and tireless devotion to propriety and accomplishment. He'll be sorely missed."

"Will the senator's body be flown home at once?"

"Well, I can't say, really, because there are some legalities and so on, but I don't imagine the German authorities will delay things too much. The senator is scheduled to lie in state at the Capitol on Tuesday, and so on, and since the police surgeon and the coroner's office have pronounced the cause of death to be a massive coronary and all, I don't suppose there'll be any delay to speak of."

"Thank you, Miss Randall. We now switch you to Washington, where George La Salle, our Capitol corres—"

Wagner reactivated the Chopin.

Sic semper tyrannical old farts, he thought.

It was three minutes to six when he walked into Morfey's office.

"Groot said you wanted to see me."

"Oh. Yes. Sit down."

"I've been sitting all afternoon. I'll stand."

"As you wish." Morfey closed the file folder that served as the only blemish on the polished mahogany of his desk. He seemed even more pleased with himself than usual. "I suppose," he purred, "you wonder why I sent for you."

"The question went through my mind, yes."

"Two reasons. The first: your friend Pohl, whom you left in charge of the case involving the Soviet helicopter spies, and so on, is having trouble. He asked me for permission to bug a hotel room where the Russians are staying, but before I make a decision, I'd like to have your opinion, as OIC."

Wagner humphed. "Well, hell, give him the permission. You wouldn't be violating anybody's rights. The Soviets are bona fide spies."

"Well," Morfey said, "I think Pohl gives up too easily. There must be another way."

"Look, Morfey, you're not paid to be spy-master, you're paid to watch our morals. Let Pohl handle the investigation. All he wants out of you is an O.K. to listen in electronically, for cripes' sake."

"Mr. Morfey."

"Pohl's up against Gregori. And when you're competing with Gregori, you need all the help you can get."

"That's another thing, by the way," Morfey said. "Gregori has disappeared."

"What do you mean, disappeared?"

"Pohl says he dropped out of the scene, no trace, shortly after you were put on TDY with Groot."

"Well, that's very flattering. I'm taken off a case, so the Ivans remove their hotshot from it, too. I get more recognition from the opposition than I do from my own people." He chuckled.

"Which brings me to another matter," Morfey said, unamused. He tapped the folder with a finger and said, "Your dossier."

"You keep a dossier on me?"

"Well, not really," Morfey smirked. "It's a report on

your misbehavior. It's to be sent to Washington tomorrow. I wanted to include your comments. We try to be fair, you see."

"Misbehavior? What misbehavior?"

"Your intimidation of Miss Pomeraine. I believe the full committee will want to review the incident, since she's such a prominent journalist. Now: do you have anything to say for the record?"

"Zounds. Egad. Even gadzooks, maybe."

"Well, now, what's that supposed to mean?"

"It's cow dung a la mode. And so are you."

Morfey came forward in his chair, his cheeks flushed and his eyes hot behind their horn-rims. "Now you listen here, Wagner: you seem to forget who and what I am."

"How can I forget a six-foot anus?"

"I'll have your pension for this, Wagner. You can't talk to me like that."

"I'm just getting started." He felt the fury rising, billowing, an intense fireball rolling and boiling somewhere behind his belt buckle. It was elemental, beyond confinement or regulation. It was like the searing prelude to a terrible sneeze, to an orgasmic release of long-stifled angers and contempts.

"Who do you think you are? I mean, really—"

"I'm the patootie who just drove, top speed, damned near three hundred miles in a pouring rain, and in the midst of a top-secret intrigue of unprecedented international ramifications, to hear you announce you're going to tell Washington I've been a bad boy."

"You were violating the First Amendment. You were denying the press its constitutional freedom to report the news—"

"Morfey, I'm sick up to here with your ham-fat face and your foppish ways and your congenital need to butt in and screw up. And I've decided to blow the whistle on you."

"Just what do you mean by that?"

Wagner was, in the turbulent inner heat, asking himself the same question. But all the weeks and months of meddling and pettiness had converged in this moment, and he knew that he must—at any cost—remove this obscene wart on the ass of the world. The words seemed to come from a source all their own:

"I've hoped that I'd never have to reveal this. But I know your secret."

"Secret? What secret?" Morfey snapped.

"Don't give me that evasive crap, Morfey. I've got the whole story on tape. I've also got pictures."

"Story? What are you talking about, anyhow?"

"Your thing. The thing you've been doing. The thing you think nobody knows about. Well, I know about it."

"What thing?" Morfey's eyes wavered.

Wagner manufactured a pained smile, full of *Weltschmerz* and resignation. "All men have their secrets, Morfey. Even I have a skeleton or two in my closet. But nothing like yours. No, sir. You're unique."

"Unique? I—what are you—?"

"Stop putting me on, Morfey. Would you like to see some pictures? Pictures of, ah, you know what . . . ?"

Morfey's face became very red, and he licked his lips. "I've done nothing to be ashamed of."

"Well, as the saying goes, nothing's wrong or shameful as long as the participant is willing. As long as it feels good." He winked elaborately.

"That doesn't make sense."

"It was just a saying. To illustrate that one man's pleasure is another man's sin."

"You don't have anything on me—"

"Right here in my pocket." Wagner patted his jacket. "Full-color pix. Want to see them?"

"I'm a happily married man," Morfey said, distraught.

Wagner didn't know, but he said, "I know."

"What do you want of me?"

"Silence. Withdrawal from my life. Your return to the States."

"The States? I can't just tear up my family and go back home simply because a seedy peeper is blackmailing me."

"Suit yourself."

"No *way* will I give up this job." Morfey's chin thrust forward.

"All right."

"You can't scare me," Morfey huffed.

"All right."

"I haven't done anything wrong."

"Of course not. I'm sure your wife and boss will agree."

"Show me one of the pictures."

Wagner slid a hand inside his jacket. "Sure—"

"No. Wait, don't. I don't want to see it."

"Whatever you say."

"How much time will you give me?"

"One week."

"One *week?* Are you out of your mind? I've got—"

"You've got one week to get out of Germany. Or I mail one of the pix to Mrs. Morfey and another to your committee chairman."

"You're a filthy, blackmailing scum, Wagner. You're the most reprehensible man I've ever known—"

"I don't respond to flattery."

"You're ruining my life, my career, in just a few minutes. You walk in here and threaten me, and my life is ruined, and I haven't done anything wrong."

"Then don't leave Germany. Stay right here. Sue me for slander. Defamation. Blackmail. Exhibiting pornography on a military post. Spitting on the sidewalk."

Morfey stood up, his fingers extended and pressing the desktop. He blinked twice. "Can we, ah, discuss the matter? Maybe strike a deal or something? I'm not a rich man, but—"

"No deals. No discussions. You are a rotten little bugger, and I want you out of my life. Out of Europe."

"Wagner—"

"You have one week."

He turned on his heel and strode out of the office, just the proper amount of indignation in the jut of his jaw, the set of his shoulders.

And an insane urge to laugh in his chest.

31

He didn't give Morfey another thought, since Morfey had been rendered a eunuch by his own secret sins. But he thought a lot about Stuttgart.

The idea had been with him since he'd passed the city on his way to Heidelberg, and so on the return trip he left the Autobahn and, after questioning a slab-faced traffic cop, found his way to Klootstrasse 18.

Stuttgart was the largest industrial center in southwest Germany, with auto plants, electrical engineering centers, machine construction, textile factories, chemical plants, and God only knew how many other clang-and-bang creations, and Klootstrasse seemed to be the grubbiest street in the grubbiest corner of the grubbiest section of all. The lashing rain had turned to a drizzle, cold and clinging, and the streetlights threw their light to no avail, as if they'd been set aglow in wads of indigo cotton. As he eased the BMW to the curb, he could see only the dark angles of the rows of houses, the skeletonlike dockside gantries and the mill chimneys making black traceries against the blackness of low-rolling clouds.

He sat in the dark for a time, listening to the far-off

traffic sounds and considering his reasons for being in this unlikely corner of a sooty nowhere. And, as usual, when he'd named his reason he had his method.

Huddling against the chill and damp, he left the car and made his way to the door of No. 18, a place without character whose bricks, streaming with wet, were chalked with dim and ancient graffiti. The door led to a vestibule in which there were four mailboxes, each bearing a name card that was barely legible in the wan light of a ceiling bulb. He squinted at these for a moment, then climbed a set of stairs that must have been painted in 1699 and last washed shortly thereafter.

The door opened after his second knock.

"I'd like to see Frau Mahlmann, please."

The woman was a warped version of Lotte. She held a frayed bathrobe close around her and, with her free hand, pushed back a strand of graying hair.

"I'm Frau Mahlmann," she said. "Who are you?"

He held up his wallet, giving her a glimpse of his American Express card. "I'm Wilhelm Koenig from the Bundespolizei. I'd like to ask you a few questions."

"Again? How many times are you people going to bother me with your questions?"

His mind picked that up, turned it around a bit, then followed the lead. "Oh. You mean the others. They were local cops. I'm from the Bundespolizei."

"You're all cops to me. But, really now, I haven't any idea what she's up to. I haven't seen her in months."

"May I come in, please?"

The woman stepped back, her expression that of an old campaigner who's been sorely put-upon. "Well, I suppose you can. But I haven't anything to add."

She had already contributed a great deal, of course, and Wagner felt the same sense of excitement that had been energized when he'd learned that Gustav Kahn and Emerson Gurney were sufficiently well acquainted to get angry at each other. But his curiosity, running on full throttle now, had to be completely satisfied.

The woman stood in the center of the combined living

room and kitchen and regarded him out of dull eyes. There was a trace of alcohol in the air, stale and cheap. "So what do you want?" she said.

"First," he said reassuringly, "I have no intention of causing you or your daughter trouble. I simply think she might unknowingly hold the key to a matter I've been investigating. I've discussed this with her in Kitzbühel, but I believe there might be a thread dangling here."

"In this place?" She peered woodenly about her.

"It's only a hunch. And I really am sorry to bother you with it."

Frau Mahlmann gave him a glance that revealed, for the first time, the barest hint of interest. "I must say," she said, "you're certainly more polite than that other clod."

"You mean the other policeman?"

"He was a surly bugger."

"What did he want?"

"He just barged in here, saying he was from the police and he wanted to look through Lotte's things. No explanations, no nothing."

"Lotte has a room here?"

"I have only the two bedrooms. She keeps some clothes and things in the one. Sleeps there sometimes when she comes to see me. Which isn't very often, I tell you. It's so hard, and I'm so alone. You'd think a daughter'd care more than that."

"Young people tend to think only of themselves, I'm afraid." He paused, then: "What did the other policeman look like?"

"Oh, I don't know. They all look alike to me."

"Tall, short, fat, thin—"

"He was tall. Big shoulders. Tinted glasses. Moustache. Big nose. Arrogant. A little older than you."

"Would you mind if I looked around Lotte's room?"

She waved a thin hand. "Help yourself. Want a drink?"

"No thanks. I'll just take a quick look and be on my way."

The room was small, with dark woodwork and a looming wardrobe. A small marbletop night stand was beside the bed, a lamp with a frayed green shade and an alarm clock with one hand its only adornments. The bed was carefully made, though, and its blue print spread gave the place a dot of hopefulness. There was a dresser and a mirror in the corner by the window and a kind of leather-strapped sea chest at the foot of the bed. A worn throw-rug on the wooden floor, and that was it.

It was a very melancholy place, and Wagner's depression was acute. He went through the wardrobe first, but it revealed nothing beyond a few outdated dresses, a sweater, two blouses, a twill raincoat, and three pairs of shoes that needed new heels. There was a stack of magazines beside the shoes—ski journals, mountain-climbing gazettes, and a few fashion catalogs. He kneeled and riffled through each of these, waiting with each to see if anything fell out. Three subscription mailers were the only fruit of this search. He did, however, give a moment to reading the lead paragraphs of some of the articles bearing Lotte Mahlmann's by-line. He was not the world's leading judge of editorial values, but he could see that Lotte would never win the Nobel for literature. She seemed to know her subjects, though, and there was even a picture of her in one of the archery magazines, standing beside the bullseye and staring into the camera. He liked her better when she smiled. He also liked her better without her clothes on.

"Finding anything?" Frau Mahlmann asked from the doorway.

"No, not yet."

"Take your time. I'm not exactly going to the queen's ball." She chuckled, then coughed dryly, sending a cloud of gin vapors his way.

He opened the sea chest and rooted through several layers of blankets and towels that reeked of mothballs. Below these, his hands touched papers, and he brought them out and held them to the light.

"How long has your daughter had these, Frau Mahlmann?"

The woman padded across the room and took the

papers from him. Her glassy eyes considered each of them, slowly and methodically, and then she stared at him mystified.

"I've never seen these before," she said.

"When's the last you looked in the trunk?"

The woman's eyes pondered the past, and she said finally, "It had to be last spring, when I put away the winter blankets."

"When was the other policeman here?"

"A couple of days ago. In the last week, anyhow."

"Did he go through this trunk?"

"Sure. He went through everything."

"Did you watch him all the time he was here?"

"Not exactly. He didn't want a drink, either. So I had my little drop—helps me to sleep, you know, and enriches my blood—while he was in here."

"So he could have left these papers here, right?"

"I wouldn't say could've. I'd say he had to. It had to be him. Nobody else has been in that thing since spring."

"All right then. Do you mind if I take these with me?"

"Why should I mind? They don't mean anything to me. Or to Lotte."

He took out his wallet and placed ten marks on the night table. "For your trouble," he said. "Buy yourself a gin on me, eh?"

"Well, now, I'd say that's right decent of you, Herr Koenig."

"My pleasure."

"You're not like any cop I ever saw."

"We're not all ogres, Frau Mahlmann."

He stood there, gazing about the room, his eyes probing for meaning he might have missed, but he saw only poverty and the matte colors of surrender and despair. He was thinking of Lotte Mahlmann, the boy-thin athletic young woman whose joy in life was to see herself unclothed in mirrors, as if the fact of her nakedness proved the fact of her existence. There was so much to look for, so much assurance to be sought, when your roots were in a dull green room in a grimy side-street canyon in a wilderness of brick. He felt a gathering understanding of Lotte as one living the life he had lived all those years ago, in all those gone days among the bricks and coal dust of Buffalo, in the times when baseball cards and aggies and a stack of Blue Book magazines represented the sum of his private possessions.

"Your daughter is very pretty, Frau Mahlmann."

She followed him across the front room to the door, saying as she went, "It's such a waste, her wandering around. She could have been a journalist. She was very fine at writing, you know. And such an athlete. Like her father, a good man, an outdoorsman. Did you know he was a game warden and forester? He taught Lotte many things about the forests and mountains. He loved her very much. Then he died and I had to come here because I couldn't get along with my sister, Lara. This place belonged to my parents, years ago, and this was the only block for miles to come through the American air raids. Isn't it strange how, with all the bombs and fire, a place as ugly as this was untouched? Oh, God, what a world."

"Lara? That's an unusual name—" He felt the sense of discovery.

"My sister Lara is an innkeeper in the Tyrol."

"Lara Stoeckler-Lindl? Of the Edelweiss Hof?"

"You know her, eh?"

"Yes."

"A good woman. Talented in business. But she can't bear me. Or Lotte, for that matter."

"Lotte is her niece, then."

"Yes. But Lara doesn't like to admit it, I tell you."

"Well, all families have their little problems."

"I suppose." She glanced toward the pantry.

"Thanks again for helping, Frau Mahlmann. And thanks for letting me have these papers."

"It's nothing. Who cares about a lot of political garbage about that fellow—what's his name?"

"Goodman. Robert Goodman."

"An American, yet. Why would a German policeman

leave pictures and propaganda about an American politician?"

"That's what I'm going to find out, Frau Mahlmann."

"The world is mad."

"It most certainly is. Good night."

32

Groot was out of sorts again, what with the miserable weather and the irritating distraction represented by Morfey and his summons of Wagner to the throne room. What made the incident all the more vexing was the sure knowledge that, no matter what the reason for the call, it couldn't possibly have been of importance. Morfey was an opaque pig, all caught up in self and pomp, and something would eventually have to be done about him. Very few of the satraps Congress has foisted on the Company were of any talent or consequence, but Morfey was the absolute worst of the lot.

Ah, well...

He stood at attention, with his hand over his heart, as the bugler played taps and the casket was elevated to the loading port of the Air Force transport. The music wavered in the gusts of wind and rain, and the flag draped over Senator Logue's coffin had to be discreetly restrained by the huge soldiers, six American and six German, who flanked the catafalque. The plane had been flown from Dulles to München-Riem for the express purpose of returning the late senator to the national rituals in Washington with all the glitter and fanfare accorded a fallen hero.

The rotten son of a bitch.

His eyes, squinted against the rain, roamed restlessly about the great airfield. The President had not come to Munich, announcing instead that the press of business in Frankfurt precluded any deviation from his schedule. He'd told the media that the funeral for Senator Logue would be held the day he, the President, returned to Washington, and he'd deliver a eulogy at that time. Meanwhile, the senator was to lie in state in the Capitol Rotunda.

The President had sent a message, though, and it had been read for him at plane-side by Amy Randall, as ranking member of Congress and longtime friend of the deceased. She had just finished this, and the machinery had begun to whir, and the bugler had begun to play, and the whole scene had become grossly boring and lugubrious and, well, a bunch of crap.

The pneumatic lift approached the access port and hesitated, and there was some fiddling about with the controls, and then it lurched and achieved the correct position. There was more fussing at the yawning hole, and exchanges of salutes, and during this, Groot's eyes fell on Amy, whose handsome back was in the rank ahead of him in the formation of diplomatic, congressional, and military notables who'd assembled to wave the senator good-bye. And, as he watched, he saw, in the tangle of wind-whipped topcoats, the little finger of her right hand curl and lock with the little finger of General Dirk's left hand. They were standing very close in the rain-lashed ranks, and the flapping of fabric offered excellent cover for such goings-on.

Oh, lord, Groot sighed silently, she's screwing Dirk now.

He tried to picture Dirk making love to Amy, but it only made him want to laugh. He couldn't imagine Dirk making love to anybody, since somewhere in the process the chairman would have to bend, and General Dirk looked as unbent as a girder even when sitting down.

Well, maybe he screwed standing up.

Groot felt a smile forming despite himself, and he hoped he wouldn't break into laughter.

But, God, what a vision: Dirk and Amy going at it like two totem poles.

To break the drift toward hysteria, he examined the row of embassy people, and he realized that there was only one he recognized among them all. Old Arthur Finkel would always be in the State Department, even on Judgment Day. But he looked very old now. And tired. *Like all of us,* Groot thought.

He found that he was suddenly and unaccountably annoyed by the newly discovered intimacy between Amy and Dirk. Only moments before, the idea had caused him nearly to choke with hilarity, but now he was irritated and depressed, like a schoolboy with an unrequited crush. Amy Randall's peccadillos had never before affected him one way or another, mainly because he himself was never able to see sex as all that worthy of the mystique accorded it by civilizations. To him, sex had always been a pleasure to be enjoyed as it happened, like any other occasion of the senses—from an ice cream sundae to an Arizona sunset. He saw no more commitment in bringing a woman to orgasm than he saw in guiding her through a rumba. The body was there to be enjoyed, and if Amy chose to sample as many enjoyments as possible, it was no more to him than when or how she brushed her teeth.

But Dirk was something else again. Dirk, with social, economic, and cultural credentials dating from Plymouth Rock, was everything Groot was not. And because Dirk had so much, it now seemed unfair that he should also have acquired a share of Amy. Groot was sufficiently realistic (and honest with himself) to recognize his peevishness as the resentment born of envy; yet the realization that he was capable of envy only intensified his bad humor. Envy connotes inferiority of position or capability, and Groot had never considered himself inferior to anybody—especially two-dimensional flip-charts like the general.

So why was he so cranky?

Standing in the wind and rain, he sought for an answer to that question, and after a time he thought he had it: he had never, for a moment, considered Dirk to be someone Amy could be interested in. The fact that he'd been proved wrong was disturbing evidence that he had developed a blind spot where Amy Randall was concerned.

He should have known from the first that she had something going with General Dirk. The fact that he hadn't known was cause for vague and testy alarm.

Groot had come to the airport with Amy and Dirk, and now he waited while they both climbed into the big Mercedes, and then he took the jump seat between them and the driver.

As the car picked up speed, the chairman said, "There's a brandy flask with cups in the bar beside you, Groot."

Groot became busy, setting up drinks, and Amy and the chairman rode in silence, each gazing absently out opposite windows. There was an atmosphere in the car he couldn't define.

"It was a very awkward time for the senator to die," Amy said at last.

"No time's a good time when you're busy," the general said, bland and preoccupied.

Groot said nothing, handing the others their drinks.

"He does leave a serious gap in the majority power structure," Amy said. "We've got Senators McDonald and Bianco, of course, but both are carrying big loads—McDonald with his antitrust disassembly of GE and Du Pont, and Bianco in those godawful, messy hearings on energy policy. That leaves Kowalski and Federman, and both have their problems. I'd sure hate to see either McDonald or Bianco taken off his big-publicity gig, but I'm certainly not crazy about the other two on Armed Services."

The general shifted in his seat and, continuing to stare out the window, said, "They're both meatheads. And for that reason, I might just be able to live with them. It's the smart ones who cause the trouble."

Amy took a sip from her cup, and then, gazing directly at Groot, said, "Any problems from your point of view?"

"You mean due to the senator's death?"

"Mm."

"None that I can see."

General Dirk said, "I should think not. As chairman of the CIA Oversight Committee, he gave you a very hard time."

"Well," Groot said, studying his brandy, "if it isn't a Logue it's somebody else. The Company has been the congressional whipping boy too long for any replacement of Logue's to ease up on us. Congressional karate chops are a way of life around our shop."

Amy, brooding and philosophical, said, "I don't mind saying that I wish it could have been Robert Goodman instead of Senator Logue. If somebody had to drop dead in all this, why couldn't it have been Goodman, for Pete's sake?"

"It wouldn't have helped a bit," Groot said.

Amy glanced at him. "Why?"

"You can't kill an idea," Groot said. "You might kill a man, say, to stop him from speaking or acting, but the idea that makes the man what he is goes on. It wouldn't have done a particle of good, for instance, for someone to have assassinated Hitler in 1933."

"It sure would have changed history a bit," General Dirk said crisply.

"Not in its essentials," Groot said, shaking his head. "Nazism had to run its course, like a fever, and if Hitler had died, his colleagues—his successor, whoever it might have been—would still have captivated the hearts and minds of a Germany crying for simplistic answers. You have to remember that Hitler was a symptom, not the cause. And it's the same with us. If somebody were to cancel Goodman, he'd only become a martyr, the spiritual focus of an idea that would persist in millions of angry, unhappy American hearts. No, Goodman should be kept alive, because a live Goodman can make mistakes—be

224

defeated. A martyred Goodman becomes a lasting, unbeatable symbol for the discontented to rally around."

The General's gaze came in from the passing scene and regarded Groot in hooded speculation. "Miss Randall," Dirk said, "tells me you're a hotshot. She says you are a very wise and trustworthy man."

"Miss Randall is most kind."

"I tend to make allowances for the old fraud," Amy smiled, glancing at the chairman.

"She also tells me you think oil's the trump card."

"Absolutely."

"Well, that makes you a very wise man, Groot."

Groot permitted himself a small smile. "Thank you, General, but it really doesn't take a genius to see that the world's oil represents the remaining slice of pie on a boardinghouse table."

Amy chuckled. "Metaphors aren't really your thing, Groot."

"I suppose not. But somebody's going to grab the pie."

"And risk getting a lot of forks in the back of his hand, eh?" Dirk said, his expression unchanged.

"Well," Groot shrugged, "none of the forks will be ours. The United States couldn't fight its way out of a Kleenex box. You should know, General. I've watched you, as chairman of JCS, presiding over the American Götterdämmerung. And I'm truly sorry. It must be very difficult for you—a very sad duty."

Did the general's eyes widen, almost imperceptibly? Groot thought so. And there was something in Amy Randall's glance that told him he had said exactly the right thing at the right time. Groot was almost certain that he had just passed some kind of test.

There was no more conversation for a time. The long black Mercedes glided creamily through the heel of Bogenhausen-Parkstadt and headed for the bridge over the Isar.

The general broke the silence with a question: "Miss Randall tells me you're upset over the Task Force Twelve thing. Why?"

225

Groot said, "Because the Soviets can misread it as a belligerent act. The Soviets are in a currently amiable mood vis-à-vis the Mideast and Eurasia, but they're not likely to look kindly on our playing with our boats in their bathtub."

"Miss Randall's right: your metaphors are stupid."

"So sue me," Groot grated, suddenly and inexplicably annoyed by this pompous, beribboned store dummy.

To his surprise, Amy Randall snickered and slapped him lightly on the knee. "Well, I'll be damned," she said. "Groot-baby's got some fire after all, eh?"

Groot snapped, "You better believe it, Amy-baby."

She laughed aloud, that musical sound that endeared all the talk-show audiences. Even the general smiled, a kind of crinkling of the leather around his fastidious moustache.

"Don't be angry with me, Groot," she chortled. "I was only teasing you. Really I was. But I admit it intrigues me to see you sore. I've never seen it before. It becomes you."

General Dirk handed back his cup. His gray eyes had a glint of amusement in them. "Miss Randall's touched on my single greatest doubt about you, Groot. You always struck me as being, well, namby-pamby. Afraid of unpleasantness. That sort of thing."

"Well, I've had plenty of doubts about you, too, General."

"I daresay. So let's strike a truce, shall we? We're all on the same side, after all."

"We can't afford a war, General. We absolutely can't afford a war. I tried to feel you out on war in your meeting recently, but you wouldn't commit yourself. Your philosophy wouldn't show. Your image was blurred. I worry about people like that. Especially when they have armies and navies at their fingertips."

"Relax, Groot. No nation can afford a war. Wars—large wars as tools of national purpose—are truly obsolete, now that we have the abject realities of universal nuclear parity. But every nation has been looking for alternatives. And what we see shaping up is a system of national terrorist squads—trained cadres of people skilled in sabotage and commando tactics, who, when their nation must work its will on another via violence, can move in, do the job, and then get out."

"Like the French Force d'Intervention, eh? Like the Israelis at Entebbe."

"Correct. What do you do when terrorists seize some of your citizens and fly them to another country for ransom? You send in a small group of commandos to seize them back. If the other country kills all your people, you can disavow the raiders; if you succeed, and you extricate your people, the other nation is not about to launch a full-scale war to retaliate against your small-scale retaliation, so to speak."

Groot, calm again, looked out the window and sighed. "To achieve such a capability you have to have first-class intelligence. The Israelis were successful at Entebbe because their intelligence people had first-class information on where the hostages were, the disposition of unfriendly troops—that kind of thing."

"Precisely. And that's why Miss Randall and I hope to convince President Randall, after his reelection, that the U.S armed forces must go into high gear to develop such a capability. Our Army, Navy, and Air Force are structured for World War Three. Since we won't have World War Three, we'll need a U.S.-type Force d'Intervention."

"And to have a capable force like that," Amy Randall said, "we'll need a strong CIA, directed by a strong and skilled professional."

"Well," Groot said, "lots of luck."

Amy laughed again and finished her drink.

The car pulled up at the Maximilianstrasse entrance, and the chairman and the congresswoman alighted and hurried through the rain to the doorway, where they were met by the squad of earnest-faced sycophants. Groot stayed with the car until it had entered the garage, and as

227

he strolled across the concrete cavern for his own VW, he was deep in thought and smoking one of his smelly cigarettes.

The President's appearances at Bonn and Frankfurt had been generally well-received by the Germans, and the press coverage had been upbeat, both in Europe and in the States. Ellie Pomeraine, assured now of a good future, had leisurely filed her sidebar story on Emerson Gurney—doing a thoroughly interesting and informative job, she didn't mind telling herself—and then had gone on to gathering background material that might be useful in the Amy Randall biography.

Amy, bless her hypocritical little heart, had commissioned her to do the book, not as an "as-told-to," but as an officially authenticated and approved God's-eye-view bio in the William Manchester tradition. It meant a book entirely hers, a book that would be assured great public attention and reviews by all the critics who count, and the advance royalties would probably be astronomical.

Ellie was sprawled on the chaise, alternately relishing all this and watching the President on TV, when Groot came in.

"Hi," she said, leaning to turn off the set.

"Is there anyone else in the house? The German girl, or anyone?"

"No," Miss Pomeraine said. "Only the Secret Service types lurking in the bushes outside. And since Amy isn't here, I rather suppose they're taking naps."

Groot put his briefcase on the reading table and took a chair by the large fireplace, whose lazy flames made wriggling light patterns on the ancient ceiling beams. He stared into the glow for a time, still thinking, as he'd thought throughout the drive from the Vierjahreszeiten.

"Would you like a drink, Groot?"

"Mm? No. Thank you. Not now."

"You look like a man with a lot on his mind."

He glanced at her, his eyes metallic in the firelight. "What are you doing here, Miss Pomeraine?"

"Amy invited me, if that's what you mean." She was watching him, her eyes careful. "It's her hideout, and, like you, I'm one of the welcome ones."

"Who else is welcome?"

"What do you mean?"

"Who else comes here?"

"Nobody. Only that girl—Irma Berchthold."

This was true, Groot knew, since the Secret Service boys gave him copies of the Amy Randall log. But something was going on, and it was dangling a string that bothered him. Not to know everything was to have a loose end, and loose ends were what always lay behind the failure of any operation.

"Miss Pomeraine," he said softly, "it's absolutely fundamental to the national security that you tell me the truth. Is Miss Randall seeing anybody? A man?"

She flicked a piece of lint from her slacks with a delicate motion of a forefinger. She did not look at him. "I don't know. And I'm not sure I'd answer if I did. It really isn't any of your business."

Groot stood up and studied the staghorns mounted above the fireplace. His voice was low and hoarse. "You must not let your new-found financial and social coups turn your head from reality, Miss Pomeraine. The acceptance in the royal court, the agreement on the biography, the other perquisites, can all be taken away from you."

"By you?" Her eyes were suddenly defiant.

"By me. I set them up for you in the first place. So I can just as readily do the opposite."

"Big deal. I knew Amy years before you did."

"I think not. Miss Randall looked you up on my recommendation. She hadn't given you a thought in a long time. And I recommended you only so that you might do a job for us."

"I don't do jobs for you CIA creeps," she sneered. "I'm a journalist."

He regarded her mildly. "You are not a journalist, Miss Pomeraine. You are a renegade, a disgrace to your profession. You lost your claim to being a journalist when you agreed to take a retainer from the West German Gehlen Service. Journalists investigate and report, Miss Pomeraine. But they do not investigate and report for a spy service, as you did. They do not warp stories into propaganda, as you did."

"I was starving. I needed the money. You know the jam I was in."

"Of course. But please don't strike those noble journalist poses, Miss Pomeraine. Being a hypocrite myself, I can't stand hypocrisy in others."

"Well," she said, annoyed, "I'm finished with all that now."

"Not until I say so. We're not done with Wagner yet."

"I am."

"Not yet."

"I like him too much. He's a nice guy. A little dumb in some things, but pretty damned sharp, mostly. His problem is that he wants to be decent and the world won't let him. And I dig that. Because that's the way it is with me."

"Even so, I want you to continue your affair with him."

"He has something to say about it, you know. And I have the idea he'll throw me out on my tokus."

"I want to know who killed Ziggi Rattner, and why. I want you to tell me as soon as Wagner finds the answer to that question."

"Suppose he doesn't tell me?"

"That's why I've hired you. You're a journalist." He smiled frostily. "You're a famous investigative reporter. You are also, I hear, easy to talk to in bed."

"Who told you that?" she asked brittlely.

"A partial list: Tom Garson, Luigi D'Orio, Fred Temple, Allen Rich, the Right Reverend Steven Tremaine, Betty Lou Danforth, Aaron Balder, Susan Doubet, Senator Gregory Sims, Congresswoman Amy Randall, and, of course, your latest conquest, Irma Berchthold." He paused. Then: "Would you like more?"

"You're a real louse, aren't you, Groot."

"No, Miss Pomeraine, I'm really not. You may not believe this, but I do not enjoy preying on the sins and weaknesses and duplicities of others. I do enjoy serving my country. This is the only way I know how."

"Well, you're still a louse, is all I can say. You're worse than my ex-husband. He used to lay every broad in the block and justify it as research for his writing. 'How can a novelist explain life if he hasn't tasted it?' he used to whine. The rotten phony."

Groot smiled dimly. "According to my list, you weren't exactly sitting home nights yourself, Miss Pomeraine."

She stared at him wordlessly. Then, after an interval, they both began to laugh softly.

"I don't like to be rough with you, Miss Pomeraine," he said. "But I really do have to learn more about Rattner's murder. And you'll be paid well."

"O.K. I'll tag along. But after Wagner, no more."

"All right. But let's not forget my first question: Is Amy playing around with a man? I must know. If she is, I've got to be sure it's kept quiet, discreet, unknown to anyone but us. She'd doing great politically, and a tawdry affair or a blackmailing male whore could cause all kinds of nasty complications, publicity-wise."

She examined her well-shaped hands, thinking. "Well," she said, "I'm not crazy about snitching, but the fact is, Amy's got a thing with General Dirk."

"He comes here? The Secret Service has no record—"

"Naw. She goes to a place he has in Bogenhausen."

"How does she get out of the house without the Secret Service knowing about it?"

"I come to visit. She puts on my clothes, goes out the French doors in the back, drives off in my car. She comes back the same way."

"What about the Secret Service man on duty at the French doors?"

Ellie Pomeraine smiled conspiratorially and said, "Add him to my list, pal."

33

It was all very Gothic.

The cemetery was on a hillock on a knee of the Kaisergebirge, at the rim of a churchyard with tilted stone crosses and weathered angels whose sculpted faces were drawn in sorrow. The rain came down in a steady drumming, and the little knot of people at graveside clung together under black umbrellas made shiny by the storm. The great valley, spreading below and beyond, was gray with mist and sad little houses and restless autumn trees, giving substance to the pastor's mournful portrayal of the world as a vale of tears.

Then it was over, and the casket was lowered and the dirt was flung, and Rollo Stoeckler-Lindl was tucked in for his ride through eternity. The people brushed Frau Lindl's cheek with their lips, shook hands with the pastor, and went off to their cars, parked behind the white church with the golden onion-top steeple. There was a slamming of doors and the vooming of motors and the crunching of tires on gravel, after which the knoll returned to its solitude and lonely dripping sounds.

Wagner, driving his BMW at a respectful rate to the

232

highway on the valley floor, gave Frau Lindl a sidelong glance.

"Are you all right?"

She nodded. "Yes," she said in a voice still heavy with tears, "but—so many memories. He was a beautiful little boy, and we had many good times in those old days."

"Well, hang onto those memories. They're Rollo's legacy." He wondered if he sounded as phony as he felt. That beautiful little boy had tried very hard to put him in that box on that rainy hill, and he found it difficult to work up a sense of loss over the murderous creep.

"Yes," Eva Whitney said from the back seat, "death's a beginning, not an end."

Wagner wished silently that he could believe that.

"I wish I could believe that," Frau Lindl said. "I've tried to be a good Christian all my life, but when things go wrong and the world closes in, I forget everything I ever learned."

Eva Whitney murmured, "As the grieving father said, when asking Christ to heal his dying child, 'I believe. Forgive thou my unbelief.'"

"Yes," Frau Lindl sighed, "that says it all, doesn't it?"

They made for the inn, withdrawn into their separate contemplations and listening to the rhythm of the windshield wipers. The Mercedes was behind again, a black dot in the rain, and Wagner felt an almost benign glow for whoever was driving it. Such loyalty. Such indefatigable tenacity. Such devotion to duty. Such a pain in the ass.

He glimpsed Eva Whitney in the rearview mirror, pale and thoughtful and smooth-skinned and glossy-haired and young, and he wondered about her. She'd been the only one of the Edelweiss employees to bring Frau Lindl condolences, and since Wagner and the cook had been the only men around who showed an interest in the old lady, Wagner had been more or less pressed into service as one of the "makers of the arrangements," as the round little undertaker from Kitzbühel had phrased it. He and Eva had been busy until almost three this morning, attending to phone calls, death notices, cards to friends—even one to Frau Anna-Marie Mahlmann in Stuttgart—and inane chats with Pastor Kleine. He knew she had to be bushed by now. As a matter of fact, he wasn't doing so hot himself, what with all his horsing around in recent days.

When they delivered Frau Lindl to her door, she hesitated, her eyes brimming. She took each of them by the hand and said, "You both have been wonderful. I don't know how I could have done without you. God bless you." Stifling a sob, she disappeared behind the door.

Wagner, turning to the young woman, said, "Well, now. How about a drink or something?"

She thought about that, her eyes averted. "I'm very tired—"

"Come on. A cognac should help."

"I'm not allowed to drink at the bar or in the lounge."

"Well, I have some whiskey in my room."

She glanced at him, and their gazes met and held while she evaluated the suggestion.

"Come on," he said. "Just a fifth or two."

"All right. Why not?"

They went upstairs and he took her wet coat and hung it in the wardrobe. She stood by the window and looked out at the valley, a gray wash of swirling rain and unhappy mountains. She folded her arms in that way of hers and said, "It'll be snowing soon."

He handed her a glass and said, "Drink this. It takes away your urge to kick the cat."

She sipped, her eyes solemn, and he saw that they were green with gold flecks in them, and they were large and had long, natural lashes. Her lips had a curious pout about them, and, in this light, she was like a Renoir, smooth and pink and full of inner fires.

She said, "You're a kind man, aren't you."

"I once wanted to be. But now I just pretend."

"You weren't pretending with Frau Lindl. You were really concerned about her."

"I owe her something. I feel guilty about it. It might go away if I treat the old lady nice."

"You're not really that cynical. You talk hard, but I can tell you aren't really like that."

"Maybe. But the world's leading altruist I ain't."

She turned her large eyes from the valley and regarded him with a moody dignity. "I'm very lonely," she said. "I wonder if you'd just hold me for a time."

He put his arms around her, and her head was in the hollow of his shoulder, and he could smell her clean warmth.

"I don't have anybody at all," she said. "And when I saw Frau Lindl by the door, old and alone and full of pain, I saw myself in the years ahead."

He had no idea of what to say, so he improvised. "Your faith. That's the answer. You've got to have faith that everything'll work out all right." (Wagner, Incorporated—Norman Vincent Peale Division.)

"I know. But it's the aloneness. Or loneliness. Being alone in your heart, coping in your heart, with nobody to talk to about it or to care about it." She sighed, a small rising and falling against him. "I can't explain it, really."

"So who's asking?"

"I'd better go," she said, her voice muffled by his jacket.

"Yeah."

"You're much older than I am, you know."

"Nobody knows that better than I do."

"You're very warm."

"It's my electric support-hose."

She laughed softly.

"Will you be kind to me, too? Without pretending?"

"We're having a special on that today."

"Then I won't go."

They went to bed and made love, lingeringly, and they slept through the rainy day—a deep and restoring sleep.

And Wagner knew he had found, not only a lover, but a friend as well.

October 18

"Hello?"

"Herr Wismer?"

"Speaking."

"There's sunshine on the bay."

"What is it, Groot?"

"I believe we've fairly well established our thing. The country is alive with rumors of the assassination plot. I have tapes and memos from Wagner to substantiate the Akim Ri aspect, the law-enforcement people are scrambling madly to locate and arrest Ri, the media are hounding the authorities for hard facts, and already there have been dark and brooding editorials in the Stateside press—warning that a democracy has no accommodation for decisions by violence, or palace coups, or whatever. It's working quite nicely."

"I hear a 'but' in your voice, Groot. A reservation."

"There's a single dangling string. I don't know yet who killed Rattner. There is somebody else working our side of the street, I'm afraid, and I don't know who. Or why."

"Well, it doesn't really matter, so long as President

Randall is reelected. Rattner had many enemies, you know."

"Still—"

"Our goal is all that counts. If we achieve that, then Rattner's killer simply did us a service. Earlier than needed."

"I suppose. But I'm going to keep Wagner going until I find out more."

"Just don't let him go too long. He's a very tenacious, resourceful, plodding fellow. They are the dangerous ones, always."

"Very well. Good-bye, Herr Wismer."

"Good-bye, Groot."

34

Wagner had walked Eva to her quarters late in the afternoon, and they shook hands formally at her door. She was really quite pretty, and he felt a peculiar blend of gratitude and astonishment—gratitude, in that he had found, at last, someone who wanted to be with him for no more reason than he was what he was, and astonishment over the fact that the someone was so unassuming and guileless.

It was an altogether alien experience, and he wondered if it might signal the love that everyone talked about so much and seemed so unable to find. She was in no way an ordinary woman, and he became as sentimental as a schoolboy when he remembered her heat and tenderness, her incandescence, in the soft twilight cast by rain-washed windows. But the most improbable thing of all was that she expected nothing of him, asked nothing of him, tended not even to speak unless he spoke first.

In all the years and all the women, he'd never before experienced this undemanding acceptance of himself as a man; before, he'd always been a foil, or a route to other things. With Eva Whitney, his primary utility—usefulness—was that he took away her aloneness. And that, as

Runyon would say, was more than somewhat.

So it was with a sense of having found himself that he went to the door of Gurney's suite and rapped against the time-darkened oak. There was a shuffling and a fumbling and when Gurney finally opened the door Wagner could see that he was very drunk.

"Well, slap my ass if it ain't the publicity gaucho."

"Hello, Gurney. Mind if I come in?"

Gurney bowed and waved an extravagant arm toward the room, a spacious area featuring a vaulted Tyrolean ceiling, carved paneling, leaded windowpanes, and arched alcove. "Come on in and pull up a drink."

"Are you alone?" Wagner asked, looking around.

"I'm always alone," Gurney beamed. "Price a fame, and all that crap. It's just me here, buyin' myself a snort."

Wagner knew he was telling the truth. The place had that air that tells of things neglected, rooms unoccupied. He could always tell when a place had been recently alive and busy, and he could as readily feel the opposite. He'd known that Frau Mahlmann had been alone; he knew that Gurney had been, too. Loneliness had its own atmosphere, an oppressiveness that was nearly tangible.

"What'll you have? Scotch? Bourbon? Vodka? Gin? Chocolate milkshake? Ha-ha."

"No drink, thanks. I've got to work tonight."

"Well, sit down, and I'll do the drinkin' for both of us," Gurney said expansively.

Wagner sat in an overstuffed chair and Gurney collapsed on a sofa, holding his drink carefully so as not to spill it.

"Somethin' on your mind, Willie?"

Wagner realized that if he was to get any reliable information it would have to be soon, since Gurney's flushed face and crooked grin made it clear that the actor's evening wouldn't be a long one.

"Tell me about Ellie Pomeraine," Wagner said. "How long have you known her?"

"The *Chronos* broad? First time I ever laid eyes on her

was the first day I laid eyes on you, as the sayin' goes. Why?"

"You're sure you never knew her, met her, heard of her?"

"Why would I put you on? If I'd a known her, I'd a made it with her. And I remember tootsies I make it with." He paused, then added, "Usually."

"O.K. Then tell me about Amy Randall again. You knew her only casually, from the old days in California. But she didn't remember you at all. Is that right?"

Gurney held the tumbler to his lips and took a huge swallow, his red eyes never leaving Wagner's. He waited for a moment until the drink hit bottom, and then he said, "What's it to you, anyhow?"

"I've got to know. I'm trying to clear up some details."

"About what?" Gurney said, wary now. "You some kind a cop?"

"What's really between you and Amy Randall?"

"None a your friggin' business," Gurney said, draining his glass.

"Then that means there is something between you. You didn't hesitate to admit you didn't know Pomeraine. If you refuse to comment on Randall, that means you know her well enough to be evasive."

"I don't know what the hell you're talkin' about. What means evasive?" Gurney's voice was thick.

"I think you and Amy Randall were lovers in the old days. She's embarrassed by that fact, now that she's a famous congresswoman and you're a famous drunken failure. But she needs you for something now, and she promised to help you get lots of publicity and reestablish your career if you simply follow the instructions given to you by somebody. My question is: What something does she want you to do, under what instructions from what somebody?"

"Who the hell are you to be askin' questions like this? What the hell kind a publicity guy has to know all this crap?"

240

"Your whole career might be riding on the answer, pal."

Gurney's florid features had fallen into a portrait of despair. He groped under the sofa and pulled forth a flat pint bottle of whiskey. Hands unsure, he unscrewed the cap and sloshed a half-tumbler's measure. He returned the bottle to its hiding place, took a long drink, and, eyes watering, said, "I get sorta confused. Who are you again?"

"Bill Koenig. I'm your friend. I'm trying to help you."

Gurney sank back against the sofa cushions and wiped his lips with the back of a hand. His eyes were filling.

"I ain't got any friends. I ain't had any friends for a long time."

"You got me. I care what happens to you."

Gurney shook his head, filled with a wrenching self-pity. "You don't know what it's like, Willie," he said, his voice just south of a sob. "You're up there, where it's all shiny and the sun's warm and people all know who you are. You drive up the Vine Street hill, slow because you're in second, see, and all the tootsies spot you in your convertible and they wave, and some even yell their phone numbers at you, and all the guys—the hungry extras with the square jaws and big shoulders—hate your guts because you've made it, and they ain't, and they gotta ball ugly old broads in Beverly Hills for the money they need to buy the clothes they need to look sharp when there's a castin' call. And you've climbed outa all that, and you walk into the classiest Hollywood beaneries and they got a special table with a star for you, and nobody asks you to pay for nothin' because they know you got it and your agent or somebody'll settle up." He took another drink and sighed heavily.

Wagner said nothing, sensing that the sodden monologue might reveal more than direct questioning would. He waited, nodding sympathetically.

"And then, somehow, it all sorta dribbles away, and there you are, doin' nightclub gigs and trashin' around, and everything's goin' television, and it's a whole new ball game. You find yourself livin' off some old sow, like the jocks at Hollywood and Vine were doin' back then, and you keep waitin', and the fan mags and the Sunday features don't call you no more. And you can't even get a job in a machine shop or drivin' a trolley, because all you know how to do is make faces and ride a horse and twirl a six-gun. And all the time you gotta keep up the front, with fancy duds and a hot car and a ritzy address and an unlisted phone so that the people who don't call you couldn't get you anyhow. So you borrow your ass off, and you rent yourself out, cash on orgasm delivered. And after a while even that don't work, and so you go to Europe and make Class Z westerns that nobody'll ever see and you put on your cowboy suit and present the President with a Indian hat and maybe you can get some of it back again. You see Amy, and she says remember the old days? And she says we can have them back, if you help me get my brother reelected and you can do that by lendin' your prestige to the scene in Munich, where all the TV cameras will be. And you know that this is your last chance, because there ain't nothin' more, and it's better to be dead than to go on livin' in these godawful places and bein' lonely and rememberin' the way it was. It just hurts too much to go on, and maybe if somethin' can happen with this last gig, maybe it'll be worth hangin' on for awhile. But if it goes like it has been, if it all goes to mashed potatoes again and there's nothin' but drinkin' alone in a godawful lonely hole, then forget it, Charlie. Count me out."

The actor sighed wetly, and the empty glass fell from his fingers to roll on the sofa beside him. He opened his eyes wide, fighting for control, but he surrendered to the forces of alcohol and fatigue, and his head lolled.

"Hey, Gurney," Wagner said gently, "I think somebody's setting you up for a patsy."

"I been a patsy all my rotten life. So what else is new?"

"So tell me what's going on."

Gurney's eyes, heavy with oblivion, blinked shut.

"Gurney. Wake up. Don't pass out on me."

"The world is a crappy place." The voice was slurred and faint.

"Gurney. Hey—Gurney."

"Up yours, C.B. Talk to my agent." Gurney's head rolled back.

"Gurney, for God's sake. Don't pass out. I haven't got time to wait for you. I—"

"I ain't got time for nothin'."

Gurney's big head came forward, and there was the sound of snoring.

"Oh, God," Wagner said, half as a curse, half as a prayer.

He wanted to see Eva. He wanted to see her because the terrible pain in Gurney's soliloquy had offered him a glimpse of the disaster that awaits those who tie themselves to a single capability, and he felt a panicky need for assurance that, with her help, he might, even in these afternoon years, find a way to climb out of the one-way chute his life had become.

But she was on waitress duty again, and he had the clock to beat.

He hurried out the side door of the inn, making for the parking area and his car. The rain had stopped, but the air was chill and the night smelled of winter.

When he reached the BMW, he stood by the door, fumbling with the keys. The leather case slipped from his fingers, and he stooped to retrieve it from the ground.

There was a coughing sound, and the ringing of metal, and when he stood up, the misty light from the parking-lot lantern showed him a ragged hole in the door panel, just below the window.

He turned, his heart beating fast, to run for cover, but there was the rasp of a starter and the whine of a car throwing gravel on the upper road. As he reached for the door handle to climb in and give pursuit, he saw another car leap out of the dark drizzle, its lights flaring suddenly, to go careening out of the lot and up the curving driveway.

Someone else was doing the chasing for him.

Someone in a black Mercedes that had been traded for a brown Volvo.

He was very angry, and he climbed into the BMW to see where everybody was going.

He knew he'd never catch up.

But it was better than doing nothing. And he had to go to Kitzbühel anyhow.

35

It was still early, so the town was alight and bustling, with the shop windows working heroically to send their cheer through the mist. Somewhere a hotel orchestra was laboring through Strauss, while along the streets the inevitable strollers paused to consider the ski boots and the jewelry and the sweaters and the antiques, their collars turned up against the night and intrusion.

Wagner turned the BMW into a municipal parking area, careful to select a space that gave free and quick access to the street. He joined the slow current of window shoppers and eased his way to a position beside the phone booth across the street from the Gipfel Gerät Kompanie. Standing in the shadows between the booth and the adjacent building, he studied the appliance store with a care still sharpened by anger.

The bleak display windows were lighted, but the store behind them was dark. The windows of the apartment above were small lattices of lamp glow, however, and as he watched them he thought he saw Lotte Mahlmann move from one room to another. He forced himself to stand and think, giving himself a little lecture on the folly of his yearning, which was to stride into the Kahn-Mahlmann domicile and, after punching Kahn in the nose, demand to know what the hell was going on.

Reason eventually prevailed, and so he went to the corner, turned into the alley, and sauntered along the cobblestone canyon in the manner of a tourist taking a shortcut. Just as he reached the loading area behind Gipfel, a door rattled, and an oblong of light came from the entrance to Kahn's apartment.

Kahn appeared in the doorway, talking in a low and urgent voice to the other man, who stepped out, full into the light.

It was the fat man with the Tyrolean hat who was in the photo with Akim Ri, and he kept nodding reassuringly in response to Kahn's comments, which the big bald man punctuated with jabs of a forefinger.

"All right," he heard the man say. "It won't be a problem. Consider it done."

"Well, then," Kahn's voice rumbled, "get with it and stay with it."

"Ciao," the fat man said.

Kahn shut the door, and the other man ambled across the loading zone to a VW parked next to Kahn's blue Audi. He climbed in and rattled off in a little storm of spray and winking taillights.

When all was quiet again, Wagner went to the Audi. First, he felt the hood, and it was so warm the drizzle was steaming. The car had been running long and hard, that was clear. Next, he removed the little chamois folder from his raincoat pocket and, in the half-light, selected a jimmy. Of all the aids all the Morfeys had taken away from him, only the burglar tools remained, and if they took those (he'd often told Dusty Rhodes) the U.S. intelligence community might just as well be turned over to the DAR. Well, they'd never take the tools from him, by God, because he'd never admit he had them.

Just as Rudi had said, the trunk was virtually filled by the bulk of a commercial amplifier. The tape recorder was there, too, as was the cassette. He briefly considered taking the tape to the record shop down the street and bringing it back after playing it through. But he decided against the idea. He didn't have the time, and he was certain he knew what he'd hear.

He ran the light from his pen flash around the trunk interior to make sure he hadn't missed anything.

He had.

A small cardboard box.

It contained a dark-brown paste-on moustache and a black wig.

As Eva had noticed, the mustache didn't quite match the wig.

Before closing and locking the trunk lid, he unscrewed the face plate of the amplifier and, with a quick snip of his wire cutters, rendered it mute.

Then, after replacing the plate, he drove back to Munich and the Klub Monika and Amy Randall's party.

36

The Klub Monika was the kind of place where the cover charge sounded like a mortgage. It was in mid-city off the Scharnagl Ring in the cellar of a plastic high-rise. It featured several acres of velvet walls and mahogany bars and cutesy interior gazebos, with potted plants and low lights and a twelve-piece band playing 1940s stuff too loud. It was large, no arguing that, and it was chic, and Amy Randall's crowd liked things that way. Even so, it seemed to Wagner to be somewhat much as a place in which to hold a get-together—even a trendy informal one—in honor of the President of the United States.

But, as Ellie Pomeraine assured him, after vouching for him at the door and taking his arm and leading him into the melee, the President probably wouldn't come anyway. After all, she reminded him wickedly, Jesus doesn't come when you give a Christmas party. She laughed very hard at her own joke, but Wagner, although he was not a pious man, thought it to be in very bad taste. In fact, he decided behind a small, masking smile, he didn't really find an awful lot in her that was anything else. She was too smooth, too brassy, too with-it, for a man of his preferences, and he wondered how he could possibly have been so ready to spend the night with her. What was surprising was that, now that he'd discovered Eva Whitney, he had taken to making such judgements— not only of other women but of things and places and values as well. In the few hours he'd known her, Eva had worked a singular intoxication on him, and everything he did and said was accompanied by a sense of new meaning and power and clarity.

He hadn't cared about much of anything, and then, with the advent of Eva, he cared about everything.

Ellie took him to Amy Randall, who was standing near a planter filled to brimming with bright fake flowers. Groot was at her elbow, and some young people, obviously of the German upper crust, clustered about them both, chattering like birds and displaying their brilliant teeth and milky skins and silken hair. Amy was presiding, as she would always preside; the cacophony and marbling colors and blaring sounds were there for her to direct and approve, and, while she pretended to listen and delight in the talk, her eyes were on him, evaluating him and, obviously, wondering who he was.

She dismissed the young Germans with a wave of her hand, which she then held out to Wagner, saying, "Ellie, who is this interesting-looking fellow?"

Ellie made the introductions, and Groot nodded hello and even shook hands.

"Nice party, Miss Randall," Wagner said.

"Roger Wagner... Are you in Government?"

"Yes. In a way."

"Your name—I know it's silly to say so, but it's familiar—"

Wagner knew she was just making conversation. Which surprised him, since she was clearly a woman who had no time for banalities. He glanced at Groot, who sipped his drink and seemed to be unwilling to grace the conversation. "I work out of Heidelberg, doing special investigations."

"Oh?" she said.

Groot decided to offer an explanation. "He's one of my people, Miss Randall."

"Aha. You're the one who violated one of Ellie's amendments." She laughed. "I'm glad to see you two have made it up."

Ellie waved her drink and said, "He violated my amendment and I amended his violation."

Amy Randall made a face. "I'm not so sure I understand that. Or want to."

Everybody laughed that vacuous party laugh. Except Groot, who continued to sip his drink, smoke his cigarette, and look sour.

Another group of beautiful young people came to curtsy before the queen, and Groot and Wagner exchanged glances. As the chattering resumed, Groot eased away and signaled with his eyes for Wagner to follow.

"You look as if you could bite the ass-end off a battleship, Groot. What's the matter?"

Groot got right to business: "I've got good news and I've got bad news."

"Give me the good news first."

"Our friend Morfey is resigning and returning to the States."

"Really? That's good news indeed."

"Odd. I thought the monster was thoroughly entrenched as a civil servant." Groot took a reflective puff on his cigarette.

"It just goes to show you: you can never tell what's in a man's mind."

"Did he give you a bad time the other day?"

"Not really. It was about the helicopter thing. Pohl wanted to bug a room Gregori's men are working out of. I was also chewed out for violating Ellie Pomeraine. Her amendment, I mean."

"A wretch. That's what he is."

"Yep." Wagner gave Groot a wary glance. "O.K., so what's the bad news?"

"It was a serious mistake, your coming here tonight."

"How come?"

"Akim Ri. The President speaks tomorrow at noon, and you still haven't led us to Akim Ri. You should be out there looking for him, not in here, socializing." Groot's pasty face showed traces of real annoyance.

The band began the sock chorus of "Marie," and the big room shook from the thunder, and the young people bounced and jiggled and whirled in their futuristic tarantella. The music and laughter and high-pitched talk provided an explosion that gave Wagner, unable to make himself heard anyhow, time to consider his real position.

He could, of course—should—take Groot aside and present a full update on the case, with particular emphasis on his discoveries at Frau Mahlmann's place, including the planted Robert Goodman campaign literature and the link between her and Frau Lindl and Rollo and Lotte and, by extension, Kahn. He could tell of the new attempt to kill him this evening; of the ever-present tail represented by the Mercedes; of the pattern that was forming, in which the Kahn group, presumably setting up an assassination for Akim Ri to accomplish, were using Gurney and Ellie Pomeraine as foils.

But there were other problems: Amy Randall herself, by inviting Gurney and Pomeraine into the act, was also being used by somebody. And the somebody had to be an American, and an American high up in the pecking order. So, if an American were behind the plot to kill the President—a plot in which foreign nationals and a rundown movie actor and an out-of-work renegade journalist were pivots—then there was someone in this room tonight who was to be feared. Perhaps it was Groot himself. If it was, it would be very unwise indeed to tell Groot anything at all; if it was not, then Groot was probably on top of things and he, Wagner, was exactly what Groot had announced him to be—the tracker of Akim Ri, and nothing more.

In either or any event, Wagner decided to play cool and close.

He might throw Groot a bone, though. He might tell

him how he'd found evidence in the Audi trunk that Gustav Kahn, wearing a phony moustache and a wig, had twice tried to kill him.

He was about to say this, in the relative quiet that accompanied the band's change of sets, but he thought he'd withhold even that tidbit.

He would tell Groot nothing. Not yet.

"It was your idea, Groot—yours and Amy Randall's—that I play nicey-nice with Ellie Pomeraine. She invited me to this crash, and, rather than risk a Supreme Court test of my daring to say no, I agreed to look in. If you don't like it, do me a favor and fire me."

"Well, say your hellos and get back to work."

"May I finish my drink first?"

"Don't get smart-ass. This is a crisis we have going."

"Well, if that's the case," Wagner snapped, feeling a return of his earlier anger, "what the hell are you doing here? The son of a bitch is your President, too, you know."

Groot was about to answer when a man with marcelled hair and dark glasses appeared out of the party-time storm. He stood before Groot and nodded wordlessly.

"What is it, Simmons?" Groot said.

"A message, sir. The office thought it of sufficient importance to be delivered to you at once." The man drew a white envelope from his double-knit jacket and handed it to Groot. After another nod, he turned and melted into the turmoil.

Groot tore open the envelope, unfolded a message form, read briefly, and went pale, a phenomenon which, Wagner thought in silly irrelevance, transformed white into whiter-than-white.

Crumpling the message and shoving it into a pocket, Groot turned without comment and made directly for Amy Randall, who was still holding court beside the large planter. The swirl of youthful admirers was still there, too, but standing stiffly at her side in the vortex was General Dirk, looking very much like a latter-day Custer making a stand against the crazies. The chairman was in mufti, but his massive head and chiseled face—staples of the Sunday supplements—were unmistakable, hovering as they did above the *Sturm und Drang*.

Wagner, curious, elbowed a path through the tobacco smoke and alcohol fumes and perfume and human heat to move into the lee of the planter, where, with the aid of the profuse and plastic foliage, he managed to be about two feet to the rear of—and unseen by—Miss Randall, the general, and the now-obviously outraged Groot. Leaning on the flower box in the manner of an inebriated guest surveying the uproar, he sipped his drink and listened.

"General Dirk," he heard Groot croak, "just what in the frigging hell do you think you're doing?"

"Watch your language, Groot. There are ladies present."

"I'm afraid you haven't heard anything yet, General. I just got a message."

"What kind of message?" Amy Randall said.

"The good general here," Groot said huskily, "has ordered the Eighty-second Airborne Division and the Hundred-first Airborne Division and the Hundred-seventeenth Helicopter Support Regiment into full combat alert. They are now loading aboard C–Fives at Rhine-Main and Fürstenfeldbruck, right out in front of God and everybody."

"What's your problem, Groot?" the general said, unruffled. "It's the Army's business to keep combat-ready, to conduct maneuvers."

"When it's supposed to be withdrawing from NATO? Withdrawing from Europe?"

"Why not? What's wrong with using a routine return to the States as a simulated combat problem?"

"Don't you see? Combined with your relocation of Task Force-Twelve, the combat alert of two crack airborne divisions and support elements can be badly misinterpreted by the Soviets. It's absolutely provocative."

"Nonsense. The Soviets have been watching us practice for years."

"That's right, Groot," Miss Randall said. "You worry too much about the Soviets. They know we don't want war. We aren't ready for war, and they are the first to recognize that truth."

"Besides," the chairman added, "why don't you let me run the military? You stick to your peeping, and I'll stick to my soldiering. Right?"

"Right," Amy Randall said, laughing.

"Well," Groot snapped, "you two can stand around in this madhouse if you want, but I've got work to do." He put down his glass and turned to go.

Amy Randall said, "Call me first thing in the morning. Groot. My brother will be arriving at Olympiapark on the dot, and I want you there with me."

"Very well."

"And don't take things so big," the general said.

After Groot had left, General Dirk and Miss Randall said nothing for a full minute. Then Dirk said, "Well, my dear, I must be getting back to my toil. It's more work to disband an alliance then it is to make it, I find."

"All right, darling. Call me. I'll try to meet you at the place tomorrow night. But call me in the morning. I need to hear your voice."

"Certainly. I miss you when we're apart."

"Well, dear, it won't be long now."

"Right. So good night."

"Bye."

With everybody leaving, Wagner saw no reason to stay and punish his eardrums further. So he followed the general through the crowd to the exit that led to the garage, where, he'd found on arrival, the Secret Service had reserved a parking place for him at the request of Miss Pomeraine, of the official party.

General Dirk, a tall and prepossessing figure among the couples careening to and from the garage, nodded stilted greetings to the security people posted at the doors and in the connecting corridor. Wagner looked them over as he went, but he failed to recognize any of them.

The garage was relatively peaceful, with no more than two or three cars snorting and jockeying for room in the sea of shiny metal and the dimly lit concrete caverns.

General Dirk headed for a GI Chevrolet parked near the main exit, and as Wagner prepared to peel off and find his BMW in the side-room stalls, he hesitated.

The chairman, spotting a dark-green VW parked in the shadows of a support pillar, strolled over to the little car and leaned against it to say something through the window to its occupant. He appeared to listen for a moment, then he nodded and slapped the car's roof in a kind of conclusive gesture. Wagner heard him say, "Good. Well, be about it."

Wagner took a position behind another pillar and waited until the general had fired up the Chevrolet and eased out the main door and into the night beyond. Then he sidled through the maze of cars, keeping low and out of sight, until he reached a place where a ceiling light gave a clear view of the man at the wheel of the VW.

It was Hans Trille, puffing on his pipe.

37

"Hey, where you going?"

He'd waited until Trille had driven off before returning to his own car, and he had just opened the door and climbed behind the wheel when Ellie Pomeraine hurried around the corner and hailed him.

"I'm going home," he told her. "I can't keep up with you young folks."

"How come you're leaving without me?"

"I didn't think you were ready to go. Last I saw, you were shaking your shimmy on the dance floor with a fugitive from Muscle Beach."

"Well, hell, Amy said she saw you leaving and you didn't even say good-night to either of us. You've got rotten manners, buddy-boy."

"Yeah."

"Aren't you going to take me with you?"

"Why? The party's here."

"As I recall, you don't exactly have an aversion to poon, pal. And poon's what I've got in mind. Your place or mine?"

"Not tonight. I did a big wash today."

"Hey, come on: we're pals, remember?"

"Sorry, lady. I'll call you. Meanwhile, thanks for the invite." He started the motor, threw in the gear, and purred out of the garage. In the rearview mirror he could see her standing there, hands on hips and shaking her head.

The rain had resumed, heavy and baleful and unrelenting, and his windshield wipers were hard put to keep ahead of it. He drove at a steady speed, since the München-Kufstein autobahn was nearly deserted.

Somewhere near Rosenheim, he decided to listen to the news, so he punched the button and waited through some dreary rock until the announcer came on with the half-hour highlights.

The creamy baritone told of President Randall's cordial reception at the Frankfurt trade fair and of his arrival in Munich this afternoon to much fanfare at Schloss Nymphenburg. The Minister-President of Bavaria had greeted him, as had dignitaries of the neighboring Länder and high officials of the city of Munich. Spokesmen said that the President was spending the evening in putting the finishing touches to his major policy speech, to be delivered tomorrow at Olympiapark. The work had made it impossible for the President to attend a gala sponsored by his sister, Congresswoman Amy Randall.

"Meanwhile," the newscaster reported in his unctuous tones, "the wave of terrorism accredited to the so-called Greuel continued in Munich tonight with the discovery of the decapitated body of Rudolph Kulka, owner-operator of a snack bar off the Stachus who had retired recently after more than twenty years as a policeman. Authorities were unable to say why Kulka, whose body was found in a trash bin at the rear of his place of business, was murdered. In other news—"

Wagner turned off the radio.

He'd never get used to it.

Never.

It always hurt so much.

The bastards.

The dirty, rotten, sons-of-bitching bastards.

It hurt more this time than it ever had before.

As he crossed the lobby and approached the stairway, Frau Lindl called to him from the door of her quarters, next to the desk.

"Herr Koenig, do you have a moment, please?"

He peered at her through the dim, midnight light of the midnight-quiet inn.

"What is it, Frau Lindl? I'm very tired, and—"

"It will take only a moment. Won't you step in, please?"

He followed her into her apartment and stood, soaking in the warmth and feeling a thousand years old, while she closed the door and hung his raincoat on a peg in the entrance arch.

"Won't you sit down, Herr Koenig?"

"No thanks. I've got to go to bed. I'm absolutely exhausted."

"If you'll forgive me: you look very bad. Pale. Are you ill?"

"No. I just got a bit of bad news, that's all. What with the bad news and being tired, I'm about ready to pack it in." He sighed and said, "What can I do for you?"

"You know how grateful I am for your courtesy and friendship and very considerable help in arranging my son's funeral."

"Frau Lindl, please: you've already thanked me."

"I know. But I'm an emotional kind of person, and I've been looking for a way—a small way—in which to express my gratitude in a, well, tangible manner. I think I've found it." She smiled wanly.

"It isn't necessary at all—"

"I know. That's why it's pleasing to me. It's more satisfying to do something for somebody when they don't want or expect you to."

"Well, I—"

"You and Eva Whitney are lovers, are you not?"

258

He gave her a quick look. "I don't know how to answer that."

She made a tiny sound, her watery old eyes hinting amusement. "You are also a gentleman, Herr Koenig. You will not say yes, because it might compromise a young lady; you will not say no, because it wouldn't be true. Ah, yes. The lover's dilemma."

He waited without comment for her to get to the point.

"You are probably wondering how I know. Well, my friend, women know those things. I had only to see you together, doing and saying ordinary things but never taking your eyes from each other."

She held her narrow and spotted hands to the stove's warmth, her eyes thoughtful. "My gift to you is my silent and hearty approval of your affair. My cooperation in it. I have already spoken to Eva, have already invited her to use the back stairs as a route to your room."

"I really don't know what to say," he said, meaning every word of it.

Frau Lindl shrugged. "Then say nothing." She glanced at him over a bony shoulder, pulling her shawl closer to her. "I know I must sound Victorian—absurdly prudish—about this matter, but, you see, I am truly a product of those times, that thinking. I have never been able to accept the license, the promiscuity, of these modern days, and it has always been unthinkable for me, the idea that our young people may live together, make children together, without the responsibilities that go hand-in-hand with the privileges."

Feeling like a grotesque Andy Hardy, he said, "I assure you, Frau Lindl, I have only the best intentions toward Fräulein Whitney."

"Of course. But I want you to know that all this represents a rather important concession for me to make. And I'm making it because my son's death has caused me to look at a lot of things. And you, unknowingly and by your kindness, helped me to realize that I, too, have left a lot to be desired in my relationships—with my son, my sister, my niece. I wanted so much for my son to be

259

someone like you. I pressed at him to be worthy and lovable, and I pressed so hard I had little time to give him love. So, I daresay, feeling unloved, he became unlovable. Rollo was as much a victim of my demands of him as he was of the shot that killed him."

"You're being unnecessarily hard on yourself, Frau Lindl."

"I think not. I've also been wretched to my sister, Anna-Marie, and her daughter, Lotte. Anna-Marie has always had what I call 'man trouble.' She's been wild, indiscriminate, since our days as children. I'm much older than she, of course, and as her big sister I gave her some very bitter treatment. And Lotte, I've treated as scum. Even Rollo felt sorry for the girl, what with an errant mother and a severe and judgmental aunt. No wonder she followed in her mother's footsteps. No wonder she failed her opportunity to marry a man of repute and accomplishment to go off with that gross man in Kitzbühel."

She paused, and Wagner said, "All families have their little problems."

"That," she said, glancing at him fully again, "is what my sister said you told her."

He knew he was showing surprise.

"Rollo's death put me in touch with Anna-Marie again. She called this evening to give her sympathies. I saw how cruel I'd been to her and Lotte and I told her so. We cried a bit, and we talked, and when I mentioned family disagreements she spoke of a visit she'd had from an uncommon policeman named Wilhelm Koenig. And she described you, and said how kind you'd been, and we agreed that for some reason you'd entered our lives to help us see the truth, and that the time for angers and resentments has passed. So, my dear Herr Koenig, I really owe you quite a lot. I want you to go now and enjoy as much of your life as you can. Take your time to enjoy and cherish that lovely girl. Because there is so little time for all of us in this world."

He nodded, bemused by the strange little scene, filled

as it was with German sentimentality and priggishness. Still, the old lady had obviously been terribly moved by her experience, and far be it from him to be indifferent to an old woman's yearning to make amends.

"Well," he said, "you're a dear lady, and I hope you can find some solace in all this. And you can rest easy: Fräulein Whitney and I will be discreet. We'll do nothing to cause you embarrassment."

"I'm sure. Meanwhile, you'll not be disturbed. I'll see to that."

As he took his coat from the peg and prepared to leave, he said, "By the way, Frau Lindl, you mentioned that your niece, Lotte, had been engaged to some kind of nice fellow. Who was he?"

She sighed and shrugged again. "A man of considerable achievement as an aviator war-hero and, since, as a police officer. Perhaps you know him, being in that work. Herr Trille? Hans Trille?"

"I've heard of him, of course. Lotte threw him over, did she?"

"No. Lotte, I'm sorry to say, became addicted to drugs. Her mother to alcohol, her to drugs. Sad, sad, sad. But Herr Trille found it necessary to break the engagement, naturally. Being a reputable public official, he could not afford to associate with a drug addict. Sad."

"Yes, very sad. Well, good night, Frau Lindl. And thank you again."

October 18

"Hello?"

"Groot?"

"Speaking."

"There's moonlight on the bay."

"Herr Wismer. I was just about to call you."

"I have the news you've been waiting for."

"News?"

"I have determined who is trying to kill Wagner."

"Who?"

"An attempt was made on him this evening. Before Miss Randall's party. Someone tried to shoot him in the parking lot of the Edelweiss Hof. The shot missed. I followed the would-be assassin."

"Well, who was it?"

"Gustav Kahn."

"You're sure?"

"I followed him to his apartment in Kitzbühel."

"That's a very peculiar development."

"Yes, isn't it."

"Puzzling."

"Mm. You say you were going to call me?"

"Ah. I was. Routine."

"You were going to call? But not now?"

"I mean, I had planned a routine check-in with you. Now, with this new development, I want to sort things out a bit before we talk further."

"All right. Call me when you're ready."

"Yes. Good night, Herr Wismer."

"Good night, Groot."

38

It was cold in the room, and through the curtains he could see the mountains in that twilight that lingers for a time before dawn. The rain had finally stopped, and he knew there'd be mist in the high valleys, and ice where the green ended and the titanic cliffs began. Somewhere in the silence outside a bird called, far up and lonely.

He sat at the small table, with the hooded lamp making a pool of light on the papers before him. He'd been there for two hours, staring at the diagram he'd drawn, reading and rereading the police files of the various personalities, adding and subtracting and fitting and piecing. And no matter how he placed the pieces, they added up to the same conviction: there could be only one motive, and in light of that motive, there could be only one Who.

As he had worked, there'd been recurring thoughts of his friend, and he tried to convince himself that Rudi had died precisely when God, or the Fates, or Kismet, or Batman and Robin had wanted him to die. It was a terrible thing to lose a friend to savagery: it was an even more terrible thing to realize that he'd deliberately involved Rudi in the savage business that had killed him.

He did not want to be responsible, so he laid it all on Universal Wisdom. But it didn't help.

Eva was sleeping. She had been sleeping like a child since subsiding, fulfilled. She lay curled under the huge feather quilt, her hair a dark cloud on the pillow. He looked at her from time to time, puzzled over what she had become to him.

He had wanted to sleep, too, and he had held her close for a long time after her breathing had become deep and even. But his mind wouldn't give up, choosing on its own, it seemed, to fret and tug and poke and pull over the scraps of intrigue he'd spread on the tablecloth. And so, softly, so as not to awaken her, he'd wrapped himself in his robe and sat at the table, staring.

It was there. The outline was taking shape.

The Amy Randall party had made the difference. It had brought him the dimensions he'd been missing.

There were still some dangling strings.

But it was there. He knew it. By laying it all out, piece by interlocking piece, and then adding the final, mad guess, it came together in the only pattern to make sense. A terrible, sane insanity.

Which method it would be and how to thwart it was his immediate problem.

Later, when the dawn light filtered strong through the leaded panes, she came up quietly behind him to rest her head on his and to slide her arms about him.

"You're so troubled," she whispered.

"I have so little time to understand it all."

"Come back to bed. Let it alone awhile."

"I can't. Today, after noon, it'll be done. I have only a few hours."

"Can I help?"

"No. But I've been thinking about you. I want you to leave this place. I'll give you five hundred dollars. Call Hertz or Avis or somebody, rent a car, and drive to the Adlershof Hotel in Nesselwang. Register as Mrs. Steven Cartwright of Wilmington, Delaware. The desk man is reliable, and the name means something to him. If anyone should ask, you're waiting for your husband, who's due to arrive in another car. Wait three days. If I don't show up by then, take the rest of the money and go home to Colorado. Have a good life."

"Frau Lindl tells me you're a policeman. Is that true?"

"In a way. I hope I can explain things soon. Meanwhile, take the money"—he counted out five hundred-dollar bills—"and do as I've told you. O.K.?"

"Are you in danger?"

"I don't want to take the slightest chance that either of us is. So get dressed, pack your things, and get going. I'll see you in Nesselwang."

"Frau Lindl owes me wages."

"I'll explain to her. I'll tell her we're eloping and will be in touch with her later."

She came around and sank across his lap, and he held her.

"Be careful," she said softly against his throat.

"Sure."

"I've just found you."

He thought about this, and how strange and good it was that she hadn't asked about anything—hadn't, in the way of women, probed for what he was up to. But habit, like savagery, is an absolute that insists on absolutes. And so he found it possible, as always, to speculate on her willingness to leave his secrets to him.

Was it because she knew about them already?

Oh, God, he heard himself saying, please don't let her be just another trickster. Let her be what she seems to be.

"Is that your real name? Steven Cartwright?" she asked him.

"No."

"You're an American, though."

"Yes. I'm an American."

"I don't really care what your name is."

She swung to her feet and, leaning, kissed his forehead. Then she went to the wardrobe and busied herself with dressing. She remained silent in that way of hers, freeing

266

him to return to his contemplations. Only when she was at the door did she speak.

"I'm on my way to Nesselwang, Mr. Cartwright."

"All right, Mrs. Cartwright. Next stop: Colorado Springs."

"Don't get bent."

"I promise." He gave her a slow, reassuring wink.

She gazed at him for a long moment, then she was gone.

He began to dress, but as he went his eyes kept going to the table. It was there. It had to be.

It had begun to show form when he'd seen the junction between Ziggi Rattner and Gustav Kahn. In what must have been his twentieth reading of their profiles, the framework had finally begun to assemble. Ziggi and Kahn had both been stationed at the sappers' school at Murnau toward the end of War Two. Connection. Each was, presumably, familiar—if not expert—in the use of explosives. Connection. Both were on the rim of the Munich underworld, with police records and overlap of time, locations, and jail experience. Connection. Rattner had been hired by somebody solely to report a plot against the President. Period. Reasons to believe this: (1) he'd worked with U.S. intelligence, whose officials would tend to listen to him and his warning; (2) he'd been killed immediately after issuing the warning, meaning that the plotters had never meant to use him beyond that initial function. The other killings, of the bouncer, of the butler, and the efforts to kill Roger Wagner, alias Wilhelm Koenig, had been to close off possible identifiers of the culpable. Who was culpable? Kahn, of course.

But who was behind Kahn?

Who had hired Kahn to hire Akim Ri? Who had hired Kahn to set up Rattner, Gurney, Pomeraine, Wagner? Who had hired Kahn to superintend the arrangements for, and conduct of, one of the most ambitious international intrigues since the Kennedy assassination?

267

There was only one way to confirm that.

But it would have to wait until he'd confirmed the method of assassination. The how had to be determined first.

Would Akim Ri in fact try to shoot President Randall?

Or would explosives expert Gustav Kahn try to blow him up?

Which assassin would be the phony?

Once given the answer to that question, the Who would become apparent.

He could have called from his room, of course, but conversations through extensions and switchboards enjoyed about as much privacy as a barbershop debate, and it was his practice to avoid them whenever possible. So he went to the lobby and used the pay phone in the insulated booth off the service hallway.

It took a lot of time to locate the president of the Army Wives Association. He called the public information officer at Wolfratshausen, the Army's big installation south of Munich, and there was considerable fussing around with base directories and some haggling on intercoms between the duty noncom and someone in the O.D.'s quarters, but he finally acquired the name and phone number and got her on the first try.

"Hello-o?"

"I'm trying to locate Mrs. Ernest T. Greene, president of the Army Wives Association."

"I'm Mrs. Greene. Who's calling?" The voice suggested Middle America and shady suburbs and PTA's, and he thought of Eva Whitney and was suddenly homesick.

"This is Louis Frammsville, and I'm a research assistant on *Chronos* Magazine. I'm sorry to call you so early in the morning but we're trying to beat a deadline."

"That's perfectly all right. I've been up for ages, getting my husband off to work and all. What can I do for you?"

"I'm checking out a few facts for a story being prepared on President Randall's visit to Munich and the various ripple effects and so on. And right now I'm prepping some sidebar stuff on Amy Randall, who, according to the VIP itineraries handed out by the White House advance party, is going to address your group the day after the President returns to the States."

"Yes," Mrs. Greene said, "we're delighted. Just delighted."

"What'll she be speaking about?"

Mrs. Greene laughed, and it was a sound full of genuine good humor, and he suspected that she was a woman he would have liked. "I wish I could say, Mr. Frammsville, but with somebody as busy and important as Miss Randall you don't just call her up and say, 'Hey, what's your subject?' I mean, with somebody like that you just let them do their thing, you know?"

"So you didn't ask her to speak on any specific subject. And she hasn't told you what she'll talk about. Right?" He spoke as if he were making notes.

"That's right. We're glad to have her under any conditions. It's done marvels already, prestige-wise. You wouldn't believe the attention it's getting, and reservations for the luncheon at the Officers Club are simply astronomical."

"I'll bet." He got down to what he really wanted to know. "How is it that you invited Miss Randall to speak? It wasn't known until only a week or so ago that she'd be coming to Germany. That means you must have moved pretty fast to send her an invite and get an acceptance.

Mrs. Green laughed again. "Well, that's what's so unexpected and surprising and exciting about it all. We have this annual meeting, see, and we always have some prominent Army man, or whatever, come to talk to us, and it's a kind of tradition, and, well, this year we were going to have Samuel F. Willoughby, assistant chef at the Pentagon's dining rooms, who was going to tell us how they prepare the meals for the brass and what all the luminaries like in the way of special dishes, and like that, you know? And then on a Sunday evening at home my husband gets this phone call from Washington, and the next thing you know I'm talking to the office of the chairman."

"Chairman?"

"You know: General Dirk, chairman of the Joint Chiefs. Well, I almost died, I'll tell you."

"Why?"

"Well, my goodness. My husband's only a company commander in an infantry regiment and here I am talking to somebody in the JCS."

"No. I mean why did the chairman's office call you?"

"It was a Colonel Carruthers, or somebody. And he said that the chairman had learned how Miss Randall would be visiting Germany and wanted to meet some of the service people's wives and families, and he would consider it a special favor if I, as this year's president of the AWA, would extend her an invitation to speak at our annual luncheon. Can you imagine General Dirk asking *me* for a favor? Heavens."

"It does seem unusual, doesn't it." He rattled some phonebook pages so that she might imagine him busily making more notes.

"I'll say," Mrs. Greene said in her All-American way. "I said the same thing to Colonel Carruthers. I'd think Miss Randall would be traveling home with her brother, the President, after the summit and all. But the colonel said she planned to stay over a day or two, just to talk to military families."

"I see," he said, adding, "What's Miss Randall's schedule at Wolfratshausen?"

"There'll be the luncheon, and then a tour of the base, and then cocktails at the Officers Club and supper at the NCO club. Then she'll fly to Heidelberg that night for a visit with the command there the next day."

"O.K.," Wagner said briskly. "Anything else I ought to know, Mrs. Greene?"

"Golly, I don't think so. Is all this going to be written up in *Chronos*? I mean, wow."

"I'm not sure. I'm just a researcher. Somebody else does the writing."

"Oh. Well, I sure hope we can get a plug for AWA in there. Wow."

"We'll do our best, Mrs. Greene. Thanks a lot for your help. And again: my apologies for calling you so early."

"Well, sure. Thank *you*."

He hung up, remaining in the booth and thinking about all this for nearly five minutes. He thought he could confirm his main suspicion right now, this very moment, by making one more call.

But if such a call confirmed his theory now, before he also knew the method—the how—he'd only get himself killed.

And that would be very inconvenient.

His first move was to have a quick cup of coffee with Frau Lindl, who was delighted (and relieved) to learn of his plan to elope with Eva. She gave him a little hug when he left, and it cheered him to be so well liked by this old woman, with her blue-dot eyes and slow smile and lilies-of-the-valley scent. His next step was a visit to the Von Hoffman Foundation Library in Kitzbühel. Perched behind the inquiry desk was a prim little man with owlish spectacles who watched his approach with all the cordiality of a house detective.

"May I help you?" the man asked, as if he rather doubted Wagner could read at all.

"Do you have anything on the United States Government? Organization, elective system, how Congress operates—that kind of thing?"

The man seemed to consider this to be worthy of first prize in the World's Dumbest Question Contest. His nose wrinkled and his magnified eyes showed a glint of contempt. "That would be readily available to you on the reference shelves, sir. Down that aisle, second stack on the left."

"Thank you, Your Highness."

It was not readily available. There were a number of German-language essays on the subject of America, bound in expensive leather and carrying publication dates that made them only a little less up-to-date than Caesar's Gallic Wars. There were several sets of encyclopedias,

271

likewise archaic, and a U.S. Government manual issued in 1957. But in a corner, barely visible in a rank of soft-bound reports, was a slim little booklet published the previous autumn by the League of Women Voters Education Fund, and on page 81, under Appendix B, he found exactly what he was looking for: the Twenty-fifth Amendment to the U.S. Constitution, followed by a discussion of its provisions and the controversy that had swirled about them. .

He read it all, very carefully. Three times. And each time his heart pounded more heavily.

There it was. The Why.

It held together, by God.

Now fully aware of the odds against him, now alternately excited and depressed, he went to the library's south wing and dug out a volume on ballistics, from which he copied a table and a chart. Then, after consulting the International Who's Who to confirm that Dirk and Trille had indeed been ETO contemporaries, he left the library for a visit to a hobby shop near the post office, where he bought a razor knife to be used in case he had to go the cutting route.

Next stop: Munich.

October 19

"Hello?"

"Herr Wismer?"

"Herr Wismer is not in at the moment."

"This is Groot."

"Who?"

"There's sunshine on the bay."

"What can we do for you, Herr Groot?"

"I must talk to Herr Wismer."

"Sorry. He's out."

"How soon will he be back? This is most urgent."

"I can't say. He comes. He goes."

"Is he on Wagner?"

"I have no idea. I only take his messages."

"Well, for God's sake, have him contact me at once. As soon as he comes in."

"Of course. Good-bye, Herr Groot."

39

Groot had been up most of the night.

He was standing at the window of his room, peering down at the barren streets, which, after the days of soaking rain, were bleached-looking and antiseptic. There was a thin, drifting mist over the city, and the dawn silence was broken only by the murmuring of an occasional passing car, the rattling of a milk truck, the distant grinding of a trolley. Above the haze, the sky was royal blue and streaked with very high streamers of feathery ice clouds, already alight in a sun still waiting to rise.

It would be a beautiful October day.

The revelation that it was Kahn who'd been trying to kill Wagner—and, obviously, who'd killed Rattner—was disturbing, upsetting, frightening, gross.

But he wasn't sure he knew why.

The feeling that he was missing something—something terribly important—had been with him for several days, but with this incomprehensible deviation of Kahn, this mystifying rebellion of an old walking horse, the sensation had become acute; painful, actually.

If there'd been time, he would have placed a special team on the matter, of course, giving them top-urgency authorization to discover what Kahn was up to. But there was no time. The President was to speak today, then fly home today. And even Herr Wismer was nowhere to be found.

Things were beginning to wobble for lack of control, and Wagner, wherever he was, whatever he was doing, represented the single control factor. All else was defense: the Secret Service, the lavish and intricate security systems emanating from the presidential epicenter, the cordons, the street police and the crowd-control squads, the helicopter patrols—all were negatives, all were antimeasures. The positive regulation of events which Kahn had provided was now unaccountably not to be trusted, and Groot had the distinct sense of impending disaster.

He had to think. He had to see the answer.

That the life of the President was now on the line, he was now certain. The good graces of the only woman he admired stood to be lost. He could not let either of them down.

One thing was clear: Wagner had to be found and protected at all costs. Wagner, the single remaining link to the forces that seemed to be careening, must be given the hours left to search, find, and cancel.

Dear God. If the man would only call. If, only, even Wismer would call. . . .

Where are you, Wagner? Why don't you call, Wagner? Why must you be such a lone wolf, Wagner?

I need more information, Wagner. I need to know what you know.

He lifted the phone and tried the Edelweiss Hof again. But the woman on the switchboard said Herr Koenig had checked out.

So he got Kevin on the Secret Service hot line and asked him to alert all agents to watch for Wagner. Then he called Hans Trille and asked for an all-points on Wilhelm Koenig.

The message: *For God's sake, call home.*

Call home, you romantic, single-handed son of a bitch. Daddy needs you.

40

He had cleared the border at Kufstein and was steaming at flank speed on the Munich Autobahn. The day had dawned brilliant and crystal, and the granite towers of the Alps behind him seemed to be pasted against a sky of unrelieved sapphire velvet. It was already mid-morning, and the clock was running severely against him.

The policeman who'd checked his credentials at the border had waved him through, but a phone had been ringing, and as he drove off he thought he'd heard someone calling out. Instinct—always that suspicious, anxious, hard-working, never-quiet Gut-Society for the Prevention of Cruelty to Roger Wagner—had told him instantly that somebody, probably Groot, had put out an alert for him. The suspicion was confirmed when, in the distance to the rear, he saw a dark green car, a blue police light flashing on its roof, bounce out of a parking area at the border station and take after him.

He'd put the pedal to the floor, and the BMW had easily outrun the patrol car. But now the problem was radio, and the police that might be waiting ahead. So, despite the lack of time, he left the Autobahn south of Rosenheim and headed due west, and then northwest, on back-country roads: Miebach to Reigersbeuern and then to the new cut-off around Bad Tölz, then on to the Starnberger See and a straight shot north by northeast into Harlaching. He parked the BMW there, and, keeping his eye out for police cars, took a cab to a rental agency. He would need a car, but the BMW was hot. The rental people gave him a VW, credited to his driver's license and credit card in the name of Oskar Freundt of Mittenwald, and he drove west around the Teresienweise and picked up Landshuter Allee for a fast run north to Olympiapark.

The driving had been rough, and his arms ached and his eyes burned.

He had seen many police cars and policemen, and there had been a time, on Hans Fischer Strasse near the fairgrounds, when a dark-hued Mercedes had given him a fright. If he was anywhere near right in his thinking, everybody was looking for him and nobody was friendly.

Every car, every face at every corner, had become a threat.

Fear magnifies.

He realized that he was sweating, and this, with all the other weary evidence, proved to him once again that his string had run out. He was no longer any good for this business. Even physically. He'd overstayed his usefulness, his capability. He was the wrong man for the wrong job.

Ironically, in Groot's eyes, he'd been precisely the right man for the job.

Oh, Jesus. What a world.

He parked the VW in the public plaza west of the Athletics Hall and the training fields. Happily, he found a place close to the access to the Brauchle Ring, which put only a broad grass area and the Olympiahalle between the car and the tower area. Crowds had already assembled, and the police and traffic-control people were as thick as flies, waving white-gloved hands and bawling orders and

277

moving barricades and ropes into place. He even saw Hans Trille, standing beside his VW in the blue shadows of the Olympiahalle, puffing his meerschaum and talking quietly with a big-chested uniformed officer of the Schützpolizei.

Taking care never to leave the protection of the shuffling mommies and daddies and kiddies and aunties, he made his way to an unoccupied bench under a tree near the west end of the artificial lake. He was wearing the hat and Tyrolean jacket Frau Lindl had loaned him, and so, if he were careful, he could pass casual examination as a tourist dozing in the morning light. Then, with the Zeiss glasses that had belonged to the late husband of the same ever-helpful Frau Lindl, he focused on the heights that overlooked the tower area from south of the lake.

The open sweeps of grass and the tree line running the long axis of the ridge were teeming with police and dogs.

Hans Trille, too, had decided the ridge would make an ideal spot for a rifleman.

So that took care of that.

Standing up and putting the glasses in their case, he sauntered to another point of ground that gave him a clear view of the tower and the low entrance hall, restaurant, and office building at its foot. He took out the table he'd copied in the library and, trying to resurrect the lessons of Fort Benning all those centuries ago, he began to estimate angles and windage, doing little problems in arithmetic.

Shooting at acute angles from above or below a target is a tricky business, since the tendency is almost invariably to overshoot, that is, shoot high. The tac officers at Benning had emphasized that the slant range—the distance along the line from the rifle to the target—is greater than the horizontal range, even though the sight-setting of the rifle is correct for the actual range between muzzle and target. To counter the phenomenon of overshooting, a table of adjustment had been developed, so that a sniper could estimate his effective

278

range, divide by a numerical factor, and arrive at the proper slant-range sight-setting.

With the glasses, he examined the roofs of the foothills buildings and saw policemen on them all. So low-angle slope shooting would be unlikely, if not impossible. Then he traversed the tower from base to top, looking for maintenance access ports in the shaft. He also studied the Postkorb area directly under the Aussichtskorb and its revolving restaurant, and saw that the windows or observation platforms of both were impractical, because the slope angle, close to the vertical, would be intersected by parts of the building. Any workable angle of slant in those positions would require a rifleman to adjust his sights, correct for windage, and fire while in full public view. This, coupled with the problem of escape (even with a parachute, for cripes' sake) from a tower that stood 290 meters high, made it very doubtful that a shooter would make such a try. Even by supposing the existence of an access port anywhere up to forty-five degrees above the horizontal, the same escape problem would exist. So, working with alternate ranges and alternate angles of slant, assuming a presidential target there, there, or there, even assuming zero wind, and juggling the table factors in a series of imaginary sight-setting exercises, he could find no concealment on the tower that would support a good position for hiding, aiming, adjusting, and firing.

The trees were the only place, as he'd originally figured, but they were out. It was an armed camp over there.

So, if his guess as to the true method was wrong, there was no other way for it: Kahn would have to use explosives.

He examined the tower again, speculating, wondering still another time if he'd guessed wrong and there was, ticking in there right now, a bomb for the President's lunch.

It was rotten, this business of having to guess so much.

If only Gurney had talked more.

But even then, damn it, there wasn't time.

The only thing he had going for him now was his guess.

If he'd guessed correctly, there was a chance—a very slim one—that nobody would die. If he'd guessed incorrectly, a lot of people would die.

Including Eva Whitney's new boyfriend, Roger the Dodger.

The crowds were very heavy now. The President had arrived as scheduled and was well into his speech in the Olympiahalle. Outside, a kind of promenade had been established by portable police barricades along the walks and across the lawns lying between the hall and the tower, and on both sides of this were masses of people, all in a kind of holiday mood. Bands were thumping somewhere, German and American flags were being waved by jolly-faced burghers and fat little children with creamy cheeks, balloons were bobbing, banners were snapping in the breeze, and everywhere there was noise and hilarity. President Randall might very well have been in trouble at home, and he might truly have teed-off the German Government, but, Wagner mused, he sure was a keen baby as far as the German people seemed concerned.

The presidential motorcade from Schloss Nymphenburg had drawn up in the Olympiaturm parking area, which lay just north of the tower and adjacent to the Brauchle Ring. Press and television vehicles had been accommodated in the same lot, as had a number of police escort and crowd-control vehicles. Barricades kept the plasmic crowds from this site, but there was a lot of coming and going of officials and quasi-officials, and Wagner watched these with much interest for a time.

He finally spotted Kahn's blue Audi.

It had been placed at the corner of the official parking area, and it had been admitted there, presumably, because it now sported a police-type emergency light on its roof and a decal on its trunk lid that read POLIZEI. Its blue was the wrong shade for any of the regulation municipal, state, or national police flects, but only the most curious cop would have wondered about it. There were so many

280

special vehicles of so many special hues here today—from U.S. Army recon cars to garish TV camera trucks—that it must have been a piece of cake for Kahn to slide into the restricted area.

But Kahn hadn't changed the license plates, which made it possible for Wagner to identify the car and which also gave Wagner the first scrap of evidence that his theory might be the right one after all.

Heartened slightly, he looked around for Kahn, but with no success.

A troupe of Wild West Indians, all gaudy in face paint and feathers, piled out of a red bus carrying the Krystal Film Kompanie legend and assembled before an officious fellow in horn-rim glasses and a checkered sport coat who, turning and waving his arms and shouting shrill instructions, led them to a position behind a barricade that formed part of the Olympiahalle-tower promenade. A lot of daddies and kiddies swirled after, hooting in TV cowboy fashion and trading jocular comments with the little band of film extras, who seemed embarrassed.

Wagner studied the Indians carefully, and eventually he felt discouragement and anxiety replacing his earlier hopefulness.

There wasn't a familiar face in the lot.

It wasn't coming together.

There was a roar from the throng around the Olympiahalle, and a fanfare of trumpets and a band playing Yankee-Doodle. A stirring went through the amassed humanity, a wavelike surge of excitement and old-fashioned thrill seeking. Craning, Wagner could see the central figure of President Randall coming at a slow, arm-waving pace from the great, tentlike meeting hall. Beside him was Amy Randall, radiant in a blue-gray suit, and to their rear were the white-haired, boutonniered, frock-coated dignitaries, the flower girls, and the lesser bureaucrats, all trying to look more important than they were.

The crowd began to chant "Randi, Randi"—the

President's nickname from his Viet Nam soldiering days—and the band had switched to "I'm a Yankee-Doodle Dandy." The President waved and grinned his famous grin, and Wagner watched, engrossed, as children ran to Randall with flowers and Bavarian dolls and candy canes. The President bent over, patting heads and exchanging sounds of delight with Amy, and then he was moving again, and he went into the business ambivalently loved and despised by American politicians who, inexplicably, saw magic in pressing and touching proffered hands. The hands, thousands of them it seemed, reached and waved and stretched for the slightest brush with the man their owners saw to be the richest and most powerful citizen of the richest and most powerful nation on earth.

Little do they know, Wagner thought bitterly. *Their politicians know. But they don't. They don't know we're on the run....*

Because he had nothing left to do, because his luck had truly run out, Wagner watched numbly.

Materializing from somewhere near the presidential party, Emerson Gurney, tricked out in ridiculous sheepskin chaps, silver six-guns and spurs, purple boots and chalk-white eighty-gallon hat, stood waving to the crowds. Even from where he watched, Wagner could see he was drunk.

Confusion began to close in.

Gurney came, slightly atilt, to the barricade where the movie Indians were grouped, waving their plastic tomahawks and patting their mouths with fluttering hands and hooting an idiotic chant. Gurney, flushed and grinning his crooked grin, took a chief's headdress from a box held by one of the men in the phalanx. As he prepared to turn and amble off toward the President, Gurney's red eyes focused on something in the crowd behind Wagner, and there was a flash of something like fear in the actor's puffy features.

Eyes hot and staring, Wagner spun about.

There.

There, by God!

There she was. Sidling up to the edge of the Indian party.

Lotte Mahlmann, in deerskin jacket and severe black wig and mocassins, her face painted in streaks of red and yellow and white. A hunting bow in her hand and a quiver of arrows on her back.

His mouth dry, his heart pounding, Wagner shoved his way through the roaring masses to take up station immediately to Lotte's rear.

Jostling and pushing, the crowd pressed him against her, and he took out the razor knife and sliced the bow string.

Gurney ran to the President, throwing the Indian bonnet aside and grinning a hideous grin.

President Randall, startled, stepped back as Gurney seized him, hauled him into his bearlike embrace, and whirled—turning his own back to Mahlmann.

Wagner, forcing himself to freeze, compelling himself to stand fast in a terrible moment of confirmation, watched the girl through eyes glazed by the realization that it was happening—happening precisely as he had guessed.

Lotte Mahlmann reached quickly over her shoulder, fingered a long, steel-tipped hunting arrow from the quiver, and brought the bow up.

She stood, staring stupidly, first at the useless arrow in the fingers of her right hand, and then at the dangling string of the bow in her left hand.

The Secret Service had rushed to the President, who watched, bemused and brushing at his rumpled jacket, as they hauled a shouting, foot-dragging Gurney toward a nearby police van.

In the uproar, Wagner thought he heard Gurney shouting, "What the hell—it's not supposed to go like this—"

41

The fat man with the Tyrolean hat was directly behind Lotte.

A switchblade was in his meaty right hand, and his arm was cocked, ready to drive the blade into the girl's leather-clad back.

He, too, however, was off-pace, confused by the turn of events, and his hesitation enabled Wagner to take two quick dancer's steps.

With a judo move, he spun the knife from the man's hand.

With a pounding jab of his shoe heel, he reduced the man's instep to splinters.

The man opened his mouth to scream, but the pain was obviously so intense he could do no more than lean against the crowd's crush, his eyes wide, his jowls trembling, saliva running.

Wagner took Lotte's elbow, and she turned marblelike eyes to stare at him, and he could see she was stoned.

Somebody pushed at the fat man and said, "Get lost, you damned drunk."

Somebody else said, "Jesus, everybody's drunk today. Even Emerson Gurney."

Somebody else said, "I wish to hell I was."

The fat man swayed on his good foot, crying soundless tears. Behind him was Gustav Kahn, huge and malevolent in his fake, off-shade mustache and his tinted glasses and his black wig.

"All right, Kahn," Wagner said. "So what are you going to do? Shoot me? Right here in the crowd? Where everybody can see you? Even the TV's watching."

Kahn rumbled, "You jimmied the amplifier."

Wagner said, "You're finished. It didn't work. Go home."

"I should have killed you first off," Kahn said.

"Like Ziggi? Like the bouncer? Like the butler?" Wagner felt a poisonous anger in his mouth. "Like Rudi Kulka? My friend?"

"So what are you going to do, Wagner?"

Wagner gave him a sardonic smile. "Ah. You know my name. My real name."

Kahn's face was set in a stubbornness whose roots were in fear. His wide mouth twitched at a corner, and Wagner could see his jaw muscles working. "I heard it around," Kahn said.

"All right. As of this moment, you and your pals are under arrest."

The crowd, oblivious of their little tableau, began to break up and flow. The President and his entourage had disappeared into the tower and were now, according to plan, rising to the restaurant in elevators that traveled six meters in a second.

"You're taking *me* prisoner?" Kahn said, nervous laughter in his voice.

"No, Inspector Trille is."

Wagner nodded his head toward a ring of policemen closing in. In the vanguard was Trille, his lean features pale and taut.

"Everybody in Germany has been looking for you," Trille barked. "Everybody."

"What for?"

"There's an all-points. Request of the highest authorities. You are supposed to contact your superior at once. A matter of national urgency."

"In the meantime, I want you to arrest this man, Gustav Kahn, this woman, Lotte Mahlmann, and this fellow with the foot problem."

Trille traded stares with Kahn. "What are the charges?" he asked Wagner.

"Murder, for Kahn. Accessories for the other two."

"Come downtown and give me the details."

"I can't. I'm under an all-points to call home, remember? I'll come by your office later."

Trille's features showed doubtful hesitation. "Well—"

"By the way: Kahn's car is parked over there." He pointed. "I think you'll find a rifle in it, or near it. A rifle that's been fired."

Wagner strode off, feigning nonchalance. When he arrived in the shadows of the big hall, he looked back, and he saw Trille and Kahn in heated discussion, heading for a gaggle of police cars parked on the grass by the tower's base. A brace of uniformed policemen were following with the limping fat man and the automatous Lotte Mahlmann.

Finding a pay phone, Wagner fished some coins from his pocket and, closing the door of the booth and lifting the phone, he found that it was his turn to hesitate. This was the conclusive move which, if it turned out as he expected, would identify the author of the little Indian production that had gone so sour.

One more step. Then one more step after that. And then it will be done.

He put through the call.

"Hendel Kompanie."

"Herr Nagel, please."

"Herr Nagel is not in today."

"Please contact him. Tell him to call Gustav Kahn. Extreme emergency." He gave her the number and hung up.

Nine minutes passed before the phone rang.

"Hello?"

"Kahn?"

"Mm."

"What in God's name is going on? What went wrong? And why are you calling me and using your own name? You know how important the code names are. No emergency warrants the use of—"

Wagner pressed down the receiver cradle with his finger, then hung up the phone.

"Well, Groot," he said aloud, "so much for your end of it. Now we'll see what the real story is."

The traffic was very heavy, but the police were efficient, and so he nosed the VW out of the parking area and into the Brauchle Ring. Driving fast, he crossed the Isar and turned south to Toginger Strasse, where he fell in with the stream of cars heading east toward München-Riem.

He wasn't sure how he'd pull it off.

He estimated that he had no more than an hour. By then the President would have finished his luncheon and his farewell remarks and would be on his way.

If his luck held, if his total guess was totally correct, there'd be a phone call. And they would be expecting him.

And if he was totally lucky, there wouldn't be a thing they could do about it.

42

Groot returned to the table, as much disturbed by the phone call as he was by the mysterious nonevent below.

The luncheon seemed to be a dreadful lull after the President's triumphal appearance in the Olympiahalle. But here, in this bizarre eating place, turning on its axis through a full circle every thirty-six minutes, the ebullience and international camaraderie had seemed to be oddly muted. Perhaps the spectacle of Munich below and the Alps in the distance, exchanging each for the other on the half-hour, was, thanks to its looming majesty, a suppressant. Or maybe even a depressant.

Whatever the cause and no matter the effect, Groot was upset, and his face must have showed it when he took his seat at the table beside Amy Randall.

"What is it, Groot?" she said in a quiet aside so that her brother, making idle talk with the minister of Land Bayern, would be unable to overhear. "What went wrong?"

"I don't know. I simply don't know."

"What was all that business with Gurney and the police and all? Obviously something went on. But what?"

"I can't tell you now. I'm trying to find out."

"What was that call about?"

"I'll have to tell you later. We can't talk here."

"You've got a lot of explaining to do, buster."

He fell silent, staring bleakly at the purple distance and sipping *eine Halbe*.

Ellie Pomeraine, exuding a cloud of expensive scent, came up to lean over his shoulder and say in an exaggerated whisper: "Where's your buddy Wagner?"

"I don't know. Why?"

"Well, heck. You told me to stick with him. But da man don't want me. He told me—politely, of course—to shove it."

"It's too late now anyhow, I'm afraid."

"C'est la guerre."

"When did you see him last?"

"At the party. In the garage at Klub Monika. He was watching those two creeps chew the rag."

"What two creeps?"

"General Dirk. And that German cop, Trille."

"Oh."

"Well, if I hear from Wagner, what do I do?"

"Forget it, Miss Pomeraine. It's too late."

She wandered off, and he sat, frozen, his mind racing.

General Dirk, he saw, was in bored conversation with the German ballerina, Elise von Lamprecht.

Dirk?

Trille?

He realized that, for the first time in his intelligence career, he'd completely lost control of a situation of his own devising.

43

Wagner left the VW in the passenger parking section in front of the terminal. The airport was doing business as usual, despite the imminent departure of President Randall and his party. The Lufthansa jet that was reserved for the return to Washington had been placed at the far end of the concrete apron, where a huge maintenance hangar formed a blue bulge on the grassy sea. Rope barriers were around the airplane, more to underscore the elemental aloofness required of the presidency than to thwart encroachments. But the terminal building and its adjacent structures were heavily policed, and access to any area beyond the commercial ticket counters, the restaurant, the restrooms, and the waiting areas had been barred by chains and ropes manned by cops and agents with bored faces and uncreased suits.

Wagner entered the lobby and glanced about. He saw a Secret Service face he recognized and so he crossed the crowded room to where the man stood, eyeing the passing suitcases.

"Hi," Wagner said, holding out his CIA ID card, "I'm

on special duty for the Company. You're Bill Coad, aren't you?"

"Yeah. And you're Wagner. Long time no see. Fort Holabird, wasn't it?"

They shook hands and Coad said, "You must be a very important fellow indeed. Did that all-points to call home ever catch up to you?"

"Yes, I'm sorry to say." He rolled his eyes in feigned frustration and then they both chuckled in deference to the little I'm-so-sick-of-working ritual.

"Are you riding with the President today, Wagner?"

"No. I'm just here to check on a few details for my front office. Where's the flight crew being briefed?"

Coad began pointing and directing with his hands. "You can try the weather-dispatch office. I heard someone say that the polar-front jetstream data had arrived from the States and that the President's Lufthansa crew was working out a westbound course that'll avoid it. If they aren't at Wind Analysis, they're probably with the flight dispatcher."

Wagner felt a small smile. "You sound like you know what you're talking about."

Coad humphed. "I was a MATS pilot for a time. So the Service puts me on all the airplane details. I don't really know a hell of a lot, but I manage to fake it."

"What's the dispatcher do?"

"Well," Coad said, his restless eyes following movements in the crowd, "he works with the captain of the airplane. I mean, getting a big crate like the President's from one place to another calls for a lot of teamwork, and the dispatcher and the captain are a team—the dispatcher keeps track of everything on the ground that pertains to the flight, while the captain does the flying. The dispatcher provides info, suggestions, sometimes direct orders, based on what he knows, and if he and the pilot can't agree about something to do with the flight, the plane doesn't fly. And—"

"O.K.," Wagner said. "I'll check at the dispatcher's office. That's probably where the crew is."

"Good to see you again, Wagner. Nice to know a VIP who gets paged all over Germany." He laughed and winked. "If any of the boys stop you, just flash your CIA buzzer and tell them I sent you."

"Thanks, Coad."

He cleared the barricades and went down a corridor that led to the operational bowels of the airport. Tidy men and women in tidy uniforms came and went from tidy offices whose labels spoke of Maintenance Control and Reservations and Weather and Inspections and Wind Analysis and, finally, Dispatching. Teletypes clattered, phones rang, slim girls with cute rumps posted things on large boards. He was stopped twice, but his credentials and mention of Coad got him through.

Wagner opened the glass door of the Dispatching Office and saw that the large room was occupied by a dozen men and women who talked quietly into phones and watched things on an electronic wall-display board. Five men, all crisp in Lufthansa flight uniforms, leaned across a long counter, listening as a man in shirtsleeves rattled some papers and made a little speech about a reserve-fuel problem.

They considered him with questioning eyes as he came to the counter, nodding amiably at them all.

"Hello," he said. Glancing at the man in shirtsleeves, he said, "Are you the dispatcher for the Randall flight?"

"That's correct."

"And this is the crew?"

"Yes. Who are you?"

"Is there any place we can talk privately?"

"What for? We're very busy here—"

The captain, a big fellow with a blue jaw and a pug nose, said, "Never mind, Kurt. This has to be the man Trille called about. Who else?"

"In the back here," the dispatcher said, nodding toward a door. "There's briefing room."

The captain looked at Wagner and said, "Let's go."

They entered a smaller room with student-type chairs, a podium, and a blackboard, all sterile under fluorescent lights. Wagner sat on the edge of a map table and waited for the others to take chairs. He recognized once again the madness of his position and what he was about to do. It was the biggest and worst of all the gambles he'd ever taken, but he was too far committed to waver now.

"Gentlemen," he said, "I have news for you. Your plot has failed. The Greuel will not be hijacking the President's plane."

The captain's blue jaw jutted and he said, "Who in hell are you?"

Wagner struck a pose of official pompousness. "As Nazi sympathizers, handpicked by Herr Trille and foisted on an unsuspecting Lufthansa and a trusting U.S. Secret Service in the name of German national security et cetera, et cetera, I find that you're not the most reliable of airmen, insofar as the duty of transporting the American President is concerned. Therefore—"

"I asked who in hell you are," the captain snarled.

Wagner snarled back. "I'm a member of CIA's counterintelligence branch, and I've just put a cannonball through your wheelhouse, sweetheart. You will not be flying today. You will be replaced by another crew—a crew appointed and passed, not by Hans Trille, but by U.S. Secret Service."

They all stared at him in a frozen silence, as if not daring to look at each other. Finally the captain found his voice. "Where's Trille? Has he been pinched?"

Ah, Wagner breathed in silent and trembling relief, *my absolute confirmation. I'm not a hallucinating maniac after all.*

"No. Nor will you be. Nothing will ever be said about any of it. The United States Government simply wants you to stop frigging around with its President. The United States Government simply wants you to go home and stop trying to force it into a war."

"We don't know what you're talking about," the dispatcher said, his anger evident.

The captain snapped, "Oh, forget it, Kurt. There's only one way to handle this." He had produced an automatic whose muzzle carried a tube silencer. "Josef," he said to one of the men, "search this fellow for a gun."

This was the tricky part, Wagner knew. Here is where his bluff had the thinnest walls.

"Put the pistol away, Captain," he said, patiently enduring the hands that patted his body. "You can't afford a ruckus. The only thing that'll save your skin is quiet obedience to what I tell you to do."

"Trille will have our heads if we don't get that airplane in the air. So if you think I'm just going home to watch TV on the simple say-so of some CIA boob, you're out of your mind. Now, you've got your choice, Mr. CIA-man: do you want it here, or in the airplane? It makes no difference to me."

"You can't afford to kill me. Instead of everybody forgetting everything, because no crime has yet been committed, everybody'll get mad and you'll be up on murder charges. All of you. Trille included."

"Mister," the captain said, "you scare me. I'll admit that. But Trille scares me more. So, I think you'd better come along to the airplane with us. We'll tuck you away, nice and quiet, until we're airborne."

"I'm not the only one who knows about this—"

"I think you are," the captain smirked. "Otherwise we'd have been up to our balls in security people and cops by now."

Lord, Wagner groaned inwardly, *of all the neo-Nazis in the world, I have to run into one who thinks.*

"Kurt," the captain said to the dispatcher, "is there a locker we can put this man's body in until we're aloft?"

"Down in the basement. Next to the perishable storage area."

"Can we walk him down there without anybody getting suspicious?"

"I don't know. The place is crawling with too many people. I think it would be very risky."

"See?" Wagner said coolly. "Just forget it, go home."

The captain ignored him, saying to the others, "All right, we'll have to walk him out to the airplane and hope nobody asks who he is. Once we've got him aboard we can lock him in the crew toilet until after takeoff."

"Ludwig," the man who had searched him asked worriedly, "what if he's telling the truth? What if somebody else does know? Our pretense that we're also victims of hidden hijackers will be broken, and we won't be able to come back to Germany. We'll become fugitives—"

"Good thinking, pal," Wagner said approvingly.

"Shut up, you," the captain snapped at Wagner. To the others he said, "Are you willing to face Trille and the Greuel? If not, then we carry out our orders until Trille gives us new ones. Period."

They all stood up, and the captain prodded Wagner with his pistol, and they went to the dispatching room, where the crewmen picked up their flight bags and map cases and the other paraphernalia of men who fly. The other people in the room seemed not to have moved a hair, droning as they were on telephones, or staring at the status board.

Wagner considered making a fuss, but that would only get him shot, and he had no doubt that the captain would explain him away as an unsuccessful hijacker or whatever. Besides, he wasn't at all sure that these manikins would even hear a fuss. Or a shot. Real anxiety began to form beneath his ribs. He was losing his gamble.

They went through a double swinging door and into the yellow autumn afternoon, and Wagner's eyes darted about in hopeful anticipation of a Secret Service type or two being on duty there. But there was nothing— nobody— between them and the airplane but breeze, sunlight, and concrete.

The giant aircraft was a considerable distance from the building, and it seemed to Wagner that they had walked for hours, and in his mind he could see the situation as it would appear to any security man anywhere: a group of security-approved airline personnel, ambling from a high-security building to a security-checked airplane for a security-approved flight. Routine. Undramatic. In no way suggesting that the most portentous kidnapping in history was about to take place.

The kidnapping of the President of the United States.

"Which one of you people speaks Arabic?" Wagner asked matter-of-factly.

"Shut up," the captain said.

"Which oil country do you plan to land in?"

"I said shut up, goddamn you."

Wagner was resigned to making a run for it. He'd be shot, of course. But there'd be a fuss.

Oh, God, whoever thought I'd be doing a Cagney?

How do I get into these stupid situations?

It's such a pain in the ass, being a hero—

In the distance behind, there was the squealing of tortured rubber and the high hum of a car under full acceleration. He heard some shouting, and then a crashing and the screeching of metal.

He and the others turned, staring back at the operations building and the source of the noise. A lot of people were running around, waving their arms and yelling for the police.

Coming at them, weaving and glistening in the sunlight, careening and chirping, was a silver-gray Mercedes that trailed posts and strands of airport fencing. It sped directly for them, and Wagner had the sudden and crazy thought that it was about to run them down.

But the car, rocking, turned at last, and, zooming past them in a thump of wind, it went into a skid that ended in a rattling collision with the airplane's nose gear. The great ship teetered gently and went into a slight list as its forward gear post bent and the tires blew.

They stood there, gaping, and somewhere a police siren sounded.

The door of the Mercedes creaked open and a smiling man climbed out, brushing dust from his natty suit.

Wagner said, "Gregori."

"Yass, Meester Vagner. Alexei Gregori. Et your sairvice, hay?"

"Let's stick to German, Gregori. Your English stinks."

"Thank you."

"So it was you in the brown Volvo."

The captain broke in, husky with shock. "You broke our airplane."

"Ah. So I did," Gregori said, making a rueful face. "But as you see, Captain, I am very drunk. I am most certain to be arrested for operating a motor vehicle while under the influence, eh?"

Wagner looked the captain in the eye and said, "Put your gun away, Ludwig. You won't be flying today. The President will have to go home on another airplane with another crew. And you will be writing reports on this incident for at least a month or two, wouldn't you guess?"

"Trille—"

"Trille won't make a sound," Wagner assured him. "He will do everything he can to see that this whole thing blows over."

Gregori chuckled. "So you and I came to the same conclusions about all this, eh, Wagner?"

"It looks that way. I confess I'd like to kiss your fat head."

"You're a first-class man, Wagner. I wish you were working for us."

"Which brings me to the logical question: How come you're working for us?"

"Not for you, Wagner. We've been working for us, as always. We simply didn't want you to get into trouble that would cause us trouble."

"Well—"

"The police are here, Wagner. I must now be arrested for drunken driving. Groot will fill you in. To Groot, incidentally, I am known simply as Herr Wismer." Gregori smiled at the man called Ludwig. "Well, then, Captain."

The captain tugged at the uniform sleeve of the large and angry airport police officer who climbed out of the red VW. "This man," the captain said in the whining tone of one who's been badly used, "is intoxicated. He sped out here on the field and rammed his car into my airplane."

The other crewmen chorused confirming complaints, and the big cop waved his arms and bawled, "All right, all right. Everybody shut up and get back to the operations building. Wait for me there until I put this idiot in detention. I'll take your statements then."

Gregori winked at Wagner, sighed, and climbed into the red car beside the cop. He waved lazily out the window as the vehicle sped off in a cloud of exhaust vapors and sirens and flashing lights.

The airline crew strode for the building without giving Wagner so much as a glance.

He stood in the sunny breeze for a time, breathing deeply and, for the first time in years, wanting to laugh a deep and unrestrained belly laugh.

October 19

"Hello?"

"Groot, this is Wagner."

"Where in God's name have you been?"

"Working. I want to see you."

"Well, I want to see you, too. You've got a lot of explaining to do."

"So do you."

"Look, Wagner—"

"I want to see Miss Randall, also. Set it up someplace where we can talk in private. Just the three of us."

"Miss Randall is a very busy woman."

"She'd better not be too busy for this."

"What's that supposed to mean?"

"I'll explain when we meet this afternoon."

"This afternoon? I can't get her to just drop—"

"This afternoon."

"Well, she has a place in Obermensing. A house. A block from the church. There's Secret Service people. I'll tell them to expect you at five."

"Very well."

"Wagner—"

"There's something I've been wanting to tell you for a long time, Groot."

"Well?"

"Up yours."

44

There had been a time, back in his high-school days, when Wagner had used some money earned by washing windows to take Alice Bigelow, the dentist's daughter, to Sunnybrook, where T. Dorsey was appearing. The orchestra's male vocalist was a young guy named Sinatra, who was absolutely the biggest rage ever to hit Ridley High School. Dorsey was the most of everything, of course, but this skinny Sinatra guy was something special, because he wasn't much older than everybody in Wagner's class, and they could identify with him, even though he was so famous.

It was the first time Wagner had ever seen anybody really famous close up. He could tell a famous face at the flick of a fan mag or a baseball card, but for all his familiarity with the Dorseys and their group, he'd never truly seen them. And standing by the bandstand, swaying with Alice, he'd looked up at the people in the spotlight—so close he could almost touch them—and he saw the truth that had escaped him for so long: they were just people. They had hair that needed cutting, they had a cuff link missing, they had a hicky on the chin, they had a spot on the sleeve of the nifty white dinner jacket. They breathed, they perspired, they smiled a lot but managed somehow to look lonely and bored and, well, lost.

After that night he had never again been guilty of hero worship or awe of celebrity. He had continued to like Dorsey and Sinatra and the others, but he was never again able to forget that they, too, said ouch.

So when he walked into the low-ceilinged room, with its flickering fireplace and wood-paneled walls and cutesy windows, and saw Amy Randall, Speaker of the House and sister of the President of the United States, standing regally before him, he wasn't cowed. He knew he should be; it was one thing to have been introduced, tangentially and forgettably, at a nightclub bash, but it was something altogether else to stare into somebody's eyes in their own living room.

Looking at her now, all he really noted was that there were lines under her eyes and a small round Band-Aid on one of her fingers.

She gave him her hand and said, "Good evening, Mr. Wagner. Drink?"

Groot, slumped in an easy chair by the fire, said nothing. His face was half in light, half in darkness, like a half moon, and, like the moon, it was noncommittal.

"Nothing to drink, thanks."

"Sit down, won't you?"

He sat tentatively on a Bavarian side chair and said, "This won't take long. I simply wanted you to know that none of you got away with anything. You're right back where you started."

"What do you mean, Mr. Wagner?"

Wagner gave her a level stare. "I mean your assassination plot. The one you and Groot cooked up to get your brother reelected."

She gave him a sharp glance. "I don't think I like what you're saying."

Groot said, "Oh, Amy, cut it out. Let him talk."

She glared at Groot and snapped, "Don't you dare speak to me in that tone."

"Amy, just listen to the man, will you?" He nodded at Wagner. "Go on."

Wagner said, "President Randall needs all the help he can get if he's not to lose to Robert Goodman. So Miss Randall decided to exploit the peculiar sympathy and popularity American public figures seem to get after close calls with death. She asked her old friend Groot, the CIA deputy, to set up something that would make the world think that a Robert Goodman zealot tried to kill the President. This would tar Goodman, create sympathy for her brother.

"So Groot agreed, for reasons I can only guess, of course—"

"I agreed to do it," Groot said suddenly, "because Robert Goodman as President would be an American disaster. The Soviets are docile now. They have their own problems. They don't want war. President Randall doesn't want war. If Goodman is elected, the whole delicate balance of things would be thrown out."

Outside the windows dusk was tinting the world a delicate blue. Wagner gazed out at the soft scene and went on, keeping it all in the third person, as if he were an old Norseman, passing along a saga. "So, because he feared Goodman's election, Groot agreed to set up a thing which would get worldwide publicity, throw serious stains on the Goodman movement, generate American voter sympathy for President Randall. Miss Randall had only one stipulation, I'm sure: her brother was not to be harmed or endangered in any way.

"Groot selected the President's Munich visit as the time. It was to be just prior to the election, and the sympathy element would still be strong by the time the voters went to the polls. He decided to feign a shooting try, and, to give it maximum credibility, he would use a bona fide undercover agent, who, assuming the plot to be real, would file regular progress reports on the search for the 'assassin.' To give the plot pathos and excitement and a kind of hero, Groot decided that, as the phony shot was fired, Emerson Gurney would hurl the President to the ground and shield him with his own body. Ta-da."

Groot made a small noise and shifted in his chair. Amy Randall continued to stand, sipping her cocktail.

"Groot," Wagner said, "evoked Akim Ri, a notorious assassin who had been killed in a plane crash. Ri was not really dead, the story would go, and Ri was seen in Germany. All the security agencies would set up a manhunt for Ri, the undercover agent would make believable reports that could eventually be fed to the media. And, after the case was well-established, the undercover agent could be conveniently killed so as to remove any chances he might have discerned something of the truth."

Miss Randall placed her glass on a table and said, "Groot, are you going to let this madman go on like this?"

"Yes, Amy, I am."

She opened her mouth to say more, but decided against it.

"So Groot hired Ziggi Rattner to implement the plan. Ziggi, in turn, hired Gustav Kahn to do the actual dirty work. Kahn tricked out his junky girlfriend in a wig to look like Akim Ri. She'd make fleeting appearances in Frankfurt and Munich, renting cars and so on, being certain to be seen by cops, so that the manhunt could begin.

"Meanwhile, Kahn fitted out an Audi with an amplifier and a rifle that had been fired. The idea was that, as the President walked from the Olympiahalle to the tower, Kahn would drive past on the Brauchle Ring, amplify a sound-effects tape of a rifle shot, and keep going fast. Gurney would 'protect' the President, the agent's reports would talk of Akim Ri's presence, the manhunt would be intensified."

"But," Groot broke in, "how would blame fall on a Robert Goodman zealot?"

"I found some Goodman campaign literature planted in Lotte Mahlmann's room in Stuttgart. Stuff planted by Kahn, playing cop. It's my guess that after the 'shot', a massive search would produce the blue Audi—which is registered in Lotte's name, by the way—parked in some lonely spot, perhaps, with a fired rifle in it, and the body of Lotte, dead on an overdose. A police check into her background would disclose literature that showed she idolized Goodman."

"Groot, you said nobody'd be hurt," Miss Randall said testily.

"Shut up, Amy. Go on, Wagner."

"So the world would think a German junky-radical-something, who typified the lunatic fringe backing Goodman, had tried to kill the President and, failing, committed suicide. The President would be reelected after giving a grateful speech to good ole Emerson Gurney, hero turned hero."

"So what happened?" Groot said quietly.

"So I, the undercover agent, got suspicious. If somebody really planned to kill the President, they wouldn't hire a famous killer and have him popping up all over Germany. The first anybody'd know of a real plot would be when the President was shot dead, and if the killer were ever caught, he'd be a nobody nobody'd ever heard of. So your first mistake, Groot, was to make the plot too public, with Akim Ri and all that crap. You and Rattner and Kahn threw a lot of razzle-dazzle at me there for awhile, but you laid it on too heavily."

Groot sighed and took another sip of his highball. "Anything else?"

"Sure. To keep an eye on me, you got Ellie Pomeraine in the act. And to prove to the Soviets that the whole thing was a well-intended internal plot to reelect the President—the Soviets' favorite American—you tipped them off and suggested that they assign one of their agents to keep an eye on me. They assigned Gregori, and he stuck to me like a plaster."

"So?"

"So the whole thing might have worked if you hadn't made your second mistake."

"Which was?"

"To underestimate Miss Randall's ambition. It's my

bet she wants to be President so bad she'll do anything to get it."

Amy Randall crossed the room and stood angrily before him, her eyes hot. "Of course I want to be President, you idiot. And it's my hope to run for the office after my brother's second term."

Wagner shook his head. "All through this thing I kept asking myself the same question. Why would you want the President to fly Lufthansa? And why would you not fly home with your brother? Then I heard you call General Dirk 'darling' at the party and saw General Dirk and Hans Trille in a very private conversation. Those seemingly innocent incidents, held against Groot's plot and the U.S. military moves in the Mideast, showed me the real plot."

Groot came forward in his chair. "Real plot?"

"Motive, Groot. Motive. The Why. The Why leads to the Who. And seeing the Why I saw that Miss Amy Randall had decided to do you one better, Groot. Why not really get the President out of the way? Why not, while everybody's so busy looking for Akim Ri, have phony Arab terrorists kidnap the President, fly him to some point in or near the Middle East oil fields, and hold him for ransom? And—"

"That's enough, you lunatic!" Miss Randall's face was chalky.

"—and, in all of the American national rage, with all the demands for action, General Dirk, exploiting an unprecedented opportunity to stabilize the U.S. energy problem for a few critical years, could send in the Navy task force planes and Marines, as well as the 82nd Airborne and the 101st, to 'rescue' the President. But the President wouldn't be found, and while the weeks, months, of search went on, the U.S. would have effectively occupied the Middle East oil lands. Ta-da."

"I warn you, Wagner—"

"Shut up, Amy."

"The Soviets might raise holy hell, but, being short of

306

oil themselves, couldn't very well start a war—especially when, in the world's eyes, the Americans were logically and rightfully trying to find their President. Meanwhile, with Vice President O'Toole fatally ill and unable to perform as President under the Twenty-fifth Amendment, Miss Randall, as Speaker of the House, becomes President, as provided by the Presidential Succession Act of 1947. On the eve of an election, yet. I don't know what the Constitution stipulates in such a case, but I'm willing to bet that, in such emotional circumstances, Miss Randall would be retained in the presidency by popular demand, if nothing else."

Wagner sighed. "So Amy talks to Dirk, who arranges to have Amy speak before the Army wives, thus giving her a reason to stay behind when the President flies home. Next, Dirk enlists an old pal, Hans Trille, to set up an air crew. And Trille, to assure security, orders Kahn to eliminate the links, from Ziggi Rattner to me. But Groot's friend, Gregori, keeps protecting me, because whatever else is going on, he knows I'm working to get Randall reelected. And that's what his bosses want."

"What happened at the Olympiaturm?" Groot said.

"Trille and Kahn felt it was necessary to have a real killing, to increase the uproar. With blood actually flowing, everybody would practically throw the President aboard the airplane. And when the airplane got upstairs and far away, a voice in Arabic would come on the radio and announce the kidnapping. Radar would lose the plane as it disappeared into the mysterious East, and so on."

Groot said, "So who was supposed to get killed?"

"Gurney and Mahlmann. Kahn would park the Audi near the tower with the rifle in it. He'd take the amplifier out and put it in another car nearby. He'd sound the shot. In all the confusion, Lotte, writer for an archery magazine, would nail Gurney with an arch. Then, in all the hullaballoo, one of Kahn's boys would slip Lotte a shiv and then disappear in the crowd. The rest would be the same: Lotte's body, leading to the Goodman literature."

There was a long lull, in which the fire's crackling was the only sound in the room. Outside, the soft blue evening had turned deep purple, and somewhere a church bell rang, alone and unheeded.

Groot laughed softly and said, "Well, Amy, you're a pistol, you are. I didn't realize you cared so little for your brother."

"Oh, shut up."

"I've always known," Wagner said vaguely, "that history wobbles on the greeds of individuals. Darius. Alexander. Caesar. On and on, to the Hitlers and the Goodmans. But I never *really* knew it until now. Being here. Looking at you. Know what I mean?"

Miss Randall, standing by the window, turned to give Wagner a curious stare. "What evidence do you have to prove all this?"

He shrugged. "Not a shred that would stand up in court. I've been flying by the seat of my pants all the way. But it's all true, give or take a detail here and there. It's all true because nothing else makes sense. Motive always determines who premeditates a crime, right, Groot? Well, I thought and thought, and the only motive that fits is your motive, Miss Randall. And all I need for confirmation is a look at your face."

"Well," she said bleakly, "my brother's on his way home. And nothing's changed."

"One thing's changed," Wagner said. "You creeps aren't going to decide who's to be the next President. The American voter's going to decide. Like always before."

There was another period of quiet.

Miss Randall cleared her throat finally and said, "I suppose you have a price for keeping all this out of the Sunday supplements."

"Yep," Wagner said.

She smiled bitterly. "There's nothing new in the world.

Our patriotic, ingenious, plodding Mr. Wagner is a blackmailer."

"For me to keep my mouth shut, here's what you will do: first, you'll get that poor old klutz Gurney into a drying-out hospital, and then you'll see that lots of your West Coast buddies give him lots of work."

"What else?"

"Second, you'll have your brother fire General Dirk tomorrow morning. Third, you'll have Groot put on pension. Fourth, you'll send all your jet-set pals to Frau Lindl's Edelweiss Hof in the Tyrol. You'll see that the Edelweiss becomes the in-inn. And fifth: take my CIA job and shove it up Groot's ass. If you don't meet these demands, I'll give the story to Ellie Pomeraine or some other fearless journalist. It might not get to court, but can you imagine what the media would do with the *charges*?"

As he was walking out, Groot called after him, openly amused.

"Are you going to vote for President Randall, Wagner?"

"Me? Hell, I'm not even registered."

45

After Wagner had left, they sat without speaking. She kept her eyes from him, staring into her drink, and he stood by the fire and thought about all the years and all the treacheries. He was filled with a sense of self-contempt and a futility, and he knew the acid taste of enormous effort wasted, weeks of work gone for nothing.

"I suppose you'd like an apology or something, Groot."

"For what? My own stupidity?"

"You weren't stupid. You were doing what I asked you to do."

He gave her an empty glance. "My stupidity lies in my willingness to fall under your—spell, I believe the poets call it—all those years ago."

"You and I are much alike, Groot."

"Too much so. And that's where I failed. I should have seen that you'd reach for the brass ring—that you'd use me, ride me like a horse, while you reached for what you really wanted."

She put down her glass and sighed, a long breath that spoke of weariness and testy impatience. "All those people, Groot. All those millions of voters—eating, drinking, working, building, laughing, crying, birthing, dying—they go through the world oblivious of the world. They grub around and watch TV in their underwear and drink beer out of cans and follow the baseball scores, and they don't even know who's running for office, let alone who to vote for, unless some smooth network ham eyeballs them out of the tube and gives them shots of the gaudiest political news to have been fabricated that day. They watch the cop shows and whodunits, and scratch their butts and go to bed, and so when there's an election all they see is another dramatic show whose characters are dull nudniks in gray suits talking about unpleasant things like inflation and taxes. The American voter doesn't know his behind from a bass bassoon, and he only reacts to spoon-fed, melodramatic contrivances that come through the tube. Well, I was going to get their attention, by God. I'd give them the biggest suspense show in history, and they would put me in charge and let me save their asses while they went on slugging beer and checking league standings."

Groot lit a cigarette and stared into the blaze. "All the while you were planning to kidnap your own brother. That's what got me, I think. If I need an excuse for my stupidity, that's it: I didn't realize how little you care for your brother."

"Oh," she said, "Randy's O.K. But politically he's a cow plop. I could run the country better with my eyes shut. Besides, we didn't plan to hurt him. Just keep him out of sight for a couple of years."

"You don't really think that, do you?" Groot said, looking at her.

"Well, why not?"

Groot smiled his dim smile. "That's where you've done a bit of underestimating of your own, Amy. They'd have killed your brother in the first ten minutes. All you needed was illusion, really; the illusion of your brother's being held somewhere. Do you have any idea how difficult it is to kidnap somebody and keep him hidden? Your

311

pals—Dirk, Trille, Kahn, Trille's other Nazi thugs—they didn't need a live President; they didn't even need a Middle East oil country in which to hide him. All they needed was the illusion, to be fed to those irate TV watchers, guzzling their beer in their T-shirts, that some dirty Arab terrorists had stolen their President and beautiful, gutty, brilliant Acting President Amy Randall was goddamn well going to get him back."

They fell silent again, and after a while Groot had the impression she was dozing. But then she stirred and said, "They were going to crash-land the plane in a stretch of desert, so it could be found, along with the bodies of the official party and members of the press. There would be a letter demanding a hundred million dollars, the release of all terrorists in jails anywhere, and the permanent closing of Wall Street, as a kind of symbolic triumph of the oppressed Third World. President Randall would have been released only then."

Groot nodded. "When they were planning the murder of others you don't think for a moment your brother would have been spared, do you?"

"I had many promises from Dirk and Trille."

"You know your real mistake, don't you?"

"What's that, Groot?"

"You didn't let me plan all of it."

"It's all academic now."

"Yes. All we can do now is hope that the T-shirts will reelect your brother. You'll do your Congress thing, and I'll fade away, the old soldier."

"Like hell you will. You're going to plan every move I make from now on. You're my kind of man, Groot. As of now, you're my man."

"God help us all," Groot said, meaning it.

46

He walked into Trille's office without announcement.

Trille, puffing on his pipe, was showing a paper to a big detective, who leaned on the desk and tried to appear as if he understood. The inspector, seeing Wagner, dismissed the man with a wave and then nodded at the oak chair.

"Where's Gregori?" Wagner said, sitting down.

"The drunken driver?"

"Mm."

"Released. You wouldn't believe the pull that man has, whoever he is."

Wagner studied Trille's face for a time, then said, "You Nazis just never give up, do you."

Trille took the pipe from his mouth and examined its bowl. "Well," he said, "you'll have to admit it was a hell of an idea for grabbing the oil before the Communists do."

"When did Dirk and Amy hire you and your fly-boys?"

"Dirk's an old friend of mine from his earlier days in Europe. We think alike. Actually this whole plan was mine in the first place. Dirk and I share a great concern that the Western world will die for lack of oil. I gave him this plan, but the time was never right. Until now, when everything was in conjunction, as the horoscopes say."

Wagner nodded. "I see." He changed his position in the chair, trying vainly for some measure of comfort. "You killed my friend, Rudi Kulka."

"Gustav Kahn killed Kulka."

"Kahn was under your orders from the moment Ziggi told him of Groot's phony little plot. When Ziggi told Kahn, Kahn told you."

"Why would Kahn do a thing like that?"

"He's a member of the Greuel, and you're head of it."

"The Greuel doesn't exist. It's Sunday-supplement fiction."

"Yeah. Sure it is."

Trille touched a fresh match to his pipe and, while puffing industriously, said, "So what's on your mind? You're here to press charges against Kahn and Mahl-mann. Against me, perhaps?"

"No," Wagner said, "I'm here to give you your instructions."

Trille smiled. "You're giving *me* instructions?"

"Mm-hm. I want everything to revert to its original condition before the President came to Munich. Except for a few items I'll tell you about. But in the main, I want peace and tranquillity to reign as the Sunday supplements say, so that the American electorate can vote undistracted for its next President. My pressing open legal charges against you would only cause a great furor and distraction, as the Sunday supplements say."

"It certainly would."

"So, Trille, here's what you're going to do: first, as head of the Greuel, you will order the usual Greuel penalty for Gustav Kahn. He murdered my friend, Kulka, and I am therefore sentencing him to be punished to the full extent of the law under which he has lived."

Trille's face remained expressionless.

"Second, you will see that Lotte Mahlmann gets full medical and rehabilitation treatment for her addictions.

"Third, you will resign from your police post and you will disband the Greuel and you will retire from all forms of public or political life."

Trille said, "And if I don't do all these things?"

"I'll kill you."

Trille laughed suddenly. "You? You will kill me? My dear Koenig, don't be naive. I've been a soldier. I've been a policeman. My life has been threatened many times. Besides, I could arrange your death before you even return to your car from this office."

"Let me be more specific, Herr Trille. I won't kill you. The Greuel will."

"Oh? How will you arrange that?"

"I have a friend in the Soviet Intelligence apparatus who has provided me with an official Soviet document that reveals Hans Trille, ostensibly an official of the Bundespolizei, is, in reality, a longtime Communist and Soviet spy. If anyth   happens to that lovable Yankee swine, Rog   my friend will see that the original of this very   uly manufactured document falls into the hands of the German press."

Trille leaned forward in his chair. "My people would never believe a phony document like that."

"Then why do you look so worried all of a sudden?"

Trille placed his pipe in an ashtray, his eyes clouded.

Wagner said, "No fooling, Trille. If, after the disposition of the Kahn case, there is a single indication of Greuel activity anywhere, the document will become public."

They traded appraisals. Then Wagner stood up, straightened his necktie, and went to the door.

"I'm not worried about you, Hans-baby," he said. "You always were one to keep his head."

Wagner was leaving the police building when Gurney came out the door, too, bleary and ridiculous in his rumpled cowboy costume. There was a terrible, dark weariness in the man's face, and Wagner felt pity.

"Hello, Gurney. You've been sprung, eh?"

The actor paused on the steps, one hand holding the railing, his eyes peering into Wagner's in a red, agonized search for clues as to what might have happened to his life.

"Oh, hi, Willie. Bad Day at Black Rock."

"It sure was. Were the police tough with you?"

"I don't think so. All I know is that President Randall himself asked them to let me go. 'Mr. Gurney had merely been carried away by the occasion,' I think he put it. 'We all have times when we overindulge,' I think he said."

"How do you know what he said?"

"He sent a note to the cops by messenger. Want to see it?" He began to fumble in a pocket. "They gave it to me. A souvenir, they said."

"Don't bother. I'm glad you weren't held."

"I shoulda been. Not for drinkin' but for goin' along with Amy's ego trip."

"She took a lot of people in, all right." Wagner checked his watch, then asked, "What'll you be doing now? Finishing your picture?"

"Sure. A contract's a contract. After that, I have a date to drink myself to death. There ain't anything else."

Wagner said, "You put your life on the line out there, Gurney. You put yourself between the President and Lotte's arrow."

"I took one look at that broad and knew what she planned to do. It all came to me, like. And I figured that if I helped get President Randall in that fix I'd have to get him out of it. Besides, think of the publicity I'da got. I might not be worth anything alive, Willie, but I coulda been worth somethin' dead."

Wagner cleared his throat. "Well, I make a prediction: I predict that there'll be a pronounced upswing in your career. Big things are coming your way."

"And I predict they'll find Pluto's a big ping-pong ball."

"Never fear, Emerson Gurney: you'll live happily ever after."

He took the old ham's hand and gave it a good shake.

316

47

"Good morning. This is the Adlershof Hotel."

"Good morning. Do you have a Mrs. Steven Cartwright of Wilmington, Delaware, USA, registered there?"

"Why, yes, we do. Room Eight."

"Can you connect me, please?"

"Of course. One moment."

"Hello?"

"Mrs. Cartwright?"

"Yes, Mr. Cartwright."

"Doing anything today?"

"No. Just papering the guest room."

"How about a little trip over to Colorado?"

"Can we make it on four hundred dollars?"

"Four hundred? What happened to the other hundred?"

"I bought a new suit."

"You've got to cut down on this spending. We can't afford a new suit every time you just feel like it."

"Well, you have your golf."

"Yeah, but that's good for business. Keeps me in good with the clients."

"Hey."

"Mm?"

"I miss you."

"I'll be right there."

UNDER THE EYE OF NIGHT
By Robert E. Mills

PRICE: $2.25 LB718
CATEGORY: Occult Novel (Original)

If you can imagine the Godfather meeting the
Exorcist, UNDER THE EYE OF NIGHT is even
more terrifying! The mafia murders a young drug-
runner, whose father has black powers that he
turns against the mob. Then a series of bizarre
events threaten to destroy the once-powerful
family. One by one they are possessed by an
unspeakable evil, and one by one they die—a
dense fog envelopes one victim and kills him...the
sounds of a slurping beast follow another...a car
mysteriously fills with water and drowns another.
The force is more horrifying than anything the
mob could create—and totally beyond their
control!

MOMENT OF THE PREDATOR
George Bernard

Author of "Inside the National Enquirer" and "Confessions of an Undercover Reporter".

PRICE: $2.25 LB807 (cc:50)
CATEGORY: Novel (original)

A shocking and suspenseful novel of a vendetta against America by the PLO. Supermodel Dianne Spain—daughter of a prominent Nazi scientist entrusted with the heinous mission of murder and mayhem—is earmarked for destruction by the PLO. The plan is for Yasir Arafat to blow up the World Trade Center by pushing the detonator button while he is making a speech at the United Nations! The author actually went inside the PLO to write this work of fiction that is steeped in frightening reality.

Mr. Bernard is a frequent contributor to the National Star.